Matt Beaumont lives in a house with a woman and some children. He still drives a blue Saab, though he is thinking about changing it.

For more (mostly made up) information about the author, go to www.LetsTalkAboutMe.com

BY THE SAME AUTHOR

e
The e Before Christmas
The Book, the Film, the T-Shirt

matt beaumont

Staying Alive

HarperCollins*Publishers*

Words from 'Sort It Out' are quoted by kind permission of its writer
and publisher. Words and music by Joakim Ahlund. © 2003 Universal Music
Publishing. All Rights Reserved. International Copyright Secured.

This novel is a work of fiction. The names,
characters and incidents portrayed in it are the work of the
author's imagination. Any resemblance to actual persons,
living of dead, events or localities is entirely coincidental.

HarperCollins*Publishers*
77–85 Fulham Palace Road,
Hammersmith, London W6 8JB

Special overseas edition 2004
1

First published in Great Britain by
HarperCollins*Publishers* 2004

Copyright © Matt Beaumont 2004

ISBN 0 00 716703 2

Set in Palatino by Palimpsest Book Production Limited
Polmont, Stirlingshire

Printed and bound by
Griffin Press, Netley, Australia

For Sam, spaceman of the future

acknowledgements

Kiss-flecked thank yous:

To all at HarperCollins, especially Susan Opie, Nick Sayers (since gone over to The Dark Side), Sara Walsh, Ben North and James Annal, and to my agent, Lavinia Trevor. They helped make this book what it is. The corollary, of course, is that they must also take full responsibility for any errors, discrepancies and rubbishy boring bits.

Doctor Sophie Robertson, who took time out from saving precious young lives to help me with the medical stuff. And if there are any mistakes in this regard, it's because I listened carefully to her detailed and thoughtful advice and then ignored it.

Susan Aslan for her sound legal advice.

Ken Morrison for his unsound sexist joke.

Holly Beaumont for the loan of her dolls.

Jack and Anita Grayson for Javea. Their hospitality knows no bounds. No really, check it out for yourself; they'd love to see you.

And to Maria Beaumont for all her love and brilliance, and also for unselfishly giving me the premise for this story. I hope I did it justice.

Finally, thanks to Bono, Beyoncé Knowles and Bobby De Niro for their – no, now I'm just making it up.

_____nov.

one: **like on the telly?**

I point the camera at . . .

Sophie Dahl's prone and virtually naked body.

The dawn-lit terraces of Machu Picchu, high in the Andes.

Elvis/Lennon/Tupac as he emerges from a cave deep in the Hindu Kush.

None of the above, actually. They're there to make me seem big and clever.

The truth now.

I point the camera at a multi-pack of Schenker Alpenchok bars. I angle it carefully – experience has taught me to do this to avoid catching the glare from the fluorescent tubes that line the rim of the Safeway freezer display. Hell, am I *good* at this? The box shows Heidi patting a cow on the foothills of the Matterhorn. She beams at me through the viewfinder – a big happy-dairy-girl smile.

Exude sexy ice-creaminess, baby . . . Mmm, yeah, that's working for me big ti—

Something crashes into my thigh. A shopping trolley, the type that hitches up to an electric wheelchair to make the HGV menace of supermarket aisles. I should know; I've been dead-legged by enough of them. An old lady is at the controls. A lime-green hat sits on her head. It's shaped like a turban and makes her look like the Mekon – as if Dan Dare's archenemy just popped into Safeway for baked beans, loin chops and loo roll. 'What've you done with the frozen veg?' she snaps.

'I'm sorry, I don't work here,' I reply, rubbing the fresh bruise.

'You lot keep messing with the freezers and I can't find

anything.' She scrutinises my lapel for a badge proclaiming name and rank.

'Really, I don't work here,' I protest. 'If you ask—'

'What are you doing, then?' she says, spotting the camera. 'You shouldn't be taking pictures. You're a spy, aren't you? You're from Tesco.'

'No, I've got permission . . . I work for an advertising agency.'

My trump card, though I don't produce it as if it's the ace of spades – more like the three.

'Adverts? Like on the telly?' She sounds impressed.

I nod. And smile – it's rare that I impress anyone with my career choice.

'I've been wanting to have a word with you,' she says, her eyes narrowing. 'I saw your one for the funeral plan. I signed up, but I'm still waiting for my free carriage clock. It's been weeks now.'

'I— *We* don't do that one,' I explain.

'Oh, you're ever so charming when you want to sell us something, but the minute you've got us you don't want to know,' she spits.

My mobile vibrates against my hip and I pull it gratefully from my pocket. The Mekon looks on with distaste. 'They cause cancer, you know,' she says. Then she hits the throttle, running over my foot with her wheelchair's solid rubber tyre and trundling off into the fluorescent Safeway sunset – taking no prisoners in the quest for world domination/frozen peas. I look at the phone display. Maybe it's Sophie Dahl's people calling to tell me her body is prone, very nearly naked and waiting aquiver for my camera's attentions.

Funnily enough, no. It's work.

'Hi, Jakki,' I say.

'What are you doing?'

'Getting grief about a funeral plan.'

'You what?'

4

'Never mind. What's up?'

'You'd better get back here. Niall's having a shitfit. You've fucked up, apparently,' Jakki tells me. 'Something to do with invoices. Don't ask me to explain. He wants to see you.'

'Well, he wants me to do store checks in five different supermarkets before tomorrow's meeting as well. Which is it to be?'

'It's serious. You'd better come back . . .'

'OK.'

'But don't come without the ice-cream shots.'

Silence, but only because I'm stifling a sneeze.

'You all right, Murray?'

'I'm coming down with something, you know.'

'Got the sniffles? You're such a wuss,' she laughs.

'Am *not*.'

Sitting behind her desk manning the phones and diaries she has no concept of what it's like out here in the field. Every time I head for the supermarket freezers I risk death from hypothermia. I'm the Captain bloody Oates of advertising.

I end the call and as I re-aim the camera at the ice-cream display, the sneeze finally explodes. Definitely coming down with something. I look through the viewfinder and wonder if the Schenker Foods brand group will spot the shiny glob of snot on Heidi's embroidered bodice.

two: **nobody died**

I'm sitting in a conference room on the seventh floor of the Canary Wharf Tower, wondering how I'd like to die . . .

  1.   Peacefully, boringly in my sleep . . .

God, that is so *me*.

  2.   Surrounded by loved ones as I utter some carefully
        chosen, though seemingly spontaneous last words:
        Megan . . . Forgive her for she knew not what she . . .
        uuugggghhhhhh . . .
  3.   Alternatively (and, let's be honest, more likely): *Nurse*
        . . . is it time for my enem . . . uuuugggggghhhhhhhh . . .

That's the trouble with final words. Timing. Surely the hard part is catching that moment when there's just enough breath left to squeeze out the ultimate sentence. With all the distractions of being terminal – pain, drugs, tubes, iron lungs and whatnot – the chances are you'd miss your cue. But that's not the worst that could happen. No, imagine coming out with your killer epilogue and then . . . you *don't* die. You linger. Maybe for hours. Or days. Picture the awkwardness. Lying there knowing what they're thinking: *'Well, he's delivered his punchline. He should at least have the manners to get off the stage.'* No, best keep it zipped.

Where was I? . . . Meeting. Seventh floor. Canary Wharf Tower. Wondering how I'd like to . . .

6

4. Beneath several tons of sub-standard Stalin-era concrete, seconds after having pulled newborn triplets *and* their mother from the rubble of a collapsed apartment building, making me:
   a) a Hero of the People in post-quake Uzbekistan.
   b) a Millstone of Guilt around the neck of Megan Dyer as she watches the news coverage. Tough – the burden is something she'll have to learn to live with.
5. At the controls of a 747, having wrested them from the grasp of a bug-eyed Arab before banking the jet inches clear of the Canary Wharf Tower as its paralysed occupants look on with unutterable gratitude.
6. No, no, *no*. At the controls of a 747 as I plunge it *into* the Canary Wharf Tower whose paralysed occupants look on with this final thought flashing through their brains: *Is that Murray Colin in the cockpit?*

Silly. I don't like flying. I'm not exactly phobic, but every time I climb aboard I have to work hard to banish visions of the jet plummeting into, say, a tall building. Therefore:

7. *Nothing* that involves heights.
8. Or depths. Diving, submarines, stuff like that. I may be poor at altitude, but I am flat-out terrified of slowly running out of breathable air while being trapped at the bottom of—

I can't think about *that* one without breaking into an icy sweat. Change the subject, Murray, *change the bloody subject*.

9. From a spectacularly massive coronary – '*My God, nurse, his heart literally burst!*' – while my body is entwined with:

7

a) Megan Dyer's
b) Megan Dyer's
c) Betina Tofting's, whose thigh – as she allows her skirt to ride up it – looks alarmingly similar to Megan Dyer's.

Betina catches me gazing at her legs and yanks at her hem. Feeling shabby, I look away at Niall Haye circling his telescopic pointer around the phrase *'Consumer expectation/Taste delivery synchronicity'*.

'I'd like now to discuss the crucial point at which the consumer and the brand interface,' my boss says, turning from the screen to me. 'Murray, perhaps you'd like to take us through the results of your store checks.'

Perhaps I bloody wouldn't. Why does he say that as if I've got a choice? *Perhaps what I'd really like to do is shove that irritating telescopic pointer up your—*

'Thanks, Niall, I'd love to,' I reply as I reach for the A0 sheet of Polyboard that has spent the last ninety minutes leaning against my chair. This is its Moment. I prop it up on the table and take the Schenker Foods brand group on a tour of five different supermarket freezer cabinets. In a bravura display of top-notch store checking I somehow managed to complete my mission before returning to the office for my bollocking – something to do with invoices, indeed.

I'm beginning to suspect that advertising isn't all it was cracked up to be. When I was a goggle-eyed undergrad the recruiters tempted me with talk of drugs, models and shoots on sun-kissed beaches. No one mentioned the store check. Eight years in, the number of lines of coke that I've snorted off models' sun-kissed bottoms runs to not even single figures. Yesterday, by contrast, I completed my ninetieth store check. No, as a career choice advertising does *not* do exactly what it says on the tin.

And if ad people can't even be straight with one another . . .
Well, it begs questions, doesn't it?

'Thank you, Murray, that was *fascinating*,' Haye says as I sit down.
Hard to believe that anyone could, but Niall Haye finds pictures
of supermarket freezers *fascinating*; almost – but not quite – enough
to make him forget that I really did mess up on the invoice front.

Betina Tofting smiles at me for the first time in nearly two
hours. This has nothing to do with her forgiving me for staring
at her legs. It's because she too was riveted by my presentation.
She's probably no more than twenty-five, a good two-thirds of
her life still before her, yet that life revolves around Schenker
Foods' new line of adult choc-ices; nothing else exists for her.
I smile back as if I feel the same way.

She says, 'They are *excellent* photographs, Murray,' in a Danish
accent that's incapable of irony. Her sincerity puts a glossy red
cherry on top of my whipped cream of a depression . . . Is this
as good as it's going to get? Murray Colin, the world's finest
store checker. You want an oil fire extinguished, call Red Adair.
You need a guaranteed thirty goals a season, stump up several
million for Van Nistelrooy. You're after flare-free snaps of ice-
cream packaging, Murray's your man.

Haye segues to the final item on the agenda: the media plan
for the European launch of ChocoChillout. As he explains in
excruciating detail how he proposes to blow an advertising
budget big enough to buy every child in Africa three square
meals a day, inoculations and a PlayStation 2, I mentally compose
a letter to the Chief of Internal Security in North Korea.

Dear Sir/Madam,
   I appreciate that you must be busy and I apologise for tearing
you away from your important work. However, should you be

9

looking for new and imaginative ways of extracting essential information from the many detainees you have in your care, I believe I may have just the thing.

Forget sleep-deprivation and attaching electrodes to genitals. I humbly suggest that just thirty minutes in a locked conference room with Niall Haye, his telescopic pointer and a selection of overhead projections will have even the most recalcitrant counter-revolutionary screaming for mercy and telling you everything you wish to know – as well as, I hazard, some stuff you didn't even think to ask about.

Should you be interested, Mr Haye could be in Pyongyang on the next flight – sanctions permitting, of course.

Finally, I would like to take this opportunity to pass on my very best wishes to everyone at your end of the Axis of Evil.

Yours et cetera . . .

Job done.

I close my eyes.

No, Niall, I'm not going to sleep. I'm concentrating deeply on your exciting proposal to spend   5.2 million giving the lucky citizens of Benelux no less than fifteen opportunities to hear a voice-over promise a sensously silky taste adventure (in Dutch, Flemish and French).

Never mind how I'd like to die. What will surely kill me is terminal cynicism.

12.36 p.m.

The meeting *finally* breaks up.

I grab a bottle of mineral water from the middle of the table and take a swig, washing down the three aspirin that I've placed on my tongue. My glands are up like feisty walnuts and I feel rough, much worse than yesterday. I shouldn't be here.

Niall stands up and announces lunch. My cue to scurry ahead to reception and organise the taxis. Before I leave the room he grabs my arm. 'You won't be joining us at the trough today,' he hisses. 'I'd like you to spend your lunch hour going through every invoice you've issued over the last twelve months. The rest of the board and I would like to know just how many of our clients you've wrongly billed.'

It was a mistake, Niall. An accident. Slightly less than three thousand pounds demanded of the wrong client. Nobody died, for God's sake.

'Of course,' I say. 'That's exactly what I was planning to do.'

12.41 p.m.

'You look peaky, babe. Not up to the lunch?' Jakki says with concern (at least thirty per cent of it sincere) as I arrive at my desk. She has me down as suffering from hypochondria, but it's nothing so serious – just a touch of flu.

'It's not that. Niall's put me on punishment duties.'

'Jeez, it was only an invoice. Nobody *died*. He sends out the wrong ones all the time.'

'Yes, but he does it deliberately. Did you know that Schenker was billed for the new boardroom table? *Thirteen* grand. He bunged it on the budget for their last commercial. He even put the agency mark-up on it.'

'At least you weren't ripping anyone off.'

'More fool me, Jakki. If I'd been ripping someone off I'd have probably got a rise . . . Anyway, I need to go through a year's worth of billing now.'

'I'll give you a hand.'

'You don't have to do that.'

And she doesn't. As secretary to four other account supervisors besides me she has enough bum-numbing rubbish to deal with.

'I don't mind. You'll be doing me a favour. If I go out I'll only end up buying a double cheese and sardine melt and some-

11

thing with triple-choc in its name. No bloody willpower.'

I let her pull up a chair next to mine. She could do with losing a little weight.

'Well, I can't find anything,' I say.

'Hmm,' Jakki murmurs. She lost interest some time ago. She's still sitting beside me, but now she's looking at the pictures in Italian *Vogue*.

'The independent Murray Colin Commission hereby concludes its investigation into the administrative record of Murray Colin, and hereby finds that Murray Colin has billed impeccably.'

'Hmm,' says Jakki.

'That was one too many herebys, wasn't it?'

'Uh-huh . . . What do you think I'd look like in this?' She holds up a picture of a model who's thinner than the paper she's printed on. She's wearing two squares of chiffon, each the size of a pocket tissue.

'Gorgeous,' I say.

'Who am I trying to kid? I'd look like Mrs Blobby. *God*, I can't hold out any longer,' she announces, standing up and pulling on her coat. 'I've got to get food. Want anything?'

'You could get me a Mars.'

'Is that all?'

'Yeah. Hang on, I'll give you some money.' I stand up and reach into my trouser pocket. I freeze as my hand touches something – it isn't loose change.

'What's up?' Jakki asks.

'Nothing . . . Nothing at all. You go. Forget the Mars.'

Well, I'm not going to tell her I've just found a lump, am I?

12

three: **fifteen weeks, four days and an indeterminate number of hours**

At least, I think it's a lump.

I stand in front of the long mirror in my bedroom and lower my trousers and underpants. I unbutton my shirt and lift the tails out to my sides to reveal myself in semi-naked glory. Nothing glorious about it, actually. My body is thoroughly average. No flab to speak of, but no corrugated sheet of abdominal muscles either. Just a gently bowed curve of stomach descending to an untidy clump of mid-brown hair. Every once in a while I consider shaving it off. Nothing to do with vanity. No, the thought appeals to my sense of neatness. But . . . *shaved pubes*. There's something pervy about that. A bit porn star. And I can't stomach the idea of being knocked down by a car, getting rushed to A&E and the medics discovering that I groom *down there*.

Doctor:	*Take a look at this, nurse.*
Nurse:	*My God, a depilator. Is he a porn star?*
Doctor:	*What's it say on his admission form?*
Nurse:	*Advertising executive.*
Doctor:	*He's most likely just your run-of-the-mill pervert.*
Nurse:	*Shall I call social services?*
Doctor:	*We'd best be sure first. I mean, he could be a pro cyclist. I understand they shave. Something to do with aerodynamics, apparently.*
Nurse:	*No, he hasn't got the six-pack to be a cyclist.*

13

As a rule my sense of neatness is pervasive, all-consuming, but in the ongoing face-off between shaggy and trim, shaggy wins every time.

My eyes travel down a little further to my . . . You know something? I don't know what to call it. I've never felt comfortable with any of the standard terms. Penis sounds too formal – a bit sort of *Presenting His Excellency Lord Penis, Duke of Genitalia.* Willy, of course, is too cute. Cock? Too blunt, macho, in-your-face. There are dozens of other words for the thing – well, *thing* for one. Then there's knob, todger, schlong, pecker, love truncheon. *Love truncheon.* Not even in my dreams. None of them feels right. And before anyone suggests it, I am *not* going down the road of personalising it, giving it a pet name. So I'm not left with much. But I'm looking at it now. Like the rest of me, it's nothing special. Thoroughly average, I suppose, though I've never taken a ruler to it. But that isn't why I'm staring at myself in the mirror, my trousers round my ankles. I reach down to my . . . Balls? Bollocks? Knackers? Testicles? Same problem. I'm stuck whenever I have to refer to anything in the . . . er . . . meat 'n' two veg region (*meat 'n' two veg* – truly horrible). My solution to date has been to avoid any reference if at all possible. It has worked well enough for thirty-one years, but now . . . Well, I've got a lump. Or something.

I think I read somewhere that men should check themselves once a month, like women are meant to examine their breasts. I also read that you should check the batteries in your smoke alarm on a regular basis. I've never done that either. Frankly, I've never felt happy about the idea of self-examination, and only partly because I'm not especially fond of molesting myself. My principle objection is that the doctors – men and women who, let's not forget, undergo only slightly less training than architects and London cab drivers – are advising the rest of us – a bunch of barely informed *amateurs* – to do the checking. Where is the logic, please? Why the billions blown on teaching hospitals the size of Devon if they end up making us do the work?

But I'm checking now. Feeling with my hand. Very tentatively. My left one . . . *Just say the word, Murray.* My left *testicle* is lower. Though I've never paid it the kind of attention I'm giving it now, I think it has always been lower. It's also bigger. Definitely bigger. I don't think it has ever been that. I take it between my fingertips and roll it gently as if it's a bingo ball and I'm looking for the number. There it is. My fingers weren't deceiving me in the scrabble for change at lunchtime. I quickly let go. Drop it like a red-hot pebble. As if I've turned the bingo ball and seen the number.

Six, six, six.

I've got a lump.

──────────────────────────────── 11.38 p.m.

I'm in bed, but I can't sleep.

I feel dreadful. Hot and sweaty, bunged up, achy. It's the flu. But that isn't what's keeping me awake. I've got a lump. My mind is racing, looking for explanations. Alternatives to the obvious and deeply unpleasant one. Until a moment ago none had offered itself. But the one that does now is so blindingly obvious that it practically switches on the light and yells *Eureka!*

Megan left weeks ago. Three weeks, two days and (quick glance at the alarm) just over nine hours ago since you ask. It was weeks – OK, precisely twelve weeks and two days – before that when we last did it. That makes fifteen weeks, four days and an indeterminate number of hours without sex. That's over a quarter of a year without any kind of release. Nothing so much as a . . . *Say the word, Murray* . . . Nothing so much as a *wank*.

The lack of sex has surely caused the lump. I must be backed up, overstocked, whatevered – there's almost certainly a correct medical term for it. It's probably only a matter of days before

my right testicle swells in a similar manner. If I don't do something soon they'll be as big as satsumas – or full-blown oranges.
Well, I can do something right now. If only to rule out the possibility.

━━━━━━━━━━━━━━━━━━ wednesday 5 november / 1.33 a.m.

It didn't work.

Oh, it worked in as much as I managed to shuffle through
some mental reruns and get the job done. But nearly two hours
on the lump is still there. Just as big – though, actually, it's
pretty small. So I still can't sleep. And now I'm in the corridor
outside my bedroom. I'm standing on a chair checking the
battery in my smoke alarm.

It's flat.

four: **fancy that. outposts of the nhs that examine nothing but balls**

Blimey, I didn't know Tom and Nicole were back together.

Mildly surprised but, honestly, not *that* interested, I return *Hello!* to the pile on the table. It's only now that I see the date on the cover – July 1998. It must be a cunning policy cooked up by a Department of Health think-tank. Put ancient magazines in doctors' waiting rooms and watch as patients are transported back to a halcyon age when Tom and Nic were the golden couple and you only had to wait *two* years for a hip replacement.

I've never met Doctor Stump. He has been my GP for years, but I've been avoiding him. Doctors make me squeamish and having one called Stump is hardly likely to cure me of that. The only time I did visit, a locum was on. He was Polish. No disrespect to the guy – I'm sure he would have made an excellent practitioner in suburban Gdansk – but in South Woodford, where the East End blurs into Essex, he was no use whatsoever. Normally I take my ailments to the chemist, where I ply the pharmacist with my symptoms before leaving with an over-the-counter remedy. But I couldn't see myself dropping my trousers in Superdrug, so here I am.

Up on the wall the green light blinks. I'm on. I walk into the shabby surgery and sit down. Stump caps his biro and looks at me from behind his desk. Then he coughs. It isn't a polite throat-clearing *ahem*. It's a prolonged, spewing-blood-into-a-hanky, Doc Holliday affair that doesn't look as if it's

17

going to finish any time before lunch. 'Can I get you some water?' I ask. He glares at me angrily – like *Who's the doctor round here?* – so I sit back and wait. As he tries to catch the spittle with a billowing cotton hankie, I wonder if I'm doing the right thing. I mean, the lump . . . It's probably nothing. The thing is, it doesn't hurt. I've squeezed as hard as I dare squeeze one of my own testicles (a word I'm growing increasingly comfortable with) and there's no pain. If it were something bad, surely it would be painful. By bad, of course, I mean cancer. Pain is the first thing I think of with regard to that disease. Cancer hurts. Like hell, by all accounts. Yet I feel nothing. So what am I doing here? Wasting precious NHS time, most probably.

Then again, if it is something bad, what am I doing *here*? Why am I entrusting my health to a doctor called Stump? It's like calling a new brand of sweetener Anthrax and expecting the public to sprinkle it onto their cornflakes. And look at him retching into his hankie as if he's spent the last few decades ignoring his own profession's very sensible advice on smoking. He can't even manage his own cough and I expect him to help me?

No, whichever way I look at it, coming here was a poor idea. Best I leave now, let him get on with the three old ladies in the waiting room, all of whom looked as if they might die in their seats if they don't get immediate medical attention. I stand up, but with the hand that isn't preventing his lungs from spilling into his lap Stump waves me back into my chair. With an effort that turns his face purple he finally strangles the cough and says in a voice awash with phlegm, 'What can I do for you, Mr . . .' He searches for the name on my file. '. . . Collins?'

'It's *Colin*,' I say. 'Like Cliff Richard.'

'What, it's not your real name?'

'No, I mean it's Cliff *Richard*, not *Richards*. I'm Colin. No S.'

'What can I do for you, Mr Colin?'

I've been giving my next line a fair amount of thought. Actually practising it in front of my bedroom mirror. Much like I used to mime to Smiths songs when I was fourteen. (And now I think about it, *Doctor, it would appear that I have a growth on one of my testicles* sounds like a Morrissey lyric, one he rejected as being *too* gloomy – that and the fact that finding a plausible rhyme for *testicles* would have been beyond even his considerable lyrical gifts.) But now I'm here – on the stage, in a manner of speaking – I can't say it. So instead I mumble, 'I've got the flu.'

'Well, what do you expect me to do about it?'

I don't answer.

'I suggest you go home, take some paracetamol and sleep it off,' he says.

I don't move, though.

'Is that it?' he asks. 'You've got the flu and you just came to tell me?' He picks up his pen and writes something on my file – *time waster* probably.

'No,' I say quietly.

'What then?'

I still can't say it.

'Speak up.' He's irritated now. 'I've got a waiting room full out there.'

Yes, three old ladies and the Grim Reaper.

'It's my . . . I've got a . . .'

He nods by way of encouragement.

'I've got cancer.' *There*. Said it. It's out now.

'Really?' he asks, genuinely curious because, well, there's no note of it in my file. 'Where? When was it diagnosed?'

'It hasn't been . . . Not exactly. But I've got a lump.'

'Where precisely?'

I can't say it.

'Give me a clue.'

'It's . . . It's on . . . My . . .' No, still can't say it.

'Somewhere rather personal perhaps?' Stump hazards.

I nod.

'Why don't you point?'

Good idea. I point.

'You'd better drop your trousers.'

'Do I have to?' I ask.

'Well, you could just describe it for me, I suppose,' Stump says.

Excellent. Relaxed now, I say, 'It's on my left . . . er . . . you know, my left one, and it's about—'

'I was being facetious, Mr Collins—'

'It's Co*lin*.'

'Whatever, if we're going to make any progress at all today you really will have to take your trousers off.'

Damn.

Still traumatised, I buckle my belt and zip up my flies. Stump noisily peels off his surgical gloves and sits down. He picks up my file. 'Smoke, Mr Collins?'

'No,' I say fairly honestly. I'll share in the very occasional joint, my one weedy concession to my inner Jimi Hendrix – I'm sure he's in there somewhere – but I've never touched a cigarette.

'Drink?'

'Only socially . . .'

. . . And not much of that these days.

'How's your general health been?'

'Fine, I suppose. Apart from the flu.'

'Are you stressed?'

'Well, I've got a lump,' I say, not adding, *You cradled it in your bloody hand. How do you think it makes me feel?*

'I meant generally,' he explains.

I should be, shouldn't I? Advertising is one of the more stressful businesses. At least, that's what everyone in advertising would have you believe. Maybe it is if you have to make knife-edge decisions about the fate of multi-million-pound marketing budgets, but I don't do that . . . I lurk around freezer displays with a digital camera.

It wasn't always so. There was a time when I lived on an adrenal diet of tension. It lasted for about six months. I was an account supervisor in the fast lane, whizzing past blue and white signs pointing me in the direction of Rapid Promotion and Big Corner Office. It couldn't last. After its initial rubber-burning burst of speed, my career stalled. I'm languishing on the hard shoulder now, watching younger models scoot by in a blur of alloy wheels. I'm only thirty-one and they're not *that* much younger, but life spans in adland are measured in months, not years. Strangely, while this state of affairs depresses me, it doesn't stress me out.

'No,' I tell Stump, 'I'm not stressed. Generally.'

'Testicular cancer is the commonest form of the disease in young men, you know,' he says, leaning back in his chair and ignoring me sinking in mine. 'Having said that, it's almost certainly not cancer. One big testicular clinic saw over two thousand lumps in a year. Less than a hundred of them were cancers. Incredible, eh? There are *testicular* clinics. Fancy that. Outposts of the NHS that examine nothing but balls.' He's rambling and I'm not feeling comforted.

'If it isn't cancer, what is it?' I ask.

'Could be any number of things,' he replies vaguely.

I need some help here. 'Like?'

Seems he needs help too because he leans over to a pile of books on the floor and examines the titles. After a moment he pulls one from the middle, a big, dusty softback that looks as if it hasn't had its spine bent in years. 'Wonderful book, this.

21

Excellent pictures,' he says, flicking through the pages. He stops, peers at the print for a moment, then reads, '"Testicular swellings commonly misdiagnosed as tumours" . . . Blah, blah . . . "Seminal granuloma, chronic epididymo-orchitis, haematocele" and so on and so forth . . . See? Any number of things.'

All of which are not only unpronounceable but also pull off the difficult feat of sounding more terrifying than cancer.

'I'm going to refer you to Saint Matthew's,' he says.

'The cancer bit of Saint Matthew's?' I whisper.

'Heavens, no. They'd try to have me struck off for wasting their time. You'll see a general surgeon. Maybe a urologist.'

What's a urologist? He's not going to tell me and I'm not about to ask.

'You'll get an appointment within the next couple of weeks – try and keep it. And cut out the cigarettes. Ridiculous habit.' To emphasise the point he launches into a fresh fit of coughing.

'I don't smoke,' I remind him.

'Well, better not start,' he says through the hacks.

I scrape my chair back – I think we're done. 'You really shouldn't worry unduly,' he says as I stand up. He manages to sound annoyed rather than soothing, as if what he'd really like to say is *Pull yourself together, man*.

I look at my watch: nine thirty-five. Sorry, doctor, but I *should* worry. Niall Haye is big on two things – store checks and punctuality – and I'm very late.

_____ 11.03 a.m.

Niall Haye is big on *three* things: store checks, punctuality and contact reports. When I arrived at my desk and checked my e-mail there were seven from Haye. *Seven* times he demanded to know the whereabouts of a contact report. Fair enough. It is a week overdue. I'm typing it now.

to: niall.haye@blowermann-dba.co.uk

       g_breitmar@schenker.com

       s_gilhooley@schenker.com

       b_tofting@schenker.com

cc: brett.topowlski@blowermann-dba.co.uk

       vince.douglas@blowermann-dba.co.uk

re: Contact Report No. 37

Brand Group Meeting:	23 October
Venue:	Blower Mann/DBA
Present for client:	Gerhard Breitmar, Sally Gilhooley, Betina Tofting
Present for agency:	Niall Haye, Murray Colin

Despite having a potentially malignant growth on one of his testicles, plucky Murray Colin took the client through the results of his store checks. There were general oohs and aahs of appreciation and it was unanimously agreed that there is no one better at shooting in tricky supermarket lighting conditions.

Niall Haye presented draft 27 of the ChocoChillout script. There was much discussion about whether the voiceover should read 'a sensuously silky taste adventure' or 'a silkily sensuous adventure in taste'. After failing to reach a consensus, the group agreed to put the matter to research so that a bunch of housewives in Solihull can make the decision.

(Action: NH)

Niall Haye presented the launch media plan. The chart (consisting of the usual Xs in boxes) was generally well received. Sally Gilhooley requested that the Xs in the central column be moved two columns to the left. Betina Tofting agreed, and further suggested that the X immediately below the X at the top right be moved to the box below. Gerhard

Breitmar endorsed these proposals and added a request for the Xs in the extreme left-hand column to appear in red rather than blue. Murray Colin slept peacefully.

> (Action: nobody – on the basis that in two days' time no one would remember what anyone else had said and that, besides, all the Xs could be put in a very big hat, shaken vigorously about and tipped in a heap on the floor, where they would make the same amount of bloody sense.)

Before the meeting broke up Niall Haye invited Gerhard Breitmar to climb onto the table, lower his trousers, kneel on all fours and have his strapping Hunnish behind peppered with kisses by the account team.

Murray Colin
Account Supervisor

I click *send* . . . But only after I've completely rewritten it to make it as dull and harmless as every other contact report I've ever written. My hand goes into my trouser pocket and touches the lump. Thankfully, an incoming e-mail takes my mind off it.

brett.topowlski@blowermann-dba.co.uk
to: murray.colin@blowermann-dba.co.uk
cc:
re: love your contact reports . . .

. . . reading them always makes me thank my sweet lord jesus I wasn't at the meeting. question: is a betina tofting a self-assembly dining table from ikea? another question: fancy buying me and vin bonfire beers tonight?

Taken at face value it reads like the e-mail of a friend. I know better. Brett Topowlski is a copywriter. Vince Douglas is his art director. Together they are a creative team. I, on the other hand, am a suit. Creative teams *do not* buddy up with suits. We're like the Bloods and the Crips. This is because, while it's a creative's job to come up with ideas that are *out there*, it's a suit's function to water them down until they're as bland as every other ad on the box. ChocoChillout is the perfect case in point. Draft one was well *out there* and barely on the legal side of the Obscene Publications Act. Draft twenty-seven is wallpaper – and not even patterned, not even as interesting as, say, a magnolia-painted woodchip. Suits 1, Creatives 0.

No, Brett, Vince and I could never be true friends. They only want me for my access to expense-account beer. However, it doesn't stop me being drawn to them, and especially to Vince. He's an entire Victorian freak show in a single body. He's a bad car crash, one where the firemen are cutting the corpses from the twisted wreckage: you know you're not supposed to look but you can't tear your eyes away.

But it's an experience I won't be enjoying tonight.

I hit *reply*.

murray.colin@blowermann-dba.co.uk

to: brett.topowlski@blowermann-dba.co.uk

cc:

re: love your contact reports . . .

Can't do beer tonight because

1. I'm broke.

2. Megan is coming round to pick up stuff.

3. There's a distinct possibility I've got cancer.

Sorry.

Murray

I send it, but only after deleting item three.

A couple of minutes later:

what bloke wouldn't pass up getting ratted with his mates so he could wait at home for the bitch that dumped him? you sad cunt.

Brett is right – I *would* sooner hang around at home for the bitch that dumped me.

five: **you've been wanking, haven't you?**

I stand in my living room and survey the rock-star chaos. The discarded Stolly bottles, the dusting of coke on the coffee table, the TV lying on its side – well, watching it the right way up is for squares, dude. And, stone me, is that a peroxide groupie wedged down the back of my sofa cushion? How long has she been there?

Actually, most of that was rubbish.

OK, all of it was.

A part of me – the deeply repressed, inner-Jimi-Hendrix bit – would love to be able to say that my flat is a temple to debauchery and that in the post-Megan fallout it resembles Hiroshima at tea-time on 6th August 1945.

I can't, though, in all honesty.

Because I stand in my living room and see . . . Neatness, a pleasure dome of just-so spick and span-ness. No dust or greasy finger marks and certainly no used socks, half-empty takeaway cartons or exhausted vodka bottles. No drugs on the coffee table – just a few magazines, the spines of which are precisely parallel to the table's edge. And while I've got some fairly cool CDs, they're stacked in order. Not in some esoteric rock bloke arrangement, but alphabetically (Smith, Elliott *pre*ceding Smiths, The). This conforms to no rock 'n' roll rulebook I'm aware of.

I could say that this outbreak of tidiness is because Wednesday is my cleaner's day, but that too would be a lie. I haven't got a cleaner. This obsessive order . . .

It's . . . *Me*.

My inner Jimi Hendrix doesn't stand a chance. If I were a pie

27

chart, *Cleaning Impulses* would be a huge slice taking up well over seventy per cent, while *Playing Guitar, Screwing Girls and Drowning in Own Vomit* would be a negligible sliver. I've always been like this. I'm well-known for it and I barely have to clean any more – household grime sees me coming and emigrates. When we first lived together Megan found this side of me endearing and I was a talking point among her girlfriends. One evening she answered the phone to Serena or Carol or whomever to be told, 'I wanted to speak to Murray, actually. Does he know how to remove encrusted limescale from the base of a tap?' I spent a memorable thirty minutes extolling the unbeatable combination of Limelite ('Not the liquid, mind. It's got to be the Power Gel.') and an old toothbrush while Megan looked on with an indulgent smile.

After a time however, the indulgence petered out and I became an irritant. There she was busy making the world a better place, while all I seemed to fret about was who was going to keep it dusted. Over time a nagging tension developed between the forces of Pledge and There's-more-important-things-to-worry-about.

When she left so did her mess. Order returned. No more work files heaped about the living room like badly planned council high-rises, no more damp knickers draped on the central heating and no more scented candles dripping irksome dollops of wax on hard-to-clean surfaces. I should have been happy, shouldn't I?

Well . . . *No*. I was devastated. After a dust and disorder-free week I couldn't stand the vacuum (I refer to the *emptiness* as opposed to my excellent Dyson upright) a moment longer and headed for Wax Lyrical where I bought a fresh stock of smelly candles. Then, inexplicably, I found myself in the Knickerbox next door, six-pack of cotton bikini briefs (assorted colours) in hand. No, it was perfectly explicable. I was going to take them home, rinse and wring them out and leave them dangling from the radiators – a Comfort-fresh reminder of what used to be. As I was about to pay I realised what a pathetic gesture it was. Megan was gone and I'd have to get used to it. The knickers stayed in the shop and, though I was already lumbered with the candles, they've remained wrapped up in a kitchen cupboard.

And now I stand in my living room and survey the germ-free perfection that is a tribute to my hermetically sealed single-hood . . . And when Megan turns up in half an hour, a reminder of the tedious dust buster she left behind.

I know what has to be done.

Deep breath – *You can do this, Murray.*

I start by taking the back of my hand to the magazines, flipping them to a wanton seventy-three degrees to the edge of the coffee table.

7.45 p.m.

She should be here by now.

As I wait I look at the mess that I've painstakingly created and it's taking every ounce of willpower to resist tidying up.

I need a distraction. My hand goes in search of one, snaking into my trouser pocket and feeling for the—

I have got to stop this. Stop worrying *unduly*. Pull myself together.

I go to the bedroom, fetch the cardboard box containing Megan's belongings, and put it on the coffee table. One more thing. I root around the kitchen until I find the scented candles. I unwrap one and light it. I immediately blow it out. It's lavender. She *hates* lavender.

7.53 p.m.

'What's that horrible smell?' she says as I let her in.

29

Though I dumped the candle in the bin, the bouquet has lingered.

My ex has an implausibly sensitive nose. The one and only time that I lit up a joint while home alone she busted me, picking up the scent as she walked out of South Woodford tube. 'I'm a *solicitor*,' she declared. 'I work with the police, the CP-bloody-S. Do you have any idea how much you could be compromising me?' It was like going out with the drug squad's star sniffer dog – the one that can smell the heroin in the baggage hold as the plane *takes off* in Islamabad. I couldn't get away with a thing. One night she climbed into bed about an hour after me and as I stirred she said, 'You've been wanking, haven't you?'

'Have not,' I mumbled sleepily while simultaneously shifting my hip onto the small sticky patch on the sheet.

'Don't lie, Murray,' she snapped. 'I can *smell* it.'

I follow her as she walks through the hall and into the living room for the first time in three weeks, three days and nearly six hours. She must have been in court today because she's wearing a sober-ish grey suit, white blouse, glossy opaque tights and shoes that tread the fine line between sensible and sexy. I feel something stir. In my gut *and* down there. You cannot imagine how gratifying this is. I've got a lump, yet I'm getting *aroused*. Any sign of a normal sexual impulse (even if it's lusting after my depressingly unavailable ex) is surely also a sign that I don't have cancer. I mean, cancer and sex drive, they're mutually exclusive, aren't they? But I have to stifle it because this is neither the time nor the place. No, it *is* the place – at least two of my happiest memories consist of spontaneously doing it with Megan in this very living room (having first spontaneously draped a towel over the sofa to avoid troublesome stains) – but it is clearly not the time.

'You can tell I've moved out,' she says jauntily. 'It looks really . . . *tidy*.'

'Does it?' I reply, deflating, probably visibly. 'I haven't cleaned in ages.'

She raises a sceptical eyebrow, then says, 'How have you been?'

Well, since you decided to move in with a QC who probably earns thirty times my salary and is old enough to be, if not your father, then your considerably older brother, and since you chose to announce the joyous news on the very day that I'd been out and blown six and a half grand on a ring with which I was going to get down on my knees and ask you to be mine forever and ever and ever, and since you're now twizzling your hair around your finger in a manner that is guaranteed to make me melt like a Mars Bar in a Glasgow deep fat fryer, I feel like rubbish . . . If you must know.

'I'm getting over the flu,' I say, going directly for the sympathy vote, before adding, 'but I'm fine, thanks . . . You?'

'You know – busy. How's work?'

'Oh, the usual juggling act of exotic shoots and five-hour lunches.'

'Still taking your orders from Mammon, then?'

'Well, from Mammon's little helper . . . You know . . . Niall. Can I get you a coffee or something?'

'No, I'd better not stay. I'm in court first thing – my client fled Nigeria after she'd been raped by an entire army platoon and now the Home Office wants to send her back there. *Un*believable.'

This brief snatch of conversation pretty much sums it up. Why Megan left me. I lack commitment. Not the emotional kind – splurging six and a half grand on a ring more or less settled that one. What I lack is her passion for justice. While she is using her degree to make the world safe for the poor and disenfranchised, I'm using mine to feed them choc-ices. It doesn't take Naomi Klein to argue that, while it undoubtedly delivers a sensuously silky adventure in taste, ChocoChillout won't even begin to address the iniquities in the continent of Africa.

It's not that I don't believe in the same things as Megan. I do. Mostly.

Up to a point.

I always encouraged her crusades on behalf of victims of police harassment and the fascist asylum laws, but that wasn't enough. My trouble was that I could never bring myself to make the leap to actually *doing* something. It was never quite the right time to give up my comfortable salary and the job that – even if I don't *love* it – is a pretty cushy number. Besides, how was I going to make a difference? Social work? Sorry, but I'm too easily scared – show me a pug-faced dad accused of beating up his kids and I'd be hiding behind the six-year-old. Voluntary Service Overseas? What skills can I offer? Do they need an expert store checker in Eritrea? I do have fantasies about joining a crack earthquake rescue team (see How I'd Like to Die, Item Four), but – *come* on – I also quite fancy the idea of having dew-drenched sex in a spring meadow with Uma Thurman. Doesn't mean it's going to happen.

(Number one: it's far from certain that Uma would be agreeable. Number two: where can you find a spring meadow that isn't saturated with pesticides these days? And – much more pertinent, this one – number three: faced with the *reality* of alfresco sex, I'd flee. Said meadow could be miles from the nearest homestead and I still wouldn't be able to get it up – well, a skylark might be watching.)

I did once make a personal sacrifice and take a stand. I gave up a Saturday – valuable *housework* time – to accompany Megan on the last big protest before Gulf War Two. I wasn't comfortable though and she could tell. Issues simply aren't that black and white for me – my politics are coloured not red, orange, blue or green, but a vivaciously vague shade of grey. (In the opinion polls, I'm one of the fourteen per cent that always votes Don't Know, the true third party in British politics). While Megan and thousands of others were yelling 'Blair out!' and 'No war!' I was looking vainly for a small group chanting (quietly, so as not to bother anyone), 'We're not sure, we're not sure.'

In the end she couldn't live with an armchair liberal and dumped me for the real thing: Sandy Morrison QC, defender of the wrongly convicted, champion of the underdog and regular star of *Question Time*. He was on it last week. He was brilliant. And his hair looked fabulous – like a lion's mane. He was maddeningly articulate too. *Bastard*. Call me bitter, but it struck me then that taking a stand for society's losers must be a doddle when it gives you a seven-figure income.

I look at Megan and I wonder if Sandy Morrison QC is waiting outside in his Bentley Arnage T with its six-point-eight-litre engine which delivers four hundred and fifty brake horse-power, making it the fastest production Bentley *ever*. How do I – an automotive illiterate – know all about Sandy Morrison's *one-hundred-and-seventy-grand* car? I read about it in the *Mail*. They were doing one of their *so-called-lefty lives in lap of luxury* stories, and had got wind of the fact that he'd recently traded up from a Jag. But he hadn't completely sold out. He'd bought one in lush socialist red.

Megan looks at the box on the coffee table and asks, 'Are those my things?'

'Uh-huh.'

There isn't much. Some soppy compilation CDs, half a dozen books, a pair of jeans, a bra that ended up in one of my drawers for reasons that have *nothing* to do with anything unsavoury, and some photos from our last holiday – they were taken with my camera so strictly speaking I should keep them, but I'm making a point.

I didn't put in her garlic crusher. I want to keep something of hers. Besides, it might give her a reason to call me.

I did slip the ring into the box. She doesn't know about that.

* * *

The evening had gone like this:

'Megan, I've got something I want to say.'

'Me too. You go first.'

'No, you.'

'OK . . . Look, there isn't an easy way to tell you this so I'd better just do it . . . I've . . . I've met someone . . .'

After that, 'Will you do me the honour of marrying me?' seemed a tad superfluous.

She picks up the box and clasps it to her chest.

I *will* her to spot the VSO booklet that I carefully placed beside it on the coffee table (at a cocksure fifty-eight degree angle), but – *damn* it – she doesn't. She doesn't notice the application form for a job with Waltham Forest Social Services either. Instead she looks at me searchingly.

'Murray . . . Are you really . . . all right?'

No, I am not all right. The moment you've left I'm going to surround myself with snapshots, holiday souvenirs, the set of aluminium espresso cups that we bought together in Camden Market (the ones we never used again after the third-degree burn to my bottom lip), my copy of the Complete Seinfeld Scripts *which you said would always remind you of me – and will thus always remind me of you – your garlic crusher, the other bra that I didn't put in the box and several other mementos of our five years, eight months, one week and three days together. Then I will swallow an entire bottle of paracetamol and wash it down with the ouzo we bought in Kos, before dying weeping, broken and about fifty years before my due date.*

All of which I manage to condense into a shrug.

She looks at me sorrowfully and says, 'You need to—'

'What, get a life?'

'I wasn't going to say that. But you do need to do something with yourself.'

I've heard this before, though never delivered with such pity. *You need to do something with yourself* was Megan's cry throughout

34

the five years, eight months, et cetera of our relationship. Towards the end it was uttered with increasingly desperate shrillness. She had a point. All she wanted was for me to have a dream, a direction, to stop drifting. She wasn't the only one. *I* wanted me to stop drifting – still do. But I've never been one to take destiny by the scruff of its neck and give it a jolly good shake – or even to tap it on the shoulder and utter a polite *ahem*. A few years ago I thought my job was The Thing, but it wasn't long before I realised my heart wasn't in it. I turn up and go through the motions, but I lack the desire to make anything of it. But what do I possess the desire to do? I've asked myself that one enough times. I've come up with answers too. Lists of them. In the fond belief that committing something to paper will make it seem more tangible and therefore achievable. I remember my last one, written shortly before Meg left:

1. Pony trek up Andean spine of S America

I should point out that the only horse I've ever ridden was pink and had a slot for the fifty-pence piece . . . But, you know, think Big and all that.

2. Write Bill Bryson-ish book of pony trek (drawing attention to plight of indigenous peoples, threatened tree frogs, etc.)
3. Return Elgin Marbles (NB: check first)

The *NB* was a reminder to check whether it was Elgin that had stolen them or Elgin that wanted them back. I was *pretty* sure that Elgin had nicked them, but you know how these things can go pear-shaped for lack of basic groundwork.

4. Buy old bus. Refurb as mobile drug rehab unit (double-decker/make it residential?)

5. Mobile soup kitchen?
6. Mobile *potage* kitchen? (Sell lobster bisque/vichyssoise to City workers at £7 per portion)

Because it was clearly getting pretty stupid at this point, I took a coffee break. That was when I noticed my kitchen hygiene was slipping below its usual operating theatre standard and wrote:

7. Clean kitchen cupboards
8. Ditto hob
9. Mr Muscle Kitchen Spray
10. Cif Cream (lemon)
11. Flash Wipes
12. Plain digestives
13. Gold Blend (decaf)

I probably needn't add that items seven to thirteen were made reality within hours, whereas numbers one to six have yet to progress from back-of-an-envelope status.

'I'm fine, Megan,' I say now. 'I've got all sorts of things in the pipeline.'

'I hope so. Just don't leave them in there too long.'

She turns to go and I ask, 'Do you want a lift?'

Now, why did you say that, because it's only going to lead to her asking you . . .

'You've finally had the car fixed?'

See what I mean?

'Um . . . No . . . But I could call a minicab.'

'It's OK. I'll get the tube.'

I follow her to the front door. She opens it and says, 'Bye, then. I'll give you a call if there's anything else.' She dips forward clumsily and kisses me on the cheek.

Then she's gone.

I return to the living room and open a chink in the curtain.

I watch her cross the road and walk in the direction of the tube station. But she stops fifty yards away beside a gleaming red Bentley and climbs in.

The woman I was meant to be with.

Megan and Murray.

M&M.

Two little peanuts nestling in their chocolate and candy shells.

Gone forever.

(Unless she comes back for the garlic crusher.)

Now it's Megan and Sandy.

M&S.

Two items of sensible cotton underwear nestling in a . . .

It really doesn't bear thinking about.

And she doesn't even know that I wanted – *want* – to marry her.

And that there is a statistically slight (according to Stump, who hardly seems the reliable type) yet distinct possibility that I have a disease that begins with C and has been known to *kill* people.

I listen to the sound of fireworks fizzing and popping all over South Woodford. It's as if they're celebrating the fairy-tale union of Meg 'n' Sand.

God, this self-*pity*. Megan was right. I have *got* to do something with myself.

Well, I can take care of that right now. I start with the magazines, adjusting them so they are once again in perfect alignment with the table's edge.

9:17 p.m.

I switch off the vacuum cleaner and turn on the stereo. Solace in song. A disc is already in the slot so I press *play*. It's Caesars. 'Sort It Out'. A nice, bouncy tune. And, now I listen to it, lyrically apt.

37

I'm gonna smoke crack
'Cause you're never coming back
I'm gonna shoot speedballs
Bang my head against the walls
I wanna sniff glue
'Cause I can't get over you.

Yes, that is *sooooo* . . . not me. If, on the other hand, it went, *I'm gonna spring clean, Wanna spray some Mister Sheen* . . .

six: **it's kind of personal**

I wake up and the first thing I think – apart, obviously, from *Damn, forgot to set the alarm* – is that it has been five days since Megan came for her stuff. I wonder why she hasn't been in touch about the ring. Or the garlic crusher. I tip myself out of bed and make a coffee. Then, still in my pyjama bottoms, I head downstairs to the hall and grab my post. No Jiffy Bag containing a jewellery-box-shaped lump. Just the usual crap.

Back in my flat I sit on my sofa and open . . . *taran-tara!* . . . a Barclaycard statement:

BALANCE FROM PREVIOUS STATEMENT	£977.74
PAYMENT RECEIVED – THANK YOU	30.00 –
JP STEIN OF HATTON GARDEN	6,499.00
MONTHLY INTEREST AT 1.385%	13.12
NEW BALANCE	**£7,459.86**

Bugger.

I've spent the last few weeks filing this under D for Denial. I have no idea how I'm going to pay it. The truth is that I had no idea when I walked into JP Stein and picked out the chunky diamond in an eighteen-carat setting. I figured that the moment Megan said *yes*, the world would transform into a magical place where it chucked down in Ethiopia like an August bank holiday, George W embraced Osama B on the White House lawn and credit-card bills were quietly forgotten.

Which I'm sure would have happened if she had said *yes*.

So, if you're upset about the sad state of the world, you know who to blame.

No, that's not fair. The fact is that she never got the chance to reply because I was too wet to ask the question.

I crumple the statement and toss it across the room. Then, unable to fight the Cleaning Impulse, I retrieve it from the floor and put it in the bin. I return to my post and open an *exclusive* invitation to become the proud owner of a Capital One Platinum Card . . . an *exclusive* invitation from Renault to test-drive a Mégane . . . and an *exclusive* invitation to an appointment at Saint Matthew's Hospital in Leytonstone.

Something else I'd filed under D.

Actually, I'm not in denial. Over the last few days I've persuaded myself to take up Doctor Stump – a *wise* and *experienced* general practitioner – on his reasonable and statistically based suggestion that I almost certainly DO NOT have cancer. It's probably a straightforward case of seminal granuloma and, honestly, how bad can that be? It sounds like a nourishing high-fibre supplement, available at Boots, Holland and Barrett and all good health-food shops. Whatever, I bet it's something that clears up with the help of a non-astringent ointment. No, I'll surely be putting unnecessary pressure on an already stretched health service by showing up for the appointment.

I bin the letter and switch on the TV.

Hyam.

Richard Hyam-Glass. Ex-junior minister for something or other, convicted of taking bribes after having unsuccessfully sued Channel Four, which had made the original accusation. The sleaziest aspect wasn't the lying or even the backhanders – he was a politician and they're part of the job spec. No, his one truly despicable act was to shove his thirteen-year-old daughter into the witness box to lie on his behalf. She provided the false alibi that very nearly won his libel trial.

I remember feeling sorry for her, being scarred in public by her own father, branded a perjurer when she'd barely grown out of Barbies. I wonder what she's up to now. Languishing in a rehab clinic for teenage junkies? I doubt it. Probably lounging around the grounds of a Swiss finishing school.

Finally rumbled, Hyam-Glass did his time in a five-star Hampshire jail, where he wrote an *'achingly confessional'* (the *Mail*) and *'poignantly repentant'* (*The Times*) memoir. Now he has found redemption. A canny producer read his book, studied the jacket photo – which showed a handsome face etched deeply with the lines of *suffering* – and decided to re-launch him as daytime telly's Mr Empathy.

You might wonder why I remember some relatively minor politician's fall from grace so vividly. Well, I lived and breathed it vicariously through Megan. She was a junior in Channel Four's legal department at the time. For her it was the clearest case of good against evil since Superman versus Lex Luthor. The TV channel's cause looked hopelessly lost, but at the eleventh hour their barrister put in a barnstorming performance. He stood up, cleared his throat and reduced the plaintiff's key witness to tears as he showed her to be nothing more than a brazen liar. Of course, that she was only thirteen might have helped him. At the time a saying about candy and babies sprang to mind, but I didn't mention it to Megan.

I wish now that I had. The barrister was a bloke called Sandy Morrison.

I watch Richard Hyam-Glass bounding up and down the steps on his set, allowing his audience one or – if they behave – two words in edgeways. The show, like all these things, has nothing to do with giving *ordinary people* a voice and everything to do with providing a TV studio large enough to contain its presenter's bloated ego. He's tossing out *empathetic* phrases: *emotional credit account* and *the long and winding road to closure*. He could be talking about anything that entails trauma – which these days does mean *any*thing – and I have to look at the caption to see what the topic is. *Living with cancer.*

I switch off the TV – *not* because I'm in denial, but because I'm late for work – and head for the bathroom. I run the shower and climb in. I squeeze a dollop of gel into my hand and soap my body. Same order as always: face, shoulders, arms, torso, groin . . . I can feel the lump and I don't know if it's an effect created by the blast of water bouncing off my scrotum, but it feels as if it's alive, like it's setting off on an impromptu growth spurt for the benefit of my soapy fingertips.

Stupid. Of course it isn't growing. But I'm panicking now. I rinse off, towel myself dry and dress. Then I head for the office. But not before I've retrieved the letter from the bin.

———————————————————————————————— 10.54 a.m.

'You're late. *Again*,' Haye snaps. 'And you've got soap in your ear.'

'Sorry – I seemed to run out of time this morning.'

'Well, don't let it happen again. This isn't the image Blower Mann likes to project to its clients.'

Haye is big on four things: store checks, punctuality, contact reports and the image Blower Mann likes to project to its clients. To give him his due, soap in ear surely breaches the spirit, if not the letter of the Blower Mann dress code.

'Anyway,' he continues, 'it's assessment time. I've got you down for a thirty-minute slot on Thursday morning. Make sure your diary's clear.'

After I'd left uni I got a letter from Blower Mann informing me I had an interview with one of their group account directors – Niall Haye. *Wow*, I thought, *Niall Haye*. Of course, I'd never heard of him, but what a *sexy-cool* name – a twinkle-toed Irish footballer's name, an edgy author's name, a *rock star's* name.

Never be seduced by a name.

Got that?

Never.

Niall Haye is a drone. Of all the drones in the hive, he is the droniest. A hundred-grand showbiz Porsche sits in his designated parking space, but it can't conceal the man's total lack of colour.

And if any one thing has killed my ambition it's the fact that twice a year he sits me down for my assessment and dangles the promise that if I work *really* hard then one day I could turn into *him*.

'Thursday, Thursday,' I burble as I feel the bump of the hospital letter in my jacket. 'Er . . . I can't, Niall. I've got a hospital appointment . . . Sorry.'

'Nothing I should worry about, Murray?'

His uncharacteristic display of tenderness surprises me and the words, *Er, it's almost certainly nothing, but I'm having a very minor lump checked out,* almost spill out . . . but not quite. What I say instead is, 'It's nothing really . . . It's kind of personal.'

Which is a mistake because, now I think about it, Haye is big on *five* things: store checks, punctuality, contact reports, appearance, and the prevention of personal affairs impacting (his favourite verb – though, of course it isn't actually a verb; just a word that he and his kind have press-ganged into performing against type) on work. Worse still, the linking of a hospital appointment to the phrase *it's kind of personal* surely has him picturing a visit to an STD clinic.

'You of all people,' he says, 'should not be taking your bi-annual appraisal lightly. If I may use my favourite analogy—'

Let me guess. Space, the final frontier?

'—a career is rather like interplanetary travel—'

Bingo!

'—The slightest misfire on your rocket's trim controls—'

Trim controls, trim controls . . . Must have left them in my

43

workstation. In my desk-tidy perhaps? Oh, I was forgetting; this is an analogy.

'—and you'll miss your destination by light years. Your ship, my friend—'

Pur-lease, Haye – I am not your friend.

'—has yet to leave the launch pad. If you've any interest at all in achieving lift-off, you'll reschedule the hospital.'

Oh yes, how I'd love to cancel an urgent investigation into a potentially life-threatening disease so I can listen to you marking me out of ten on my performance across fifteen key criteria.

'I'll do my best,' I say.

He turns and walks briskly away, all things-to-do-people-to-see. I can't believe how jaded I feel. A thirty-one-year-old burn out. Yet there's one thing that gives me hope. I do, after all, have a dream, though not one of which Megan would approve. I'm not sure I entirely approve of it myself. This is how it goes:

Haye: *Murray, something huge has come up, a gold-plated revenue opportunity and a chance to make the world a better place.*

Colin: *What is it, Niall?*

Haye: *Before I tell you, I need to know I can count on you one hundred and ten per cent. You'll be playing on the A-team, pissing with the big boys, and I need to know you're up for it.*

Colin: *You know I relish a challenge, Niall. Show me your biggest executive urinal and let me hose down that porcelain.*

Haye: *We've been appointed to handle Mr Muscle.*

Colin: *Fantastic! Stupendous. This is the one we've been waiting for.*

Haye: *Isn't it? We've got the whole lot. The kitchen spray, the bathroom cleaner, the entire kit and caboodle.*

Colin: *Even the oven spray, the drain cleaner and the handy orange-scented kitchen wipes?*

Haye: *Their entire product portfolio is ours and I believe there's*
        only one man who can handle it . . . (Unnecessarily over-
        played dramatic pause) . . . Murray, this is your baby.
SFX: *Manly backslaps and high fives.*

It isn't always Mr Muscle. Sometimes it's Cif, sometimes Dettox.
Other times, as a sop to my ex, it's an as yet un-launched range
of eco-friendly products that really do make the world a better
as well as a cleaner and more fragrant place.

Murray: *Can you believe it, Meg? Thanks to me the Midlands and*
         the Southeast have been officially pronounced germ-free,
         and it's been achieved without any increase in CFC and
         chlorine levels.
Megan: *Oh, Murray, you really have made the planet safer for*
         our unborn child and you've done it without sacrificing
         market share. Come here and let me smother you with
         kisses.

Whatever, I honestly think that being given control of a big-
spending household cleaner account would give my life
meaning and purpose. I imagine the factory tours where I'm
shown how they mix the chemicals that cut through grease,
yet leave no unsightly powdery residue. I picture myself in a
white protective suit being allowed a glimpse of the aggressive solvents that, if they weren't so busy breaking down
baked-on filth, could be used by some crazed despot for his
WMD programme. I dream of brainstorming sessions where I
lead a crack team of marketing pros and detergent boffins in
search of the Holy Grail: a multi-surface cleaner suitable for
kitchens *and* bathrooms. It's a question of fragrance. You may
or may not have noticed, but kitchen cleaners smell entirely
inappropriate when you use them in the bathroom and vice
versa. It's only a little thing, but a one-product-fits-all solution

must be out there . . . If only they could find the right scent.

I'm rambling. My point is that, sad to say, the task – the job of Detergents Tsar – would be more than advertising. For me it would be evangelism.

seven: **i have done this before, you know. that's why i keep my nails short**

Why Saint *Matthew*? He started out as a tax inspector, didn't he? Hardly a name to comfort the sick, and surely it only reminds the dying of death duties.

The place is vast; an industrial sprawl reminiscent of a Soviet uranium facility in the Siberian wastes – except somehow it ended up in east London. It must take the health budget of a third-world country just to heat and light the place.

Where's Outpatients? Is it the same as A&E or is it something different? I wonder this as I walk past a group of three old men in winceyette pyjamas smoking by a fire exit. Don't think I'll be asking them.

The story goes that a minor royal – the Duchess of Chingford or something – turned up to cut the ribbon on a new paediatric ward in the early nineties and she still hasn't found her way out. Never mind pegging out on trolleys in corridors, people must die simply trying to find the right department – unless they've had the good sense to pack a rucksack with food, water and Kendal Mint Cake.

I'm walking around in circles. I know this because the chain smokers are looming into view again.

————————————————————————————— 9.55 a.m.

By the time I find the right Outpatients I'm nearly half an hour late. I'm tired and footsore, and I'm wishing I were significant enough to qualify for Blower Mann's corporate BUPA membership. I'm also worried that I've missed my slot. I shouldn't be. This is the NHS and they're running well behind.

My appointment is in one of Saint Matthew's new bits. The reception area has floor to ceiling windows and a bracing view of big trees, though I think I can make out a tall chimney stack between two sycamores. Hospital incinerators always unsettle me. I know they put old bandages and stuff in them, but what else? I mean, if you'd asked the commandant of Auschwitz about his, I bet he'd have said, 'Ach, zose zings? Zey are just for burnink ze garden rubbish und votnot.' Hospitals bring out the paranoiac in me. I've seen *Coma* too many times. Show me a couple of doctors chatting by a coffee machine and I'll show you a conspiracy. I'm scared of flying, but I'm *terrified* of hospitals. And it's an entirely rational fear. Statistics are used to soothe the nervous flyer: *you're far more likely to get knocked down by a car* and so on. But when it comes to nervous patients they're flummoxed. *Hospitals are perfectly safe – more people die in . . . Er . . . Die in . . .* Die in *what*, then? Look at it this way: even if you get whacked in a car crash there's a fair chance you won't die in the wreckage – no, they rush you to a *hospital* to do that.

I badly need a distraction. I reach into my briefcase, fish out the *Guardian* and open it at random – 'MIRACLE' CANCER DRUG DISCREDITED IN TRIALS. Why didn't I buy the *Daily Sport*? Right now I could do with a light-hearted lap-dancers-abducted-by-aliens-for-intergalactic-sex-orgies story. Ironically, I have a sudden urge to take up smoking – nicotine might be just the ticket. Without even moving my eyes, though, I can see three NO SMOKING signs. I look at a kid in a baseball cap on the far side of the waiting area. He's got no eyebrows, which suggests that he's most likely bald beneath the hat. Jesus, *cancer*. He's trying to read a Spider-man comic, but it's obvious his heart isn't in it. How old is he? Nine? Ten? He should be in school. Or bunking off. Whatever, he doesn't deserve to be here. At least his mum is with him. I don't often wish for my mother, but I'd like her to be with me now. What am I thinking? No, I wouldn't. She'd be crying. When I gashed my shin at scouts she was hysterical. I needed two stitches and a tetanus. She required treatment for shock and was kept in overnight for observation. I had to catch the bus home *on my own*. Could she cope with cancer or, rather, with the *faintest* and most *wafer-thin* outside chance of it? Forget about it.

But I wish someone were with me.

A few weeks ago that someone would have been Megan. Situations like this bring out the best in her – her innate empathy makes her a natural Florence Nightingale. Last night I came close to calling her – I got as far as dialing the first five digits of her mobile. I couldn't go through with it – I *hate* to seem needy.

The *engagement ring*. How needy must that have made me look? She must have found it and seen it for what it was – a cheap (six-and-a-half-grand-cheap!) shot at emotional blackmail. I picture the scene:

Megan: *Jesus, Sandy, have you seen this? He thinks he can buy*
         me. He just doesn't *get it.*
Sandy: *Have a heart, darling. He must be—*
         (The rest of his answer is drowned out by . . .
SFX: *£6,499 of diamond solitaire being flushed down a toilet.*

I need that ring back – with or without Megan attached. I still have no idea how I'm going to pay for it. I've started buying lottery tickets – £20 blown on them today – because odds of fourteen million to one must be better than no chance at all.

Can't think about all that now. I return to the newspaper. With eyes closed I flick past the cancer drug story. When I open them again I'm staring at RADICAL QC CAMPAIGNS FOR REFUGE and a picture of Sandy Morrison. Well, who the hell else? He's standing outside an asylum centre in Highbury that's facing closure. The neighbours can't stand the place, apparently. Sandy is one of them, but he's swimming against the NIMBY tide and is all for it. Normally I'd be sympathetic to his argument, but seeing his handsome face makes me want to round up every last refugee, load them into containers and truck them out of the country. And if a certain *radical* lawyer gets caught up in the mêlée and ends up being shipped to a crime-ridden tenement in Tirana . . . Acceptable collateral damage, if you ask me.

My mobile beeps. The receptionist glares at me and points at the MOBILE PHONES MUST BE SWITCHED OFF sign, which is competing for attention with NO SMOKING. I don't care though – being in possession of an active mobile could be an imprisonable offence, but at least mine is dragging me from the excruciating thoughts swimming about my head. I turn away so she can't see me lift the phone to my ear. I listen to the message. It's Jakki: 'Niall wants to know where you put the Schenker job-start file. Call me when you can.'

Haye was miffed when I didn't reschedule my appointment – which guarantees me a column of fat zeros on my assessment, as well as about a dozen pesky messages on my mobile. Well, sod him. I'm having some quality *me* time.

In a hospital.

With some sick people.

I switch off my phone with a decisive flourish just in time to hear the receptionist call out, 'Mr Collins?' She's squinting at a folder with – I presume – my name on it. 'It's *Colin*. No S,' I say on autopilot, though I don't know why I bother.

'Doctor Morrissey will see you now,' she says. 'Third door on the left.'

Just what I need – a doctor whose namesake is pop music's singing suicide note.

Doctor Morrissey doesn't have a bunch of gladioli sticking out of his trousers and a comedy quiff. In fact *she* has very short hair indeed. She's young as well. Which is reassuring, actually – if I were on some critical, tumours-sprouting-out-of-his-ears list, surely I'd be seeing a battle-scarred senior consultant. With her Peter Pan haircut and pert features she's quite elfin. No way would an elf pull the literal graveyard shift.

'Take a seat,' she says pleasantly with a hint of a West Country accent – not one of the Manchester Morrisseys, then. 'Why don't you tell me why you're here.' She must know why I'm here. Hasn't she got some notes, a letter or something? Do I really have to explain? She seems to sense my discomfort and says, 'I know you've found a lump . . . On one of your testicles. I just need to know how long you've been aware of it.'

'A couple of weeks. Maybe three,' I say.

'That's good. Our biggest headache is when men find something and then ignore it for months. Why don't you let me take a look?'

I knew she was going to ask me that. In fact, I showered twice this morning because I knew someone was going to ask me precisely that question. So much for all the preparation because I feel extremely uncomfortable now. I hated it enough when sixty-something Stump had me drop my trousers and felt me up. Twenty-something, not unattractive Doctor Morrissey is an entirely different proposition and I imagine a lot of blokes would be thrilled at the thought of her small and fragile hands down there. Not me, though. I suppose I'm shy. Or uptight and repressed. Whatever, I'm someone who needs to be on very familiar terms with delicate feminine hands before I'm comfortable with them touching me below the waist. Again she senses my awkwardness and says, 'I have done this before, you know.

51

That's why I keep my nails short. You can take your trousers off behind the curtain if you like.'

I'm sitting on the edge of an examination couch, a needle in my arm, and under the circumstances I feel remarkably relaxed. Doctor Morrissey is taking blood. 'We'll do some tests for tumour markers,' she explains matter-of-factly. 'They indicate the possible presence of cancer cells.' I flinch at the mention of the T- followed closely by the C-word. 'Of course, you most likely don't have cancer,' she goes on, and I relax again because I believe it from her. 'It's much less common than you might imagine. It looks like you have some sort of growth down there though and we need to get to the bottom of it.'

She knows that I have *some sort of growth* because she sent me to a room along the corridor where a technician gave me an ultrasound scan. This, bizarrely, is what sparked my sense of calm. Ultrasounds – to me, anyway – are Good Things. My only experience of them was when Liz Napier, a senior account director at work, brought the print-out from hers into the office. A small, fuzzy black and white image that drew a gaggle of cooing onlookers. I peered at it too. I looked at the snap of the perfectly formed foetus that everyone agreed was sucking its thumb, though all I could see was something that resembled a photo of Greenland taken on a particularly cloudy day by a satellite equipped only with a disposable Kodak. But of course Liz didn't give birth to Greenland. She had a perfectly formed, thumb-sucking baby girl called Carmen. That's why ultrasound scans equal nice, warm and pleasant, even when they're looking for cancer. So what if this has no basis in reason? It's a sturdy-looking straw and just try and stop me clutching it.

Doctor Morrissey has helped to ease my stress as well. She has told me several times that I most likely don't have testicular cancer and that even if I do, the cure rate is up in the very high nineties when it's caught early enough. I'm choosing to go with her because she's pleasant and competent and seems to know what she's talking about. She takes the needle from my arm – very competently, I might add – and says, 'OK, we're done.'

I stand up, roll down my shirtsleeve and pull on my jacket. I bend down to pick up my briefcase and my Lotto tickets tumble out of my pocket and onto the floor. She picks them up and hands them back to me. 'You're the optimistic type, then,' she says.

'More like desperate, actually.'

'Well, if it's any consolation, the odds of there being some-thing seriously wrong with you are almost as long.'

Almost? Only bloody *almost*?

Bloody Morrisseys. Why do they always have to drag things down?

eight: **absolutely dandy**

I pick up the tray of drinks from the bar and fight my way across the room to Brett, Vince and Kenny. Kenny is Production Geezer. The man without whom the glittering mirror ball we fondly call *advertising* would come crashing to the dance floor. He's the man responsible for seeing to it that Brett and Vince's lovingly crafted adverts make it into print. Always *just* in the nick of time. And usually, to his immense credit, the right way up.

As I sit down it only takes a moment to figure that the conversation hasn't moved on from ten minutes ago. The question: How would you spend a Lotto win? It was sparked by my fumbling for a twenty to cover the round and pulling this week's hopeless punt from my pocket.

'You're mad, Vin,' Kenny pronounces. 'Why would you risk blowing it when you've just won at fourteen *million* to one?'

'Egg-fucking-*zactly*, you tubby twonk,' Vince says. 'If I've just won at fourteen mill, I'm gonna fancy my chances at twos, ain't I?'

Vince's Lottery Dream: '*Hit the casino and put the fucking lot on red.*' Which, naturally, struck me as deeply insane, though I didn't say so. Partly because, as is often the way with Vince, his logic has a perverted appeal. But, no, I mustn't get sucked into this way of thinking. It's *profoundly* insane.

'You're mad,' Kenny repeats. 'You've got your millions. Why piss it away?'

'I wouldn't be pissing it away,' Vince says. 'You're forgetting the *secret*.'

I must have missed this when I was buying the round.

'You gonna tell us what this secret is, then?' Kenny asks.

'The secret is I couldn't fucking lose.'

'Yeah, but what is it?'

'If I told you it wouldn't be a secret, would it?' Vince says.

'More like there ain't no secret,' Kenny mutters, draining his glass. 'Here, stick another one in there, Murray.'

Hey, wow, you noticed I'm here.

Brett says, 'Give him a break, Kenny . . .'

What, you're buying this round?

'. . . He hasn't said how he'd spend his win yet. Tell us, Murray. Then you can get the beers in.'

'Er . . . I don't really know,' I say, because . . . Well, I really don't know. I don't have a dream, unless you count getting Megan back (not sure a lottery win would do it) or being promoted to Account Director (Detergent Brands). Endless lists on the backs of envelopes have more or less proved that I'm devoid of credible ambition.

'There must be *something*,' Brett prods. 'Just make it up.'

He's right, there *must* be something. Even Vince, who usually never projects beyond the next ten minutes, has an ambition.

I'm not talking about putting it all on red, which as far as I could tell, came out of nowhere. I'm referring to the Official Vince Douglas Dream. Vince is like every creative. None of them wants to be doing ads forever. Nearly every copywriter I know is working on his Novel (though they're so conditioned to thinking in thirty-second chunks that they rarely make it past page two). Similarly, every art director wants to Direct – preferably Cate Blanchett and Halle Berry in a twenty-first century *Thelma and Louise*, but, frankly, they'd take *Police Academy 12* if it came down to it.

Vince is the exception. He longs to break out of ads, but he has no wish to become the next Ridley Scott. His dream involves cunning, bravado and a miniature submarine. Ironically, it was inspired by a film – an action flick about a sunken nuclear sub. The crew spent a couple of hours running out of oxygen while outside Kurt Russell or Chuck Norris or whoever attempted rescue in a little yellow submersible. I can't give you much more detail than that because I didn't see it. I'd sooner have typhus-dipped slivers of bamboo shoved under my fingernails than sit through one minute of a film about my personal idea of hell. Vince saw it seven times though, munching his popcorn and thinking, *What if you put the docking mechanism on the top of the rescue sub instead of the bottom and went up instead of down?* In short, this is the plan: buy sub, sail up and down Med on lookout for millionaires' yachts, dive beneath them, dock, make hole, climb in, clear the loaded sods out of boat and home, cruise off into deep blue yonder.

Sounds slightly more insane than putting it all on red, but . . .

I cannot stress enough how *deadly serious* he is about this. He has spoken to submarine makers and even drawn up a business plan – which he only just stopped short of taking to the small-business advisor at NatWest. He even nags Brett to begin every one of their TV scripts with *Open on miniature submarine* in the hope that he'll get to shoot it and do some real live research. Bizarrely, their *Cats Undersea* script for Pura Kitty Litter came within a whisker's breadth of making it onto the telly. As far as I can tell – though I have to say I'm no expert in the field – his plan is more or less flawless. Every time someone proposes a *but*, Vince has an immediate and convincing answer.

There is one problem, actually. Everyone that Vince has ever shared a beer with knows about it. If Trevor McDonald ever announces, 'And now let's go to our reporter in Monaco for more on that daring underwater robbery . . .' a couple of thousand people will scratch their heads and try to remember the name of the drunk who was sounding off in the pub about magnetised docking tubes.

'I'm sorry, Brett. I pass,' I say finally. 'Don't know how I'd spend it.'

'What're you asking him for?' Vince sneers. 'You *know* what he'd do. Buy a Volvo, a cottage in the Cotswolds and invest the rest in the fucking Nationwide.'

Well, I'd have said the Woolwich, but it doesn't seem like such a bad idea.

'Leave him be. There must be something you wanna do, Murray,' Brett says.

'I've always fancied the idea of pony trekking in the Andes,' I say nervously.

'That is fucking *cool*,' Vince splutters – to my amazement because to the best of my recollection I have never had an idea that *I* would consider cool, let alone Vince.

'Is it?' I ask, wincing as I wait for the rug to be whipped from beneath me.

''Course it is. Buy your conk candy at source. Cut out the middleman—'

That isn't what I had in mind, as it happens.

'—Here, you fancy joining me in the gents for a toot?'

I'm stunned. Is he offering me a *line*? Of *cocaine*? Because I don't believe he's suggesting we repair to the toilets for an impromptu trumpet recital. Either would be unprecedented, actually. Vince only has me around to pick up the tab. I'm not here to *join in* – with drug-taking or lavatory jam sessions.

'Er . . . no thanks,' I reply. 'I'm . . . um . . . detoxing.'

He looks at me as if I'm mad.

Well, I'm hardly going to tell him that few things are more terrifying to me than the prospect of snorting white powder of indeterminate origin up my nostril. A very, very, *very* occasional joint is the furthest I've ever dared travel down the road to junkie hell. And my answer wasn't a lie. I *am* detoxing. Since my visit to Saint Matthew's my body has been, while not exactly a temple, a lot more spick and span than usual. I haven't had a single burger and right now I'm drinking Sprite – though there is no reason for Brett, Vince and Kenny to suspect that it isn't a V&T. The new regime isn't because I think I'm actually ill, as in *ill* ill, really it isn't. But these things – lumps and what have you – serve as a warning, don't they? Shape up or ship out, so to speak.

And, well, I'm shaping up.

Vince arches a brow and says, 'You don't even burn the candle at one end, do you, matey?' Then he turns to his partner. 'What about you, B Boy?'

'I'll pass,' Brett replies. 'I'm sick of waking up with the three a.m. nosebleeds.'

'Kenny?'

'Drugs is for mugs,' Kenny replies, draining his eighth pint of mind-altering lager. 'Reckon I'll be off.'

'Whatever,' Vince says as he staggers off in the general direction of the gents. I watch him go, envying his complete inability to live beyond the moment. As Kenny hauls himself to his feet and takes his leave, Brett asks, 'You OK?'

Well, I've got a lump in my trousers that may or may not be cancer and I'm on the eve of visiting the hospital to get the verdict, but, that apart, I'm absolutely dandy.

'I'm absolutely dandy. Why do you ask?'

'You've seemed a bit spooked lately. And you asked for that last lot of script changes like you couldn't give a toss. I kind of missed your usual cheery *Hey, guys, the client's made a tiny suggestion that'll improve the core idea immensely* bollocks.'

'That was because I *couldn't* give a toss . . . I'd just had my assessment.'

'Not good?'

'Haye reckons my career might be helped by a visit to the Job Centre.'

'He's firing you?'

'No, but I guess my name's pencilled in for the next *efficiency-focused downsizement*.'

'Take it as a compliment. The man's dull as fuck. I've had livelier conversations with the automated menu on the Odeon booking line.' He gives me a hearty slap on the back – I think I've just risen in his estimation. 'Know what you need?'

'What's that?'

'A fuck,' says Vince, back from the bog and full of the joys of Colombia.

This – their uncanny ability to complete each other's thoughts – is what marks them out as a team.

'I was going to suggest a new girlfriend, but it amounts to the same thing,' Brett says.

'You wanna grab your secretary,' Vince goes on. 'She's gagging for it.' He gestures in the direction of Jakki, who's on a Breezer binge with her mates from the office. I like Jakki, even if she has given her name its pop-star spelling. But I don't fancy her any more than she fancies me.

'I couldn't,' I say.

'Gimme one good reason,' says Vince.

Well, she works ten feet away from me which would make things awkward the morning after, she's a bit on the plump side, she likes Enrique Iglesias, which isn't the end of the world but it could form a potentially insurmountable stumbling block six or seven months into a relationship, and she loves sardines which, though they're a rich source of omega acids, have an unfortunate habit of repeating. . . . Oh, and her first name isn't Megan and her second isn't Dyer.

'I dunno . . . I just don't think it's a good idea to get involved with girls you work with,' I say.

'What's the fucking point of having birds at work if you ain't gonna get involved with 'em?' Vince says.

'Murray's a one-woman man, Vin,' Brett says. 'Even when the one-woman *done gawn* left him fucking weeks ago. He deserves our sympathy.'

'Deserves a slap on the arse more like. Spineless twonk.

Fucking *suit*.' Having whacked the nail painfully on the head, Vince stands up and heads for Jakki's crowd.

Like a fly heading for shit.

I don't mean that at all. Vince is a bit fly-like – certainly when it comes to attention span and personal hygiene – but the girls are *not* shit. They're extremely nice, if slightly the worse for wear. I'm just not feeling too grand at the moment – entirely because of my dire assessment (reiterated so succinctly only moments ago by Vince) and *nothing* to do with the . . . you know . . . *lump*. I'm sure that if I were drunk I wouldn't feel like dragging everyone down with me. Perhaps I should trade in the Sprite for a grown-up drink.

'Bevy?' asks Brett, reading my mind.

'I'm all right, thanks,' I reply, changing it.

'Vin isn't the cunt he makes out, you know.'

'Oh, really?'

'He's got his sensitive side. Did you know he's a dad?'

'You're kidding,' I say, watching him work Jakki and her friends like they're King's Cross hookers.

'Yeah, he got this flaky PA at Miller Shanks pregnant. Bit of a shock at the time. Vin's never been too choosy, but she's the type who'd look at Prince William and think he's a common little twat. How she ended up in a locked toilet with the V-Bomb is one of the great unsolved mysteries. Mind you, she's the most staggeringly *stupid* person I've ever met. She thought Doctor Pepper was a Hungarian tit surgeon on Harley Street . . . You think I'm kidding? I read the letter she typed trying to book a consultation.'

'Vince, a dad,' I say, still unable to wrap my brain round the concept.

'He couldn't believe it either,' Brett says. 'He was in denial until the baby came out. No need for DNA – she was his Mini Me. She's three now.'

'What's she called?'

'If Vin had had his way, she'd be Diddymu.'

'Excuse me?'

'Name of a nag. Came in for him at forty-to-one on the day she was born. Mum obviously wasn't having that. They couldn't agree and rowed about it for two months. In the end they compromised. Went for two names. Mum chose Scarlet.'

'What about Vince?'

'Bubbles.'

'That's the name of—'

'Yeah, Jacko's chimp. I told him he was mad; he was writing out a permit for adult therapy right there on her birth certificate. I mean, if they had to have two names the least they could've done was make one of them Kate.'

'Does he have custody?'

'Fuck, no – he makes Fagin look like a model carer. But he's very hands-on. Takes her to toddler ballet every Saturday and brings her to all-night edits at Moving Pics.'

Bang on cue, Vince reappears with Jakki. His hand is on – what else? – her bum and I'm trying – *struggling*, frankly – to picture him cosseting a tiny bundle of humanity; *his pride and joy*.

'Here, Jakks, do something with your soppy boss, will you?' he says, shoving her in my direction. She lands in my lap, where she stays, giggling. She smells icky-sweet – Dune mingling with the Bacardi marketing department's notion of passion fruit, which at least masks the sardine sandwich she had for lunch. I pull her upright and she slides off onto the bench seat beside me.

'Leave him alone, Vince, he's lovely,' she slurs, putting an arm around my shoulder. He takes her advice and leaves me alone, heading back to her mates. Jakki looks me in the eye and says, 'You OK? You've been very ... *distant* lately.'

'Have I?'

'Yeah ... I notice stuff, you know. I'm like a radio. I pick things up.'

'I'm fine, Jakki. Just a bit under the weather . . . You know, tired.'

'You wanna pull yourself together,' she snaps suddenly, pulling her arm from my shoulder. 'You don't know how bloody lucky you are.'

What did I say?

She starts to cry.

What did I say, for heaven's sake?

'My uncle's got cancer,' she says through drunken sobs.

'I'm sorry, Jakki,' I say, though she'll never know how truly sorry I am.

'He had this lump on his forearm for ages. He used to joke about it – said it was his extra muscle – but it's cancer. They cut his arm off at the elbow last week. He's having chemo now. They reckon he'll be OK, but you're *never* OK after that, are you?'

No, I don't suppose you are.

'It's like a *knife* hanging over you—'

OK, I get the picture.

'—a ticking time *bomb*—'

Shut up, for God's sake.

'—a *death* sentence. It's so sad.'

Sad? It's tragic, *girl. You do not want to know how much that little nugget of family news is churning me up inside.*

'I'm sorry about your uncle, Jakki, really sorry, but . . .'

But what? She looks at me for a morsel of comfort.

'. . . But I've got to go.'

I stand up, grab my jacket and leave the bar.

10.01 p.m.

Outside the icy air whacks me in the face. I suck it in, but it doesn't make me feel any better. My legs are shaking and I have that sharp, pre-sick taste in the back of my throat. I try to swallow but my mouth is too dry. I can't shift my mind off tumescent, throbbing tumours.

I need to get home. *Now.*

I see a taxi – a rare sight in Docklands at this time of day. A rare sight at *any* time of day. Docklands is placed next to Papua New Guinea in the cabdriver's atlas. I stick my arm out. Barely slowing, the taxi swings through a dizzying U-turn and pulls up in front of me. The driver's window slides down and a cheery voice calls out, 'Where to, chief?'

'South Woo—'

The rest of the word comes out as a stream of vomit that pebble-dashes the Rimmel poster on the cab door – it looks as if Kate Moss has suddenly quit extolling longer, lusher lashes in favour of drawing attention to the horror of eating disorders.

'Drunken fucker,' the cabby shouts as he accelerates away.

I wish – I truly, truly wish.

nine: **i said run!**

What am I doing here?

It's barely an hour since I gave the taxi a spray job. *Here* is nowhere near South Woodford. *Here* is Barnsbury Square, Islington. I have no idea which house they live in, but it's surely close. I start in the northeast corner and set off. Halfway round I spot the Bentley. I can't be far away. Resisting the urge to give the car a good *kicking*, I look at the houses. They're only terraces – albeit nice, *big* terraces – but each one must be worth over a million. I walk along the iron railings that separate them from the pavement and peer down into the basement wells. Most of the windows are shuttered, but light pours out of one – shining like an irresistible *come on*. I stop and look inside. A couple sits at a rustic pine table. In front of them are half-empty glasses and dirty plates decorated with scraps of rocket, Parmesan shavings and smears of glossy, dark brown sauce.

I look at the couple. He's thirty-ish, deliberately unshaven. A chunk of surgical steel glints in his eyebrow, paint splatters his jeans. A decorator? Eating rocket in Barnsbury Square? More likely he spends his working days in a barn-like studio off Old Street roundabout which he shares with canvases and *objets trouvés* – AKA *shit from skips* according to Brett, who's something of an art critic. She's long and angular in a way that a scout from Storm would describe as *momentous* before booking her on the next flight to Milan. Her hand is on his leg and they're laughing.

I remember that. Laughing. With Megan. Her hand resting casually on my thigh.

Jesus, what the *hell* am I doing here?

Did I really think I'd see her and *him* through an un-curtained window? And even if I did, what was I proposing to do? Ring on the doorbell and invite myself in for coffee? Slip a burning, petrol-soaked rag through the letterbox? I should have known that the journey would leave me feeling embittered, not to mention bitterly cold – it's mid-November and all I'm wearing is a flimsy suit.

I half turn to walk back the way I came, but before I can take a step, a second woman comes into view. I only catch her as a blur out of the corner of my eye, but in our five years, eight months, one week and three days together her every molecule was processed and stored in my head so that – however brief the glimpse and obscure the angle – she's instantly recognisable.

I turn back and look at Megan. She's putting a fresh bottle of wine on the dining table. She's laughing, too, sharing in the hilarity with the artist and the model. *He* isn't far behind her. His arms reach around her waist as she refills the wineglasses.

Sandy *sodding* Morrison.

Queen's *bastard* Counsel.

I try desperately to recall the last time that Megan and I had friends round for dinner. Did we rustle up something with Parmesan and wilted rocket? Was there wine, marinated olives and lashings of laughter? Did we ever invite anyone to dinner at all? Because right now I honestly can't remember doing so. Not once.

My tears make her appear in soft-focus and, therefore, more perfectly beautiful than ever. Silently I plead with her to look up and see me. She doesn't, though, and as my hysteria subsides I'm glad. She surely thinks little enough of me as it is. I don't need her to add *pathetic stalker* to my list of failings. I turn again and this time I stride purposefully away.

But I stop when I reach the Bentley. I don't know why, but I peer inside. He's a *scruffy* git. One hundred and seventy grand spent on the car and he treats it like a dustbin. The ashtray is overflowing and belongings cover the seats and floor. My car is *spotless*. OK, it doesn't happen to . . . you know . . . *go*, but you won't find so much as a sweet wrapper in the ashtray. How can Megan live with such a slob? I know my . . . er . . . *orderly* nature irritated her towards the end, but did she really have to rush so madly to the other extreme? It's like . . . I don't know . . . Brad Pitt, for example, dumping Jennifer Aniston and going out with a really fat girl with dull, lifeless hair. Like he's got a point to make and he wants to rub it in his skinny, glossy-maned ex's face. I bet Jen would be cut to the quick and, well, I'd be totally with her.

My eyes tour the car's interior. I can see old newspapers (the *Guardian* of course), exhausted fag packets, a bag of Murray Mints (*Murray* Mints – *way* too Freudian), a fat, dog-eared law book and . . . a white, lacy bra. It's there on the back seat next to a crumpled pair of 501s, three soppy compilation CDs and a few snaps of Megan and me frolicking on a beach in Kos.

She made such a fuss about coming to pick up the last of her things – *'You know how I've got to have all my stuff around me'* – yet now it's obvious that she didn't really want them; she simply didn't want them to be anywhere near *me*. The realisation hurts me almost as much as *'Murray, I've . . . I've met someone.'*

I can't take this. I'm about to walk away for good, but something else catches my eye – a small rectangular box in the rear foot-well. Though most of it is hidden beneath the driver's seat, I can make out the glint of the elegant gold lettering stamped into its lid. I can't actually read it in this light, but I *know* what it says: J.P. STEIN OF HATTON GARDEN.

So she never found the ring. It must have jostled out of the carton along with her other things and it has lain on the floor ever since. This new knowledge takes some of the edge off my hurt – at least she and Sandy haven't been holding the sparkler up to the light, admiring its *exquisite* (J.P. Stein's adjective) cut and laughing at the sad, clingy mug that bought it.

But I need the ring back. I've had two letters from Barclaycard threatening to turf me into the bottomless pit of credit-card hell if I don't cough up. The summons can't be far away. Jesus, yes, I *need* it. I stand back from the car and consider my options. They're limited. I could return to the house, knock on the door and say something like, 'Hi there, Sandy. Look, I know it's a bit late and I live several miles from here, but I just *happened* to be passing and – loved you on *Question Time*, by the way. Terrific point you made about electoral reform. Anyway, as I was saying, I was just passing and I remembered that thing in the *Guardian* about the asylum seekers' centre. Really good that you're taking a stand. You haven't got a petition to sign or something?' Then, when he disappears to find it, I nip into the hall and grab the car keys that just happen to be lying on the table . . .

I don't think so.

Which leaves only one course of action and I feel my heart race at the prospect.

Come on, you can do this. How many times have you watched those Police, Camera, You're Nicked You Recidivist Twat shows and seen cocky little twelve-year-olds do it on CCTV? Piece of piss.

I glance up and down the street for late-night dog walkers or – far less likely these days – coppers. No one. I'm alone.

But I can't do *this*. I'm the bloke who breaks into a cold sweat when he pads his expenses. I don't have a criminal bone in my body. I *so* cannot do this.

Course you can, because if you don't it's CCJ time. And eviction – have you any idea at all how you're going to make the rent this month? You'll be lucky to borrow the price of a cup of tea after your creditors have finished stripping the flesh off your bones.

Shaking, I take my jacket off and wrap it around my right forearm, making sure that one of the shoulder pads covers my fist. It offers scant protection, though. I rue the day that fashion designers tired of the shoulder-pads-of-an-American-footballer aesthetic – what I really require is a pad big and broad enough to land a helicopter on . . . as worn by Dex Dexter in *Dynasty*.

Jesus, this is no time for a delve into the history of men's fashion, 1980 to the present.

I suppose I'll just have to make do, then. I pull my arm back behind my shoulder and hold it there.

Go on, pussy, do it.

I close my eyes and swing. Though I can't actually see it, I'm sure my arm is cutting a menacingly sweeping arc on its descent towards the car. One worthy of Lennox. Or Brad in *Fight Club*—

Fist connects with car. There is no give, though – no implosion of glass.

Just a sharp, burning pain that shoots through my hand and up my arm before coming close to blowing the top of my head off.

Who told you to close your eyes when you punch, you wanker? That was the door pillar you hit.

I cry out in agony, but luckily the blaring of an alarm drowns me out.

You are such a pillock. It's the alarm on the fucking Bentley. Run!

I stagger back from the car, which has sprung into hi-tech life. Its indicators are flashing wildly and its muscular red body is shaking visibly with the vibrations of its banshee security system. I look down at my fist. The jacket is still wrapped around it, but I can make out a dark patch of blood spreading through the fabric. I hear a front door open and I turn to see Sandy Morrison QC illuminated by brass coach lights. His dinner guest – the artist – is at his shoulder and between them I can make out . . . I think . . . Megan.

I said run!

I set off as if my life depends on it.

Which I suppose it does.

By the time I reach Highbury & Islington station I'm wheezing audibly and my lungs are burning with pain. It's nothing compared to the excruciating torture going on in my thighs, which haven't had to pump so hard since some dim and distant school sports day. This agony, in turn, fades into insignificance next to the paroxysms of pain firing off in my hand. I look down at it. It's so red and sticky with blood that I can't make out where it's cut. I try to flex it, but nearly pass out with the effort. I'd throw up again if it weren't for the fact that Kate Moss is already wearing my guts on her cleavage.

As the pain recedes slightly it strikes me that there is virtually no movement in my ring and little fingers.

Something else hits me – where the hell is my jacket?

ten: **trance is the *bollocks***

I arrive at Saint Matthew's only eight hours early for my appointment.

But I'm not here to see Doctor Morrissey.

This is A&E.

I walked, of course.

All the way from N1 to E11.

My wallet *and* my tube pass were in my jacket.

It was a slow, freezing walk, every step jarring fresh pain into my fingers. Despite the agony I didn't want to come to the hospital. No, I wanted to crawl home to bed in the hope that half a night's sleep would somehow set things right. Bed is where I'd be now if halfway across Hackney Marshes I hadn't realised that my front door keys had been in – where else? – my jacket.

I read in the *Standard* that this is Britain's busiest casualty department. Apparently it boasts the longest waiting times and the most assaults on staff, and the doctors here know nearly as much about tweezering bullets from crack-crazed gangstas as the guys on *ER*. Seems I've caught the place on a quiet night though – not a single lurching drunk with a pint glass embedded in his head at a jaunty angle. Even so, I'm told that I'll have to wait at least an hour.

I sit down on a chilly perforated steel bench and watch a girl drop some coins into a vending machine. She waits a moment before pulling out a Styrofoam cup of steaming liquid. She cradles it in her hands and walks it to the bench facing mine. I watch the vapour rise from the cup and – even though it's almost certainly whatever the NHS passes off as coffee, and by definition undrinkable – I *want* it.

I've never felt so cold in my life. The ambient temperature in A&E would be comfortable enough in normal circumstances, but my body is so iced up that I'd need to sit in an industrial bread-oven to have any hope of bringing warmth to my bones. Right now a cup of whatever passes for coffee represents my only chance of raising my temperature. I stare at the girl. She's vaguely familiar. But she has long purple hair and the grime-encrusted look of homelessness. All my acquaintances have addresses and hair colour that passes as natural – even when it isn't. But she *does* look familiar. I dismiss it – probably gave her a quid once outside the station. She takes a tentative sip from her cup. Her caution isn't surprising – she has a ring through her bottom lip, which must make drinking hot beverages an ongoing hazard. I've always wondered about body piercing. Doesn't it compromise everyday activities? Things like eating, peeing, sex, breast-feeding, navel de-fluffing and walking unhindered through airport metal detectors. Or, for that matter, getting work. All those rivets would surely hinder her prospects of a job in . . . say . . . account management at . . . for example . . . Blower Mann/DBA. She peers back at me through the gaps in the lank curtain of fringe, and . . . Is that a sneer? She must be reading my mind. And if she's thinking, *God, not long past thirty and already he's thinking like his mother*, well, I wouldn't blame her.

She takes another sip of her steaming coffee-style beverage.

I *so* want some of that.

Hang on. Not *every*thing was in my jacket. Haven't I got some money in my trousers? I shake my legs gently and experience a wonderful sensation. Chinking change. I stand up and reach my left arm across my body in an attempt to feed my hand into my right pocket. Left hand to right pocket is a manoeuvre that I suspect even a bendy Mongolian contortionist would have to think about – a knackered and stiff-with-cold me doesn't have a prayer. I look at my bloody right hand and wonder if it's up to it. I have no choice but to try so I gingerly feed it in. I've got no further than an inch when I feel a jolt of pain as my little finger catches the lip of the pocket. I try to strangle the *Aagh!*, but I'm too late. The admissions clerk doesn't look up from his computer, but the girl does and she calls out, 'You OK?' I nod my head, but I guess I don't look too happy because she adds, 'Wanna hand?' I shake my head and look down at my pocket – there *must* be a way of getting in there.

This is like a rubbish 'based on a true story' TV movie; Luke Perry and the bloke who used to be Pa Walton as rescue workers standing at a cave entrance, post-landslide.

Luke:	*There must be a way of getting in there.*
Pa Walton:	*We gotta find it, son. If we don't rescue the change from Murray's pocket there's no tellin' how long the guy will hold out.*
Luke:	*I got it! You can get the chopper to drop me on his waistband and I can abseil down from a belt loop.*
Pa Walton:	*That's pure crazy. No one's ever made a climb like that . . . and lived.*

'Whatever it is, you ain't gonna get it with that hand.'

I look up. It isn't Luke or Pa Walton. The studded girl is in front of me.

'It doesn't matter – it's only some change,' I mumble.

'Let me,' she says and she thrusts her hand where no girl has been since . . . I was going to say Megan, but, actually, Doctor Morrissey was fumbling around my groin only eight days ago. Her hand, though, wasn't decorated with weeping scabs and a tattoo of what looks like a cod.

Moments later it re-emerges from my pocket clutching nine or ten one pound coins, a fifty-pence piece, two tens and assorted coppers. 'If you were gonna get a coffee with this, don't bother,' she says. 'It tastes like a rat pissed it out.'

'As long as it's hot I don't care too much.'

I reach out for the money.

'It's OK, I'll get it. Milk? Sugar?'

She's eighteen. She has ambitions. She wants to be a tattooist. Or a psychiatric nurse. Or an environmental terrorist. Or a model. Or a contestant on *Big Brother*. Or a bus driver. Or – truly fanciful, this one – a long-haul flight attendant ('*Chicken or Beef? Nah, don't bother, mate – they both taste like a rat shat it out.*') But she's between jobs at the moment. She loves dogs but not cats, ecstasy but not acid and *The Matrix* though not the sequels. And she *stinks*. BO, KFC, B&H, Woodpecker and – ever so faintly – piss all jostle for my nose's attention. She smells because she hasn't had a bath or, I suspect, a change of clothes for some time. This is because she lives in a squat in a condemned tower block on the Cathall estate in Leytonstone.

I study her as she talks – and she hasn't stopped for over half an hour. A thin film of dirt lies over the skin on her face, and her pores are clogged with enough black grease to lubricate the drive shaft on a sixteen-wheeler. Her teeth are chipped and stained the colour of the 'before' set of dentures in a Denclens ad. She has a cold sore on her top lip – roughly the shape of Cuba, though obviously not as big. She's wearing the world's baggiest jeans so I can't tell, but I'll bet she hasn't waxed lately. I wonder what she'd look like if she scrubbed up, but not for long – she's *way* past scrubbing up.

'What are you doing here?' I say, getting a word in edgeways at last. I've been curious because she has no discernible signs of injury or illness. Perhaps she's come about the cold sore – but at nearly three in the morning?

73

'It's the only place round here you can get a coffee this late,' she explains. 'And it's quiet – tonight it is, anyway. These three Dutch guys moved into the squat and they play trance all night.'

'I hate trance,' I murmur sympathetically.

'Trance is the *bollocks*, man – but the arseholes've only got one CD.'

Like you can tell one from another, I don't say on account of the fact that it would be exactly what my mum would say.

She doesn't need to ask why I'm here – though, curiously, she hasn't expressed any interest in *why* my hand resembles a clumsily butchered chicken quarter that I've found in a dustbin and stuffed up my sleeve for a rag-week-type jape.

A voice calls out, 'Mr Colin?' I look up to see a tired-looking doctor scanning the reception. I rise from the bench, but before I follow him I turn to the girl. 'Thanks for getting me the coffee ... And for the company.'

'No problem. Take care of yourself, yeah?' she replies with apparent sincerity.

'Thanks – you too. What's your name, by the way?'

'Fish.'

That would explain the cod.

'*Fish* ... That's really ... Er ... I'm Murray.' And then, because I haven't been able to shake the feeling, 'You look familiar, you know.'

'Shouldn't think so. Unless you're the twat from Tesco who keeps moving us on from their ATMs.'

'No, that wouldn't be me ... Bye, then.'

'Yeah ... See you 'round, man.'

I almost ask for my change – the coffee was only 50p – but I stop myself. My life is at a fairly low ebb, but I still think she needs the money more than I do.

Maybe she'll use it to buy soap.

But I doubt it.

It seems like an hour since I last checked the time, but it was only two mintues ago. I've been sitting on the wall outside my flat for just over forty-five minutes. I walked here from Saint Matthew's. After the doctor had finished I looked for Fish – I was going to ask her for a pound for the bus fare – but she'd left. Now my body is even colder than it was when I arrived at the hospital, which I didn't think would have been possible. There is an upside, though – my right hand is so numb that I can't feel any pain for the first time since I punched the car. A bandage covers the four stitches in my knuckles. My ring and little fingers are strapped and splinted. Seems I was wrong about my body's lack of criminal bones. I have at least two, both of them fractured.

My peripheral vision catches something and I quickly look round to see movement through the window of the ground-floor flat.

At last.

I shake my legs to check that they're still capable of move-ment before slipping off the wall, climbing the steps and ringing the bell to flat A. I see a hand part two slats in the venetian blind of the bay window, and my neighbour's eyes peer at me through the gap. I hope they belong to Paula and not to her slightly scary girlfriend, whose name I can never remember. After a moment the intercom gives a farty buzz and I lean my shoulder into the door. Inside, a yawning, crusty-eyed Paula is standing in her doorway. She's wearing a long, baggy T-shirt printed with a picture of, surprisingly, Sigourney Weaver (skin-head *Alien 3* model). Surprising because Paula goes to great lengths to avoid the shaved head and swagger of stereotypical dyke-ness – obviously all the effort goes out of the window when she goes to bed.

'Bloody hell, Murray, what happened to you?' she asks.

I guess I don't look my best, then.

'Oh, nothing much. I fell . . . outside the office. Spent all night in casualty – it was like Piccadilly Circus,' I say. I didn't want to lie, but there was no way I was going to tell her the truth. 'Look, I'm sorry to bother you, but I left my jacket at work and my keys were in it. Can I nick my spare set back?'

'Yeah, of course.' She disappears into her flat.

A minute later she's back with a key ring.

'Are you really OK?' she asks.

'Yes, *really*. Thanks for these,' I say, jangling the key ring.

'Murray,' she says, 'do you mind if I ask you something?'

Here we go. You want to know how I've been coping since Megan dropped me for a barrister with a highly developed social conscience, TV charisma . . .

'I hope you don't take this the wrong way—'

. . . a million-pound house close to several cabinet ministers . . .

'—I'd hate you to be upset—'

. . . and an impregnable (to idiots, at least) Bentley.

'—but would you mind having your TV on a bit quieter? We could hear everything the other night and Apollonia—'

Apollonia! How could I forget?

'—is a really light sleeper.'

Fine – so you really couldn't give a damn that I'm a miserable, lovelorn wreck – one, by the way, coping manfully with a potentially cancerous tumour – and that my one and only comfort is to watch repeats of Seinfeld *on Paramount with the volume right up to drown out my sobs as I cry at all the bits that Megan used to laugh at hysterically. Well, fuck you too.*

'Yeah, sorry, Paula, I'll keep it down.'

—————————————————————————— 7.34 a.m.

As my (very, *very* hot) bath runs I go to my wardrobe to choose some clothes. I pull out a mid-grey suit – one of several

76

mid-grey suits I possess. I hold it up and wonder if it's suitable attire for the kind of appointment I've got in less than three hours. It looks a little formal for a cancer verdict. It's more the other kind of verdict – you know: 'And how do you find the defendant?' It will have to do, though. I've got a meeting in Croydon this afternoon. I shouldn't think I'd get past Schenker security in anything other than mid-grey. At the height of post-9/11 fever they had a walk-through metal detector in their foyer, but now they've replaced it with a spectrometer.

Needless to say, Niall Haye loves it there – Croydon is his spiritual home. He needs only the flimsiest excuse to board a train for the Schenker Bunker. This afternoon's is a slimmer-than-slim excuse for a meeting – we're presenting draft thirty-two of the script, which is all of *three* words different to thirty-one – but I'm duty-bound to attend.

I lay the suit on my bed and go to the front room – I need to call Barclaycard, the Royal Bank of Scotland, Morgan Stanley and Goldfish to tell them I've lost my cards. (To which they'll doubtless reply, *Good – it'll save us the bother of calling on you to seize them and then casually beat the shit out of you as a warning to other piss-takers.*) I sit on the sofa and as I reach for the phone I see the red light on the answering machine blinking at me. I press *play*.

'You have – one – new message –' the familiar synthesised voice announces, 'left – yesterday at – eleven – thirty – seven – p.m.'

Beep!

'Murray, it's me,' says another familiar though less robotic voice. 'I was really hoping you'd be home, because it'd mean that what I just saw was an hallucination ... Obviously not. I think we'd better talk ... Oh, and by the way, don't you think it's about time you took my voice off the answering machine?'

Funny that. For weeks I've been desperate for Megan to call. Now that she finally has my heart . . . s
i
n
k
s.

Like A&E last night, Outpatients is quiet.

As a *morgue*.

But, hey, maybe they've cured everyone; the London Borough of Waltham Forest is now a tumour-free zone . . . Oh yeah, and it's twinned with Never Land.

Actually, given that this is my first *ever* trip to a hospital where the news could be truly dire (as opposed to being dire only in my paranoid fantasies), I'm coping pretty well with my nerves. Keeping a lid on things.

I look at the only other patient. He's a ginger nut, about my age. Needless to say he isn't wearing a mid-grey suit. He's in faded black jeans and a red and white Arsenal shirt that clashes disastrously with his hair.

Should have worn the away strip, matey.

Even so, he *isn't* wearing a mid-grey suit. Lived-in jeans and favourite team shirt seem suitable wear in which to receive *possibly life's final piece of significant news*. Not a suit in which your own mother would have trouble picking you out in a crowd.

But as I said, I feel pretty good. I'm not expecting the worst. As the pixie doctor assured me, testicular cancer isn't that common, and far be it for me to do anything uncommon. Being the original Mr Average, departing from the norm isn't my thing and I'm wearing the mid-grey suit to prove it. Last night's panic attack was silly, irrational, and totally induced by (other people's) drunkenness.

Ginger nut isn't alone. A woman is with him, her arm linked comfortingly through his. She turns to him and says, 'Fancy some tea, Mark?' He nods and they get up. I watch them amble off hand in hand. Love's young-ish dream. I wish someone had come with me. (Purely for company – I am *so* not worried.)

Obviously not Megan. Not now.

I almost returned her call before I left, but I chickened out. What was I going to say? *Let me get this straight, Meg. A man who looks exactly like me was seen in your road trying to punch in the window of your boyfriend's car? That is incredible! But what a sick bastard – going round impersonating women's exes. Some sort of weirdo vigilante for jilted blokes. Have you ever heard of such a thing?*

Somehow I didn't see that convincing her, a lawyer.

'Mr Collins?'

I don't even bother to correct the receptionist this time.

'Doctor Morrissey is ready for you. It's the third door on the left.'

Her tone is far more sympathetic than the last time I was here. Does she *know* something?

Don't be daft – hospitals, paranoia and all that.

I walk down the corridor and tap quietly on the door.

'Come in,' Morrissey's voice calls out. I ease the door open and step inside. The elfin one isn't alone. A nervous grey-haired man is sitting beside her. He's wearing half-moon glasses and he peers over them at me with moist, kindly eyes.

Wait half a bloody mo— ... I've seen that look before. *Vets in Practice* – they save it especially for dogs that they're about to dispatch to doggy heav—

For Christ's sake CUT IT OUT. Remember: HOSPITAL plus MURRAY COLIN equals gibbering PARANOIAC.

'Please, take a seat,' Morrissey says with a smile.

I smile back.

Go on, give me your worst, which I know for a fact isn't going to be bad at all. And make it snappy, because I'm a busy man – I've got three words to discuss in Croydon.

_____ dec.

one: **thoffy, thakki**

I'm flying.

(Metaphorically, of course. I don't like *flying* flying.)

'It's really good to see you smiling again, Murray,' Jakki slurs, leaning her head on my arm.

Amazing, isn't it? I am flying, girl.

I nod vigorously. Since I'm simultaneously draining my glass, most of my drink ends up on my shirt.

So what? I'll buy another . . . beer . . . shirt . . . whatever.

'I mean, you've been so down since . . .' She mouths the unutterable M-word. 'I thought you'd *never* get over her.'

I am so over her. I am more over her than any man has ever been in the millennia-long history of jilted blokes. Want to know just how over her I am? She could – even as we speak – be having deviant, unprotected sex with the entire Bar Council and I really wouldn't give a damn.

'I'm doing OK,' I say.

'So why all the time off lately? You haven't really had the flu *again*, have you?'

Course not. I have the constitution of an ox; an exceptionally big and strong ox; Super Ox. Disease sees me walking down the street and hides in a shop doorway.

'Not . . . exactly . . . I just needed a break.'

'Well, it's done you good. Mind you, Niall isn't too chuffed.'

'When is he? Fancy a trip to the toilet?'

'Excuse me?' She's shocked.

I tap the side of my nose.

'Oh, for *that*,' she says, knocking back her Breezer. 'I'd *never* do coke.'

83

'If they made it in a range of six fruity flavours, I bet you fucking would,' Vince says as he crashes between us and into the bar with the impact of a Scud.

'You what?' Jakki asks again.

'Narco-pops,' Brett says, completing Vince's thought as he, too, joins us. 'Top way to market toot to the teenies.'

'Bacardi would *love* it,' Vince says, slapping his partner on the back. 'They could hand out little sachets at the school gates.'

'Or at Busted gigs.'

'Or free with Happy Meals.'

'You two are *sick*,' Jakki says.

'No, we're marketing professionals, darling,' Brett explains, 'and our highly paid minds never sleep when it comes to seeking an edge for our clients' brands.'

'Stop giggling, Murray,' Jakki says. 'You're only encouraging them.'

'Leave him alone, Jakks. He's all right. He's our flexible friend,' says Vince.

Jakki's brow furrows so Brett explains. 'As in, "Barman, do you accept Account Supervisor?" Talking of which, you gonna get some drinks in, Murray?'

I pull myself together and order two more of the blackcurrant-flavoured Belgian beers that are tonight's novelty choice – an alcopop for those too cool to ask for an alcopop. I've already put my one remaining card behind the bar and I'm running up an Enron-sized tab.

My one remaining card: an RSPCA Visa. I got it because the idea that a small proportion of my profligacy might help some abandoned puppies and half-starved donkeys appealed to me. When the card arrived and I saw the fluffy kitten on it I let out an involuntary *aaah*. But the first time I used it – slapping it on the bill at a client lunch – I was laughed off the table and – wimp that I am – I banned it from my wallet. Now it has made a comeback. Well, in the absence of Barclaycard, Morgan Stanley *et al*, it's saving my (and with it, I hope, some poor animal's) bacon now.

I hand over the drinks and give Vince a discreet look. Brett spots it, though, and says, 'You sure? You'll do your schnozz a serious mischief.' It's as if he can sense that I'm a rookie and his concern is quite touching.

'Leave him alone,' Vince says, coming to my support for the second time in the space of less than a minute. 'First rule of the market economy: it's the consumer's inalienable right to fuck himself over.' He slips me another wrap.

I have one of those moments. You know, *those* moments. The moments that overwhelm you when you're exceptionally drunk. The sort of moment where *nothing* else matters except the here and now, and that is invariably accompanied by a slurred, spit-spattering *I love you guys, I really fucking love you*. Brett is sober enough to see it coming and he leaps in to cut me off: 'Go on, fuck off to the bog.'

 10.28 p.m.

I close the cubicle door and, despite the fact that this is my second such excursion tonight, I immediately have an anxiety attack. It may be my second time tonight, but it is also only my second time *ever*. What am I doing here? This is not *me*. Locked toilets, rolled-up banknotes and white powder that may have arrived in Britain inside someone's bottom. I'm not even properly equipped. No Amex. All I've got to cut the stuff up is a Homebase Spend & Save card. How un-cool can I get? And the lack of hipness is the least of my concerns. What if the card swipe machine at Homebase can somehow sniff cocaine and automatically cancels the reward points I've painstakingly accumulated before summoning the manager? *'We're sorry, Mr Colin, but we can't allow you to leave the store with that Black & Decker hot air gun, which is clearly intended as a weapon in a drug turf war.'*

No, I'm being silly . . . Pathetic . . . I'm being *Murray*. Like I said, this is my *second* excursion tonight. Obviously the first hit is wearing off and that's what's causing my wobbles. I can handle this. All I need is another blast. I tense my hands to stop them trembling and take the wrap from my pocket. I tip some powder onto the lid of the cistern, chop it up with the card and coax it into two little lines. Then I snort them up through the rolled tenner. I lean back against the cubicle wall and feel . . . Nothing, as it happens. I'm about to leave when I have a flash vision of *Casino* and a stoned James Woods dementedly massaging coke residue into his gums. I smear my index finger over the cistern lid to pick up the last few grains before popping it into my mouth and—

Hang on, this is Sleazy Junkie Land, a place I've *never* been. The anxiety kicks in again, because, apart from the culture shock, the coke has a horrible bitter medicinal taste and no amount of frantic salivating seems to be shifting it. Something else. I'm in a *bog* and I'm as good as licking the porcelain. Doesn't this raise some grave hygiene issues?

I'm breaking out in a cold sweat when the rush saves me, washing over me at the exact same moment as I'm being struck by the ridiculous, black irony of that last thought.

_____ 10.34 p.m.

When I get back to the bar I find Brett and Jakki in conversation. I pull up a stool and sit down next to them. I don't tune in, but instead watch Vince, who has made his way to the far side of the room. He's harassing Juliet, the public face of Blower Mann. She has a perch in reception from which she welcomes all and sundry with a shimmering Miss World smile. Vince, being Vince, is the last person to care that Juliet has a fiancé. He should be a little less blasé though, because her beloved is a scaffolder or a meat porter or a circus strongman – something that involves brute strength, anyway – and he's built like a concrete fallout shelter . . . And right now he's standing ten feet away with his back to them.

You really don't want to be putting your hand there *Vince.*

Juliet is obviously of similar mind because she shrieks and pushes him away as if he's diseased – which he may well be. Fiancé turns round, takes one look and wades in. I must say he's pretty light on his feet for a fallout shelter.

Jakki must have been watching as well because she says, 'Jesus, he's a complete bloody idiot. He's gonna get himself killed.'

'You've got to understand that Vince operates by a simple code,' Brett explains calmly. 'It only runs to one rule – he doesn't have the memory capacity to take in any more. It goes like this: F.E.A.R.'

'*Fear*?'

'Fuck Everything And *Rumble*, darling. Live each day as if it's your last.'

'But he's got his whole life ahead of him,' says Jakki, wincing as Vince ducks his wiry five-seven frame beneath a heavy right from fiancé.

'Yeah, but who's to say he isn't gonna step under a bus? Or get his head ripped off by an irritated scaffolder? He'd hate to take his last gasp in the knowledge that he'd missed out on something by showing restraint. Oh lordy, lordy, the mibs are here.'

Security has arrived. Three black-clad bouncers are attempting to subdue fiancé while another two are slamming Vince's face into the wall.

'Of course,' adds Brett as a parting comment before he goes to his partner's aid, 'the corollary is that by living each day as if it's his last, he dramatically increases the chances that it actually fucking is.'

Now, this strikes me as the funniest thing I've heard all night, a view that I demonstrate by falling off my stool with the force of my laughter.

'Murray!' squeaks Jakki.

'I'm fine, I'm fine.'

I am as well. Somehow – luck not judgement – I managed to prevent my broken fingers from taking any impact. Jakki sticks out her arm and I take her hand. But she's had too many Breezers to mount a successful rescue effort and I bring her crashing down on top of me. She lies there panting for a moment, her plump breasts moulding themselves over my face. The coke and the alcohol – as well as the fact that the sensation is undeniably pleasant – cause my brain to fast-forward through some fairly disgusting thoughts before guilt and shame regain supremacy and press *stop*. 'Thoffy, Thakki,' I say – a soft pad of boob is pressing onto my mouth, preventing normal speech. She won't be able to see me blushing but surely she can feel the heat from my cheeks that's threatening to melt her bra. She manages to peel herself off me and then attempts to push herself upright by planting a hand first in my stomach and then in my groin. Her face breaks into a drunken grin and she says, 'My God, you're *big*.'

You do not know the half of it, darling.

She sees I'm not smiling – anything but – and her grin fades. We look at each other in embarrassment. Her hand is still somehow welded to my groin. We're saved by an explosion. A thunderous crack followed by the tinkling of a thousand fragments of glass hitting the pavement outside. Something – a table? A bouncer? An art director with a death wish? – has gone through a plate-glass window.

two: **you work in *advertising*. you earn more in a week than the average filipino takes home in a year. what do you know about crisis?**

I'm sitting on the sofa in my front room with the phone in my hand. Slowly and deliberately I punch out a number. This is a call I've been dreading.

But one that I've also been *desperate* to make.

Now that I'm out of my head on drink and unfamiliar drugs, it is perhaps the *ideal* time to make it.

My mother will be asleep, of course.

So what?

I'm too hammered to care.

And I'm her *only* child.

She lives in Spain now. Javea. It's twenty minutes along the coast from Benidorm. But *nothing* like Benidorm. It's low-rise for a start. Much smaller and prettier. Terry Venables has a house there. That should tell you something. Not sure what, but something all the same. It has a thriving expat community, actually. Brits who have, for one reason or several, given up on life here. My mum went because David, her husband, my *step*-father, took early retirement. Medical grounds. He was a policeman – a detective inspector with Hornchurch CID. Twenty-five years of loyal service to crown and country. Then his back went. *Just like that.* You had to feel for him – he'd lost the job he loved and he would . . .

. . . never swing a golf club again.

They spent a couple of years of mooching around Essex's garden centres. Then Mum and DI David Finch (rtd.) packed their bags for Eldorado. After putting down the deposit on the half-built villa the first thing they did was to join the golf club. My mum is a crap golfer, but she enjoys 'a good walk'. I supposed that David was joining purely for the social side, what with his back and all.

Amazingly, though, he has managed to get his handicap down to thirteen.

I slump back with the phone to my ear. The long, rhythmic *beeeeep* of the Spanish ring tone is making me sleepy. *Come on, Mum, answer the sodding . . . phone . . . I need to . . . talk . . . to . . .*

4.14 a.m.

'—is not responding . . . Please replace the handset and try again later . . .'

You what?

'. . . The number you are calling is not responding . . . Please replace the handset and try again later . . .'

I pull myself upright on the sofa. The phone is still wedged between ear and neck. The mouthpiece is coated in drool. I lift my head and let the receiver slide down my chest to my stomach. How long have I been asleep? The room is cold. The hangover is kicking in. I peer at the clock on the VHS.

Jesus, Murray, you do not want to be awake at four-fourteen on a night like this.

I get up and walk to the kitchen, where I fill a glass from the tap and drink.

Where the hell is my mother? For nineteen years of my life – right up to the second she left for Spain – she was always there for me. Especially – *especially* – when she wasn't wanted. Doesn't she *owe* it to me – just this once – to be *there* when she *is*? My dad was rarely there when I needed him, but I'd call him now if I had a number.

He was a cop too. The desk sergeant at Hornchurch. When I was seven he came to my school assembly and lectured us on the Green Cross Code. I don't mention that because it was a seminal Freudian moment in my young life. I mention it because . . . Oh, you'll figure it out. Though I *was* quite proud of him that day, he wasn't a model policeman. He smoked and drank too much, ate rubbish and he had his ideal cop job – sitting idly behind the desk as opposed to chasing down alleys after hare-legged muggers. He was severely overweight, he had a perpetually raging ulcer, his blood pressure was off the scale and he had enough cholesterol coursing through his veins to open a burger stand.

They say that scientists have looked at the physics of the bumblebee and figured out that technically it should not be able to fly. Dad was like that. Technically he shouldn't have been alive.

Everyone told him so. Mum, me, his colleagues, his mates and various doctors. Even strangers would wince and cross themselves as he walked by huffing, wheezing, purple-faced. Finally, sick of the nagging – and maybe just a little scared – he got off his backside. He did the Allen Carr thing and quit fags. He joined Weight Watchers. He kept a fastidious record of his vastly reduced alcohol intake. He joined a gym and started doing step. And one Sunday morning, not long after the start of his new regime, he stuck on a tracksuit, opened the front door and set off on a jog. He never came home. The Nissan Sunny that hit him as he lumbered across Upminster Road was a write-off, too.

Yes, I'd call him now if I could.

I drink another glass of water before stumbling into bed. I know I won't sleep, though.

I was right. Sleep is out of the question.

I go to the kitchen and fill a glass with orange juice. Maybe that and the three ibuprofen I pop from the blister pack will do something to attack my headache. They'll do nothing to slow my heart though. I can feel it hammering against my ribcage. I wish it had something to do with all the coke I put up my nose. But the rush has long gone and I can no longer plunge myself into the blizzard of denial that comes free with every line.

This is purest, uncut panic.

I go to the PC in the corner of my living room and switch it on.

Come on, come on – so slow.

I click on the Explorer icon and listen to the beeps and burbles as the machine goes online. I call up Lycos and type one word into the search box. The same word I've tapped out every single sleepless night since Friday 21st November:

    cancer

Brett Topowlski claims the Internet is responsible for taking mankind – by that he does mean *man*kind; women are excluded from this hypothesis – to the next stage of evolution. 'Look at it this way,' he contends. 'There's an entire generation of blokes who've become ambidextrous. They've had to master the art of wanking left-handed because their right hands are too busy manipulating the mouse.' He should know. He and Vince spend their working lives being virtual sex tourists – and, fair's fair, I've spent a little time glancing over their shoulders. (I defy anyone to wander into their office with a Schenker research debrief for their immediate attention and *not* look at the image of, say, horse and rider engaging in a spot of role-reversal.)

But over the past fortnight I've made a remarkable discovery. The porn sites haven't taken over. They're outnumbered – *dwarfed* – by ones that deal with the C-word, the *six*-letter one. Tonight I carried out an experiment. I typed *tits* into the search box and hit *go*. It came up with a staggering 3,199,658 matches.

It is *nothing*, though.

Because *cancer* got me 18,073,389. Over eighteen *million* mentions of the disease that will afflict one in three of us and kill one in four.

I haven't been keeping count, but so far I must have visited several hundred cancer sites. I now know more about it than I ever did. (Not saying much, granted.) I know, for instance, that one per cent of breast cancers occur in men; that a Calgary businessman claims he was brought back from the brink by an ancient cure used by the Ojibway Indians; that over eighty per cent of lung cancers are attributable to smoking, yet only thirteen per cent of smokers will get lung cancer; that on the day Philip Morris – in an expensive corporate con – changed its name to *Altria*, some web wag re-christened lung cancer *Philip Morris*; that drinking milk produced by cows treated with bovine growth hormones increases the risk of colon cancer; that *Hosen* is the Hebrew word for strength and is also an acronym for Cancer Patients Fight Back; that frequent masturbation reduces the risk of prostate cancer; that frequent sex *increases* it; that shark cartilage, liquefied and given a pleasant fruit-style flavour, is the miracle that will revolutionise cancer treatment . . .

_____ 6.55 a.m.

The trouble is that I'm none the wiser. I fly around the web hoovering up facts, seizing on speculation and clutching wildly at every out-of-its-tree conjecture. I've looked at countless pictures of tumours the size of kumquats . . . nectarines . . . grapefruits . . . watermelons (which strikes me as wholly inappropriate. Why is it that, when dramatising their size for their dumb patients, medics invariably compare tumours to fruit? Fruit is tasty, nutritious, life-enhancing. Tumours, in case anyone hasn't noticed, are not. Better, surely, to state that Patient X is host to a malignant growth the size of, say, a hand grenade, or a decomposing, maggot-ridden rat). I've waded through turgid papers posted by academics and heartbreaking poetry penned by mothers coming to terms with their children's leukaemia. Yet I'm no closer to dealing with the only cancer I really care about.

My cancer. The one that will *kill* me.

'It isn't possible to say without a lot more tests, but without treatment you've maybe got between three and five months.' That was how Doctor Morrissey put it in her sweet, slightly yokel voice.

Between three and five months . . .

I consider myself a truly average individual – to the point, actually, of being totally *un*-individual – so I've gone for the middle ground.

I give myself four months.

Working forward from the day they told me, that's 21ˢᵗ March.

It's a Saturday.

Best keep my diary clear.

'But you must be able to do something,' I said. *Pleaded*, actually. Hadn't they told me that these days the cure rate for testicular cancer is well over ninety per cent?

Well, yes, they said . . . *Provided we catch it early enough.*

'But I went to the doctor as soon as I'd found the lump,' I said.

Hmm, they mused, *and how long had the lump been there by the time you stumbled across it?*

Well, I dunno, I didn't say. *I don't like to touch myself down there, do I?*

Unbelievably, considering all this appalling news, my cancer is still only *suspected*. They can't be *certain* until they operate to remove my testicle and then get it under a microscope. Having said that, the blood tests suggested I've got something called a teratoma. This is the less common of the two main testicular cancers, but – wouldn't you just know it? – it's the more aggressive. Given the high probability that I did have cancer, they wanted to see if it had spread. They gave me a CT scan. CT scanners are those gleaming high-tech machines that you see pictured in private health-plan brochures – photos of patients with peaceful smiles gliding into wide tubes where they'll be showered with gentle diagnostic rays of something or other. 'CT scans are amazing,' gushed the technician giving me mine. 'They give your medical team the kind of information they could only have got by slicing you open in the old days.'

Sorry, techie, but I hate any machine that tells *my* medical team I've got great big bloody growths in my lungs and liver that will kill me very soon.

'There must be something you can do,' I *implored*.

Yes, they'd like very much to lop off my left testicle and then subject me to an aggressive course of radiotherapy, chemotherapy, or both, but they feared that the cancer is so advanced that it wouldn't achieve anything other than prolong my life for a few extra months.

Well, I supposed, under the circumstances – death staring me in the face and all that – a few extra months sounds pretty good. 'Let's do it, give me drugs,' I cried – no, *screamed* – in utter desperation. That was when they sat me down and took me through what it is to go through chemo and radiotherapy. I got all the 'cancer may be grim but the treatment is invariably grimmer' stuff. You don't want to know.

I know I didn't.

'But I don't even feel ill,' I said. (Which was and still is pretty much the truth. I have a painless lump on my testicle. And a tightness in my chest, which is more than likely due to a heavy dose of hospital-related stress.)

They didn't say much then. They simply looked at me, their expressions doing the talking for them: *'You don't feel ill now? You will, boy oh boy, you will.'*

The choice, of course, is mine. To be treated and last maybe a year: time spent feeling sick as a dog. Or not: enjoy a better quality of life for a shorter time. Quality of life. *Ha!*

You really should talk to someone, they said.

I haven't talked to a soul.

Instead I came to the web, the first resort of sad, lonely *twonks*. I came in search of . . . What? An understanding? A miracle? I haven't a clue and, besides, whatever it is I'm no nearer to finding it.

No, the Internet has made things worse. The sites that have freaked me out the most are the ones that are there to console and inspire. The ones filled with personal testimonies from fellow sufferers. *Brave* struggles in the face of overwhelming pain. *Stubborn* refusals to accept the verdicts of the doctors. The worst are the ones where I read a memoir of courage and endurance and then at the end a caption: *So-and-so died on 19th June 2003.*

So hang on, let me get this straight. After all that teeth-gritting, bloody-minded effort you went and died anyway? Please tell me there's a point here.

I haven't seen myself in a single one of these sites. I am not brave or stubborn. Never have been. I've spent a lot of my life thinking about death – panicking, actually – and the only way I could cope at all was by reminding myself that while it was a cast-iron certainty, it was a long way off – I could think of it as *hypothetical*.

Not any more. Now I've got a date. I'll be gone in four months, give or take. I'll expire incoherent, incontinent and saturated with enough morphine to keep all of Glasgow's junkies in a permanent blissed-out fug. And while I wait for that to happen I'm staring numbly at my PC as a fresh site downloads. Pretty graphics in shades of pink and lilac. Pictures of smiling doctors and nurses who look like they know what the hell they're playing at. I read the menu.

ABOUT US
LATEST TREATMENTS
UNCONVENTIONAL ALTERNATIVES
YOU AND YOUR FEELINGS
WHERE CAN YOU TURN?

I click on YOU AND YOUR FEELINGS.

A diagnosis of cancer comes to most people as a shock. Your mind may well be confused with many different feelings, some of them conflicting. Some may be very negative feelings . . .

It has been written for *me*.

. . . This should not worry you, because all of them are part of the process of coping with your illness.

Phew, that's OK, then.
The remainder of the page is written as bullet points.

You may experience:

- Shock
- Disbelief
- Denial
- Anger
- Guilt

- Depression
- Isolation

I could put a big fat tick next to every item. Jesus, in the past few days I've gone through more mood swings than a country and western album. Just for starters I've done a lot of denial. Only tonight I was buying it by the gram. And I still have moments of disbelief. Moments when I think – I *really* think – pixie Morrissey is going to leap out from round a corner, probably in clown make-up, and trill, '*Da-daaa! We really had you going there, eh?*' Actually, the disbelief is overwhelming. More than anything I can't believe my bad luck.

While a drowning man supposedly reviews his life at lightning speed, I can afford to reassess mine at a slightly more leisurely pace. I'm doing a lot of looking back and all I can see is a catalogue of lousy fortune. And look at me now: up to my neck in credit-card debt, in a job that makes me loathe myself, and I've lost the only girl that ever mattered. That is not the description of a lucky guy.

Well, at least I've got my health.

Can't say that any more, can I?

I've got a cancer that only a couple of thousand British men will succumb to this year. And while the overwhelming majority of them will make full recoveries, I'm one of the forty or so who won't.

Why *me*?

Why couldn't I have found that lump months ago, before its vicious mutant cells had begun their journey around my body?

And while we're at it, why *that* particular cancer out of the dozens on offer?

Why not a little melanoma on the small of my back? A slice with a scalpel, a quick zap of radiation and I'd be back on the streets in no time. Then there's colorectal cancer, non-Hodgkin's lymphoma, mesothelioma and multiple myeloma. My chances would almost certainly be better with any of those. They surely couldn't be any worse. I'd happily number among the one per cent of male breast cancers. I could put up with the sniggers. Or how about bowel cancer? Let them hack some of my stomach out. I'd put up with that. I'd put up with pretty much anything over the deal I've been dealt. A tumour on my arm like Jakki's uncle. That's a nice treatable one. Just cut off my arm. Hack off *both* to be certain.

At least I'd be *alive*.

But, no, I've got cancer in my testicle, my liver and my lung *and I don't even smoke*. I can't even shrug and admit I was asking for it. Well, thanks a million, God, Buddha, Allah, Krishna, the fairies at the bottom of the garden, whoever the fuck.

I thought I'd plumbed the depths of my self-pity in the days after Megan left.

I had no idea.

And I'm *terrified*. The website doesn't mention that one, does it? All-consuming, mind-curdling *fear*. More than anything else, I'm frightened . . . Of the impending pain . . . Of losing my dignity (not that there's much to lose) . . . Of losing my *life*, obviously . . . And, strangely, of telling people. Making it real. Official.

You really should talk to someone.

Yes, but who?

I click on WHERE CAN YOU TURN? More handy bullet points.

• A counsellor

I have major issues with this one. I know, I know, *issues* – as in the raising of and the dealing with – are what therapists are all about. But I've known *me* for thirty-one years, and I have trouble talking frankly about my feelings with myself in the mirror. It would take me an age to feel sufficiently comfortable with a stranger and, well, an age is something I don't have.

- Family

I'm trying, but there's no reply at *Casa Mama*. Anyway, how is Mum going to comfort me? I know only too well how she will react. Remember the gashed shin? She will take all of the emotions listed on this website and fuse them into an incandescent ball of *hysteria*.

- A sympathetic employer

Now they're having a laugh, surely. The thought of taking my disease and the excess emotional baggage that goes with it into Niall Haye's office and plonking the whole lot down on his desk is just so ridiculous that it's almost – but not quite – funny.

- Friends

Not long after the diagnosis I drew up a list of my friends. It ran to over twenty names. People with whom I work, drink beer, watch football/films/the world go by. I read it back and for a moment I felt quite popular. But then I drew up a second list: friends that I talk to. By that I mean really *talk*. About anything that matters as opposed to just any old thing. Talk as in *'Paul, there are days when I feel so depressed that I have actually thought about killing myself,'* or *'Sarah, I'm having these destructive fantasies that I find really unsettling,'* or *'Phil, I think you should know that I've got cancer . . .'* After ten minutes I hadn't written down a single name. Not one. Every relationship in my life is essentially shallow. Enjoyable maybe, but with all the emotional depth of a puddle.

I have mates, not friends.

Why else would I be communing with the Internet? Talking to a humming beige box whose only emotional response is to crash on me.

But . . . *You really should talk to someone.*

This would be the ideal time to reach out to the Almighty. Perhaps not *ideal* – a bit eleventh hour; a bit *'For thirty-one years you never write, you never call, yet the moment you get a terminal disease you want dialogue?'* – but better late than never. As with most of life's Big Issues, I've always been hazy on the religion thing. Hedging my bets. If it's possible to be an Anglican Atheist Who Doesn't Actually Believe In The Afterlife But Would Quite Like To Reserve Accommodation Just In Case, then I'm one of those. I've never had what I could call a spiritual moment. I did once get unfeasibly large goosebumps during the singing of 'I Vow to Thee My Country', but later I had to put it down to a freak combination of a beautiful tune, extremely cold weather and a broken church boiler.

However, discovering that you're going to die very soon doesn't half cut through the fuzz. Focus becomes the buzzword and for a fair amount of the last couple of weeks I've been focusing on a search for a Supreme Being (any Supreme Being. I'm really not choosy). When I haven't been typing *cancer* into the search box I've been tapping out *God*. But while there is a plethora of mentions of Him/Her/It (49,630,352 matches at the last count), none of them has helped me to make a personal breakthrough – no road-to-Damascus (or even Dagenham) moment for me. Time being of the essence, I've had to reach the rapid conclusion that He/She/It simply doesn't exist and, therefore, believing in the hereafter is the very last word in wishful thinking.

And since there is nowhere else to go, there is no point to being in this world unless you make a mark. I haven't left so much as a greasy thumbprint for posterity . . . And if I had – me being *me* – I'd have been straight onto it with a wet wipe.

While death scares the hell out of me, the thought of the utter futility of my nearly spent existence makes me feel sadder than anything else could.

You really should talk to someone.

There is only *one* someone . . .

I sit with my index finger poised over the phone keys. It has been frozen in this position for . . . oh . . . some minutes. I really don't think I can make this call . . .

So I don't.

Instead I dial work.

'Murray Colin's line. How can I help?'

'Hi, Jakki, it's me.'

'Where the hell are you? Niall's doing his nut.'

'I'm at home. I'm not feeling great.'

'Well, get into work. He told me if you take another sickie this year he wants a doctor's certificate.'

This makes me laugh.

'It isn't funny, Murray. They're talking about redundancies, you know.'

'You're right, it isn't funny.'

It *so* isn't funny.

'Look, set off now and you'll be just in time for the Schenker review,' she suggests.

'You'll have to give Haye my apologies,' I say.

'No, *you* give them to him. I told you he's having a shitfit.'

'I'm *not* coming in and I'm *not* talking to Haye,' I snap, actually stamping my foot on the carpet.

'What is it, Murray? You're not hungover after last night, are you? Even Vince made it in and he's got twelve stitches in his face after that fight.'

Yeah, and he's only come in to show them off. How do I compete

102

with that? Pin my CT scan film on the notice board?

'Good for him,' I say. 'Really, *good* for him. I can't come in, though.'

'Do you want to talk about anything?' Jakki asks, sensing the cracks. 'I'm a good listener.'

'No, it's OK ... Thanks. I do have to see someone, though.'

'I *knew* it. I knew all that bravado in the bar was bollocks ... Murray, you mustn't look back. She's *gone*. You have to look *forward*.'

I slam down the phone – I don't want Jakki to hear me scream.

10:43 a.m.

Two cups of coffee on, I'm recomposed, phone in my fist.

Hesitantly I punch out the digits that I know by heart.

It rings twice. Then ...

'Good morning, *Bindinger*, can I help you?' asks a crisp voice.

'Er ...'

Do it, for Christ's sake!

'... Megan Dyer, please,' I mutter.

'May I ask who's calling?'

'Murray Colin,' I mumble at a level only slightly above inaudible.

The line goes dead.

Bindinger is in Grays Inn Road, Holborn, home to plenty of corpulent law firms, but it isn't the sort that has numbing hold music on its phone system. Its clients make do with silence. I doubt they complain. Mostly they're the types who are simply glad to have a lawyer – *any* lawyer. But Bindinger doesn't employ just any old lawyers. Megan Dyer is on the payroll for a start. She's a partner now. You don't make partnership at Bindinger without talent. And a bit of judicious schmoozing. And convictions (the principled rather than criminal kind). Bindinger has made its name in publicly funded cases, AKA Legal Aid work. They're not doing it to milk the taxpayer either – Legal Aid isn't the nice little earner it used to be. They're doing it because they *believe*. They've represented thieves, terrorists, rapists and murderers. *And* asylum seekers. They also take on women who've been molested by their line managers, rail-crash victims, transsexuals who want to join the Royal Marines . . . You get the gist. It's the rare sort of legal firm that actually believes what they teach in law school; that everyone is entitled to a fair hearing.

Even, perhaps, me.

'So you finally had the guts to call me,' Megan snaps as I'm connected.

'I'm sorry. I've wanted to ring you back, honestly . . .' (A lie. I've been terrified at the prospect of replying to each and every one of the half-dozen messages she has left since that night in Barnsbury Square.) '. . . but I've had a lot on my mind.' (True, so bloody true.)

'Jesus, what were you playing at that night? It was you, wasn't it?'

Silence.

'I thought so. You scared me to death. And have you any idea how hard it was to stop Sandy calling the police?'

Oh, so Sandy Morrison QC – fearless exposer of police brutality, corruption and incompetence in countless bravura court performances – gets a tiny-weeny tap on his one-hundred-and-seventy-grand car and he wants to go blubbing to . . . the cops?

'I'm sorry . . . Tell him I'm sorry . . . I don't know what the hell I was doing—'

'I know I didn't leave you in the nicest circumstances, but I'm really angry with you, Murray, *really* angry.'

'I'm sorry.'

'Is that it? *Sorry?*'

'No . . . Can I see you?'

104

'I don't think that's a good idea.'

'Please . . . There's something I need to talk about—'

'We are *not* getting back together.'

'It's not that, honestly. I'm just having a bit of a crisis and I don't know who else I can talk to.'

'God, listen to yourself, Murray. *A bit of a crisis*. You don't know the meaning of the word. AIDS is killing hundreds of thousands of Africans. Kids as young as six are toting machine guns in Rio. Women in Pakistan are being gang raped in court-sanctioned punishments. Do you know what I'm doing today? Defending a Bangladeshi guy who punched some thug who'd beaten up his nine-year-old son and put a turd through his letterbox? You work in *advertising*. You earn more in a week than the average Filipino takes home in a year. What do you know about crisis?'

Well, give me half a chance, Megan, and I'll tell you.

three: **they asked me to feed their fish**

The wine bar on High Holborn is packed with lawyers, accountants, IT pros and other office escapees. Fun is being had. And amidst it all Megan is *sobbing*.

'I'm sorry,' she blubs. 'You don't need this.'

'It's OK,' I say, reaching my hand across the table and squeezing hers.

'I feel terrible . . . I'm sorry. You need someone to be strong for you . . . Not falling . . . apart . . .'

She fumbles in her bag for a tissue. She looks beautiful. Puffy eyes, streaked mascara and a dribbly, reddening nose could *not* look more becoming on anyone else.

Bloody hell, I . . . Love . . . Her.

It strikes me that this is the first time in weeks that I have felt good. Well, good-*ish* – everything's relative, isn't it? Getting the words out wasn't as hard as I'd thought it would be – helped by the fact that Megan is one of the very few people to have seen me with my trousers off. And it *is* good to talk. It has made me feel as if I can cope with this – no idea how exactly, but I feel as if I *can*. And . . . Sorry, but this is really flip . . . As a man desperate to get his ex back into his life in *any* shape or form, I couldn't have scripted it better.

'Right,' she says, dry-eyed again, 'here's what you're going to do . . .'

This is the more familiar Megan. The unflappable, tack-sharp version that I love just as madly as the disintegrating, tear-streaked one.

'. . . You're going to take me through everything that's

106

happened. Every test you had, everything the doctors told you. There must be something we can do.'

There must be something we can do . . . She said *we*.

I tell her the story. About the ultrasound, the blood tests and the CT scan. About how the cancer is spreading even as we speak via my body's lymphatic system. (Until a couple of weeks ago I didn't even know I had a lymphatic system. Does everyone have one or is it just me? I'm still not certain what it does, apart, that is, from spread cancer cells.)

'And they're certain, are they?' she says as I conclude. 'Doctors aren't perfect, you know. They do make mistakes.'

No doubt she's thinking of the teenager she represented a year or so ago. The one who went into the operating theatre for a tonsillectomy and came out minus a pair of ovaries. Megan helped her win a fortune.

'What about the treatment options?' she asks. 'If there's any kind of chance at all, you've *got* to take it.'

I give her the facts – those given to me by the team at Saint Matthew's and embellished by long trawls on the Net. I explain about the futility of surgery. About the radio- and chemotherapy that will do little more than buy me some time.

I'm crying now. That's how it works, then. Her renewed show of strength has allowed me to revert to type.

'What about your mum?' she asks. 'Have you told her?'

I've been trying her all day. Finally I phoned her neighbour – Mum gave me her number for emergencies, and I guess this qualifies. Mum, apparently, has gone off with David in a camper van. He's a cowboy nut and they've gone to Almeria – spaghetti-western country. Judith-next-door doesn't think they'll be back for a couple of weeks: *'They asked me to feed their fish.'*

'Don't worry, Murray,' Megan soothes, taking my face in her hands. 'You and I are going to go back to that hospital and have them go through everything again.'

'What's the point?'

'There's *every* point. You've been going through this on your own. I can't imagine how hard that's been. And you can't possibly have been in a fit state to take it all in properly and ask the right questions. Maybe things aren't as bad as you think. And if they are . . . Well, I want to hear it for myself.'

I'm still crying, but over her shoulder I can make out a group of people I recognise – some of Megan's fellow lawyers from Bindinger. They're looking at her and exchanging nudges and whispers. They might be right-on and motivated by purest altruism, but they're clearly not above a juicy bit of office gossip. I can't resist it. I take her hand and pull it to my mouth, showering her palm with slobbery kisses. Though she's unaware of her colleagues' scrutiny, she pulls away from me and I feel cheap and stupid. She reaches into her bag and takes out her mobile.

'I'm going to phone Sandy,' she announces.

What, and grass me up for kissing your hand?

'We're supposed to be having dinner with Ben Elton tonight, but he'll have to go on his own. There's no way I'm going to let you go home by yourself.'

The room is bathed in dazzling white light as I lounge naked on the cool bed-linen. Megan walks towards me, naked as well.

'It's going to be all right now,' she murmurs as she lies down beside me.

'Is it?'

'I promise.'

She raises her left arm and holds it above us. She twists her hand slightly from side to side, making the chunky diamond on her finger sparkle.

I wake up to pitch-blackness. The only light in the room comes from the display on the radio alarm. I climb out of bed and creep to the door. I open it a crack and peer out into the sitting room. Snoring softly on the sofa is Megan. I watch her for a minute before returning to bed. I sink my head into the pillow, close my eyes and compile a top-ten *I love Megan because* . . .

10. She stayed tonight.
9. She always knows *exactly* what she wants . . . Except in shoe shops. She's worse than useless in shoe shops.
8. She stayed tonight.
7. Whitstable, May bank holiday 2001.
6. The twirly thing she does with her hair.
5. I'm feeling . . . very . . . tired.
4. She . . . stayed . . . to—

five: the pharmaceutical industry is mired in the shite with the arms dealers and big tobacco, murray. they're little better than a mob of sallow-faced pushers outside a wee kiddies' playground and it depresses the *hell* out of me

_____ friday 12 december / 7.40 p.m.

One week on.

One week nearer death.

Though it began with such Megan-heavy promise, it hasn't been a vintage seven days. Yes, she's back. Sort of. She's here in a kind of lawyer capacity. That was how it felt when we went to Saint Matthew's. She took notes on the same pad she uses when she's interviewing her clients and she grilled the doctors as if we were in one of those discovery hearings you see in Grisham movies.

Dyer: *When you characterise the alleged tumour on the liver as a metastatic cancer, that's just a fancy way of saying it's a secondary growth, is it not?*

Doctor: *Well, yes, but—*

Dyer: *And given that it's secondary, and therefore less advanced than the primary, and further accepting that the liver is capable of regeneration, then surely it is feasible to operate.*

Doctor: *It's terribly complicated. Let me exp—*

Dyer: *Answer the question, please. Is surgical intervention a viable option?*

110

> Doctor: *I suppose, all other considerations aside, yes it is, but —*
> Dyer: *'Yes it is.' Thank you, doctor. Now, shall we move on?*
>   *The alleged tumour on the lung, also metastatic . . .*

OK, I'm exaggerating a little for dramatic effect, but it's not that far off the mark. There were several moments when I expected her to leap up and shout 'Objection!' and at one point Mr Hersh, the timid senior consultant urologist, looked so flustered that I thought he might be better off taking the fifth.

Lawyers, eh? In all of my dealings with them – professional as opposed to personal – the chances of getting a straight answer to a direct question have been slim to non-existent. Ask a lawyer if she'd like sugar in her tea, and you'd better have a spare hour to listen to the answer with all its sub-clauses, riders and disclaimers. Yet when a lawyer starts *asking* the questions, well, aren't those tables turned? Suddenly the only colours in her palette are black and white and merely to speculate that there might be some shade of grey is tantamount to heresy.

Yet for all her incisiveness, Megan's efforts didn't change a thing. They simply put into sharper relief the stark fact that in a very short while I'm going to die.

She wants me to take the treatment option on the basis that even the most minuscule chance is better than none at all. I could point out to her how out of character she is being. Megan is above all a realist. She's not a clutcher of straws. There's no pie in *her* sky. She spends her working life dispassionately assessing her clients' chances and then gently shunting them towards their best – or oftentimes their least worst – option. But this past week her estimable powers of reasoning seem to have packed their bags and gone on a long holiday – backpacking in Laos where they're completely uncontactable. She has, in short, gone a bit *weird*.

Yes, I could point this out, but I haven't . . . Not yet, anyway.

Well, the fact that she is so uncharacteristically hoping for a miracle suggests that . . . maybe, just maybe . . . she still . . . you know . . . *cares*. And the only reason I haven't yet ruled out treatment – and all the grief that goes with it – is because I'm drawn to the fantasy of lying in a hospital bed and focusing through the morphine haze on Megan stroking my hand as she reads me the *Seinfeld* episode about the soup nazi. Kind of, *I'll take the radiation hell as long as you go through every second of it with me.* The last word in emotional blackmail, I suppose.

My motives are *that* selfish.

Well, I think I can be excused. I am *dying* here. How am I supposed to cope with *that* alone? You hear of people reaching an accommodation with death, accepting their fate and getting their affairs in order. I've read dozens of their stories on the Net. I'm not one of them. No bloody chance of that. I *panic*. The only way I've found to deal with it is by handling it in chunks. One day at a time like an alcoholic. I daren't look forward. I do spend a good deal of time looking back. Which, I'm afraid, only ever leads me to sink into a dank pit of regret.

So pardon me if in my misery I selfishly grab at whatever little morsel of pleasantness I can. And so far the only one I've come across is Megan Dyer. In fact, it's only because I'm so desperate to keep her as close as I possibly can that I'm here now – in a pub a couple of hundred yards from Lincoln's Inn. I'm sipping on a beer as I wait for her . . .

. . . and . . .

. . . Sandy Morrison.

Megan – honest and open as the day is long (apart, of course, from the three or so months when she was CHEATING ON ME) – has told him everything. He – the *perfect* combination of empathetic and self-secure – is *very* understanding. '*I've never seen him so distraught. His heart bleeds for you, Murray.*' This evening he's going to prove as much by turning up to buy me a drink and share my pain. He also wants to give me the benefit of his knowledge. *'He has first-hand experience of cancer . . . No, he's never had it, but he was close to someone who did. Perhaps what he's got to say could really help.'*

Well, we'll see about that, won't we?

I'm sorry if I seem cynical.

But I don't give a damn how wise and saintly he is.

As far as I'm concerned he'll always be . . .

THE BASTARD THAT STOLE MY GIRLFRIEND.

'Here's how it works, Murray,' Sandy booms as he winds up for an explanation. 'Take a barely known condition that hardly any bugger suffers from, PR the pants off it so that the world and his wife thinks they've got it and then market the drug to treat it. It's worked like a dream with depression. I mean, forty, fifty years ago who the hell suffered from *depression*? Then GlaxoSmithKline, Pfizer, Eli Lilly and the rest discover chemicals that play with the brain's serotonin levels and – hey-*presto* – we're all told we aren't just a bit fed up, we aren't simply having a bad day at the office, but we've got this *chronic* disease called depression. And – whaddya know? – they've got just the pill to make us feel fine again. Now we're Prozac-ed up to our eyeballs. Flog the disease *then* flog the cure. *In*credible, eh? You'd have to admire 'em if they weren't so bloody heinous. The pharmaceutical industry is mired in the shite with the arms dealers and Big Tobacco, Murray. They're little better than a mob of sallow-faced pushers outside a wee kiddies' playground and it depresses the *hell* out of me.'

Looks like you need some Prozac, pal.

'I know it's probably not what you want to hear—'

Well, now you mention it, it isn't, Sandy. I was kinda hoping that you were going to give me a rare insight that would actually help me to . . . you know . . . cope with my terminal condition. If I'd wanted a

113

diatribe against the military/fags/drugs/industrial complex, I'd have bought a copy of the Socialist Worker, *thank you.*

'—but I reckon you're a smart guy—'

God, now you're patronising me.

'—and you'd prefer to know precisely what you're dealing with – however ugly the brute.'

Megan and I have been listening to this for nearly an hour now. Megan has barely said a word and is totally in his thrall.

Bastard.

I have to say he's brilliant. He's a courtroom natural, though I suspect he modifies the language a touch for *m'lud*. If I were a jury I'd be mesmerised – *Those pill-peddling fiends! Guilty as hell!* – and I can see why TV producers love him. He has his facts neatly marshalled, an answer for everything and that impassioned, R-rrrrolling delivery that has worked so well for Gordon Brown and Billy Connolly – well, Billy Connolly, anyway. But he's not so Scottish that he requires subtitles.

He's a looker, too, for an old bloke.

Bastard, bastard, bastard.

'That's bang on, Sandy, but Murray has a very tough decision to make – incredibly tough,' Megan says, at last getting a word in and moving the conversation back onto the only item on the agenda – *me*. 'And he has to make it fast,' she adds.

'Aye, the Big One. Well, there's a point to my ranting, Megan, my sweet.'

Now you're patronising her.

'You've been dealt a pretty shabby hand, Murray. Cancer in the old wedding tackle—'

Wedding tackle? Hardly, matey. Not now that you've nicked my bride.

'—But before you decide whether to have your body pumped full of toxins so deadly you'd hesitate to give 'em to a lab rat or before you choose to be zapped with radiation so dangerous that those doing the zapping will be hiding in a lead-lined bunker, you need to know what's motivating the guys in the white coats—'

The prospect of making me a little better, perhaps?

'—And believe me, it isn't the prospect of making you a well man.'

Oh.

'No, they're up to their necks in the cesspit with the drug companies. They have a symbiotic relationship, y'see? The pharmaceutical industry needs warm bodies and the medical establishment supplies them. In return for their trouble the doctors get highly paid consultancies and jet-skiing junkets to Nassau Beach dressed up as *international seminars*. Take chemotherapy. The NHS spends untold-fucking-millions on the drugs, but how well do they actually work?'

'It's pretty refined,' Megan says. 'I've done a lot of reading these past few days and it's buying a life for more patients than ever. There are side-effects, but—'

'Exactly, the *side-effects*,' says Sandy, all triumphant and I-rest-my-case-ly.

'The point is that increasing numbers are living long enough to suffer them,' she says with – I'm very pleased to note – just the slightest hint of irritation.

'Who's to say they wouldn't live that long *without* being marinated in poison?'

'Look at the statistics, Sandy.'

'The statistics don't fool me for a second. The first thing I learned at the bar is that you can take any figure under the sun and make it prove any damn thing you like. No, my sweet, the statistics are furnished by doctors, who, as I've demonstrated, are card-carrying members of the pharmacological conspiracy.'

'Well, I don't honestly see what option Murray has,' Megan says through – I'm delighted to see – ever so slightly gritted teeth.

''Course he has an option. Let me tell you about a friend of mine—'

At last, the much heralded first-hand experience of cancer.

'—Not so much a friend, as it happened, more a friend of a friend.'

OK, second-hand experience, whatever. I'm listening.

'The guy had cancer in his bowel, poor sod. Anyway, he had a few yards of intestine hacked out and started radiotherapy. After a month his gut was burned to buggery and he couldn't even take a sip of tea without throwing up. Then it struck him, *Hang on, this would be the same radiation they used to carbonise all those souls in Hiroshima and Nagasaki; the very same radi-bloody-ation that if it didn't fry the poor bloody Japs in the blast gave 'em cancer – aye, cancer – twenty, thirty, forty years down the line.* That's when he walked away from it. Found himself an acupuncturist and six months later he was bungee jumping into a ravine in Middle Earth, AKA New Zealand.'

'That's amazing,' I say, picturing myself bouncing merrily at the end of a rubber band – I'm terrified of heights but at this moment I am *so* ready to bungee jump.

'Aye, amazing is the word, Murray.'

'So, how is he now?' I ask as I fumble in my pocket for a pen – I want the name of that acupuncturist.

'Well, he died last year. Tragic business. But the point is the guy had eighteen months in which he lived a *life* and where he wasn't beholden to some jobsworth technician with a radioactive laser beam. It's about *quality of life*, Murray.'

God, don't get me started on quality of life.

I feel too deflated to say anything. No matter – Sandy hasn't finished yet.

'You've got to be *clever* about this, Murray. It's *your* life and the smart thing to do would be to take control of it. What do *you* want from whatever time you've got left? You can either go out there and get it – bloody *revel* in it – or you can lie on some hospital slab screaming for the opiates.'

'Sandy!' Megan rebukes.

'No, however harsh, the boy's got to hear it.'

Megan has slipped into the stiff-bodied, clamp-lipped pose I recognise from having pissed her off myself countless times in the past. But this time it wasn't me. She has her head buried in her handbag in which she's rooting for a lip salve. She mutters something. It's hard to make out, but it sounds a little like *Bullshit.'*

'What was that, my sweet?' Sandy asks.

'Nothing, Sandy,' she replies with a taut smile. Then, 'No, it wasn't nothing. I'm sorry, but I don't agree with you.'

'It's unarguable, girl.'

'Bullshit,' she mutters again.

'What was that, Megan?' I ask hopefully.

She ignores me and stares him in the eye. 'Has it crossed your mind that if your silly git of a friend of a friend had stuck with the radiotherapy he might be alive today?' she suggests.

'Ach, have you not been listening to a thing I've said?' Sandy spits – clearly not a man used to having his advice spurned.

'I heard every word,' Megan answers. This time the teeth are *definitely* gritted. Then she looks at me and says, 'Murray, I know the thought must be terrifying, but I really think you should phone Saint Matthew's the first chance you get and book yourself in for treatment.'

I look across the table at Sandy coolly sipping his beer and Megan icily applying blackcurrant balm to her lips. The silence . . . Oh, yes, you could take a Stanley knife to it. My stomach is churning. Mostly because I am very, very scared, but also, strangely, because I feel just a tiny bit elated.

'I'm going to do it,' I say very quietly.

'God, I can't tell you how relieved that makes me feel,' Megan sighs.

Sandy, to his credit, visibly stops himself from saying what is really on his mind and makes do with, 'Well, it's a very tough call you're making and I can only wish you luck.'

Och-aye the fucking noo to that.

six: **two jacuzzis (!!)**

What does she see in the guy?

Well, obviously *apart* from the Mills & Boon looks, the rebel-liously tousled hair, the swagger, the towering *presence*, the intellect, the wit, the expansive and richly enunciated vocabu-lary, the (right kind of) celebrity, the big house in N1, the fact that he has managed to buy the big house without selling out on his principles, the A-list address book, the car that not only *works* but is also a *Bentley*, the fact that he's almost certainly *not* in a state with his credit cards . . .

I've been awake for less than a minute and already I'm depressed. So I had the thrill of seeing them come close to arguing? It didn't last and once it had passed I felt cheap for having exploited it. And with whom did she go home? I look at the unrumpled half of my bed, though clearly I already know the answer to that one.

I force myself up and take some ibuprofen. Hangover? I wish. My chest is *hurting* this morning. It probably won't be long before I'm seeing the doctor at Saint Matthew's who specialises in nothing but pain management. Kind of Torquemada in reverse. Nice work if you can get it.

I go to the kitchen and switch on the kettle. While I wait for it to boil I head down to the hall to pick up my post. I leaf through the small stack of envelopes: a phone bill, letters from Barclaycard, Goldfish and Morgan Stanley – writs? Threats to remove cards from wallet/caps from knees? – and a hand-written envelope with a Spanish stamp in the corner. I sit on the stairs and tear it open. Two sheets of paper are wrapped around a photograph. A picture of Mum in a lairy floral sundress standing in front of a tall cactus. She isn't alone. David has his arm around her. He's wearing a poncho and a black Lee Van Cleef hat and he's biting on a thin cigar.

Git.

I don't like my stepdad. A bit of a cliché, that one. Kids aren't supposed to *like* the person that steps into the picture when one or other parent quits. I'm following in the tradition of Snow White, Cinderella and the cheesy brats in *Stepmom*. You know what? I don't care. Because however flawed, fat and feckless (at least when it came to road sense) my dad was, he was always a better man than David Finch.

Not that it ever looked that way on the surface. While Dad sat on his backside at Hornchurch nick, collecting the money for the station pools syndicate and palming off paperwork to whoever he could, David was out there catching the bad guys. He was the star detective. His conviction rate was exemplary. Though he's flashy in a diamond-geezer way, underneath the gold chains he's a handsome sod as well. He's bald, but he carries it like Sean Connery rather than Bobby Charlton. As a result he was never out of the local papers. And while Dad was lumbering onto the stage at my school to give us the Tufty Club lecture, David was having his nose powdered by the *Crimewatch* make-up girl as he prepared to talk the viewers through the reconstruction of a rape in Saint Andrew's Park.

No contest, really.

OK, so Dad wasn't exactly Dixon of Dock Green, but DI Finch was no Morse either. Something we don't talk about in my little family: at the time he left the force, David was being investigated. He'd won a string of convictions thanks to the evidence of one bloke, a housebreaker who'd spent only slightly less of his life in jail than out. Then the bloke discovered God. Good news – *there is more joy in heaven over one sinner that repenteth* and all that – for everyone except David. Dazzled by his shiny new conscience, the grass felt obliged to confess. He told a reporter on the *Hornchurch Gazette* that he'd only testified because David had let him off the hook on more than a dozen burglaries. He claimed that he hadn't even heard of three of the guys he helped to put away until David came along with the script.

Prospects didn't look good for my stepdad as the inquiry dragged on. After the grass had blazed the trail an assortment of cons crawled out of the woodwork with accusations of bungs, brutality and fitting up. Then David's back went. *Just like that.* What dumb luck, eh? To add to his other woes he was pensioned off a sad and hollow man.

I didn't like him, but I have to say that I felt sorry for him at the time. But I was only seventeen and I didn't twig for years that the rules and regs of internal inquiries prevented investigations being continued against *former* members of the force. Which was convenient.

So was Detective Inspector Finch corrupt . . . bent . . . a *slag*? You the jury will have to decide. Well, a proper one never got the chance, did it?

As I gaze at the photograph it strikes me that the black hat is pretty appropriate. I put the snap down, pick up the letter and read Mum's neat but cramped hand.

Dear Murray
How are you?

Hmm, where would you like me to start?

I hope you're not working too hard. I phoned you the other night, but you were out. As usual! Anyway, here we are in Almeria! David is in his element. He's 'walking in the footsteps of his heroes'! John Wayne, Gary Cooper, Alan Ladd. Mind you, since they had the real Wild West right on their own doorsteps, why did they come all the way over here to make their films?

121

Good to see you've been paying your usual amount of attention, Mum. They didn't. It was the spaghetti westerns that were made in Spain. You know – the Clint with no name, crap dubbing, weird music . . . Oh, never mind.

It's all a bit lost on me. I'm afraid! You know what I'm like. Give me a mushy old Barbra Streisand video to curl up with any day! But the weather is gorgeous so I'm just enjoying the chance to top up my tan while David gallivants about playing cowboys and indians! Honestly. I think you'd really enjoy yourself out here with him.

No I would not and if you were at all honest with yourself, you'd know it, Mum.

We've bumped into an absolutely lovely couple. They're called Jimmy and Christine, though she insists I call her Chrissy. They're retired like us. You'll never believe this, but he's an old friend of David's. The two of them go way back and are off the whole time gassing about the old days, but Chrissy and I don't mind a bit. They're staying in a lovely hotel. Five star! Much more comfy than our grotty camper! So while the lads are off, Chrissy and I sit around the pool sipping cocktails or nip off to the salon for a treatment or two! Perfect! Anyway. Chrissy and Jimmy are really the reason I'm writing. They've asked us to spend Christmas with them at their villa in Marbella.

Hang on . . . Marbella? Jimmy wouldn't be that sort of old mate, would he? How did he earn a crust, then? Importing exotica from Colombia or the Lebanon? Offering . . . ahem . . . security to twitchy East End nightclub owners? Whatever, I bet he isn't a retired judge.

They showed us some snaps of their place and it looks absolutely magnificent. Gold and marble everything, two Jacuzzis (!!) and the most stunning porcelain leopards standing guard at their front door. They've also got that famous painting of the water lilies above their fireplace. It looks like it might be the original, but I didn't like to ask! Anyway, we've said yes to their kind invitation and we'll head down there in a week or so. Obviously I didn't pack nearly enough, but Chrissy says not to worry because there are some lovely shops in Marbella.

Lovely, that is, if you don't mind looking like an Essex gangster's tart.

But I do feel a bit guilty about waltzing off.

Mum, please don't feel bad on my account.

I asked Judith next door to feed the tropicals.

Oh.

She says she's happy to traipse over to ours, but you never know, do you? I must call her and tell her to buy more fish food. And I'll get her something lovely in Marbella. I know you said you weren't planning to pop over for Christmas

I did say that.

so I know you won't mind.

Course not. Why should I mind? I'll just go through the operation and the chemo and radiation hell on my own while you piss off to Marbella with Dodgy Dave and his mate who's probably a second-cousin-once-removed to the Krays. No, Mum, please don't worry about—

'You OK?' a deep-ish voice asks.

I look up to see . . . What's her name? . . . What *is* her bloody name? . . . *Apollonia*, that's right . . . Apollonia from the downstairs flat standing in her doorway. She's looking at me as if I'm

123

a loon. Which I am – I've only just realised that I've been conversing *aloud* with Mum's letter.

'Yeah . . . Apollonia, I'm fine, thanks.'

Apollonia! What kind of a name is that for a girl with a truck-sized Harley-Davidson that requires an HGV licence just to lift it off its side stand?

'Letter from my mum . . . I miss her,' I add, feeling myself blush.

Apollonia grunts, throws me a scary look and stomps out of the front door. I stuff the letter into my dressing-gown pocket and stomp – though not in half as virile a fashion – back upstairs to my flat.

Why do I feel so angry?

Because my mum has abandoned me? Since I *did* say I had no intention of joining her (and, more to the point, *him*) for Christmas and since she doesn't even know I'm sick that's hardly fair. Maybe it's because, actually, she abandoned me less than a year after my dad died when she took up with DI David Finch. And then, *again* – just to rub salt in – when she went to Spain the moment I was safely out of the way at uni. Why did I choose Newcastle? If I'd applied for, say, Middlesex and stayed at home she might never have left. *Newcastle*. Three years spent freezing to death while Mum flew off to the sun with her *fancy man*.

I sit on the sofa and flick on the TV. I surf through the channels to . . . Cartoon Network . . . *Deputy Dawg*.

Just hang on one cotton-pickin' minute, Musky, I see a pattern emerging here.

Two women in my life.

Both leave me for handsome, charismatic, telegenic men working in some sense or another with the law.

I don't know what's more depressing.

The double rejection.

Or the fact that I've only had *two* women in my life, one of them my mother.

Or the realisation that, with the final taxi drawing up to the rank, two is all I'm going to get.

Still slumped on the sofa, remote in hand.

I was planning to get the car fixed today (it's probably the alternator . . . It usually is . . . What, by the way, is an alternator?), but there doesn't seem much point. My car became terminally ill some months ago. I think it was trying to tell me something.

I could do some cleaning.

But, again, what's the point? That is depressing – the realisation that ultimately I'm going to lose the war on filth. I'll be gone soon and the dust particles will be holding victory parades in my living room, messing the place up with ticker tape and drinking toasts to the cancer cells, their allies in the Microscopic Axis of Evil.

Best stick with Cartoon Network for now. *Powerpuff Girls*. Mutant toddlers with superpowers. I can relate to that. The mutant bit anyway.

seven: **back in the land of the living**

I've done it. I've just booked my orchiectomy.

Which sounds horticultural – as discussed on *Gardeners' Question Time* – but which sadly is not even remotely floral. It's a surgical procedure; one that is, I'm assured, relatively quick, simple and painless. That's as maybe, but it still involves being drugged into unconsciousness and having a man in a mask take a lethally sharp knife to me. And whichever way I look at it there's no escaping the maths: when I wake up I'll have one less testicle than I had when I went to sleep.

I'm fully prepared to believe the doctors when they tell me that I'll be able to '*perform perfectly normally, sexually speaking*' with just the one. And I have to admit that at this point in my life my opportunities to perform *at all* are nil, and are likely to remain so in the *very short time I have left*. All that being the case, why does the impending loss of one little testicle freak me out so? I think the answer lies in the word *freak* – as in, that's what I'll be. OK, I've never been one for public displays of nudity, or even one for public displays of very tight trousers, so no one need ever be aware. But that won't stop *me* knowing. I'll know that down there I'm lacking, abnormal, out of kilter. A bloody freak.

So I really can't believe that I've gone through with it – booked the op. And I can't believe that all it took was a three-minute phone call. As if it's a weekend break in Brighton or a table for two at the Ivy. What am I talking about? *Nothing* like the Ivy. Unless you're A list (and you can guarantee that your date is at least B), you can't get a table there for about eighteen months. The National Health Service, I've discovered, doesn't even vaguely resemble your typical celebrity restaurant because (quite apart from *not* doing fish and chips for over twenty quid a portion and *not* holding the best bed – the one furthest from the bagpipe-lunged geriatric – for Sir Elton John and David Furnish) they've reserved me an exclusive and very private operating theatre for tomorrow.

TOMORROW!

But this is the *NHS*. When it comes to keeping the plebs waiting, it's supposed to be *exactly* like the Ivy, isn't it? Why haven't I joined the queue behind a lady with a crumbling hip and a bloke with an ingrowing toenail? What the hell's got into them? Too much of this kind of behaviour and they'll get a reputation for efficiency. But this, I'm finding out, is simply how the NHS acts when it's confronted with someone who is very seriously ill indeed. And I find their sense of urgency the most depressing thing of all – do I really need to be reminded how bad things are? Mind you, I'd feel just as miserable if they sat on their hands. Poor old NHS. It can't win, can it?

A few minutes after putting down the phone I'm still staring at it. I'm unsure what to do now. I'm sitting at my desk, so I suppose I should get on with some work. But how can I work? *Advertising – remind me, please, how do you do that again?*

I hear a *ting*. Someone has sent me an e-mail.

brett.topowlski@blowermann-dba.co.uk

to: murray.colin@blowermann-dba.co.uk

cc:

re: where the wanking-fuck are you?

while you've been hanging around dog tracks or crack houses or wherever it is you go when you're not here, that twat haye has got us up to draft 38 on chocochillout. i repeat, draft THIRTY-FUCKING-EIGHT. even in my long experience of crafting gold into turds, this is

UN-FUCKING-PRECEDENTED. if you have even the tiniest scrap of decency about your person and don't wish to see YOUR ONLY TWO FRIENDS in the creative dept drown in a scummy, foetid swamp of cretinous script rewrites, you will do something about this. we're DYING here.

That's how you do it. It's all coming back to me now. *Advertising: take one good idea, add two pinches of enthusiasm and slowly smother the living daylights out of it.* Brett's e-mail has also reminded me that adland is a self-contained universe. Nothing exists outside of it and within it concepts like *drowning* and *dying* take on new meanings . . .

'Murray, you're here . . . You're *early* too.'

I look up. Jakki is flinging her bag onto her chair, shrugging her coat from her shoulders and, without even knowing it, saving me from drowning in my own scummy, foetid swamp of teary philosophising.

'Good weekend?' she asks.

'You know, so-so,' I lie.

'Hey, a load of us are going to Mr Ryan's tonight,' she says. 'They do a half-price menu on Mondays. Fancy coming?'

'I can't.'

'Aw, why not? You haven't been out with us for ages.'

I can't tell her that I've been ordered to go nil-by-mouth from this evening onward. It won't do me a lot of good showing up at the hospital tomorrow stinking of house red and deep-fried Camembert, so I say, 'I'm really broke at the minute.' This is true. I doubt I could afford even Mr Ryan's half-prices.

'You should get Niall to give you a rise. I just bumped into him by the lift. He seems in a really good mood today.'

'I need to see him, actually,' I say, hauling myself to my feet.

9.04 a.m.

'Come in, come in,' Niall says without looking up from his

computer screen. I walk into his office and sit down on the compact Bauhaus sofa he inherited when our CEO traded up to something more CEO-sized. He's reading an e-mail. He's smiling, so I guess it isn't from Brett. Finally, he sits back and says, 'Murray, you're back in the land of the living. You've finally rid yourself of the dreaded lurgy?'

I nod because he must be referring to the *chronic flu* that I've been phoning in with for the last few weeks.

'Good, good, because you need to get yourself back into the loop. ChocoChillout is hitting fresh peaks . . .'

That's not how Brett would put it.

'. . . And there's something else. I want to sign you up for a little pitch team I'm putting together. It's a *fantastic* opportunity. Winning this one would fill a gaping hole in our portfolio.'

There are a few chasms in the Blower Mann client list. As yet we have no car account, no beer, no airline, no cigarettes, no anti-smoking lobby group. (In the absence of both, we'd take either.)

'I'm going to pick up the brief from the client tomorrow morning,' he continues, 'and I'd like you to join me.'

'Tomorrow. That's what I wanted to see you about,' I say. 'I . . . Er . . . I need some time off.'

He stares at me for a long moment, then says, 'You're taking the mickey now. I'm throwing you a lifeline. An opportunity to redeem yourself. And you want more *time off*?' He shakes his head sorrowfully. '. . . No matter. I'm sure there are half a dozen account supervisors who'd jump at the chance to help me bring the Mr Muscle business to Blower Mann.'

Aaaaaggggggggggghhhhhhhhhhhhhhhhhhh!

Better make that *Aaaaaaaaaaaaaaaaaaaaaaaagggggggggggggggggggg- gggggggggggggggghhhhhhhhhhhhhhhhhhhhhhhhhhhhhhhhhhhhhhhhhhhh hhhhhhhhhh!*

It's the one I've been waiting for.

Praying for.

I can't believe that God has chosen this moment to reveal Himself to me. And that He is a cruel and heartless bastard who revels in the perfect black timing of his punchlines.

'I'm sorry, Niall. It's just that I've got to go into hospital . . . But I can be back at work by the end of the week,' I say, unable to keep the desperation out of my voice. 'I can help you out then if you like. Mr Muscle . . . *Wow*. It's a fantastic product and I know loads about the sector. Maybe I can—'

'No, no, you go, Murray,' he says, giving me a dismissive wave. 'Don't worry about us. I'm sure we'll somehow struggle on without you.' His phone is ringing and he looks at it eagerly, ready to move on, get me out of his life.

'I'm really sorry,' I say. 'It's just that I've got to have an operation.'

He picks up the phone. 'Hullo, Niall Haye . . . *Gerhard*, glad you phoned. Draft thirty-eight. We're just putting the final touches to it. Checking it ticks all the boxes, presses the requisite buttons . . .'

'Yes, I'm having an operation, Niall,' I go on. 'I've got cancer, you see.'

'. . . Oh yes, we're terribly excited about it. Give us a couple more days and we'll get it over to you . . .'

'It's in my testicles, my lungs and my liver. I've only got a few months left.'

'. . . Now, Gerhard, how would you like a trip to the opera? Some first-rate tickets for *La Boheme* have come my way . . .'

I stand up and walk out of his office.

eight: **you risked a criminal record for a garlic crusher?**

Only eight shopping days to Christmas. Unless you count Sundays, which I suppose you should these days.

Don't know why I thought that.

'Hey, only nine shopping days to Christmas. Unless you don't count Sundays. In which case only eight,' I say.

Megan smiles weakly. 'Murray, I've been meaning to mention something . . .' She's twizzling her hair. A fat, black ringlet is twined around two fingers and she's tugging on it anxiously. This is an I've-got-something-tricky-to-broach twizzle as opposed to the regular absent-minded one. No matter. Megan twizzling in any shape or form always brings a pleasant tingle.

'About last Friday . . .' she goes on.

'Yeah?'

'I'm sorry about Sandy. He was a bit . . .'

Arrogant? Condescending? Full of shit?

'. . . I dunno . . . A bit *overly* focused.'

I guess that's one way of putting it.

'That's OK,' I say.

'Anyway, I had a go at him about it when we got home. He does feel bad.'

So he should.

'He really shouldn't.'

'Well, I'm sorry . . . *He's* sorry . . .'

'Forget it, Meg.'

Blimey, I haven't called her that in a while.

131

The conversation trails off as we both contemplate our surroundings. We're in Saint Matthew's . . .

Why does no one call it Matt's? Like Saint Bartholomew's has become Bart's? That's a teddy bear name, isn't it? Big, cuddly Bart the bear. I guess Saint Matthew's just isn't that kind of hospital.

David Beckham Ward. No, really. With adidas paying squillions to name football boots after him, I doubt he's even noticed that a hospital in the place of his birth has slipped his name on a ward. We're sitting on the edge of a bed. *My* bed. In a couple of hours or so I'm going to be put to sleep and when I wake up I'll be an ounce or two lighter. How much does a testicle weigh? Not a lot, surely, even when it has a tumour attached. 'All being well you can go home tomorrow morning,' the surgeon told me with a matey smile a few minutes ago. 'Oh, and we'll pop in a prosthetic while we're at it so you'll still be man-shaped down there.' Isn't that reassuring? I'll soon be wasting away on a diet of drugs and radiation, but I'll still be man-shaped. I've had some blood taken and I've signed the forms, though not before Megan had scrutinised them, making sure I wasn't giving them free rein to whip out a kidney and auction it on eBay. The nurse has brought me a green backless gown, but I haven't changed into it yet. I'm not quite ready to place my bottom on display, and strut the corridors mandrill/sad-sick-bloke style.

'How are you feeling?' Megan asks.

'Fine,' I lie.

She squeezes my arm. Either she's telepathic or she has spotted that my hands are maintaining a tight grip on my knees to prevent from shaking. At least my left hand is. My right is still splinted, bandaged and not up to gripping. As a result it's bouncing up and down on my leg like a hyperactive toddler on tartrazine supplements. The two healing fingers jar painfully on my kneecap and I wince.

'That'll teach you to pick scraps with Bentleys,' Megan says.

At least she's joking about it now. Maybe it's a good time to . . .

'Megan . . .'

No, keep it light. Don't go there.

'. . . Never mind. It's no big deal.'

'No, go on.'

Fuck light. Go there.

'Did you. Don't quite know how to put this. Is. Did. When. Have you—'

'You're not making a whole heap of sense, Murray.'

'Have you. Did you. When you . . .'

She nods at me encouragingly.

'God, sorry. Let me start again. You know your stuff in Sandy's car . . . Did you find anything . . . you know.'

She looks at me blankly. Definitely not telepathic, then.

'You know.'

'Sorry, Murray, I don't.'

'Did you find anything . . . that you didn't necessarily expect to find?'

'Like what?'

'Anything that wasn't yours.'

'No. The morning after your . . . er . . . *episode*, Sandy cleared my stuff out. He said having it lying around the backseat was asking for trouble. Anyway, it was just my bits and bobs. Nothing else. Why? Was something of yours in there?'

'Kind of . . . *Yours* really . . . No, mine, I suppose . . . Technically.'

'Well, God knows where it'll be now. The weekend after you attacked it, Sandy took the car to be valeted.'

Oh, I know exactly where it'll be now. Sparkling exquisitely on the ring finger of some lucky girl whose bloke works in a car wash.

'Was it important?' she asks.

Only important enough to have Barclaycard on the verge of sending round the boys with baseball bats.

133

'No, not really,' I say.

'What was it?'

'Nothing. Forget it.'

'It can't have been *nothing* if you've brought it up after all this time. Tell me.'

Megan, as ever, pursuing the quarry like a terrier after a rat – a terrier with a bloody law degree, the scariest kind. Should never have gone there.

'Was it the reason you tried to break into the car?'

'It was . . . It was . . . Your garlic crusher.'

'Excuse me? You risked a criminal record for a garlic crusher?'

'Yes. *No.* Of course not. I hit the car because I was *upset.* I've told you that already. I only just thought of the garlic crusher. I can't remember if I put it with your stuff or not.'

'I haven't seen it. It must still be at yours. Keep it. Sandy's got one.'

Of course he bloody has. Probably a silver Georgian garlic crusher, part of a very rare and complete set of handcrafted eighteenth-century kitchen accessories. Or a one-off Philippe Starck garlic crusher with no discernible place to pop the clove because it has been cunningly disguised as a Martian landing module. Whatever, it won't be an ordinary garlic crusher. Like the garlic crusher you left behind; the garlic crusher you've moved on from.

'If I find it I'll send it to you,' I say. 'I don't like garlic.'

'I know. Five years together, remember?'

Five years, eight months, one week and three days, actually.

Time for a change of subject. 'I really appreciate this, you know. You coming with me, I mean. You didn't have any trouble getting the time off, did you?'

'Not really. A partners' meeting that'll somehow manage without me. And I was supposed to be at Holloway to meet my husband killer – *alleged* – but she's not going anywhere in a hurry.'

'Did she do it?'

'He *so* deserved it. If the jury doesn't pin a medal on her, I'll consider myself an abject failure and get a job in . . . I dunno . . . advertising or something.'

I don't smile.

'*Joke*! Anyway, what about you? I presume you got off work OK.'

'Er . . .'

'You haven't told them yet, have you?'

'I told Niall everything yesterday.'

'My God, that must have been tough. How did he react?'

'He . . . Um . . . He wasn't listening. He was on the phone to a client.'

'Jesus, Murray. You've got to sit him down and tell him. You need all the support you can get at the moment. I know he's a bit of an arse, but even he would be sympathetic . . . Wouldn't he? Look, is it because . . . Are you embarrassed about telling people? Because it's testicular.'

Embarrassed barely begins to cover it. It's not nearly a long-enough word to explain how I feel about the world knowing the root of my illness – add another three or four syllables and you might be close. I can't even bear Megan, the woman with whom I've been more intimate than any other, knowing.

'*Embarrassed*. Don't be silly,' I say.

'You *have* to talk to him. All this,' she says, gesturing at our environment, 'is going to take up a lot of time. And what happens when . . .' She peters out.

'When what?' I think I know, though.

'When . . . *If* . . . If you get too sick to work? I know it's hard, but you have to think this through. Running away is just going to make it tougher.'

'I'll talk to Haye. As soon as I get out of here. *Definitely*.'

She raises an eyebrow. It's one of those eyebrow lifts she's seen barristers use on juries to convey in a single economic movement, *You and I know, of course, that the witness's last answer was a complete and utter direct-from-his-backside fabrication.*

I think back to work. To yesterday and the Mr Muscle moment. Maybe I can save things. Patch things up with Haye and spend my last few weeks of relative health going all out for the Big One. Maybe one day, not long from now, Haye will tearfully invoke my name in graduate training sessions as a shining example – *'He was riddled with cancer, wracked with pain, yet nothing could deflect him from his goal: Murray Colin refused to die until he'd brought a market-leading degreasant to this advertising agency.'*

'What are you thinking?' Megan asks.

'Oh, nothing much,' I reply, because she'd only laugh if I told her. 'Meg, can I ask you something . . .?'

Keep it light, for God's sake keep it light.

'. . . Why do you think . . . it didn't work out . . .? You know, us.'

Oh, well done, my son. Bravo. What happened to light? That one was the conversational equivalent of suet pudding . . . with extra suet.

'Whew! Jesus, Murray. Where did that one come from?' Megan is flustered. 'How . . . You want to . . . talk about this? Now?' Very flustered.

The last time we talked about *this* was weeks ago. Nine weeks and two days to be exact. The Sunday she left. Actually, we didn't *talk*. It wasn't a conversation as such. Not unless you define *conversation* as the exchange of insults in voices loud enough to constitute a public-nuisance offence. The wounds are still raw – pustulent and weeping on my part.

'Look, I don't think it's a good time,' she says.

She's right. It isn't. Because she'll either pull her punches on account of the fact that I'm dying – *It wasn't you, Murray. It was me. I wasn't right for you* – or she'll tell me what she told me nine weeks and two days ago – i.e. the truth – and I don't want to hear that. Even so, I must look disappointed because she puts her hand on mine and says, 'We will talk . . . If that's what you really want. Later.'

'OK,' I say.

'OK,' she says.

We sit in silence for a few minutes.

Then: 'I need a loo, Murray. I'll be as quick as I can. Will you be all right?'

'I know they haven't given me long, but I think I'll last the duration of a piss.' It comes out a bit more sarky than I'd intended. All the same, she laughs . . . *Oh, yes, Murray, you still got it, baby.* 'I'll be fine,' I add. 'Go on.'

I watch her walk to the end of the ward and out through the double doors. Her jeans look tighter on her than they used to. She's paying the price of sharing Sandy's two-Michelin-star lifestyle. Still a great bum though. I feel a slight tightening in my chest. Simple separation anxiety? Or the tumour on my left lung deciding, at last, to flex its muscles? Who knows? For sure, though, I'm not imagining this. The sharp ache starts at my collarbone and goes all the way down to the bottom of my ribcage . . . on my *left* side. The fear returns. It had more or less evaporated over the course of a normal (kind of-ish) conversation with Megan. I need a distraction.

I get one.

The double doors swing open and a wheelchair rolls through them. It's hard to believe that it contains a living person, but it does. I think. He is a loosely connected set of bones in a green hospital gown. His head is a skull. A layer of thin, grey skin is stretched tautly across it like shrinkwrap. His scalp is covered by an incongruously cheery scarlet and yellow bandana. He looks old, but the Eminem logo on the bandana suggests that probably he isn't.

The porter pushing the wheelchair manoeuvres it between the two beds opposite mine. He parks it and without a word to his cargo he spins on his heel and walks away. A nurse walks

137

by and gives the man a smile. 'Back already, Darren? The radiologists must be quiet today. Sit tight and I'll get you back into bed in a minute.'

Sit tight. Darren isn't going anywhere in a hurry. I look at him. I can't help staring. At his glazed, hooded eyes and thin blue lips. At the deep grooves between the bones in his forearms – canyons that would once have been filled with muscle. At the ID tag small enough to slip round the wrist of a baby. At his slumped, unmoving pose on the patched vinyl seat of the wheelchair. His eyes flicker, then look at me. His mouth twitches – barely – at the corners. The best attempt at a smile his wasted muscles can manage.

This is the reality. Not some lame fantasy, where I lose a bit of weight, come over a touch queasy and Megan mops my brow. Did I really agree to come into this because I saw it as some kind of elaborate exercise in M&M re-bonding? Because I thought it might drive a sliver of a wedge between her and Sandy? I think I bloody did. And I think I must be completely out to lunch, George III, loop-di-loopy, *off my fucking trolley.*

This man – this husk curled up in a wheelchair – is the barely living embodiment of the *cure.* The only thing I can find in mitigation of my own fluffy-brained imbecility is that no amount of coded caveats from doctors, anti-medical rants on the Net or steaming Celtic diatribes from Sandy Morrison could have prepared me for what I'm looking at. How long before I am him? A couple of weeks? A couple of months? It doesn't matter because I'd rather . . . I don't know what.

I *do* know I want nothing to do with this.

'I'm really sorry,' I mumble. To the poor irradiated man who looks as if there is no point to his continued existence unless it's to discover just how much a human being can take. To the operating team I'm about to inconvenience. To David Beckham. And to Megan, who, of course, isn't around to hear it.

I get up, put on my jacket and leave.

nine: **yoo berra gerrootta thuh fookin ruhrd**

If this were a movie – a not particularly good movie; not even good enough to have Luke Perry playing me – the minicab driver would say to me now, 'What's up, boss? You look like you've seen a ghost.' He doesn't, though. He doesn't say anything. He just glances at me nervously in his rear-view mirror. Probably hoping he'll manage to negotiate the three sets of lights that separate his cab from my flat before I vomit on his furry acrylic seat-covers. It's touch and go, actually. If we get a run of greens . . .

As the cab pulls up I throw a tenner into the driver's lap and dive for the door. Out on the pavement I lean uneasily on my gate.

Right, here's what you're gonna do. You're gonna go in there, have a shower, put on a nice boring suit and go to work. Say sorry to Haye. Beg forgiveness for dicking him about of late. Plead for a slot on the Mr Muscle team and promise him you'll work your cancer-ridden bollocks off from here on in. Pretend this morning – this whole fucking cancer thing – never happened.

A woman walks towards me hauling a shopping basket on tiny wheels. She stops abruptly, stares at me and decides to cross the street. A wise move on her part. I *must* stop this thinking-out-loud thing or I can add getting sectioned to my list of woes. I fumble for my keys and walk unsteadily up the steps.

139

Toast.

Coffee and *toast*. Maybe something in my stomach will quell the nausea and get rid of the deathly taste of the hospital. I haven't eaten since yesterday afternoon and I am *starving*. In the hall I look at the pile of post that Paula-downstairs has arranged into a neat stack. Bills.

Kiss my arse, bills.

I head upstairs and open my front door.

CRAAAASH!

What the hell was that?

I freeze in the doorway. I've been scared from the moment I clapped eyes on the living dead guy at the hospital, but the fear I'm feeling now is different. This is a petrifying, *immediate* fear. Still rooted to the spot I look down the corridor that leads to my living room. The doors leading off it – to my bedroom, bathroom and kitchen – are ajar, but not open enough to give me a view inside.

What I should do now is quietly close the door, head back downstairs and phone the police. That would be the smart thing. That would be the standard cowardly Murray thing. But this hasn't been a standard morning.

So I quietly close the door and . . . tiptoe down the corridor. I reach the bathroom. Dry-mouthed, sweaty-palmed, I peer into the gloom . . . Nothing. Just my thin selection of toiletries on the glass shelf, my stupid plastic duck on the rim of the bath. I edge my way on to the bedroom. I push the door open . . . to see my carefully made bed (which I turn down in the evening, though I stop short of popping a mint thin on the pillow). No sign of life.

I stop and listen. *Really* listen. I hold my breath and listen like I've never listened before. I can't hear a thing. I think . . . the only person in this flat is . . . *me*.

CRAAAAAAAAAAAAAAAAAAAAAAAASH!

I jump, knocking the back of my head against the wall.

140

Idiot! That noise isn't in your flat. It's outside. The bottle banks across the street. They've been full to overflowing for weeks and the truck with the little crane on the back has come to pick them up. Stupid, stupid, stupid idiot!

My heart slows and I feel myself relax. I rub the beginnings of the bruise on my head and make for the kitchen. Water in kettle. Granules in mug. Bread in toaster. That's what I need now. I open the kitchen door and—

Jesus-effing-Christ-who-the-hell-is-that?

His back to me. Number two cut. A line of studs in the top of his left ear. Home-made tattoo on the side of his neck. Filthy camouflage jacket. Filthy, filthy scabbed hands tipping the ceramic jar containing teabags onto the counter. Adding them to the Rich Teas, macaroni, balls of dried green tagliatelle, brown and white sugar and instant coffee that are already spread across the surface. He's emptying every one of my storage jars looking for . . . money?

What does he think I am? Some geriatric who banks with a biscuit barrel?

He's oblivious to my presence. What is he? Five-six, five-seven? Given that he's got his hands full of PG Tips Pyramid Bags (excellent tea delivery, but rubbish in a fight), and I have surprise on my side I could take him on. Couldn't I? Or I could walk out of the flat and do what I should have done in the first place. Call the police.

Take him down, pussy. You're the son of a copper. You have law enforcement in your genes.

I have *cancer* in my genes.

OK, OK. Cancer. AND law enforcement. Take the scruffy little bastard.

Right. Yes. OK. Here goes. Right.

'Excuse me.'

'Excuse me'? What the fuck's 'Excuse me'?

He swivels and sees me. He freezes against the counter. I'm

still frozen in the doorway. His face is ashen. Maybe natural. Maybe he's as scared as I am. We stare at each other. Two rabbits caught in each other's headlights. He's young. Can't be twenty yet. His right hand fumbles behind him on the counter. It makes its way through the mess – the *mess*! In *my* kitchen! – of teabags, coffee, sugar and pasta, then over the lip of the worktop to the drawer handle. The drawer that contains cutlery, a fish slice, a wooden spoon, something to shave the rind off lemons . . . *knives*. He's sweating. Little beads of the stuff are coalescing on his grimy forehead. He *is* frightened. But doesn't that make him doubly dangerous? Funny that. I've never felt more terrified in my life . . . or *less* dangerous.

His hand works its way into the drawer. His eyes never leave mine as he fumbles blindly among the contents. The hand comes out flashing silver and he yells, 'Yoo berra gerrootta thuh fookin ruhrd.'

Well, yes, I'd better, but my . . . legs . . . won't . . . move.

He rushes me. Legs finally agree to do something but it's too late. He's on me, piling me into the doorframe, one forearm crushing my chest, the other pushing cold metal into my throat.

'Just . . . go,' I rasp. 'Please.'

He doesn't move except to push harder on my chest . . . and into my neck.

'Whorra yer dee-in, yer daff fookin bitch? Thuh cunt's hame. Lezzgeh thuh fook ootta hee-ah!' His accent takes me back. To university. Newcastle. Bigg Market. Chucking-out time on Friday nights. Vicious, fearless, paralytic men in Magpie shirts who liked nothing better than a weedy student they could kick about the pavement.

Geordie waits for a response from . . . Me? No, *the daft fucking bitch*. He's not alone.

I look down at his scared, angry face as he stares at me. 'Yer fookin stupid . . . Fook it!' he shouts to his unseen partner. Parting words, because the pressure from his arm eases on my chest and his hand falls away from my neck. I see the gleaming tapered blade extending from his grip. Or, rather, I see the gleaming tapered aluminium handle of Megan's garlic crusher. I crumple as his knee hits my groin. He stumbles past my descending body and pushes it roughly aside. I twist round in time to see the corner of my small pine dining table rushing towards my head.

ten: **do smack, rob banks, screw everyone**

Gnnngghh . . .

A groan. Me, I think.

'Thank fuck . . .'

A girl's voice. Do I know it?

'. . . I thought you were dead.'

I *do* know that smell.

I'm lying on the floor. My head is pressed onto my shoulder, forced there by something sharp that's digging into my ear. That would be the table leg. I can't see anything. The bastard blinded me. *Hang on*. My eyes are closed. I open them . . . But I still can't see a thing – and they *sting*. The bastard *has* blinded me. I bring my hand to my face and rub my eyes. They feel sticky. Wet.

'Here, let me,' says the familiar-ish voice. I sense a body crouching over mine. The smell grows stronger . . . BO . . . KFC . . . B&H . . . A hint of Woodpecker . . . A subtle undercurrent of piss. Something damp dabs tentatively at my forehead, then smears across my eyes. 'You're covered in blood. Fuck knows what he did to you.'

I try opening my eyes again and slowly focus on the face that's peering at mine. 'What the hell are you doing here?' I ask.

Fish jumps back from me, moving out of the door and into the corridor.

'You're OK, man. I'm off,' she says, her body edging towards the front door.

I try to raise myself up from my back and onto my elbows,

144

but as I lift my head I feel a needle-sharp pain shoot from one temple to the other. A wave of dizziness wafts over me and I flop back to the floor.

'You are OK?' she asks.

'I dunno.' I lie on the floor panting slightly, trying to get air into my lungs. My hand goes to my groin. It's sore, but I remember the Geordie psycho just planted his knee there. I wonder if cancer can be made any worse by being physically attacked. I watch Fish twitching in the corridor uncertain what to do. Run? Hang around a bit, then run? She's wearing the same clothes she had on at A&E. I don't know what she's doing here. No, I *do*. I don't know why she stayed, though. Because she's all compassion? She's a *daff fookin bitch*? I *do* know that I don't want to be on my own now . . . I don't want her to go.

'Don't go,' I say.

'You're gonna call the cops, intcha?'

'I won't . . . I promise. Not unless that psycho comes back.'

'He won't. *Twat*. You won't call the cops?'

'No. No, I won't . . . Get me some water . . . Please.'

11.15 a.m.

Fish was supposed to be keeping watch. Not her forte, because instead of craning her neck like a conscientious meerkat, she was in my living room, headphones on, going through my CDs. 'You ain't half got some shite. Who the fuck are the Cranberries?' She asks this as if they're the Glenn Miller Band and I'm her granddad.

'They were . . . Never mind. A bit *Oirish* if you're into trance.'

'I listen to other stuff as well,' she says indignantly. 'You've got that Kenickie album. I love that.'

'You do?' I'm surprised. It's a bit more jangly-guitary than I had her down for. It's also a bit rubbish.

145

'I wanted to be Lauren when I was twelve. I thought she was the bollocks.'

'Morrissey,' I say.

'Who?'

'I wanted to be Morrissey when I was twelve.'

'Who're they?'

'*He* was . . . Never mind.'

'Go on, sing some.'

'No way. I don't sing.'

'How could you have been Whateverhe'scalled if you don't sing?'

'You might have hit on something there.'

We slip into silence as we finish our coffee – made from granules that Fish somehow separated from the rest of the stuff spilled on the counter. We're sitting on the two pine chairs that go with the small pine dining table; furniture there isn't room for in my tiny kitchen. I look at the mess. It's going to take me *ages* to clean up. This, though, is a good thing; the distraction of a domestic challenge.

Fish peers at the cut on my forehead. 'You wanna have that looked at, man,' she says. 'It's quite deep, you know.' She reaches forward and pokes at the bruising around the wound with a filthy finger. I pull away, wincing. 'Probably need stitches,' she adds, obviously picturing another trip to her favourite all-night coffee bar.

'Forget it,' I say. 'It'll be fine.'

I've had enough of hospitals for . . . Er . . . Make it a lifetime.

'I'm going to get cleaned up. Want me to run you a bath when I'm finished?'

Well, somehow it seems the right thing to ask.

––––––––––––––––––––––––––––––––––– 12.12 p.m.

I sit up to my neck in hot, foamy water. I wonder . . . Lots of

146

things, actually. But especially why Fish trusted me not to call the police. Then again, why should I trust her? On the other side of the locked bathroom door she could be finishing off where her and her mate left off. Cleaning me out. Then again, with things the way they are, would it matter a jot if she were?

_____ 1.19 p.m.

I feel surprisingly clear-headed given the knock. Hopefully no concussion, then. The cut is about an inch long. It gapes slightly and runs vertically from my hairline to a point midway above my left eyebrow. It probably does need stitches. I've covered it up with a square of kitchen paper folded into a pad. A Band-Aid at each corner holds it in place. The paper is decorated with _Mr Men_ characters. If I don't want the world to see me looking like something they made on _Blue Peter_, I'll have to go to the chemist and buy a proper dressing. And some antiseptic.

I've cleaned up the kitchen. Mopped the blood from the lino, swept the crap on the counter into the bin, though I did first pick out the tea bags and undamaged biscuits. Now I'm heading for the living room.

Shit.

Fish and her mate had a laugh in here. My CDs and books are scattered across the floor. There's no sign of my TV, VCR, PC and telephone – the flashy phone stroke fax stroke answering machine stroke teasmade stroke all-over body massager that I bought when I had sunny visions of Megan and me working from home. The stereo is untouched – only because Fish was busy with it when I disturbed them. The sash window is open. I guess that's how they got in. Through the garden and across the flat-roofed extension at the back of Paula's flat. I go to close the window and see my appliances on the roof a few feet below. I think about climbing out on a salvage mission, but not for long. It's raining and has been for long enough to void the

147

warranties under the weaselly *Invalid in event of contact with moisture* caveat.

I turn round and survey the mess. The *mess*! What is it with thieves? Isn't it enough for them to take away your stuff? Do they really have to turn everything upside down while they're at it? I know they're under a certain amount of time pressure, but a little consideration wouldn't go amiss. It's one thing to take the TV, but another entirely to knock over the stand and scatter the carefully ordered videos and DVDs willy-nilly. And they might have thought to wipe their bloody feet.

Fish appears in the doorway. She's wearing my dressing gown. 'Fancy a cup of tea?' she asks.

'Have you any idea how much work goes into keeping this place tidy?' I snap.

'Sorry.'

'Sorry? *Sorry*?' I march across the room to where the yucca plant lies on its side. 'Look at this. Potting compost everywhere. You've trodden it in too. I'm going to have to shampoo this carpet now and I'll *never* get it all out, you know.'

'You wanna share a joint?' she asks.

'Excuse me?'

'I said do you want some smoke?' she says, producing a small polythene change bag containing Rizlas and a lump of brown resin.

—————————————————————————————— 2.16 p.m.

'So where are you living now?' I ask, passing the remains of the joint to Fish.

Her tower-block squat was finally dynamited a couple of weeks ago.

'We're not really anywhere,' she replies dreamily.

'You're sleeping rough?'

'S'pose. Here and there.'

'So where are you gonna meet your mate?'

'I'm not gonna meet him. If he sees me again I'm fucking dead, man.'

Join the club.

'Why Fish?' I ask. 'Is it your surname?'

'Nah.'

'Is it short for something?' (Fishella? Fishina? Who knows?)

'I just liked it,' she explains – not the name on her birth certificate, then.

'There was a rock singer in the eighties called Fish . . . *Fish* from Marillion.'

'Any good?'

About as crap as they came.

'He was . . . *brilliant*,' I say.

'*Knew* it was a cool name,' she sighs.

We drift into slightly stoned silence. Fluke are grinding out 'Atom Bomb' on the stereo – one of the few CDs in my scattered collection that we both like. I look at her as she stares into space through the slits in her fringe. I expected more of a transformation when she emerged from the bathroom. I thought vaguely that she might float out looking like a pierced and plum-haired Audrey Hepburn. Apart from having cleaner pores, though, she looks much as she did – just a bit more vulnerable in my fluffy white dressing gown than she was in the world's baggiest jeans and battered DMs. At least she smells fresher.

3.04 p.m.

Bzzzz!

'I'll . . . get . . . it,' I say in slow motion.

Fish doesn't hear me, being as she is, on another planet – in a distant galaxy. I smudge out the second joint in the ashtray and haul myself to my feet. I stagger dizzily to the front door and press the button on the intercom just as the buzzer gives another angry snarl.

'Murray . . . Are you there?'

Busted.

'Hi, Meg.'

'Are you going to let me in? I'm soaked out here.'

'Er . . . Yeah.'

I buzz her in and open my front door. She bounds into the hall and up the staircase. 'God, I've been worried stupid. I am so glad to see you,' she says, flinging her arms around my neck – she *is* soaked. 'I had every security guard searching every inch of Saint Matthew's. Why didn't you answer your mobile?'

'I switched it off in the hospital. They're not allowed.'

'What happened? Why did you just walk out?'

'It was becau—'

'Your head! What did you do?'

'I . . . fell. In the kitchen.' Best to leave it at the heavily edited version for now.

'And what's that smell? . . . Shit, you're stoned, aren't you?' Bloody Megan and her bloody nose. Though, I have to say, she could be blocked up with several gallons of catarrh and still have figured that one out. 'C'mon, you and I are going to talk,' she says, pushing past me and heading for the living room. I slump against the front door, close my eyes and wait for . . .

'Jesus Christ, who the hell is *she*?'

I join her in the living room. This does not look good at all. Something I've learned in advertising: presentation is all. Overstating it, obviously, but the way things *look* is fairly important. I have to admit that as presentation goes, this is bad. If it were a *presentation*, half the slides would be missing, the remainder would be upside down and I'd have misplaced my notes on the way to the meeting. Megan is staring at Fish who has crashed back onto the floor in a mild dope-coma. Fish's – *my* – dressing gown – a Christmas present from *Meg* – has split open at the front leaving a wedge of mousy pubic hair on display.

Not a natural magenta, then.

I'm trying to stifle the giggles. Really I'm trying.

'This is not a joke, Murray.'

'No, no, Murray, it's OK. It's *fine*, really. But let me get this straight. You're refusing life-prolonging – possibly life-*saving* – treatment for your cancer. You're also refusing treatment for your head injury, having been beaten up in a burglary, which you're *refusing* to report to the police. You've spent an afternoon smoking mind-altering *carcinogens* with your attacker's teenage girlfriend who's called *Fish* and is now lying off-her-face in your living room. Oh, and all of your appliances are on Paula's roof benefiting from the effects of a ridge of low pressure over the South East.'

'Listen, Meg, it's—'

'No, it really is fine. I just wanted to reassure myself that you were OK. I feel so much better now that I've seen you, a picture of fucking normalcy. Just call me if you suddenly have an urge to do something truly insane like saving your fucking life.'

Not for the first time in our relationship, but almost certainly for the last, Megan slams my front door and storms out of the house.

I stand in silence for a moment before returning to the living room. Fish has finally risen to her feet and is trying to get her brain engaged. I wonder how much of Megan's and my . . . er . . . discussion managed to pierce her purple haze.

'Girlfriend?' she asks as I slump onto the sofa.

'She was.'

'Wants to get it on again?'

'I somehow doubt it.'

151

'Shame. She's a babe.'

Hear hear to that.

'She freaked me out, though. She was mad.'

'Well, I kinda messed her about today.'

'And what was all that stuff about cancer? She's not dying, is she?'

'There you have it . . . basically . . . in a nutshell. A collection of dumb cells decided they'd had enough of following the same old boring genetic code day-in day-out. So they've gone off on a live-fast-die-young, hotel-trashing rock-star tour of my body. They'll ultimately kill me, their host, of course, and they've therefore signed their own death warrants . . . But that's dumb cells for you.'

There's nothing like a good sob story to knock some sense into a stoner. As I finish mine I see that it has worked a treat on Fish. She's sitting on the edge of the sofa rocking back and forth like an extra from *One Flew Over the Cuckoo's Nest*. 'Fuck . . . That's mega . . . Four months . . . That's mega, man . . . Fuck.' Her new mantra. Then after a few circular chants, 'She's a bitch, man, getting mad and walking out on you.'

'I can see her point. She wants me to have the op and she's been taking time off to, you know, help me through it. No one else has been there for me. And we're not together any more, so it's not like she has a responsibility. I suppose I should've at least hung around the hospital to explain. She's entitled to feel . . . er . . . frustrated.'

'You're definitely not getting the treatment, then?'

'No way. I don't much fancy dying ten times over before I peg out for real.'

'Is it that bad?'

Silence . . . Then she says, 'Johnny's got this idea about dying.'

152

'He the nutter you broke in with?' I ask.

'Nah, one of the Dutch guys who used to be at the squat. He's from Stockholm or somewhere.'

'One of the Swedish Dutch?'

'Yeah, that's it. Anyway, he reckons we should all be told when we're gonna go. Not too early or anything. Like maybe six months before it's gonna happen.'

'How would that help?'

'He says if we knew the date, we could all go apeshit for the last bit. Have a mad fucking party. Do smack, rob banks, screw everyone . . . He says fuck the consequences 'cause . . . Well, there aren't any when you're dead. Johnny's fucking mental, though. He reckons the Pope was flying one of those planes that hit that building in America. Says that's why he doesn't appear in public any more.'

'He does appear in public.'

'He reckons it's a robot.'

'He might have a point,' I say quietly.

'What, you reckon the Pope's like a Dalek or something?'

'He might well be, but I wasn't talking about that . . . Your mate sounds like this bloke at work. He's got this motto: F.E.A.R.'

'Fear? What's that?'

'Fuck Everything And Rumble.'

'That your motto now?'

'No, not yet,' I say, thinking of Niall Haye . . . Mr Muscle . . . Tomorrow's half-cooked plan. Not one that would have either Vince or Fish's Scanda-Dutch friend bigging me up, but it's the best I've come up with and it does give me a small thrill of excitement.

'Anyway, fuck, you've got some serious shit to deal with. You don't need me around,' Fish says, suddenly flustered, suddenly freaked out by being in the same room as a dead man. 'I'd better go.'

'Go where?'

'I dunno . . . Don't worry. I'll be OK.'

'You might as well stay. You can sleep on the sofa. Anyway, I put your clothes in the wash, so unless you're planning to hit the arches in my dressing gown . . .'

'I couldn't . . . Honestly. It ain't fair on you. I mean—'

'I'm starving. You fancy a pizza?'

eleven: **out of the silo**

I've been practising on the way to work. Rehearsing the New Improved Murray (now with added Go-getting-ness and the unbeatable power of Proaction^{TM}). I'm standing in front of Haye's desk and I'm ready. Psyched, focused, primed . . . But he's on the phone. He's looking at me as he speaks; I don't think he likes what he sees. Bruised and bandaged head, strapped fingers, probably not the image Blower Mann wishes to project to its clients – at least I got rid of the *Mr Men* kitchen roll. He ends his call at last and says, 'I thought you were in hospital.'

'I was. I . . . Um . . . I decided to cut it short. You know, I could see that things were getting busy at work.'

I look for a sign that he's impressed by my self-sacrifice. Not a glimmer.

'What happened to your head?'

I'm glad he asked that because this one will surely garner me some sympathy.

'Oh, it's nothing much,' I say. 'Yesterday morning I walked in on a burglar at my flat. Actually, it was pretty frighten—'

'Every time I see you it seems you have another ridiculous injury . . .'

Oh yes, wide green acres of sympathy replete with little hillocks of empathy and a babbling brook of concern.

'. . . If you'd been at work – *where you should have been* – you'd never have tangled with the fellow . . .'

There is a quite undeniable logic to that.

'. . . Anyway, I'm snowed under here. What is it you want?'

155

This is my cue. I clear my throat and say, 'Well, I was hoping I could take some of the load. Maybe help out with the Mr Muscle pitch. It's a product category I know a lot about. I'd be happy to do anything. *Anything* . . . Round up some market data, sit in on the focus groups, run some store checks—'

'Hang on, Murray, let me get this straight. You expect to wander in and out of the office willy-nilly and have first pick of the juiciest projects?'

'Well, no, but—'

'Because I'd love to accommodate you. You know, perhaps relieve you of some of your more mundane chores so you can work exclusively on the glamorous new business pitches.'

I suspect he's being sarcastic now. It isn't going at all how I'd hoped. This played a lot better in my head on the tube, where the mental Niall Haye wasn't even mildly sarky – was quite warm and receptive, actually, especially at the end bit of the fantasy where he made me pitch team leader and gave me a pay rise. There's only one thing for it: the truth. 'I'm sorry I haven't been on the ball lately,' I say, 'but there's a lot going on in my life at the moment. I've got ca—'

'Let me stop you there, let me stop you *right there*. All this . . . this *personal* stuff has no business in the office. Compartmentalise, Murray, *compartmentalise*. It's the secret of getting on.'

'But I've got—'

'Now, I've put an excellent team together for Mr Muscle and I'm not going to disrupt it to accommodate your whims . . .'

Excuse me, you pompous git, but Mr Muscle is not a bloody whim, all right?

'. . . Having said that, I'm glad you want to get back with the programme because there's plenty to be getting on with. ChocoChillout is about to receive its target coordinates and come out of the silo . . .'

Who else but you, Niall, could elevate a 200-gram choc-ice to the status of an intercontinental ballistic missile?

'. . . Betina Tofting needs to be taken through the new script – draft forty . . .'

Wow, the day before yesterday it was only up to thirty-eight. Is this a new world record, Norris?

'. . . I can't do it. There's Mr Muscle to take care of and L'Oréal is going critical. I'm flying to Paris at eleven . . . Which leaves you. You look more like a football hooligan than an account director . . .'

I am not an account director, remember? I have conspicuously not been an account director for some years now, time spent watching those younger and dumber than me earn their sodding account director's stripes.

'. . . but, sadly, you're all I've got. The meeting's at twelve. Don't be late.'

I nod and dislodge the small tear that's been lurking at the corner of my eye.

9.26 a.m.

I'm sitting at my desk. I'm seething. My anger is directed, of course, at Niall Haye for being so, well, Niall Haye, but also at myself for being so, well, *me*. Why couldn't I tell him? Why couldn't I say that terminal cancer tends to make *compartmentalising* a little bloody difficult? Why, even now as my life fades to black, am I still so *wet*?

As I rage I gaze at draft forty. It looks indistinguishable from draft thirty-one, the last version I paid any attention to. I've no idea how I'm going to take Betina Tofting through the changes when I can't even spot them myself. Maybe she can take *me* through them. Yes, that would look professional.

'Murray, you're here!' cries Jakki as she returns to her workstation. I swivel round to face her and she gasps, 'Fuck, your *head*!'

'Bumped into a burglar at my flat,' I reply casually, successfully

157

managing to convey not a single shred of the dizzying terror of the experience.

'Shit . . . *God* . . . That is my *worst* nightmare. Apart from the one where I get gang-raped, beaten, slashed, put in a bin bag and left for dead in a skip. What happened?'

'I'll tell you later. How's it been here?'

'Absolutely *mad*. Niall's got us all running around on Mr Muscle like blue-arsed whatsits . . .'

Not all of us, Jakki, not all of us.

'. . . God, it's only a bottle of bloody spray, but the way he's acting you'd think it was the cure for . . . I dunno . . .'

Don't say it, please don't say it. Not the C-word.

'. . . AIDS or something . . .'

Thank you.

'. . . Anyway, I'm surprised he hasn't dragged you into it.'

'Oh, someone has to keep the resident clients happy,' I say. 'I've got to get my head round this ChocoChillout script.'

'Haven't they shot that yet? Seems to have been going on forever.'

'Draft *forty*. I can't see what's new about it. I'm supposed to be taking the client through it in a couple of hours.'

'You could always show them Draft One. I liked that.'

She's joking, of course, but I look at her as if she has given me the secret of eternal life.

'*Joking*,' she says, registering my expression and panicking.

'Are Brett and Vince around?' I ask as I get up.

'No idea . . . Murray, I was *joking*,' she calls as I head for the lift.

I'm standing in the doorway to their office on the creative floor. No Brett, only Vince. He hasn't seen me. He's huddled over the Mac, trying to force a DVD into the slot. As I wait for him to finish I look around the office. Brett and Vince have rewritten the rules of interior decoration. Actually, they've torn them up and trampled them into the dirt. The room is like a scrap yard. The only place where order exists is on the wall behind Brett's desk. This has become a shrine to Vince's heroes. He's a crime junkie. He keeps up with who's who in the underworld the way other blokes follow football transfers. The wall is papered with photographs of villains, most of whose scowling faces mean nothing to me. Vince can give a potted biography of each and every one of them, and I'm surprised the Met hasn't yet utilised him as a database. Pride of place goes to a laminated shot of Brian Sharkey complete with Vince's typeset caption: THE BADDEST MUTHAFUCKA THAT EVER MUTHAFUCKED. Even I've heard of Brian Sharkey. To return to the football analogy, Sharkey is the closest thing crime has to a David Beckham. He's a tabloid dream – not only is he extremely wicked, but his name is God's gift to head-line writers. Having said that, there've been few Sharkey stories for a year or two. He's rumoured to be retired. Or dead.

Strangely, given his reputation, Sharkey is the only villain on Vince's wall who doesn't look like one. The photo shows him as a young man in naval uniform. Crime was his second career choice because he spent a few years serving Queen and Country onboard a Polaris submarine. As Vince tells it, the Navy turfed him out. He reckons they caught him dealing heroin to fellow crewmembers. I suppose that if there's any truth in it, then the MoD hushed it up. They wouldn't have wanted taxpayers to think that their expensive nuclear deterrent was being operated by the cast of *Trainspotting* in sailor suits. It only dawns on me now that Sharkey the submariner, rather than some rubbish action movie, must be the true inspiration behind Vince's dream of becoming an underwater highwayman.

He's at the end of his rope with the DVD. He's trying to bludgeon the wafer-thin disc into the Mac with a copy of the Yellow Pages. I decide to intervene.

'Vince, I think you have to switch the computer on first.'

I duck as the disc frisbees past my ear and into the corridor where it catches Della the creative secretary a glancing blow on the cheek. She ignores it, an occupational hazard. I look at Vince, now slumped in a chair. I wonder how he'd ever manage at the hi-tech controls of a miniature sub.

'Where's Brett?' I ask.

'Gone to a J&J meeting,' he replies. 'He's presenting our new Baby Oil ads – more lubed dolls than you can shake a dick at.'

No need to ask why Vince isn't with him. He isn't allowed near clients, particularly ones in the doll-lubing business. He's the three-dimensional doppelganger of Muttley. Not the image Blower Mann likes to project to the people paying its wages. More than that, though, he's a danger to others as well as himself. Witness the messy stitches from the bar brawl a couple of weeks ago. Clients like to have a bit of creative rough at a meeting – makes them feel rock 'n' roll – but there's a limit and Vince exceeds it by the width of Siberia. He's a self-mutilating, genital-exposing Iggy Pop to Brett's soft rock Bryan Adams.

'Don't you miss presenting your own work?' I ask.

'*Clients*! Keep me away from the fuckers – fucking bastard-wanker-cunts. If it wasn't for them I might be able to do some decent ads.'

Twisted logic that is, in its way, unarguable.

'Fancy coming to Croydon with me?'

'Fuck off. I'm a top London art director. I don't do *Croydon*.'

'Go on. It'll be fun . . . And you can take the script.'

'Draft forty? No ta.'

'No, you can take Draft One,' I say in what I hope is a tone of quiet authority.

'Draft One?'

'Uh-huh.'

'Draft One with the dribble shot Draft One?'

'Yip.'

'When d'we leave?'

I look at Vince sitting opposite me as the train rattles and sways through Clapham Junction. A dog – Muttley, who else? – with two tails. I can't believe I'm doing this. But I am . . . *I am*.

Five copies of Draft One nestle in my briefcase.

Draft One of the ChocoChillout launch script has never left the office, never been allowed within several miles of anyone who works for Schenker Foods – or even anyone who's vaguely related to anyone who merely knows in passing anyone who works for them. It . . . er . . . wasn't considered to be terribly client-friendly. In fact, if Schenker possessed an inkling that even the idea for Draft One had wafted across the creative team's minds before passing harmlessly into the ether, they'd reach for a pen to compose the letter dismissing Blower Mann/DBA from their business.

Draft One is the advertising equivalent of a black spherical cartoon bomb.

And here it is in my briefcase en route to the Schenker Bunker, its fuse fizzing merrily.

And here I am sitting opposite the advertising equivalent of Muttley as he gazes through the train window, barely suppressing a Muttley snigger.

Which makes me feel just a little Dick Dastardly.

The train screeches to a halt in Croydon. Doors clatter open as the carriages spew out their contents; business clones who, like me, are bound for various corporate HQs and are, like me, wearing safe mid-grey. The fact that Muttley in dirty jeans and

T-shirt walks among us doesn't go unnoticed, and not because he's jacketless in the biting pre-Christmas wind. No, the T-shirt reads CHRISTINA SUCKS on the front, BRITNEY SWALLOWS on the back – an apt message given what is about to take place.

As we leave the station and set off on the short walk to Schenker my mobile vibrates. I pull it from my pocket and look at the display: my home number.

'Hi, Fish. You got the phone to work, then?'

'Yeah, man. I stuck it in your oven on *low* for half an hour. Seems OK. The video's working too,' she adds excitedly, 'but . . . I think your telly might be fucked.'

'You never put that in the oven?'

'Nah, it's wide-screen. Wouldn't fit. I stuck it by the radiator. I thought it had dried out, but when I switched it on it made a kind of crackly noise and sparks came out the back . . . Sorry.'

'Never mind,' I say, and I mean it. 'You OK? No sign of your psycho mate?'

'He wouldn't come back here in a hurry. Probably thinks he killed you.'

'Good . . . Not that he thinks he's killed me. Good that he hasn't shown up. All right . . . Suppose I'll see you la—'

'Want me to cook something?'

'Can you?'

'Got a B in home ec.'

'OK, then. I'll call you when I'm on my way.'

I pocket the phone and Vince asks, 'You mates with Fish from Marillion?'

'No, just a girl who's staying at mine for a bit.'

'New bird, you saucy cunt?'

'It's nothing like that.'

'Reckon she'd fancy me, then?'

'Who knows? She might.'

'Your last one did,' he goes on. 'Proper little suit slut.'

Thankfully, I don't have to respond because the mobile vibrates again: Jakki.

'Niall called from Heathrow. Told me to make sure you got to Croydon OK.'

'Here now.'

'Are you all right, Murray? You were acting a bit . . . you know . . . *weird* this morning. I'm worried.'

'Well, don't be. Honestly. I feel really good today.'

'You sure? . . . Please tell me you haven't got Draft One with you.'

'I'll see you later, Jakki.'

As I end the call Vince says, 'She *definitely* fancies you, Muzza.'

'I don't think so.'

''Course she fucking does. She leaves a slime trail on the carpet tiles whenever she clocks you.'

'You're disgusting, Vince. Shut up.'

The phone goes off again. I look at the display and see a number that's tattooed on my brain. I flick at the off switch.

I can't talk to Megan now. We've reached the front steps of Schenker House, haven't we? Work comes first.

Vince stops, puts a hand on my arm and says, 'You sure about this?'

'Uh-huh.' (Though I have to say I'm not.) 'You?'

'I'm creative. Everyone expects me to be a fucking nutter. I've got everything to gain here and fuck-all to lose. *You're* the one who's about to slap your bollocks on the chopping board.'

Bizarrely, this is both the most inappropriate analogy and the most sense I've ever heard, and as we stand on the steps doubt climbs up my trouser leg and into the pit of my stomach.

Stop it now. That's the old Murray. Today is Day One of New Improved Murray. (Perhaps not the exact model I had in mind at nine o'clock this morning, but there are distinct signs of newness and improvement.)

'Apart from a shitload of grief and maybe your P-fucking-forty-five,' Vince continues, 'what're you gonna get out of it?'

Self-respect?

I don't say that, though. I say, 'F.E.A.R.'

'Yeah, matey, let's get it on. Know what this reminds me of? *Die Hard*. We're like the terrorists going in to fuck capitalism up its lardy arse.'

I gaze up at the eight storeys of glass and dirty grey concrete that are the Schenker Bunker. It's about as far from a gleaming Californian corporate temple as I can imagine. And, let's face it, in the league table of urbane terrorists, I'm hardly up there with Alan Rickman.

twelve: ze vacky guys behint our vunderful adwertisements

wednesday 17 december / 12.38 p.m.

Betina Tofting is showing early signs of hyperventilation. Her chest is heaving and, though the room is far from hot, she's sweating. It's just possible to make out the filigree of her bra beneath the now clinging fabric of her damp blouse. Vince is hypnotised. It doesn't take much and I guess this is just a taster of why he's not allowed out to play with clients. I notice the powdery white residue clinging to the stubble below his nose – it wasn't there before his recent trip to the gents. On a normal day this would have me stressing, but this is not a normal day and I'm willing Betina to spot it too.

A copy of Draft One sits on the table in front of her. She alternates between staring at it and stealing glances at the bustle of the Schenker marketing department outside. In the present lull I'm half-expecting her to grab the notepad in front of her, scrawl HELP ME! TWO MAD CRAZY MEN ARE HOLDING ME HOSTAGE, and press it up to the glass divide.

'I'm really not sure,' she stammers at last. 'Actually, I don't understand.'

'What don't you understand, Betina?' I ask gently and – I hope – condescendingly.

'This script is *different*. The changes are not the ones we agreed.'

'But it's a good script,' I say.

'It does not express the ChocoChillout Brand Genome,' she says haltingly, attempting to recover her composure by resorting to the marketing speak that she's at least as comfortable with as her native Danish. She reaches into a folder and pulls out an A4 copy of a lozenge filled with words like *sexy, youthful* and *futuristic* – the Brand Genome. She slides it to me across the table. 'I am surprised that you are going off the message, Murray,' she goes on, tapping on it with her pen by way of emphasis. 'We have settled these matters over very many researchings and I—'

'Look, sweetheart,' says Vince, snapping out of his rapture, though addressing himself not to her, but to her breasts, 'It says *sexy* here. The script's *sexy*. Job done.'

'It also says *healthful* and *fun*. The script is not reflecting this.'

'Looks like a shit heap of fun to me,' Vince mumbles.

This, of course, is a question of perspective.

Vince stares at Betina, no doubt finally satisfied that her only redeeming quality is her taste in bras. She stares at me, pleading silently for me to end her torture by doing the time-honoured account-man thing – agree that I have no mind of my own before scurrying back to Canary Wharf to perform her bidding. I guess that this more than anything is what's freaking her out. Not Draft One. Not even the wired menace of Vince. No, it must be confusing the hell out of her that I haven't cravenly surrendered at the first sign of resistance to an agency proposal.

Sorry, Betina, not today.

I rise to my feet and say, 'It's simple, Betina. What do you want the brand to be? A shrinking violet or a flesh-ripping Venus flytrap . . .?'

This is the weirdest thing. I've never felt a rush like this before – surely not even pitching for Mr Muscle could feel this good. It's like an out-of-body experience. I'm watching myself adopt the body language of a preacher. Listening to myself sound as if I actually *believe* what I'm saying. Hang on, I *do* believe it.

I'm watching my inner Jimi Hendrix. He has finally escaped,

and while he isn't quite simulating fellatio on his guitar, he is being bloody *mesmeric*, man.

I've dreamed of being this cogent, this impassioned, this *persuasive*. I *love* this me. I could get used to this me . . . Given half a chance.

So much for being persuasive. As I conclude my speech Betina is sinking in her seat, yearning to be someplace else, for someone to invent teleporting, and *quick*.

'Look, it's a big decision, Betina,' I muse. 'Maybe too big for you. Why don't we show it to Gerhard?'

'No, no, no, we cannot show Gerhard,' she says hastily, terrified at the prospect of putting this *filth* in front of her boss. 'He is in meetings all of the day. I think we must . . .' Her voice dies as a massive shadow crosses the table and the room darkens as if the Hindenburg has just flown across the sun. I turn to see Gerhard Breitmar – big, jovial, Gerhard Breitmar who makes Helmut Kohl look like a rank outsider in the obesity stakes – lumber past on the other side of the glass wall. He greets me with a cheery wave, opens the door and sticks his head into the room. 'Murray, exzellent to see you again. Niall has been keepink you busy on uzzer clients' projects, ja?' he booms in the faultless English with a deliberately hammed German accent that is his trademark. He always sounds as if he's auditioning for a part in *Schindler's List* – camp entertainment officer.

'Yes, Gerhard, yes, busy, busy,' I bluster, continuing Haye's lie.

'Betina is makink you right at home?'

'Absolutely. The perfect hostess.' I nod to Betina who is shrinking in her seat.

I look at Vince looking – *glaring* – at Gerhard – the *bastard* he holds personally responsible for the invasion of Poland, the whole silly beach-towel thing and, more to the point, the emasculation of his *TV* script. 'Gerhard, I'd like to introduce you to Vince Douglas. He's the art director on ChocoChillout.'

Breitmar steps into the room and acknowledges Vince for the first time.

'Ah, half ze unruly creatiff team.' He extends a fat hand and I can hear Vince's joints crack in the ensuing squeeze. 'I am alvays sayink to Murray and Niall zat ve should meet ze vacky guys behint our vunderful adwertisements.'

He looks at my battered face, then at Vince's. 'My vurt, you guys haff been in ze vars. Not fightink each uzzer over ze creatiff product, I hope.'

'Nah,' snarls Vince, 'just duffing up some client who wanted his logo bigger.'

A big belly laugh from Breitmar and then, 'Duffink up. Wery goot, Wince – ze creatiff sense of humour. Perhaps you vill enjoy zis one. I hear it at ze exec com zis mornink from our finance deerector. Let me see if I get it right.' He lowers his bulk into the chair at the head of the table and prepares to entertain us – Baron Bernard Von Manning. 'Ah, yes, I haff it. Zere are four secrets of a goot relationship . . . First: it is important to fint a voman zat cooks and cleans. Zecond: it is important to fint a voman zat earns goot money. Zird: it is important to fint a voman zat likes to haff sex. Und fourz . . .' His vast body begins to shudder at the impending punchline. The vibrations are transmitted across the table and even through the concrete floor – seismographs on the San Andreas fault line are probably registering the tremors. '. . . Und fourz: it is important zat zese zree vomen neffer effer meet.'

Betina blushes while her boss slaps the table with his hands and guffaws deafeningly. Vince is sniggering, too. Perhaps thinking that this fat Kraut isn't such a war-mongering, sunbed-stealing *bastard-wanker-cunt* after all – at least he has a decent line in reassuringly sexist gags. Gerhard recovers and administers a hearty whack to Vince's back. 'Vat's zis on your T-shirt, Wince? *Christina zucks*? I hope it is on von of our refreshink ice creams, ja?'

'Funny you should say that,' I interrupt, realising I couldn't have scripted a better cue than this, 'because Vince and I have brought a new ChocoChillout script.'

'At last, draft forty. Ve haff bin vaiting.'

'No, Gerhard, not draft forty. The original. Draft One.'

thirteen: **i still want us to be**

'You were fucking awesome in there. Fucking, *fucking* awesome,' Vince whoops as the Schenker Bunker's revolving door vomits us into the street.

'What the hell just happened?' I ask. I am dazed. And confused. What *did* just happen? Because whatever took place wasn't what I'd expected. Or, by the way, what I'd intended.

'He just bought our script, you bastard, that's what happened.'

'He can't have bought it,' I say, seriously doubting what I heard only a few minutes ago. Gerhard Breitmar, a man sophisticated in the bland ways of international marketing, cannot possibly have bought a forty-second close-up of a model giving one of his choc-ices a blowjob accompanied by a voice-over that says '*Don't spit; swallow*' as another model licks up the overspill from the first one's chin. It isn't possible. It's like peace in the Middle East . . . Cyprus winning Eurovision . . . Elton John growing old gracefully. It's just not going to happen.

'You heard him, Muzza. He gave us a green light.'

I did hear him. I *distinctly* heard him say, 'Guys, guys, guys, zis is ze script I haff been beggink you for. I say over und over to Niall zat vat I vant is ze concept zat truly gets to ze heart of ze eatink experience. "*Don't spit; svallow.*" Zat is genius! It is a *sin* to vaste a single solitary molecule of ChocoChillout! Zank gott someone has been listenink, because frankly I am gettink sick und tired of all zese endless drafts.'

'He doesn't even wanna research it,' Vince squeaks as he skips down the road. He's only a few feet ahead of me, but, actually, he's miles away. In Cannes, to be precise, picking up his little gold lion for Best Oral Sex Analogy in a Television Advertisement.

Unless . . . Unless Breitmar doesn't actually get it.

I feel the truth walk down the train carriage, tap me on the shoulder and utter a discreet cough. Breitmar doesn't see a blowjob at all. He sees a glorified eating shot. He has spent every single one of this project's (sixty? Seventy? Eighty?) meetings haranguing us to extend the sacred mouth-biting-on-product close-up. Well, now we've done it. We've given him an eating shot that lasts for the entire ad.

I look at Vince gazing dreamily out of the train window. Should I tell him? No. Soon enough someone will point out to Breitmar that he has approved an ad that casts his flagship product as a chocolate stiffy and everything will come crashing down. Until then, let him enjoy it. I reach into my pocket and switch on my mobile. After a few seconds it beeps. A message.

'Hi . . . Murray . . . I want to apologise for yesterday . . . I shouldn't have got so angry . . . You probably had every reason to freak out in the hospital . . . It's just that . . . Well, I want you to do what's best . . . And I know only you can decide what that is . . . But I can't help thinking that however tiny the chance, you should take it . . . But it *is* up to you . . . By the way, I think it's really sweet you taking in that homeless girl . . . Weird . . . I had the strangest flash of *déjà vu* when I saw her . . . Probably nothing . . . That's it, really . . . I'm sorry . . . And I'm thinking of you and . . . And . . . Call me . . . If you want to talk or anything . . . And . . . I still want us to be—'

Stupid bloody voicemail. All that digital wizardry, all those menu options, and it doesn't even allow for the natural stammers, hesitations and false starts of message-leaving, especially *important* and *difficult* message-leaving. What was she going to say?

What does she *still want us to be*? Best friends? Sheet-singeing lovers? Real Madrid's scintillating new strike partnership? Damned if I can tell at this strange and tricky juncture in our relationship. I listen to the message again . . . And again . . .

After the eighth play I'm still none the wiser. Luckily Vince cuts in before I drive myself completely insane. 'You could've lost us the business today, Muzza. You'd have been fired. You still might be when the tossers in charge find out you've been making them look like cunts,' he observes. 'What's got into you?'

Terminal cancer, mate.

'Something happened this morning,' I say. 'Niall hacked me off. I was really trying to be a good little account supervisor and he just . . .' I trail off.

'Shat all over you?' Vince says, filling in the blank admirably. 'He spends his life shitting on twonks like you. You must be used to it by now. C'mon, there's more to it than that, matey.'

'I suppose I'm sick of second-guessing what Niall or the client is going to say and then trying to say it before them. I thought it was time I had . . . You know . . . An opinion.'

'Nah, I still don't buy it. Second-guessing clients is your job. You don't stop doing your job just 'cause you feel like it. I mean, you're still wearing the suit, paying into the fucking pension plan. You've got another twenty years of not having an opinion to look forward to. You don't piss all that away for an afternoon of fun in fucking Croydon. Something's happened. Something *big*.'

I don't reply.

'Spit it out,' Vince nudges. 'What's going on?'

'Nothing. Nothing's going on, Vince.'

'You're a fucking liar.'

''Course I am – I'm an account man. Anyway, what about you?'

'What you on about?'

'You're full of surprises. I hear you're a dad.'

172

'Er . . . Yeah . . . That's right,' he says awkwardly.
'Got any pictures, then?'

Bubbles in a tutu . . . Bubbles on a donkey . . . Bubbles smeared with pizza sauce . . . Bubbles in Legoland . . . London Zoo . . . Chessington World of Adventure . . . Bubbles in (her mum's? Surely not Vince's) Manolo Blahniks . . . Bubbles curled up beneath Vince's bike jacket.

'You must be very proud,' I say, handing the photo binder back to him.

'She's a diamond. A princess. Best thing that ever happened to me.'

'You get on with her mum?'

'Like a fucking house on fire.'

'That well?'

'One with a family of sixteen Bangladeshi illegals trapped in the upstairs bedroom, screaming for help. She's a fruit bat. Nutso. Doo-fucking-lally. Thick as a paving slab an' all. But . . . You know . . . I put up with her for little Bubbles.'

'Little Bubbles,' I echo. Then, as the train pulls into Victoria, 'I've got cancer.'

'You what?'

'I've got about four months to live.'

Where the hell did that come from?

Why am I confessing to Vince Douglas (*Vince Douglas!*) in the lounge bar of a sticky-floored pub next to Victoria Station? Because, though he's elated at the meeting's outcome, he's genuinely confused about the mad experience we've been through, and the truth is the only thing that begins to explain it. And because I realised in Haye's office that I finally need to talk about this. He wouldn't give me a chance and poor old Vince, well, he's next in line. Of course, apart from a wildly uncharacteristic suggestion that I should perhaps ease off the alcohol – '*Are you sure Scotch is a good idea . . . you know . . . with your . . . er . . . condition and everything.*' – he has no idea what to say. Rendered speechless, as I almost certainly would be if the tables were turned. No matter. I've got more than enough words for the both of us. So here I am, articulating thoughts that have been swirling around my head for the last twenty-four hours.

'The weirdest thing,' I'm saying, 'the *weirdest* thing is that a few weeks ago, when I assumed I had a whole life stretching before me, I couldn't envisage myself amounting to anything.'

Vince is staring at me, nervously picking at his stitches, listening intently, but, I should think, also wishing he was elsewhere.

'All I could see were fifty years of drabness, shuffling from one pointless meeting to the next, never having another relationship that meant anything, forever living under the thumb of passionless twits like Haye. But now it's down to a matter of weeks, I feel as if I could actually . . . you know . . . *Be* someone.'

'How do you mean?'

'Be a contender. Make a mark. Go out with a bang . . .' I'm searching for something that isn't desperately corny. '. . . I dunno . . . Be remembered as someone other than Murray What's'isface, the drone in the mid-grey suit.'

'*Fuck*ing hell,' Vince says in a whisper, 'Fuc*king* hell.'

'Don't get me wrong. I'm *terrified* of dying . . . But I'm not frightened of the living bit any more.'

'Fucking *hell*, man . . . *Cancer*,' he says, still unable to shift his mind on from my initial revelation. 'In your liver. Your *lungs*. In your bollocks and all. What a *mind*fuck . . . I think I'd better get some more drinks in.'

174

As I watch him head for the bar it strikes me that I've never seen him so ashen. Or, for that matter, so sober – and after three shorts as well as a couple of lines. It's a mindfuck all right, death staring you in the face, even when it's someone else's across the relative safety of three feet of beer-stained pub table.

He returns with doubles and a determined expression – *I am gonna handle this*. He fixes me with a searching look and asks, 'You OK? . . . Nah, stupid question. 'Course you're fucking not *OK*. I mean, do you feel . . . Can you . . . Will you be . . . Aw, *fuck*. Do you know what I'm getting at?'

'Yeah, I think so. I honestly feel really good. Never better, in fact . . . If that makes any sense. I woke up this morning and decided that it was my last chance to reinvent myself. Be the person I've always wanted to be, but never dared. To be honest I didn't think I had the guts. The Schenker meeting was kind of a test.'

'Reckon you passed.'

'Reckon I did. I feel amazing. Now I can't wait to get on with it.'

'With what?'

'Oh . . . There're a million things I want to do,' I say, not being able to think of a single one now that a transfer to the Mr Muscle squad is out of the question . . . Pony trekking up the Andean Spine of South America?

'Like?' he nudges.

'I don't know . . . I really need to get my life in order,' I say lamely.

'What? Write your will? Pay off your credit cards,' he says, trying and failing to keep the contempt out of his voice.

'Jesus, my credit cards. I am so up to my neck with them.'

'So? By the time they get you into court you'll be . . . You know . . .'

He has a point.

'Do you need money?' Vince asks.

175

'To sort my bills out? Yes.'

'*No*, money to . . . er . . . reinvent yourself . . . 'Cause you can always get a loan.'

'I doubt it. I'm behind with my rent and snotty letters from the bank are costing me about fifty quid a month. My credit rating's wrecked.'

'You can *always* get a loan,' he repeats. Then he leans into me and lowers his voice. 'My dealer knows these blokes.'

'What, like loan sharks or something?'

'They ain't Bradford and fucking Bingley.'

Vince's complexion is reviving. He's reinvigorated, no longer floundering. Now that the conversation has shifted from *feelings* to *practicalities*, I guess he figures he can make a contribution.

'What do you want?' he continues.

'I don't know. Ten grand?' I say tentatively.

'You could have thirty in your hand this time tomorrow.'

'Really?'

'Uh-huh. They'll stiff you on the interest. And if you don't make the repayments, well, you can kiss your knackers good-bye . . .'

Done that already, more or less.

' . . . Mind you, don't s'pose that matters too much in your case. Shit, fuck, *sorry*.'

'No, it's all right. That's the whole point, isn't it? No consequences.'

I look at Vince's pack of Marlboro, at the slab of black type that takes up half the box: *Roken veroorzaakt van de bloedvaten, hartaanvallen en beroertes.*

'Where did you get those?' I ask.

'Nicked 'em off the Tofting bird. Must be Danish. So, what'd you do with a bunch of cash? I'd buy me a little sub. Or put the lot on red, then buy the sub.'

As he starts humming the theme from *Stingray* I look again at the health warning. Maybe it's not a warning. It could mean anything. Danish for *So they cause cancer? Ha, what doesn't these days?* I pull a cigarette from the pack and light it. I take a drag and think about money. I really don't know what I'd do with *funding*. I don't have a dream. I've drifted through my first thirty-one years on the basis that *something will turn up*. But nothing has, and the clock is counting down. I've never enjoyed the pressure of a deadline. Now I think about it, as long as I remain broke my options are limited to . . . Well, to sitting in my flat, where I can alternate between tidying up and writing lists of unachievable ambitions.

'Since when did you smoke?' Vince says.

'Since . . . oh, thirty seconds ago.'

He smiles as if this is the most reasonable thing in the world.

'You wanna get your hands on some cash, then?' he asks.

'Yes,' I say quietly. Then more firmly, 'Yes, I do.'

Because the mere thought of money makes me feel optimistic and ever so slightly energised – like simply getting it is an end in itself . . . And – who knows? – once I have it in my hand perhaps the answer will present itself. Perhaps something will turn up after all. Better late than never.

'I could make a couple of calls if you like,' Vince continues. 'You'll have to put up security. They ain't gonna bung you several grand unless they know they can collect one way or the other. You could put up your flat.'

'It's rented.'

'Car?'

I shake my head. I'd have to *pay* to have my knackered Polo taken away.

'It's a non-starter unless you can think of something,' Vince says.

I deflate. Until a few minutes ago the thought of bankrolling the last few weeks of my life hadn't even occurred to me. But now that the dangled possibility has been snatched away, I feel gutted. We both drain our glasses in silence.

'Shall we head back to the office?' Vince asks.

'What for? My work is done . . . For today at least.'

'True. Well, I'm going back. Gotta tell the B Boy the good news . . .' Then the embarrassed afterthought, 'About the script, I mean. Mind if I split?'

'No. Go ahead.'

He stands up and says, 'Thanks for today, matey. I really mean that. I owe you. Big time.'

'Don't mention it. I enjoyed every second.'

Then he shifts down to a mumble. 'Look, Muzza, if you . . . You know . . . Want to . . . Any time . . . You know . . . Whatever.'

'Thanks, Vince. That means a lot.'

It does as well. I *think* he's being sincere, though I imagine the prospect of a three a.m. phone call from a sobbing me needing to discuss my disease terrifies him.

He turns to leave and I call out, 'One thing, Vince.'

'Yeah?'

'Don't tell anyone about this.'

'Not even Brett?'

'Sorry. Not even Brett.'

He zips his lips.

_____ 3.32 p.m.

Alone now, I sit down with another drink. I take a sip, pull my phone from my pocket and dial.

'Good afternoon, *Bindinger*.'

'Megan Dyer, please.'

After a few more rings, 'Hello, Megan Dyer's office. How may I help?'

Suhira, her assistant.

'Hi, is she there?'

'She's in court this afternoon. Can I take a message?'

'No . . . No, it's OK. I'll try another time.'

A pause, then, 'Is that . . . Is that Murray?'

'Yeah, hi, Suhira.'

She doesn't reply. Just sniffs . . . Then makes a strange choking sound . . . That quickly leads to a full-blown sob. I guess Megan has told her, then.

'Please, don't cry,' I say. 'I'm OK, you know.'

Sobs morph into curtly strangled wails.

I let her continue and bask in the mild warmth of the knowledge that Megan has been talking about me. Lord knows what she has been saying, but judging from Suhira's outpouring of grief it wasn't words to the effect of *Don't feel pity for him because he is a sad and unpleasant bastard who thoroughly deserves to die.*

She squeezes out a 'So-o-o-rr-eee' between convulsions and I hear the soft rustle of a tissue followed by a loud trumpeting.

'That's all right,' I say. '*I'm* sorry.' (Though God knows why.)

'No, I'm really sorry,' she repeats, gamely getting her act together. 'I'm pathetic. It's just that you're being so brave . . . And . . . And . . .' The sniffs return.

Although nobody has ever suggested I'm brave and I'd like her to expand a little, I say, 'I'd better go, Suhira.'

'Are you sure you don't want me to give her a message.'

'No . . . *Yes.* Tell her I still want us to be, too.'

'Still want you to be what?'

'I'm not sure . . . Whatever she still wants us to be.'

fourteen: **who's mona?**

'Where did you learn to cook like this, Fish?'

'Told you. B in home ec. You like it, then?'

'*Deee*-licious. I'd never have thought that putting the starter, main course and dessert in the same pot could work.'

'I didn't learn *that* in home ec. My teacher was crap, man – no imagination. That's *my* invention. Everyone in the squat loved it.'

I should think that when you're taking a variety of recreational drugs and you maybe haven't eaten in a week, the psychedelic combination of Heinz Minestrone, frankfurters, McCain Micro Chips, mushy peas and Mr Kipling Bakewell Tarts would be a relishable feast. However, when I said *deee-licious* I was being polite.

'Seconds?' she asks.

'Couldn't eat another thing.' I don't add *ever*.

'Tea?'

'OK.'

Overlooking (and it does take some overlooking) the slop-bucket cuisine, Fish is surprisingly – and *pleasingly* – domesticated. I arrived home to a spick-ish-and-span-ish flat – not quite up to Murray Colin standard, but not *that* far short. She'd vacuumed, my CDs were back in the rack (though in an incomprehensible order) and all my electrical appliances were in their allotted places. I wonder if she was like this at the tower block. Foetid sleeping bags hung out to air. Magazines in mathematically correct alignment on the tea-chest-for-a-coffeetable. And what was her scent preference for the freshly scrubbed squat? Bracing Nordic pine or something more citrusy? Or does she, like me, find comfort in the WARNING: HAZARDOUS CHEMICALS AT WORK stench of bleach?

I wonder this as I roll a joint with the last of her dope. I look at my handiwork – loo-roll-fat at each end, anorexic in the middle – and I can't understand it. It's not as if I'm completely useless with my hands. I can fold a linen napkin into an elegant replica swan. I can sit down at a potter's wheel and turn out a perfectly serviceable ashtray. I can *knit*, for heaven's sake. Nothing fancy like an Aran sweater, but I could run you up a lovely scarf. But please don't ask me to do anything cool like *skin up*. You'd get a better joint from David Blunkett.

'How long have you been . . . you know . . . homeless?' I ask Fish when she returns to the living room with tea.

'Coupla years. Since the day I got my GCSE results.'

I pass her the joint and even though it's sagging alarmingly in the middle, she's kind enough not to comment on its appalling construction.

'Why?' I ask.

She takes a pull and shrugs – not, I suspect, because she doesn't know the answer, but because she'd prefer me not to.

'Where does your family live?'

She shrugs again.

'Do you like being homeless?'

'Love it. 'Specially this time of year when it's minus fucking twenty and you bastards with houses and warm coats are *too cold* to get your hands out of your pockets and bung us fifty pee.'

'Sorry.'

'S'all right. Didn't mean you personally.'

The phone rings.

Fish is sitting next to it. The dope is kicking in and I let her answer.

'Hello. Drug Squad. Got any good shit, man?' she asks the receiver. Then, after a moment, 'It's for you.'

Course it is. You won't have got round to sending out your change of address cards yet.

I take the phone from her.

'Who on earth was that?'

'Hi, Niall. Just a friend.'

'Well, she should learn some telephone etiquette.'

Excuse me, but this is not the HQ of Murray Colin PLC and she is not the receptionist.

'How's L'Oréal?' I ask.

'A bloody disaster. Very negative feedback on our new Elvive film—'

It's not a film, Niall. It's a television commercial. Just so you can tell the difference in future, a film is roughly two hours long, entails the purchase of tickets, soft drinks and popcorn, and provides a welcome respite from reality. A television commercial, on the other hand, is over in thirty seconds, but provides a welcome opportunity to check out what's on the other channels.

'—They think the hair shots are clichéd—'

I've seen them. They are.

'—and some silly bimbo from their strategic planning unit reckoned Milla Jovovich is *wooden*.'

She is. But who can blame her? Umpteen ads pouting drivel about hair that's two per cent more manageable and seven per cent shinier would have turned Olivier into a plank.

'As a result my mood is now poor to bloody lousy and it wasn't improved any by the call I just had from Gerhard Breitmar.'

Hmm, Gerhard. Didn't think you were calling to give me a reprieve on Mr Muscle.

'Is he upset about something?' I ask.

'On the contrary. He's bloody delighted.'

'That's good . . . Isn't it?'

'No, it is not good. Not good at all. It's a shambles. Draft *One*. What on earth were you thinking?'

'I just thought that—'

'Have you any idea of the fix you've got us into? How the hell are we going to get out of this?'

'Well, we could just do what he wants, couldn't we? You know, shoot the ad.'

'Don't be so bloody ridiculous. *Shoot the ad*. Are you completely mad?'

Very possibly.

'We haven't spent months developing a precisely targeted brand message just to throw it all away and make that piece of . . . That piece of . . . It really doesn't bear thinking about. Look, I've got a black-tie do at the Louvre to get ready for. I haven't got time to discuss this now.'

Me neither. I've got a joint to finish here.

'I'll deal with it – and *you* – when I get back on Friday. In the meantime don't go near any clients. Don't even phone them.'

Suits me.

'You can make yourself useful tomorrow by taking my car to Lancaster in Bow Road for its service. The keys are with security. Can I trust you to do that?'

'Yeah, sure.'

'I mean, you do know how much my car is worth?'

Yes, I read the all-staff memo.

'Don't worry, Niall. It'll be fine.'

'When you get there tell them to run some diagnostics on the PSM system. It doesn't feel right.'

'OK, Niall. Check the PMS.'

'*PSM. SM*. It stands for Porsche Stability Management. It significantly enhances dynamic control.'

Like that's supposed to mean something.

'Sorry. PSM.'

'OK, then. Good night.'

'Night. Give my love to Mona.'

'Jesus bloody Christ,' he says before slamming the phone down.

'Who's Mona?' Fish asks.

——————————————— thursday 18 december / 2.34 a.m.

'Wasn't it nice of Niall to let us have his car?' Megan says as she reaches over the gearshift to rest her hand on my thigh.

'Yes, wasn't it?' I reply. 'It's a Porsche. And did you know it has PMS?'

I ease the car off the slip road and onto the empty motorway.

'*SM*! It's P*SM* for heaven's sake! PSM, PSM, PSM, PSM, PSM, PSM . . .'

I turn to see Haye's face contorted with fury. He's wearing Megan's charcoal-grey court suit – the slightly butch but horny one she wore when we had opportunistic – and for me scary and, frankly, disastrous – sex in a restaurant toilet.

'. . . PSM, PSM, PSM . . .'

Ignoring the road I reach over and grab his door handle, snapping it towards me. I shove hard on his shoulder and he rolls out of the car, still screaming.

'. . . PSM, PSM, PSM, PSM, PSM, PSM – Porsche Stability Management for significantly enhanced dynamic con*troooooo-ooooooooooooooooooool*!'

In the rear-view mirror I watch his body bounce across the carriageway into the path of an articulated container truck. Megan is at the wheel and she waves to me cheerily as the huge wheels of her lorry turn my boss into raspberry jam.

My eyes snap open.

I feel excited, but I don't know why. Dreams of Megan are a common occurrence. They were when we were together and they have continued to be since we split up. These days I invariably wake from them feeling sad, then sadder still when I turn to see the Megan-less half of my bed . . .

Which tonight isn't empty.

In the vague light I can make out a body-shaped lump beneath the quilt. And a head on the pillow. And the merest glint of purple hair. Fish rolls onto her back, opens her eyes and looks at me.

'Hi,' she says. 'Sorry . . . But it's been ages since I slept in a proper bed and—'

'No, I'm sorry. I should've thought. I should've taken the sofa.'

She sits up, pushes back the quilt and slides her legs onto the floor.

'You might as well stay now,' I say.

'No, I'd better go.'

'Please . . . It's not as if there isn't room.'

She flops back onto the pillow and onto my arm that's lying across it. She rolls towards me until her head is resting on my shoulder. As we drift back to sleep I work out why I feel excited. It has nothing to do with Fish, pleasant though it is to have someone beside me.

No, it's because I've figured out how to get my hands on a thick wad of cash.

fifteen: **the best way forward for humankind: mutant antlers or giant lobster claws?**

Brett, Vince and Kenny Production Geezer are oblivious to my presence in the doorway. I've arrived at Brett and Vince's office to find them mid-debate.

'Bollocks, as per, Vin,' Kenny is saying. Loudly. 'If you had a giant lobster claw you couldn't get your T-shirt on for a start. You'd be stuffed before you'd even got dressed. It's got to be the antlers. No question.'

'You'd look like a proper cunt with antlers on your head,' Vince snarls.

'And I s'pose you'd prefer a giant pink claw where your hand should be?'

'It wouldn't be pink, you lardy twonk. Lobster's only pink when it's cooked. It'd be a kind of mottled bluey-grey colour.'

I've twigged by now that this is a variation on an endlessly fertile topic of discussion. The one that runs *If aliens invaded tomorrow and – apart from wiping out civilisation, turning all the men into zombie slaves and abducting the women for use as guinea pigs in inter-species breeding experiments – made us all mutants with either* (in this particular instance) *giant lobster claws or antlers, which would you prefer?*

'Any road, my claw'd twat your fucking antlers in a ruck,' Vince goes on.

'Would *not*. A single claw would throw you completely off balance. You wouldn't stand a chance against antlers. They're tailor-made for close quarters combat. You see them lobsters scrapping on *Blue Planet*? Donkeys of the deep, mate.'

Brett, who has yet to contribute – obviously weighing up the evidence with his usual forensic care – spots me lurking.

'What's your view, Murray?' he asks. 'The best way forward for humankind: mutant antlers or giant lobster claws?'

'What're you asking the suit for?' growls Kenny.

'Give him a break,' Vince snaps. 'He's O-fucking-K.'

Vince, my New Best Friend.

'I reckon it'd have to be the claw,' I say. 'I mean, you'd never again be stuck for a can opener.'

'Yeeesss!' says Vince.

'Wanker,' says Kenny, pushing past me into the corridor.

'Vin tells me you played a blinder yesterday,' Brett says. 'Draft *One*. Who'd've believed? S'pose you've come to tell us the Komedy Kraut has had a change of heart.'

'No. Not yet, anyway. Actually, I wanted a word with Vince.'

'Go ahead, Muzza,' Vince says.

'Alone . . . If that's OK.'

'Well, I wouldn't wanna be the gooseberry watching you two get it on,' Brett says, pushing past me into the corridor.

_____ 9.11 p.m.

I watch Vince gallop excitedly down the steps of the big terraced house that contains his flat. He reaches the car, bangs on the roof and opens the door. As he climbs into the passenger seat I notice the snowy moustache – he'd never leave home for a West End night out without first enjoying an apéritif.

'Fancy a toot before we rock 'n' roll?' he asks.

Seems I'm his new drug buddy.

'I'm OK, thanks.'

'Sure? Think of it as chemo.'

'Do you mind? I'm not in the mood for cancer jokes.'

'Sorry, mate. I thought it was quite sharp.'

'Any other night, Vince.'

The pains in my chest that I first felt during my final visit to Saint Matthew's with Megan have returned with a vengeance this evening. It feels like the onset of something and I'm frightened.

But what can I do?

Get on with things, I suppose.

I start the engine and mirror-signal-manoeuvre before gingerly pulling out of the parking space. I've driven the car from Docklands to Battersea. Several miles at a sub-ten m.p.h. London crawl. Far enough, you'd think, to get used to it. But I rarely drive, and when I do, it's in a twelve-year-old Polo. I have no idea of the engine capacity of Haye's silver Porsche, but I suspect it's considerably bigger than one-point-one litres. I don't like cars. Why else have I allowed mine to rot in the street for months? I've never felt comfortable in the company of men who speak car – I shuffle awkwardly from foot to foot switching between feelings of boredom and inadequacy. Then there are the machines themselves. I find them intimidating, especially when they have fat tyres and wings on the boot. I'm sorry. You can show me all the diagrams explaining automotive aerodynamics you like, but wings belong on aeroplanes. Or, at a stretch, sanitary towels. They have no place on car boots. And being at the controls of what Haye unfailingly tells anyone who'll listen is *the ultimate embodiment of Porsche engineering* has me scared witless. It must show, because Vince says, 'You're driving like a queer. Want me to have a go?'

'No, it's OK,' I reply. Tense as I am, I think my nerves will be slightly less frazzled with me at the wheel. Besides, for my plan to bear fruit, the car needs to remain intact for the next couple of hours or so.

Vince's wired and twitchy fingers will have to make do with the CD player. 'What's Haye listen to on his way to work, then?'

he asks rhetorically. He touches *play* and after a moment our ears are assaulted by 'Total Eclipse of the Heart'.

'Jesus buggering Christ,' he yelps, fumbling for the *off* switch. 'Goes to show, huh? You can stick it in a hundred-grand motor, but a cunt is still a cunt.'

I don't say anything. I feel unsettled because I've just discovered that Niall and I do, after all, have something in common. I didn't know he liked Bonnie Tyler . . . Look, I can't help it . . . It's just one of those things, OK?

9.26 p.m.

We're sitting at the traffic lights on the south side of Battersea Bridge. As I look at its prettily illuminated suspension cables, it strikes me that I'm enjoying a glimpse of a picturesque London that I hardly ever see. Americans who know the city only from British films must think that the place consists of the Houses of Parliament, the Albert Hall, Primrose Hill, Battersea Bridge, a few loft-style conversions in gentrified Victorian warehouses and . . . er . . . that's it. They must also be under the impression that all of these places are slap-bang next to each other and not separated by miles of drab, ill-planned, traffic-clogged concrete and tarmac. But I can see why the filmmakers go for Battersea Bridge. It really is quite beautiful.

I feel my eyes well up. Vince is smoking, but it isn't that.

I've lived in London, or at least on the edge of it, my whole life, but I've hardly *seen* it. I remember the first time my mum and dad drove me down Regent Street to see the Christmas lights, then onto neon-clad Piccadilly Circus, Parliament Square and up the Mall to Buckingham Palace. I must have been five or six. I spent the journey frantically wiping the condensation from the car window so that I could take in the sheer *wonder* of it all. I couldn't get enough. The sensation has been repeated only a few times since. My adult life has been spent shuffling from flat to tube to office, rarely looking up, rarely seeing London as a wide-eyed kid – or even as a tourist – does. But a few moments ago as I stared at the bridge I felt the same rush that I did over twenty Christmases ago. And I'm crying because – through apathy more than anything else – I've failed to appreciate what I've had in my life. And I've got bugger-all time left to compensate.

Battersea bloody Bridge.

Who'd have thought it?

I mean, it's hardly the Golden Gate.

'You know the Nine-eleven GT Two will top two hundred with a following wind,' says Vince, gatecrashing my despair and sounding like a Porsche brochure.

'Really?' I say, my head turned away from him to hide the tears.

'Yeah, *really*, and you're driving it like a cunt. What's the point of having four hundred and sixty BHP under your foot if you ain't—'

'Tell me, Vince, what does BHP mean?'

'Brake horsepower.'

'I know that, but what does it *mean*?'

'It means *power*, dunnit?'

'But where do horses come into it? Is this it? You strap four hundred and sixty horses to this car and they'd pull it along at two hundred miles an hour?'

'Yeah . . . No . . . It's like—'

'And what about the brake bit? Correct me if I'm being thick, but brakes *stop* things, don't they? How do they fit into the equation?'

'I dunno. What's it fucking matter?'

'It matters because I've spent my life feeling intimidated by blokes who spout spec on cars like they've got jobs in the formula-one pit lane. I've only just realised that they have as much clue what they're talking about as I do.'

'You wanna lighten up, matey.'

'I intend to.'

'Tonight should help.'

'How so?'

'Momo. Model heaven. It's like a bunch of 'em died in a tragic Milan catwalk massacre and their spirits went to Momo.'

'Really?' I say, far more surprised by Vince's slightly lyrical turn than by his revelation that one of London's hipper clubs is the hang-out of fashion models. I mean, they're *models*. Where else are they going to go? The Pig & Whistle for ale and pork scratchings?

'I defy you to leave the place without a hard-on,' he adds unnecessarily. 'You should cash in, you know.'

'How do you mean?'

'Well, no offence . . . And I know you reckon you're not in the mood . . . But, let's face it, Muzza, you've got a bona chat-up line.'

'What's that?'

'You fucking know.'

'Sorry, I don't.'

'The "I'm gonna snuff it any day and I gotta fuck your arse off before I go" one – only better worded than that. Obviously.'

'Obviously.'

'This guy at college used to use it. Worked every time. He had 'em forming queues to give his knob one final polish. And he was a lying twat who wasn't even ill. *You* can deliver it from the heart, mate. Believe me, you could have top international totty circling for their landing slots.'

'I couldn't do that, Vince.'

'Course you could. Before yesterday you'd've said you couldn't breeze into Schenker and hit 'em with Draft One. Think about it.'

But I *know* I couldn't. As we cross Battersea Bridge I realise that, however much I wish to reinvent myself, there remains an insurmountable difference between a guy like Vince and someone like me. While someone like me is ruminating on how a chocolate-box London landmark can sum up his life's failings, a guy like Vince is formulating strategies to get into model girls' knickers.

<hr />

10.09 p.m.

'Innit the bollocks?' Vince gasps.

Momo. A subterranean cavern in west Soho. It isn't big and – a word of warning to any claustrophobics, basketball players and especially claustrophobic basketball players out there – the ceiling is *low*. The theme is Morocco. Dark wooden stools and benches strewn with big, soft, harem-ish throw cushions. Low tables with tooled metal tops. And, of course, the music. Euro chill-out meets Afreekaaaaa. This is all a bit of a culture shock – the Pig & Whistle usually represents the outer limit of my hipness.

It's quiet. Less than half full. But Vince was right about the models. They must make up over fifty per cent of the clientele. Whether male or female, they're long, thin and scarily, off-putting-ly beautiful. And *preening*. This place should be called Me-Me. We sink into the cushions in a small alcove and are immediately joined by a waitress. 'What can I get you?' she asks briskly.

'Momo Special,' Vince says.

'Vodka and tonic, please,' I add, having no idea what a Special is.

'Organic?' the waitress asks.

'Excuse me?'

'Organic vodka?'

'Er . . . yes . . . organic, please,' I say. Then under my breath as she heads for the bar, 'As opposed to corn-fed, free-range or non-genetically modified.'

'What's that?' Vince asks.

'Fantastic, isn't it? While you're laying down the foundations of sclerosis and heart disease you can rest assured that at least the vodka is *organic*.'

'Look, it goes down your neck. You get wankered. Who gives a flying fuck?'

'What time are they arriving?' I ask.

'Should be here now. But they're a bit like Network SouthEast – best to ignore the timetable.'

'Seems an odd choice of venue.'

'What, you think these guys only hang out in dodgy East End pubs? The Blind fucking Beggar and "Knees up Mother Kray"?' Vince says, launching into a mini-lecture on his specialist subject. 'This is the twenty-first century, Muzza. Crime has gone like Gap and Starbucks. It's a fucking global concern. Half the fucking gangsters are foreign. They wouldn't know Bethnal Green if it turned up at a party with a nametag on its tit.'

─────────────── friday 19 december / 12.17 a.m.

'You figured how much you're going to hit 'em for?' Vince asks as we wait.

'I'm not sure . . . Twenty? Thirty?' I reply tentatively.

'Best make your mind up. Be sure of yourself. They're like dogs. They can smell fear like it's piss on a lamppost.'

'O . . . K,' I say . . . uncertainly.

'So, you sorted how you're gonna spend it?'

'Oh . . . Yes . . . There're a million things I want to do,' I say, hoping he doesn't want me to be any more specific.

But he's distracted now, looking across the bar. 'We're on,' he announces. He stands up on shaky legs and exchanges an over-elaborate handshake with the whippet-thin guy who has arrived at our table. He has long, black shampoo-ad hair and perfect chiselled features, and he is dressed like a bag of designer liquorice all-sorts. A thin, pink nylon jacket over a semi-transparent yellow shirt, open to the navel to display a dark crucifix tattoo. His trousers are turquoise, a spray-on, mock-snakeskin affair. On his feet are slippers. At least, I *think*. Brown check with a zip up the centre. As seen on Dad. They're either a profoundly ironic fashion statement or a monumental cock-up. Probably safer to go with the former.

'Murray, this is Clark, as in Kent,' Vince announces. It strikes me that nothing would be less surprising than if Clark, as in Kent, had slipped on a pair of scarlet Y-fronts over his crotch-hugging turquoise trousers.

'Hey, Muwway, cool,' Clark says in a polished Eton though severely R-challenged accent before launching into the same choreographed shake he has only just finished with Vince. He spots the strapping on my fingers and pulls back. We make do with an effete high-five.

The three of us sit down and suddenly I feel hopelessly square in my suit. I'm surrounded by people who've stepped straight out of a Condé Nast photo shoot and I'm sitting opposite Clark, a Technicolor Adonis with hair that would make Jennifer Aniston spit with jealousy.

Just a mo. He's wearing your dad's slippers. Why feel intimidated?

Sorry. Can't help it.

I watch as Vince and Clark close heads in conversation. Vince discreetly pulls a roll of notes from a pocket, peels some off and palms them at knee height to Clark – payment for deals past or future. This is not my world and I'm beginning to feel scared, which only adds to the ache in my chest. And, of course, I know that the situation will shortly become scarier still.

But this is what you signed up for, Murray. The thrill of the new. A bit of danger. The chance to fucking live before you fucking die. And it's free, remember? No cost. No consequences.

The deal over, Clark and Vince sit back.

'So, dude, bought yourself the yellow submawine yet?' Clark asks.

See? *Everyone* knows about Vince's dream.

'Working on it, mate, working on it.'

'Maybe Muwway can help you out,' Clark says, before turning to me and asking, 'you're like Vin's business manager, yah?'

'Huh?' What the hell has Vince been telling him? But I guess there's a tenuous equation between account supervisor and business manager. 'Yeah,' I say, 'I suppose . . .'

'*Cool*. And you find yourself a bit compwomised, cash-flow-wise?'

'Er . . . No . . .'

I glance at Vince. He's giving me a look: *F.E.A.R.*

'*Yes*,' I say. 'Compromised.'

'That's majorly depwessing, man,' Clark sympathises.

'But it's strictly a short-term situation,' I add. 'Be sorted in a few months. Completely sorted.'

<hr>

Clark was merely the warm-up act. Or the go-between. As Vince was my conduit to Clark, he is my conduit to the man with the money.

The man with the money has arrived. He's one of Vince's foreigners. East European. Too dark and with features that are too heavy, I think, to be Russian. Ukrainian or Georgian perhaps. Or a *Chechen*. Aren't they the ones who're so tough that they eat their own babies – uncooked – as an initiation rite? He's short but broad enough to compensate. Like me, he's in a suit. At first sight this offered some mild reassurance. But it only lasted for as long as it took me to realise that his would have cost several thousand pounds more than mine.

He hasn't given me a name.

And I didn't think it appropriate to ask.

Especially since he isn't alone. He's with his double. Like him in every way. Only *much* bigger – a double-size double. Double's suit would have cost a few grand more than his boss's simply on account of the acreage of extra fabric involved. Double doesn't say much. The strong, silent type with the emphasis on strong.

'So, ow muj we tokk?' the man with the money asks in a barely penetrable accent, rendered more difficult by the music, which has increased in volume as the club has filled up.

'How much? Er . . . Fifty . . .'

Fifty? Where the hell did *that* come from?

'. . . Yes, fifty should definitely cover it.'

''K. 'K.' He says, staring at me through slitted eyes. He sniffs. Smelling the air for fear, which I *am* feeling and I only hope that the scent is drowned by the heavy wash of perfume that's emanating from the legion of models. Then he stares at me . . . for what seems like a very long time.

If we were down at the bank, this is the bit where the manager would be wondering, not unreasonably, how I proposed to manage the repayments alongside all my other outgoings and asking if the Kew Gardens-sized conservatory I was intending to have built would really add value to my flat. This is an entirely different kind of grilling. A silent one where I feel as if my inner soul is being sucked out of me before being spread on the table and poked at with a pointy stick. This stare *hurts*.

Finally it stops and he says, ''K. 'K. 'K. 'K. Ees veery pozzibull.' Then he turns to Clark and snaps, 'Tell im ow wukks, Clakk.'

Clark, who has sat through the preceding few minutes with closed eyes, shimmying his body to the music, springs to life. 'Yah, cool, how it works. Sure. Wight, Muwway, listen up, dude. You get the money. With me?'

I nod.

'Wight. Then in thwee months you pay the money back, yah? With twenty-five gwand on top, yah? To cover admin, *et cetewa, et cetewa*.'

Seventy-five gwand; I mean grand. That is steep . . . But, hey, no consequences.

Nod again.

Hang on, though. Three months is too soon. You might still be lingering. You need at least four. Five to be certain.

'Except,' I say, 'I'll need longer. Five months.'

The man with the money has been watching all of this and dives in. 'Five muns? No! Four. Four! Coss you hunnerd G.'

'Get that, man?' Clark asks. 'One hundwed in four months, yah?'

'Yah,' I hear myself saying.

'Coool,' says Clark. Business concluded.

Not quite.

'One other thing. Collatewal . . .'

What's that?

'. . . Vince tells us you're putting up a Nine-eleven GT Two.'

Oh, he means the car – *collateral.*

Forcing my hand to stop shaking, I reach into my jacket and fish out the keys. I place them on the table, making sure the Porsche badge on the fob is facing upwards. The man with the money picks them up and turns them over in his hand. Then he tosses them to his double and gestures to the door. I must look confused, because Clark explains, 'Wants the two of you to go check out the wheels.'

'The reels?' I say, my confusion congealing.

'*Wheels*, dude, *wheels*.'

Oh, that was a *double-u* – wuh for wheels.

'The *car*. Yes. With you,' I say, standing up.

———————————————————————— 12.58 a.m.

I turn the corner and hope that Haye's car is still on the meter where I parked it.

It is.

197

I point it out to my companion, but he's already moving ahead of me, aiming the remote at the Porsche and plipping it open. He opens the door and the car sinks beneath his vast bulk as he slides into the seat. He starts the engine and revs it loudly a few times. He strokes the leather passenger seat wistfully, then pulls himself together. He climbs out and breaks into an unexpected grin.

I smile back – it seems the thing to do.

'Four-sixty BHP,' I say, hoping he doesn't demand an explanation.

'Boossy vargen!' he booms, slapping the car's roof so hard that I'm afraid for its bodywork.

'Pardon?'

'Boossy vargen,' he repeats.

I shake my head.

'Boossy, boossy, boossy,' he chants before sticking out his tongue and waggling it lewdly – the internationally recognised gesture for cunnilingus.

'Yeah, got it now,' I say. 'It is a *tremendous* pussy wagon.'

He puts a giant arm around my shoulder and we head back towards Momo.

 1.21 a.m.

'You fucking did it, geezer!' Vince shouts above the music. He made himself scarce during the negotiations. I spotted him a couple of times, his head bobbing into view in the sea of swaying models on the dance floor, apparently drowning, but actually thriving like an agile chub. But now he's back, forcing the cork out of a very un-Vince bottle of champagne and spilling most of the contents on both our trousers.

'Fifty fucking big ones, eh? You fucking did it!'

Yes, I did it, though I don't think I'll fully credit it until I wake up tomorrow morning with the memory intact.

I still don't quite know *how* I did it without vomiting, fleeing or both.

I especially don't know how I got through the last bit. The bit where Clark outlined terms and conditions – no loan is without its small print.

'Wight, OK, wight,' he said, flicking through a small black diary. 'Four months. Monday the nineteenth of Apwil. The agweed date. You will make payment in full on that day, yah? Ninety-five gwand. A day late, you will be wubbed out. A penny short, wubbed out. With extweme pwejudice. Dig?'

I dug. The comedy speech impediment didn't blunt the edge. I looked at Eastern Europe's answer to Little and Large – the *anti*-Little and Large. They'd been glaring at me with menace throughout. The prospect of being *wubbed out* – with or without *extweme pwejudice* – by even the smaller of these two evil bastards will have me fleeing into the bosom of my cancer. And if I by some sick miracle I'm not already dead by the eighteenth of April, then I'll be looking for a high window.

But now it's done I feel elated. Energised. Better than I've felt in . . . Oh, quite a long time. Not because I'm going to get my hands on fifty thousand pounds – which I have no idea how I'm going to spend anyway – but because I went through with it. It's as if simply asking some very bad and scary people for lots of their money was an end in itself. The equivalent of Sandy Morrison's friend-of-a-friend's pointless yet life-affirming bungee jump. Now I'm bouncing around on a metaphoric elastic band enjoying the aftermath of a rush that's definitely better than coke and . . . Think carefully about this one . . . Yes, better than sex too.

'So, when you getting the dosh?' Vince asks as he finally manages to get some champagne into my glass.

'Tomorrow. I'll get a call apparently.'

'Fifty fucking grand. You ever seen that much cash?'

'No. I've never even seen one grand.'

'I did once. Had to shoot a suitcase of loot for a *Reader's*

Digest prize draw ad. Quarter of a mill. I creamed my kecks.'

Probably not an exaggeration.

'Any road, we need to fucking celebrate.'

Watch those split infinitives, Vince.

'I thought we were,' I say, taking a sip of champagne.

'Nah, this ain't celebrating. There's someone I want you to meet.'

He grabs my arm and drags me from my seat, pulling me through the forest of slender arms and legs until we reach the bar. 'See that bird?' he says.

The counter is lined with several birds. 'Which one?' I ask.

'The tall one.'

'They're all tall.'

'Blonde, bit titsy.'

There are a few of those, so it hardly narrows things down.

'Gyppo look.'

I spot a terrifyingly beautiful blonde wearing a white peasant (well, some overindulged designer's idea of peasant) top and a flouncy, petticoated skirt. I nod.

'Me and the B Boy wanted to use her in our Courvoisier ad, but Haye and the client reckoned she was too minxy. They were fucking right. Still a pair of twats though. Anyway, come and say hello.'

'No, it's OK, Vince.'

'Fuck off. She's dying to meet you.' He hauls me along the bar, yelling out, 'Saffy, *Saffy*, this is the guy I was telling you about.'

The blonde – Saffy – turns and looks at me – I should say she looks *down* at me. I'm five ten, not usually a height that induces a complex, but I figure if I hang around for much longer in the Land of the Willowy Giants I'll have a Napoleon-scale inadequacy attack. Saffy – the blonde – stretches out her endless arms and places a palm on each of my cheeks. 'Daaarling, *sooooo* brave, pooooor baby.'

I glare at Vince, trying to summon up just a fraction of the menace of Little and Large. He leans over and whispers into my ear. 'Well, you're such a fucking dork, you'd never get the words out. Thought I'd oil the wheels for you. Go for it, big boy – she's been juicing up a storm since I told her.'

What am I doing?

What the *hell* am I doing?

Actually, what the hell I am doing is self-evident. The more pertinent question is *why*. Why am I driving a Porsche 911 GT2 along Bayswater Road at gone two in the morning? Why is the maroon leather passenger seat currently occupied by a blonde of immense beauty and chilling cool? Part of the answer is that I'm under the influence. Of half a bottle of champagne and several (organic) vodkas.

And of Vince Douglas.

And of my own lust.

They say that love is blind, but, actually, it's lust that can't see beyond the end of its own dick.

This is crazy, isn't it? Most blokes spend an unnecessarily high proportion of their waking hours (and a good many of their sleeping ones) dreaming of sex with unattainable women. I'm no different in this regard – you may recall my telling you that my particular fancy involves Uma Thurman and a lush spring meadow.

Sorted, then. Me plus model in muscular Teutonic sports car equals dream made flesh.

Surely?

The trouble with me is that fantasies are fine so long as they stay that way. Yes, I have happy visions of jogging onto the stage in a packed Shea Stadium for my third encore. However, stick me in the rock-star clobber and helicopter me into the

201

auditorium and I'd make a rabbit in the headlights cut a resolutely heroic dash.

And that's how I feel now – panicked, stressed, the complete opposite of blissed-out – sitting beside the blonde – Saffy – whose gypsy skirt is riding up her leg, though the limb in question is so long I doubt it will ever reach the top.

It's. Just. Not. *Me.*

It's not a cool admission, but I like my sex homely and comfortable. *Safe.* In the emotional sense. First-time sex with any of my count-em-on-one-hand girlfriends was an experience fraught, on my part at least, with dread. The prospect of performing with Saffy – the blonde – in her Notting Hill model pad is . . .

Well, it's just not going to happen.

Yet it *is* crazy, because in the adrenaline rush that followed my decision to forgo treatment, live life large and hang the consequences, guess what one of the items was on my mental to-do list.

That's right.

Sex with model.

See what I mean?

Lust.

Blind as a bloody bat.

'*Love* Vincent,' Saffy says in her languorously posh voice.

'He's a good guy,' I agree.

'So *cute*. He promised to let me drive his getaway sub.'

Everyone knows his plan. Even the international model set – '*Paris? Tuesday? No can do, Donatella, baby. Got submarine practice.*'

'It's *so* cool of you to give me a lift,' she says.

'S'OK,' I reply, staring unblinking at the road ahead, trying to delete the not unpleasant sensation of slender hand slithering onto my thigh.

'I mean, you must have so much on your mind. So much

. . . *baggage* to deal with. Providing a taxi service must be the last thing you need.'

Taxi service I could cope with.

'Really. It's OK. It's my pleasure,' I say automatically.

'I've done a lot of charity work, you know. Naomi, Kate . . . All us girls have been totally into the breast cancer thing. At one do we met some poor women who'd lost their . . . You know . . .'

'Uh-huh.'

'It was absolutely devastating.'

Well, for them I suppose it was.

'So, I can imagine what you must be going through . . . It breaks my heart.'

'You're very sweet,' I say.

Why the hell did I say that?

She squeezes my thigh and my leg tenses.

'You feel tense, baby.'

Well, if you'd just take your hand off my leg . . .

She strokes rhythmically up and down my thigh and I feel my knee lock. Then – *oh, thank you, sweet Jesus* – she takes her hand away. My body relaxes. I hear a click and glance at her out of the corner of my eye. She has taken her seatbelt off. She's leaning over. She's in my lap. I hear the sound of a zip.

My zip.

'Please . . . Saffy . . . *Please.*'

Bugger, she's taking that as a *yes*.

I look at her blonde mane sprawling across my thighs like the money shot in Haye's L'Oréal ad. I reach down with my left hand. But what do I do with it? Tap her politely on the back of her head? Grab her by the hair and attempt to prise her off? 'Saffy, there's something you should know,' I say.

'Mmmnng?' she replies.

'My cancer. It's . . . It's testicular.'

'*Nnnnngugghhh!*' She's choking now and I think she might

203

well throw up. She's trying to dislodge me from her mouth, but her head is trapped by the underside of the steering wheel.

I hear a siren.

Shit, the road.

I look up.

Is that a red light flashing past?

Is that a blue light?

Streaking into my field of vision.

Across the front of the Porsche.

My body lurches forward.

My head whips back.

Phhhhhhh-shhhhhtt!

So that's what an airbag sounds like.

2.21 a.m.

I'm looking at the crumpled nose of Niall Haye's pride and joy, which is buried in the side of the police car – the one that was racing across the junction, its blue light flashing. Now the cops have something else to deal with. The idiot who shot a red light and slammed into them.

The police driver is still in his seat, rubbing his shoulder. His partner climbs out and walks deliberately towards me. Should I try an apologetic smile? Or maybe polish up the old *Hey, my dad was on the force. Maybe you knew him* . . . line? I touch the control to open my window and it glides serenely into the door – even after a smash, a credit to Porsche engineering. The copper reaches me and crouches to my level.

'You hurt, sir?'

I shake my head.

'Would you like to step out of the car?'

I'd love to, but . . .

I make a gesture of helplessness at the airbag, which is pinning me against my seat . . . and which, as if by magic, chooses that instant to deflate, its job of saving my worthless life done.

I really wish it hadn't.

Officer and me are greeted by a new sight as the bag flattens like a high-tech whoopee cushion and then hangs limp from the steering wheel.

Saffy.

Her head is on my lap. Blood pours out of a cut on her ear. My flaccid *thing* lies across her cheek.

There is one consolation. It's tiny, but I'm clinging to it with all my might. At least I won't be alive to hear the courtroom dissolve into helpless mirth when I say, 'The thing is, your honour, I didn't actually *want* her to perform oral sex on me.'

sixteen: as if

I step into the Blower Mann reception.

When I made this same walk just over forty-eight hours ago I was nervous. That was because I was about to tell Niall that I wished to knuckle down and give my all to Mr Muscle, and I was unsure how he'd respond. Today is different. Today I'm the bloke who not only showed his biggest client an un-authorised script, but also – just in case he wasn't mad enough at me already – totalled his hundred-grand car. Today I know exactly how he'll respond. Today I am *nervous*.

As a kitten.

One of a squirmy bunch of kittens in a sack.

That can smell the dirty canal water drawing closer.

I'm not sure what I'm doing here, but the fact that I am must mean I'm very brave. Or unspeakably stupid. Think I'll go with brave for now. Definitely *brave*.

'Morning, Murray,' Juliet singsongs from behind a desk that's about as long and as wide as the flight deck of an aircraft carrier – and that probably cost only slightly less to build. 'You look *tired*,' she continues. 'Late night?'

I nod and attempt a smile.

I head for the lift.

Best get this over with.

'God, you are in so much trouble,' Jakki says as I arrive at my desk.

What? She can't know. Can she?

'Niall's back from Paris. Going crazy-ape. Wants to see you . . . What happened at that Schenker meeting the other day?'

Oh, the Schenker meeting. Is that all?

'I'll tell you later,' I say as I slump at my desk.

'Vince has been calling as well,' Jakki continues. 'Wants to know how you got on last night. What've you been up to, then? Anything I should know about?'

'I wrecked Niall's car,' I mumble.

'As if,' she says.

I switch on my computer and open e-mail.

One from Brett.

brett.topowlski@blowermann-dba.co.uk

to: murray.colin@blowermann-dba.co.uk

cc:

re: you dirty rascal

you and saffy! she may sound posh, but her dad was a bus driver. the word on the street (well, on sloane st) is that she polished her technique siphoning derv from routemasters. you jammy twat. drop by and tell all. vin is gagging. trust saffy was too.

Later, Brett.

A second e. This one from Haye.

niall.haye@blowermann-dba.co.uk

to: murray.colin@blowermann-dba.co.uk

cc:

re: WHERE THE HELL ARE YOU?

THE FOLLOWING ASAP, PDQ, ETC.

1. FULL DEBRIEF ON DISASTROUS MEETING W/SCHENKER SO CAN TAKE REQUISITE REMEDIAL ACTION RE MINIMISING NEG

IMPACT ON BUSINESS.

2. EXPLANATION OF CALL JUST RECEIVED FROM LANCASTER PORSCHE ASKING WHY DIDN'T BRING CAR YESTERDAY AS PER ARRANGEMENT.

I've had a thousand shouty e-mails from Niall. Probably more, actually. My standard reaction is to seethe for a bit, but then jump to whatever action is demanded. Today, though, I simply seethe. The man is such a . . . *wanker*.

He wants a debrief? I'll give him a bloody debrief. I decide to knock off the obligatory contact report, expanding the usual distribution list by adding the names of Blower Mann's CEO and creative director. I'm doing them a favour. *Honestly*. Busy, busy men, they spend too much time in shareholder meetings, strategy sessions and lunch (mostly lunch, actually). They should know the goings on of the shop floor.

murray.colin@blowermann-dba.co.uk

to: niall.haye@blowermann-dba.co.uk
        g_breitmar@schenker.com
        s_gilhooley@schenker.com
        b_tofting@schenker.com

cc: brett.topowlski@blowermann-dba.co.uk
        vince.douglas@blowermann-dba.co.uk
        marcus.blower@blowermann-dba.co.uk
        garry.mann@blowermann-dba.co.uk

re: Contact Report No. 46

Brand Group Meeting: 17 December
Venue: the Schenker Bunker
Present for client: Betina Tofting, Gerhard Breitmar (part time)
Present for agency: Murray Colin, Vince Douglas

Murray Colin and Vince Douglas took Betina Tofting through Draft

One of the ChocoChillout launch script. It's fair to say she hated it. Even so, she agreed to forward it for research, which just goes to demonstrate the enduring power of a Duran Duran lyric (you really had to be there).

Murray Colin then presented the script to Gerhard Breitmar. It's fair to say he loved it. He was especially taken with the sequence where his product spills its creamy load into the lead model's mouth. He approved it and agreed that it should be fast-tracked into production.

Gerhard Breitmar expressed concern that this new approach hadn't been presented much sooner. Murray Colin chose not to point out that if it had been, it would have rendered the process far too straightforward, wiped out the need for months of meetings and made several engorged salaries extremely hard to justify.

    Murray Colin
    Account Supervisor

I click *Send Later*, then *New*.

murray.colin@blowermann-dba.co.uk

to: niall.haye@blowermann-dba.co.uk

cc: everyone@blowermann-dba.co.uk

re: Porsche 911 GT2, whereabouts of

Niall – I didn't take your car to the garage yesterday because:

a) It states in the Blower Mann Client Charter, 'A minute not spent contributing to our clients' success is a minute wasted.' In all honesty I couldn't see how taking your Porsche to have its spark plugs changed tallied with this noble aim.

b) I couldn't be bothered.

However, last night I did take the car to Momo. I figured that with all the soul-destroying shite I've carried for you over the years, one night's joyride was the least you owed me. Once at Momo I met Saffy, a successful fashion model, and I agreed to accompany her to her flat in W11. Sadly we never made it. Our journey was terminated by the sudden appearance of a police car at the junction of Pembridge Rd and Notting Hill Gate. The police car sustained relatively light damage, though yours is now a little less than showroom sleek. In my defence, I have to say that the Porsche Stability Management system failed on this occasion to deliver 'significantly enhanced dynamic control.'

The good news – and there is always good news – is that, thank God, no one was hurt. Actually, not entirely true. Saffy sustained a nasty cut to her ear. She does, perhaps, have only herself to blame – she wasn't wearing her seatbelt.

By the way, if you want your car back, it's in a police pound somewhere in west London. Since it is no longer 'the ultimate embodiment of Porsche engineering', be sure to take a tow truck.

Murray

Finished, I hover the PC's pointer over *Send* . . .

Just as Niall has sent me a thousand-plus peevish little e-mails, I have typed a thousand-plus bitter replies. To date I have sent a sum total of none.

I've been too . . . er . . . *professional*.

OK, too scared.

The reality is, despite the radical changes in my circumstances, I still am. Cancer is mutating my insides, but it hasn't changed one thing. Deep down I'm still *me*. Probably always will be, even though *always* no longer means what it used to.

But what am I scared of? However I play this, what are the

chances of me still having a job at five-thirty this afternoon? Somewhere between nil and zero once the truth about Niall's car comes out. That being the case, the damage already being done, would I sooner shuffle wimpishly out of Blower Mann/DBA than go out in a fireball of glory?

Knowing me . . . *Yes*.

I wish I could be more like Vince. I don't want to wallow in drugged-up debauchery – *obviously* – but I'd like to swap my fear for his F.E.A.R. I think of him with his imagined lottery win. Turning it into chips and putting it all on red . . .

I look at the two e-mails in the out box . . . And at the *Delete* and *Send* buttons, just an inch and a half apart on my computer screen.

Delete or *Send*?

Black or *Red*?

Send or *Delete* . . .?

I shut my eyes and oscillate the mouse rapidly from side to side, from *Send* to *Delete* . . . From *Delete* to *Send* . . .

Then . . . *Click*.

A beat later the PC lets gasp a little *ting*. The e-mails are on their way.

I sit back and wait. Terrified. And excited.

Excited or *Terrified*?

Red or *Black*?

Terrified or *Excited* . . . ?

After two minutes and thirty-seven seconds Jakki shrieks, 'Shit on a bloody stick, Murray, you weren't kidding, were you?'

After two minutes and forty-one seconds my phone rings. It's Emma, Marcus Blower's PA. She hasn't spoken to me in nearly a year and Marcus hasn't deigned to say so much as *hullo* in more than two. I should feel *immensely* privileged.

'Darling . . . Marcus would like a word,' she says.

'Shall we put a time in the diary?' I say.

'For God's sake, just get up here now.'

I'm sitting on an ostentatiously large leather sofa – it's firm, flat and black and almost as big as a truck lay-by on the A1. The sofa is in an ostentatiously large office, roomy enough to accommodate an Afghan refugee, his extended family and any livestock he has managed to smuggle out. Of course, no Afghan will ever see this office unless it's late at night and he's clutching a can of furniture polish and a duster. Until today I have only ever seen it from behind the metaphoric velvet rope of Emma's ostentatiously large workstation outside. I was always under the impression that to gain entrance you had to *achieve* something. Be Someone. But, no, all you need do is e-mail a couple of suicide notes.

Fifteen minutes into the meeting I have barely said a word beyond a mumbled 'You wanted to see me?' Neither has Haye. He's on the sofa too, though given its size he's so far away from me that I'd need to hail a cab to reach him.

Silent though we both are, words aplenty are being spat out. By Garry Mann, short and tubby with a creative goatee to compensate for the lack of hair on his scalp. And by Marcus Blower, tall, perma-tanned and slightly shiny, looking as ever like the man Central Casting sent when they were faxed the demand for an ad agency CEO. Nearly all the words are being aimed at Haye, and I'm feeling just a tad piqued – *C'mon, fellas, I thought it was me you were firing.*

Blower: Tell us, Niall, just how long were you planning to allow a lunatic to walk the floors shafting our business up the rectal passage? What do you think we're running here? Care in the fucking Community?

Mann: And what the hell were you thinking allowing a junior suit behind the wheel of that fucking Porsche? . . . By the way,

Marcus, why is Niall driving a *Gee Tee Two* and I have to make to with a Boxster?

(*Make do* with a Boxster. Only in advertising.)

Blower: He's got it because he has over fifty million quid's worth of business in his pocket, Garry ... Jesus, Niall, if you weren't so far up so many client arses I'd fire yours right now.

Mann: We could just take his car away, Marcus.

Colin: I wouldn't worry, Garry. He won't be pulling in it any time soon.

Blower: If you've got any sense left, Collins, you'll zip it.

Colin: It's Colin.

Blower: Excuse me?

Colin: Murray *Colin* – one L, no S. It's just that if you get it wrong on the P-forty-five, I'll have a nightmare when I sign on.

Blower: Get out of my sight. You have ten minutes to clear your desk.

I arrive back on my floor to silence. *Awed* silence. People look at me, unsure whether to say anything. Torn, I should think. Wanting to avoid death by association and at the same time needing to be able to tell people they spoke to me moments after I'd sent *that* e-mail.

A small reception committee waits for me at my desk. Jakki, Brett and Vince. Jakki is red-eyed, but even in tears she has been as thoughtful as ever – she has procured a cardboard box for my personal effects. They don't amount to much.

'Thanks, Jakki,' I say.

'Fuck, I'm really gonna miss you,' she says as she leans into me and hugs me.

I look over her shoulder at Brett and Vince, both of whom are energised. I feel strangely buzzy as well. I never imagined that being fired could feel this *special*. Just now in Blower's office

213

I amazed myself. More than I did last night with the gangsters. More than I ever have. Now I'm an outlaw. A maverick. My inner Jimi Hendrix has downed a bottle of Jack Daniel's and embarked on an ear-popping solo that doesn't sound as if it's going to stop any time before Christmas. Never thought I'd see the day.

'Never thought a suit could be a role model,' Brett says, seeming to read my mind. 'Reckon we owe you several beers.'

'Reckon you do,' I say. 'Be with you as soon as I make this call.'

For the very last time I pick up the phone on my desk and dial.

'Good morning, *Bindinger*, can I help you?' asks the usual crisp voice.

'Megan Dyer, please.'

seventeen: **things**

'Aren't you frightened?'

'Terrified. Every minute of every day, Meg. But I'm also more excited than I've ever been. I'm making things happen rather than just reacting. I can't tell you how good that feels. Being in control. *Wow*.'

'Making *what* happen?'

Good question. You can tell she's a lawyer, can't you? 'You know . . . *Things*.' At this point I wave my hand in the air – meaningfully. 'Good things. You'll see. I'm not going to wimp out any more.'

Megan's brow crinkles up as she tries to figure me out.

We're in a trattoria on Chancery Lane. Nowhere special. So anonymous I still can't remember its name even though I must have eaten here over a hundred times. It's where Megan and I invariably used to meet up after work. I'm having the *tagliatelle Alfredo*. If I've eaten here one hundred and twenty times, then I've had the *Alfredo* one hundred and nineteen. I can remember the occasion I didn't, and went instead for the calf's liver in sage and butter. Bad move. I should have known that Megan's personal veal embargo extended to anyone who came within a one-mile radius of her. Megan as per usual (though, of course, the post-work tratt date ceased being *the usual* some months ago) is having lamb cutlets. A half-drunk bottle of house red sits on the table between us. Neither one of us has dared to say it. And who knows if Megan is even thinking it? But this is . . . whisper it ever so quietly . . . just like old times.

215

'What's the next *thing*, then?' she asks, picking up a lamb bone and tearing off the few remaining scraps of meat with her pretty teeth.

I've told her about being fired, although the version of last night's crash was judiciously edited to exclude the blowjob (which – I'd argue – is fair enough. It's not as if I *wanted* one). She took it in with varying degrees of incredulity, mixed, I hope, with at least a bit of admiration. I may have done no more than squeeze a pimple on global capitalism's backside, but a small coup is surely better than none at all.

'I think I'm going to spend Christmas in Javea,' I announce.

Am I? Where did that come from?

'Visit your mum,' Megan says with an approving nod. 'Good idea.'

'She won't be there. She's cavorting in Marbella with a bent copper and assorted bank robbers. I was thinking I'd just hang out at her villa. You know, chill for a bit.'

Not such a bad idea, now I think about it.

'That sounds lovely,' Megan says.

'It's only Spain. It's not exactly pony trekking in the Andes.'

'Doesn't matter.'

'Or following the Ho Chi Min Trail.'

'So?'

'You always used to have a go at me for my unadventurous taste in holidays.'

'Did not.'

'You don't have to be nice, Meg. Remember when you booked us onto that diving course at the Y so we could go swimming with the rays in the Red Sea?'

She nods. How could she forget me getting water in my ear during my first trip to the bottom of the pool? How could she forget my subsequent diver-entangled-in-kelp-while-sharks-circle-above-style panic attack in less than six feet of chlorine-fresh water? I had to miss the rest of the course. *Sweet* relief.

216

Me swimming with the rays? Come on. I get nervous paddling with the crabs.

'It was hardly your fault, Murray,' Megan consoles.

'Maybe not. But it was kind of indicative of something . . . It was my body's way of telling you what I couldn't.'

'What's that?'

'That, actually, the idea of swimming with the bloody rays terrified me . . . Look at me now. A whole world out there and where am I going for my last Christmas, my last holiday on planet earth? My mum's house. In Spain. Pathetic.'

'Don't say that. It's what *you* want to do. That's the only thing that matters.'

Funny. She didn't say that after the diving disaster. Actually, I think the word *pathetic* might have been tossed around a fair bit in that conversation.

'Anyway,' she goes on encouragingly, 'a week or two in Spain sounds perfect. Lovely. Idyllic. Don't knock it. I wish I could spend—'

'You could,' I blurt out, feeling a crackle of sparks in my gut.

'Come to Spain? I'd really, really like to—'

'Great. Shall I look into the flights?'

'I can't, Murray. Sandy—'

Should've known there'd be a *Sandy*.

'—and I are going to Edinburgh.'

'Oh.' I don't even try to mask my disappointment.

'We're spending Christmas with his parents. They're very old. Virtually—'

'Dead?'

She blushes.

'I'm sorry,' I say. 'That wasn't fair. Here's a thought. Why don't you come out on the twenty-sixth or -seventh or something? Just join me for a few days. You could probably get a flight from Scotland.'

'After Christmas we're going up to the Cairngorms . . . For Hogmanay.'

Hogmanay – Jesus wept.

'The Cairngorms? You *hate* mountains.'

'Sandy wants to take me . . . walking.'

Walking?

Walking?

I am going to lose it now.

Blow any chance I have of talking her into a change of plan.

'*Walking*? You *hate* walking. You *loathe* walking. You completely *detest* walking. We lived three hundred yards from the tube and you complained about the walk. You used to whinge about the walk to the pavement if I parked eight inches from the sodding kerb. You're going to put on a pair of stout *walking* shoes and lug yourself up the side of a big hill? In the *sleet*? You hate sleet more than anything.'

'It might not be sleeting.'

'Mid-winter in the Cairngorms? I'd say the chances of sleet are excellent. What the *hell* is going on, Megan?'

'People change,' she says, a tear rolling down her cheek.

'All I can say is that you must really love the bastard.'

'I do,' she whispers.

'Rotten timing.'

'What?'

'You getting involved with Sandy when you did. If you'd held off for a few months you could've played the grieving widow, then fallen into the arms of Robert the Bruce QC. You'd have saved yourself a sack-load of guilt.'

Jesus, Murray, that was cruel.

'Jesus, Murray,' she says through tears and gritted teeth. 'If you weren't . . .'

'Go on, say it.'

'No. *No*, I won't say it. I think it's best if we just drop it.'

We slump into uncomfortable silence. Me staring out of the

window at the wet, empty street, hating myself for losing my temper, for being so spiteful. Megan snuffling into a linen napkin, possibly hating herself for loving someone else, certainly hating me for drawing attention to it in so vicious a fashion.

I turn to her and watch her dab her eyes with her serviette. I've got to say something to fill this awful void. My mobile goes off, saving me from committing to a platitude. I pull it from my pocket and put it against my ear.

'Muwway? . . . It's Clark.'

As in Kent? Figured that much.

'Be at the corner of Bewwick and Bwoadwick in twenty and we might have something for you.'

In the day's excitement it has somehow slipped my mind that I'm supposed to be getting my . . . um . . . loan. I look at Megan. She's poking at her spinach. Angry. Upset. I can't leave her like this.

'Twenty, OK?' Clark repeats.

'Couldn't we make it later?' I say, but the line has gone dead.

'I've got to go, Meg.'

'Now? What are you doing?'

'Just . . . *things*. . . . Look, I'm sorry about losing it—'

'No, I should be apologising.'

'What the hell for? Falling out of love? It happens. *I'm* sorry.'

Sorry I wasn't more exciting, driven, dynamic . . . I could go on.

A waiter walks past and I ask him for the bill.

'Of course, sir. Will there be anything else?'

'I don't think so.'

I'm looking at Megan as I say it.

10.43 p.m.

I've been standing at the corner of Berwick and Broadwick Streets for over half an hour. Chancery Lane to Soho took me just less than fifteen minutes, so I was slightly early. No sign of Clark, as in Kent. No sign of Little or Large. Perhaps I misheard him and got the wrong address. Or perhaps I heard him perfectly clearly and I should instead have headed for junction of Bewwick and Bwoadwick Stweets – which, I suppose, would be located somewhere in Wotherhithe . . . Or Wuislip . . .

11.31 p.m.

Or Womford . . . Or Woyal Oak . . . Or Wegent's Park . . . Or Woehampton . . .

Woe is about bloody right.

I should have known this would be a waste of time. A wind-up.

I could be making amends with Megan now.

Or at least licking my wounds at home.

Instead of shivering in Soho at chucking-out time.

I've had enough. I pull my jacket across my chest and set off up Berwick Street. I reach Oxford Street and turn right towards Tottenham Court Road and the warming prospect of the tube.

My mobile vibrates again.

'Where the fuck are you, Muwway?'

'I was waiting for you for over an hour, Clark. You told me to meet you in *twenty* minutes.'

'Cowwection, dude, I told *you* to be at Bewwick and Bwoadwick in twenty. Didn't say we'd be there, did I?'

Smart arse.

'OK, OK, sorry. Are you there now?'

'Affirmative. And you have pwecisely sixty seconds to get back here or the deal is off.'

11.35 p.m.

I am *knackered*. Barely living proof that miscellaneous tumours

– and specifically a tumour in the lung – are not conducive to efficient physical performance. I stoop, hands clutching my knees, trying hard not to retch on Clark's brown slippers. They may be the spit of my dad's preferred footwear – under a tenner from Woolies – but I should think they cost Clark several hundred pounds. My heart roars. From exertion. Also from fear. But the fear of cancer is being rapidly overtaken by the terror of the patent-leather dress shoes that are lined up beside the slippers. They are huge – size twenty, if such a thing exists – and they belong to Large, Clark's escort for the evening. I'd forgotten how big he is. Tonight – as well as the standard-issue menacing glare – he's carrying a black attaché case.

'Not in the Porsche tonight?' Clark asks.

'It's in the garage,' I say between pants as I slowly haul myself upright.

'The gawage?' Clark splutters, managing to transmit his alarm to Large.

'No big deal.' The lie compounds my terror and I hope desperately that my exhaustion stops it from showing. 'The PSM system is playing up,' I explain.

'PMS? That is majorly depwessing.'

'Really, it's no big deal. Picking it up tomorrow.'

'*Excellente*, man, *excellente*. Then pwhaps you'd like to step into our office.'

I follow them a few paces along Broadwick Street and then down a dark and narrow alley. We reach a rubbish skip that masks us from passers by. Their office. Should I be thankful for the lack of streetlights? While the darkness conceals my fear, it will also hide my being bludgeoned to death should things turn nasty. Clark clicks his fingers and Large swings the attaché case up to chest height – head height on me. As Clark takes it from him and holds it up, he places his thumbs on the locks and slides the buttons sideways. As he opens the lid I appreciate what Vince meant about coming in his kecks at his *Reader's*

221

Digest shoot. Automatically my hand reaches forward towards the wadded notes.

'Just a mo, Muwway,' Clark says, grabbing my wrist. 'Wemember the terms?'

I nod.

'Apwil the nineteenth?'

'If not before,' I reply.

The bastards.

The cheap *bastards*.

Since they're presuming to make a fifty grand profit from me, they could have at least thrown in the attaché case.

No such generosity.

So here I am, walking towards the ticket barrier at South Woodford tube, clutching one thousand fifty-pound notes to my chest. None of the homeward-bound drunks would know that I'm carrying a small fortune. And if any would-be mugger should whip open my jacket between here and my flat, a branded plastic bag – THE GOLDEN BOSPHORUS KEBAB HOUSE – will be all he'll see. I found it in the skip. I did my best to clean it out, but even so, my crisp, virgin fifties will still reek of raw onions and chilli sauce.

eighteen: **he ain't worth it**

I climb up the stone steps to my building and unlock the front door. Once inside I feel relatively safe so I let the bag slip from my jacket. I peek inside it. Ten fat wads. Each one represents far more money than I've ever seen, let alone possessed.

So why don't I feel happy?

Do I have to spell it out?

Do I have to say that if it cost me fifty grand to beam Megan Dyer from the top of a Scottish mountain to my side, I'd hand over the money in a trice?

Depressed, I trudge towards the stairs. The door to Paula's flat opens a crack and then fully to reveal Apollonia. She's wearing a long black Harley T-shirt, flip-flops and a face like thunder.

'Hi,' I say.

'Thought it was you making that racket,' she snarls, nodding her head towards my flat. I hear it for the first time. A joist-quaking bass line. Not one of mine. *Trance*. Fish must have been CD shopping.

'Sorry. I'll sort it out.'

She slams the door and I head upstairs. Once at my own door I slip the key into the lock and let myself in.

'Fish, turn it down,' I shout down the corridor.

No reply so I head for the living room, push open the door and—

Jesus-bollocking-Christ-not-again.

Fish is on her back on the carpet. She can't move because her arms are pinned to the floor and a body is sitting on her chest. It only takes a moment to figure it belongs to Geordie Psycho.

223

Again he is clutching a gleaming silver object which he has pressed to her throat. This time, though, it isn't Megan's garlic crusher. Megan's garlic crusher isn't nine inches long with a serrated edge. That would be my breadknife. He's leaning towards her, his face close to hers, shouting something – I can't hear over the music. As I stand petrified in the doorway I realise that this is to my advantage – Geordie Psycho can't hear me. Since he has his back to me he can't see me either. Fish could, if she twisted her head my way a little. But she seems to be too preoccupied with the knife at her throat to look around for the SWAT team.

Ha! What's the plan, then, Officer Dibble?

Fair point. What am I going to do? I'm still knackered from my short sprint over an hour ago. My right hand is still bandaged. Geordie Psycho, by contrast, has two good hands and a knife in one of them. He also has a hostage. And he seemingly possesses no concern for health and general wellbeing – his own or anyone else's.

Hang on, matey, neither do you – for your own at least. I mean, you're gonna die soon enough. What's a few weeks early matter? And you'll be a have-a-go hero. Nice touch – beats wimping out on morphine.

Before I've had a chance to weigh it up I'm barrelling across the living room, my head down in what I imagine to be the classic battering-ram position. An unscripted *Braveheart* yell is flying from my throat. Fish turns and watches me steaming towards her, but Geordie doesn't register me until my head connects with his, sending him tumbling to the floor. Now I'm on top of him, and – where the hell did this move come from? Certainly no martial-arts movie I've ever seen – my elbow is pounding repeatedly into his forehead, pile-driver style. On what must be the tenth whack I connect with something softer and more forgiving than skull. I hear the wet crunch of cartilage and I stop. Blood is pouring from his now flattened nose and he drops the knife to clutch it with both hands. I look behind me at Fish. She's sitting up now, looking at me with bemusement and – I think – relief. I look back at Geordie. He's still holding his bleeding nose. 'Yer fookin brurk it, yer cunt.'

I sincerely hope so.

I pick up the knife from the floor and climb off him. My legs are shaking as I stand over him, but my suit trousers are fairly baggy and he's not to know that. He pushes himself backwards across the carpet until he reaches the wall. Then he raises himself to a sitting position.

I always thought that violence sucked. Violence, I'd contend, is ugly and dehumanising, and, while it might win the battle, it never wins the argument. However, I suspected all along that the truth behind my feelings might have been less dignified. Perhaps my abhorrence of violence was because I've never been terribly good at it. Sour grapes, if you like. I mean, all those playground bullies never took time out from beating the daylights out of me to attend peace workshops. No, they loved violence for the simple reason it was something at which they excelled. I loved English and history. Surely no coincidence that I consistently scored As in those very subjects, while when it came to playground bundles I was unclassified.

Now standing gladiatorially triumphant over Geordie, the breadknife in my hand looking not entirely dissimilar to a stubby Roman sword, I'm having to revise my view. Violence is actually *thrilling*. I feel energised. As if the little bit of life that I beat out of my victim has entered into me.

My forehead feels wet. I put my hand to it and realise it's bleeding. The assault on Geordie must have reopened the cut he gave me a few days ago. No pain though – the anaesthetic effect of adrenaline. I feel a thump on the floor. A broom handle. Apollonia, no doubt, on the end of it.

The music.

I go to the stereo and switch it off. Not quite silence, though. I can hear panting. Mine. Geordie's. And Fish's. I turn to her and help her to her feet.

225

'You OK?' I ask.

'Yeah . . . Yeah, I think so.'

Then she walks over to Geordie and gives him a merciless kick in the ribs.

'Don't ever take a knife to me again, you piece of *shit*.'

'I think you'd better leave,' I add.

He climbs unsteadily to his feet and tentatively takes his hand away from his nose. The bleeding has slowed to a dribble.

'Reet . . . urkay . . . I'll be gannin,' he says meekly.

Excellent. Violence not only comes with a king-of-the-world rush. It *works*. Let's face it, once you've won the battle, the argument is, well, academic. I've transformed a vicious potential killer into a slightly awkward houseguest, uncomfortable at outstaying his welcome. Except he hasn't quite finished.

'You wourrn't have owt tuh eat, would yous? Only I'm fookin starvin.'

'Sorry,' I reply with a shake of my head.

'Worraboot yer *kee*bab?'

He's eyeing the Golden Bosphorus bag that I dropped in the doorway.

'It's not a ke—'

Too late. He darts past me, knocking my shoulder and sending me crashing to the floor. I watch him fly through the door, slowing only to grab the plastic bag. I jump to my feet and follow as fast as my rubber legs will carry me. As I slam the front door behind me I hear Fish yell out, 'Come back, you idiot, he ain't worth it.'

She's wrong of course.

1.16 a.m.

I more or less kept pace with him for all of fifty yards before my body gave up. The pain I experienced earlier after the dash to meet Clark was nothing next to what I'm feeling now, watching Geordie sprint like a thief into the distance. How much faster would he be going if he knew the bag contained fifty grand rather than a kebab? Feeling utterly defeated I slump against a parked car. A navy blue Polo.

My navy blue Polo.

I pat my pockets for my keys. They're there in my trousers. Two for my flat and one for the car. This is almost certainly going to be a waste of time – I haven't tried to start it for over three months, and when I did the engine offered no more than a half-hearted wheeze before dying – but it's my only hope. I unlock the door and climb in. I put the key in the ignition and my foot on the accelerator. Then I close my eyes and turn the key.

Something happens. The starter motor rasps into action. Insufficient to get the engine going, but more than I expected. I ease out the choke and try again. This time the engine splutters and almost picks up enough momentum to get going. In a panic I pump the accelerator and it dies. Frightened of flooding it, I ease the choke back in and turn the key a third time. The starter winds up . . . The engine turns over . . . Then fades . . . Then suddenly . . . No, *miraculously* . . . surges into life. I look in the mirror at the dense cloud of black smoke that's pouring from the exhaust. I'm fairly sure that's not a good sign. But the engine is *going*. I put it into gear, lift the clutch and feel the car roll forward.

Maybe this will be my lucky night.

I pull out into the street and set off in search of a spring-heeled Geordie thug.

What the hell was I thinking? That I'd turn a couple of corners and there he'd be, perhaps leaning on a lamppost recovering his breath? He had a good five-minute start on me and he could be anywhere now. I've spent the last hour covering more or less every inch of South Woodford and even parts of neighbouring Snaresbrook. Of course I haven't seen him. Who was I trying to kid?

I feel exhausted and desperately dejected as I drive slowly up Hermon Hill towards my flat. The Polo reflects my mood. It barely has the energy to escape the thick fumes spewing from its exhaust. I drop down to third and floor the accelerator, but the speedometer refuses to register anything above twenty-five. Fittingly it's chucking down.

I sense something on my tail and glance up at the mirror. Through the rain and smoke I can see the lights of a following car. It's so close that it must be in danger of nudging my bumper. Suddenly it pulls out into the middle of the road and speeds past me . . . Like everything else in my useless life.

I watch the car – a smugly sleek and silver BMW – and I feel raw, painful jealousy as it accelerates away . . . then suddenly brakes. It slows rapidly but not nearly enough to avoid the dark blur that has darted off the pavement and in front of it. I watch the blur become an airborne figure, sent back the way it came by the BMW's nearside wing. The figure hits the road headfirst and bounces – actually *bounces* – before coming to rest in a heap near the pavement. Though I'm easily a hundred yards behind and my speed hardly makes impact with anything imminent, I hit my brakes. I stop fifty yards short of the body. I look beyond it and see that the BMW has stopped as well. I open my door and climb out into the rain. I walk towards the motionless body fully expecting someone to emerge from the BMW . . . But shockingly it starts to inch forward . . . then accelerates and disappears up the hill in a fog of spray thrown up by its tyres.

I continue towards the heap in the road. It hardly looks like a body from here. Just a pile of wet, dirty clothes. I can make out limbs, but they don't seem to be connected in any way that could be described as anatomically correct. I'm only twenty feet away now and I'm fairly certain that I'm looking at my first dead body. Something else is on the ground a few feet away from it. A white carrier bag with—

I do not believe this.

—a kebab-house logo on it.

In the blackest way possible this is my lucky night.

I'm not certain, but I think I did the right thing.

At least I think I didn't do too many *wrong* things.

Think isn't good enough, though. I have to *know*, and I spend the painfully slow drive back to my flat reliving every second of the last fifteen minutes.

When I got to Geordie's body I crouched down to look at him. His eyes were open but there was no sign of life. The top of his head was smashed open, but there was little blood that hadn't been diluted and flushed away by the rain.

I did a wrong thing then. But it was entirely involuntary. I threw up.

Next I pressed my ear to his chest and listened for a heartbeat. Nothing. So I sat back and looked around. It was after two o'clock, but this was London, and surely someone else should have driven past by now, curtains should have been twitching. No movement. No sound apart from the rain and the distant hum of traffic someplace else. It was as if this bit of suburbia had been suddenly depopulated.

Hard to say precisely why what I did next was wrong – it just *felt* that way. I stood up and retrieved the Golden Bosphorus bag. I looked inside it at the money. It was difficult at this point to think of it as *mine*. It had almost certainly been dirty money before I got my hands on it – tainted by trafficking in drugs, people or both. Now it was smeared with death. But that didn't stop me stuffing the bag into my waistband.

Then I almost did a right thing. I reached into my pocket, pulled out my mobile and dialled 999. But I cut the line while it was still ringing. Mobile calls can be traced. I didn't want to be connected with Geordie's death. Anyway, I reasoned that there wasn't any hurry. The fastest ambulance crew would still have been too late. And what was I going to tell the police when I inevitably had to talk to them? I certainly didn't want to get into the whys and wherefores of my pursuit. But after I'd driven off I pulled up at a call box and called 999 from there. Then I continued for home, my duty done, my conscience still muddied as hell.

As I park I brace myself to tell Fish the news about her boyfriend/squat mate/would-be murderer. I still have no idea what he was to her.

Boyfriend/squat mate/would-be murderer? All three as it happened. He was the first two until they broke into my flat. After that he simply wanted to kill her. Why? ''Cause I didn't follow him? 'Cause I went for the central heating and the hot bath, and left him on the street? 'Cause he thought I was shagging you? Fuck knows. Headcases like him don't need a reason.'

Earlier tonight she'd gone out for milk and fags and bumped into him outside the corner shop. He'd made her take him back to the flat. 'You saved my life, you know. If you hadn't come home when you did, I'd be dead now,' was Fish's response to the news of his demise. She took it – is this the right word? – well. Matter-of-factly, anyway. As if it was only a matter of time. The thing that amazes her is that I returned intact. 'You got lucky when you jumped him earlier,' she says as we sit on the living-room carpet, trying to ignore the large bloodstain from Geordie's nose. (I'm sorry, because this is an entirely inappropriate thought,

230

but I can't help it. When it comes to stains I *know* my stuff and that blood will *never* come out.)

'No offence,' Fish says, 'but I don't see you as a scrapper. And he's the most vicious bastard *ever*. I can't believe you went after him. Mad wanker – him, not you. He died for a doner kebab? Should put that on his fucking gravestone.'

'Not exactly a doner.' I reach into my waistband and pull out the bag. 'Have a look,' I say, passing it to her.

'Jesus. *Fuck*,' she explodes. 'You rob a fucking bank or something?'

'Or something.'

It was a front. Fish's cool reaction to Geordie's – I've discovered that his name was Andy – death. She kept it up for over an hour, but the dam broke around four o'clock. It was ugly and hysterical. But at least having to deal with it took my mind off my own discomforts – mental and physical. It stopped only a little while ago and she's asleep now. I'm sitting on the chair in my bedroom watching her.

I tried to sleep, but my body hurt despite my having tipped the last of my aspirin, paracetamol and ibuprofen into my stomach. And when I did finally drift off I started to dream of the Megan-shaped hole in my life, watching it fill up with crap.

So I gave up.

I stand up and pull the covers around Fish's shoulders. Then I head for the living room and sit down at my PC. I switch it on and try to ignore that *bloody* stain as it goes online. Then I head for lastminute.com – which is grimly appropriate – and check out their prices for flights to Alicante.

nineteen: **i know where i can get one**

I open the curtains, put a mug of coffee onto the bedside table and gently rock Fish's shoulder. She opens her eyes and looks at me.

'Hi . . . How do you feel?' I ask.

She shrugs.

Then looks at the rain beating relentlessly against the window.

'Fucking shit. Happy fucking *Christmas*,' she says.

Which more or less sums it up.

'Fancy going away somewhere?'

'Fancy anywhere other than here.'

'You got a passport?'

'Yeah, sure. Us runaways never leave home without it.'

Oh well, it was worth a shot.

Then with a hint of a grin she says, 'I know where I can get one.'

twenty: **whoops-a-fucking-daisy**

I stand with my hands clamped over my ears, trying to block out the alarm, which is the loudest I've ever heard. I hope to hell it isn't the kind of security system that's wired to a police station. Mind you, I don't suppose there's any need for that – it's so deafening that the NYPD must be able to hear it.

This was a *mad* idea.

This, actually, has been something of a mad day.

Which, given the high levels of insanity in recent weeks, is quite a statement.

After Fish got up we went to a florist where she bought a scraggy bunch of white carnations. Then we walked to Hermon Hill. We would have driven – I thought I could coax one last journey out of my car – but when we reached the spot where I'd parked, it had gone. It took me a moment to realise it had been stolen. Which almost made me laugh. How far was the thief going to get in it? Hardly the motor for a *joy*ride. The old me immediately knee-jerked into life – *call the police, insurance* – but then my inner Jimi Hendrix kicked in and told me to shut the fuck up, before embarking on a psychedelic, feedback-happy version of the national anthem.

I found the spot easily enough. One of those yellow police signs was standing on the kerb; the sort that appeals for witnesses. As Fish laid the bouquet at the foot of the nearest lamppost I looked around nervously, waiting for a police snatch squad to leap from nowhere and bundle me into a van. No, I didn't feel comfortable being there. Scared, guilty, more than a little sad for the Geordie psycho – all of that. Fish stood there

233

for a minute or two, adding a few of her own tears to the pouring rain. Then she said, 'C'mon, then, let's fuck off out of here.'

We headed for the station and got the tube to Hampstead. We walked through the rain to Frognal Lane. Our destination was a detached house hidden from the road by a garden planted with lush evergreens. I followed Fish through the gate and after scoping the place for a minute, she picked up a reproduction millstone – a doughnut of rock twelve inches in diameter – from a flowerbed. I watched her, wondering what she was going to do with it. Then in a remarkable display of strength she hefted it through the pretty, multi-paned window next to the front door.

I must be very naïve. I honestly thought she had a key.

'What the hell are you doing?' I shouted, but the alarm had kicked off and she couldn't hear me.

She took off her jacket, folded it, laid it across the vertical spikes of glass and climbed deftly through the hole.

Leaving me on the doorstep.

Which is where I am now.

Wishing I was someplace else.

Someplace I can't hear the world's loudest burglar alarm.

Another planet, then.

The wailing stops as abruptly as it started. A few seconds later the door swings open and I'm greeted by Fish. 'It gives you three goes at punching in the code. I got it first time,' she says proudly. 'The dozy gits haven't changed it in years.'

She turns and I follow her into the house. It's as impressive on the inside as it was from the garden. A big, wood-panelled hall, a wide staircase with ornately carved banister spindles and newel posts. Above the hall table an oil painting of a feline woman reclining on a chaise longue. No idea of the artist, but not Rolf Harris.

A question popped into my head on the tube when Fish first

revealed that her parents live in Hampstead. It strikes me even harder as I gaze at the opulence surrounding us. It is, of course, *Why did you leave this for a cardboard box?* I didn't ask it on the train and I'm not about to now. Whatever it was that made her flee must have been dire. If she'd wanted me to know, she'd have told me.

'Go in the front room. Make yourself at home,' she says. 'I'll go upstairs and look for my passport.'

'What if someone comes back?' I ask.

'They won't.'

'How can you be sure?'

'My dad's a Chelsea fan. He takes my kid brother to home games. They've got Middlesbrough today – I checked.'

'What about your mum?'

'Don't worry about her. It's December.'

'So?'

'She spends December in Italy. Any excuse to get out of this shit-hole.'

Of course. Christmas and the time-honoured tradition of mothers fleeing their children, leaving them to bake their own mince pies.

'What if someone heard the alarm and called the police?' I ask.

'Can tell you haven't done this before. This is Hampstead. The bigger and more expensive your house, the less of a fuck you give about your neighbours. Believe me, no one's calling the cops.'

She bounds up the staircase. A girl with a mission. I follow her suggestion and head for the sitting room. I flick on the light and take it in. The heavily ruched curtains. The excess of embroidered and tasselled throw cushions. The monumental slab of white marble fireplace. The grand piano, its lid covered with photo frames. Three sofas so vast and plumped that if you lost your change in them you'd never ever find it again. Though I don't suppose they worry about stuff like that round here. It's a *shit-hole* fit for *Hello!*.

I flop into one of the sofas and . . . several seconds later I'm still sinking. When I finally come to rest – touch bottom – I think about lighting a fag (that's right. I'm a smoker now. I bought my first packet this morning), but it doesn't seem to be the right thing to do. *So* me. I'm even intimidated by soft furnishings.

I sit and listen to the distant noise of Fish. It sounds as if she's tearing the house apart. She said the family's passports were kept in a box in her father's study. Perhaps hers wasn't with the others and she's turning the place over.

She told me nothing about her family before today and very little on the way here. Her dad is 'something in TV' – judging by the address, not a studio technician. Her mum is 'a point-less pisshead'. Her little brother was 'born with a silver spoon up his arse.' That was all I got. The gritted teeth through which she told me that much made me shy away from probing any deeper. I am very curious though.

No time to dwell on the matter because my mobile goes off. It's Jakki.

'I can't believe they did it to you, the *bastards*,' she blurts before I've even said hello. Her outburst shatters the squishy bliss of my bask in the sofa. I'm surprised. She was upset in the immediate aftermath of my firing yesterday, but nothing like this. And once we'd had a few leaving beers she'd perked up. By the time I left her, Vince and Brett to meet Megan she even seemed to be sharing my sense of triumph. So I have no idea what has brought on this attack of grief.

'It's cool, Jakki,' I reassure her. 'Please don't be upset because I'm not.'

'But it's just so cruel. To do it to you when you're . . . God, it's *disgusting* . . . When you're . . .' She can't get the words out and I'm putting two and two together and coming up with Vince, way too much beer and a flapping mouth.

'What's Vince told you?' I demand.

'That you've got . . .'

'And who the hell else did he tell?'

'Just Brett. Don't blame him, Murray. He only told us because he cares.'

'And what, he claimed that I got fired despite the fact they knew I was ill?'

'Well . . . Kind of. He actually said they did it *because* you were ill. You know . . . They thought you'd have a bad effect on morale. Isn't that how it happened?'

'No it is *not*. They don't know about it. Jesus, I am seriously pissed off about this, Jakki,' I rage, ignoring her growing sobs. 'This is *my* business. *My* life – what's bloody left of it. *I* decide who knows.'

'Sorry.'

'It's not your fault. I'm not mad at you,' I say, calming down a little. 'You haven't told anyone else, have you?'

A long, painful silence. Then: 'It was just the one person. Honestly.'

'*Who*?'

'Stevie Tyler,' she says weakly. 'No one else. I swear.'

The name rings a bell. *I know.* Steve Tyler. Drug-ravaged Aerosmith front man. She couldn't mean him, surely?

'Who's he?' I ask.

'*She* . . . She works for . . . *Campaign*.'

'Jesus *Christ*,' I explode as the penny finally drops.

Over the next few minutes I drag it out of her. Yesterday evening she returned to work in a state of drunken distress. She stormed into Blower's office, determined to upbraid him for his brutality. He wasn't there, but she did bump into Stevie Tyler, the *Campaign* reporter assigned to cover Blower Mann among other agencies. Jakki only knows her from having to serve her coffee on her regular visits, but it didn't stop her spilling the beans.

'You could have told anyone, Jakki,' I yell. 'Your mum. One of the cleaners. A bloody priest. *Anyone*. Why did you have to tell *her*? You might as well have rented a helicopter and showered the West End with leaflets.'

'I told her off the record. That means she can't report it.'

'For Christ's sake, it means she can't report that *you* gave her the story. After that she can write anything she bloody likes. What else did you give her? My shoe size? Inside leg measurement?'

'Nothing . . . Just your phone number. She was *really* concerned. She wanted to talk to you . . . You know, to see if there was anything—'

I cut her off.

I'm standing now. At some point I must have jumped to my feet. I've been this angry before – rarely – and my usual inclination is to jam a fat cork in it until eventually it settles. This time, though, I want to lay into someone. Vince would be ideal. I make do with pacing the thick Persian rug. I feel nauseous though, and I have to stop and steady myself. I put my hands out and lean on the piano. I close my eyes and listen to Fish tossing furniture upstairs. The nausea fades and I find myself wondering why I'm so upset. What's the big deal about people knowing?

From the moment I fled the hospital I've felt in charge of my life – for the *first* time in my life. I may be making some bizarre decisions, but at least they're *mine*. I have no faith in my power to resist and I'm afraid that once everyone knows I'll be sucked back into the flow of things and meekly go along with *other people's* choices.

I'm buggered now, though. The pre-Christmas *Campaign* will probably carry a small item on me. I've never been in the advertising mag. I've never done anything remotely interesting enough to warrant it – ACCOUNT SUPERVISOR SUCCESSFULLY COMPLETES 100th STORE CHECK wouldn't have been much of a

238

headline. But I've finally achieved something that makes me newsworthy. I've got a disease.

Of course, all of this makes escape even more pressing. I hope Fish can find her passport. But even if she can't I'm on the first plane out of here.

It's gone quiet upstairs. Maybe I should go up and see how she's doing. I'm still leaning on the piano and I look at the photographs that cover it. Pictures of a happy family. Handsome dad, immaculate mum and toothsome son. No Fish – obviously the victim of some Stalinist airbrushing. Either that or this isn't her family home and she simply fancied an afternoon of upmarket housebreaking.

But Fish *is* in these pictures. I pick up a silver frame containing Mum and Dad sitting on a veranda against a backdrop of what can only be described as Tuscany. And there she is. She's in her dad. Unmistakably. The same strong mouth. The same tiny cleft at the tip of the nose. And – take away Fish's riveted brows, draw back the curtain of hair – the same liquid eyes. I stare at the picture . . .

. . . And feel my jaw drop.

I know this man. He has been in my living room on several occasions.

Something in TV all right.

Richard Hyam-Glass. Daytime telly's Mr Empathy. Former minister and bung-taker. The shit who persuaded his daughter to perjure herself at his libel trial. The shit who persuaded *Fish* to perjure herself. My mind rewinds to the first time I saw her. Now I know why she looked familiar. Of course, when her picture was splattered across the front pages she was only thirteen. Her hair was its genetic mousy colour and her face was free of grime and metalwork. And, of course, she wasn't called Fish. What was her name? Damned if I can remember now. I fast-forward to Megan meeting her at my flat – stoned and dishevelled in my dressing gown – and experiencing an incomprehensible flash of recognition. Megan spent every day of Hyam-Glass's libel trial in court, and studied Fish at close quarters while Sandy Morrison annihilated both her and her father's case.

I'm still staring at the picture when I hear a noise behind me and jump. 'C'mon, let's get the fuck outta here,' Fish says for the second time today. As on the first occasion at Hermon Hill I don't need a further invitation. We crunch across the broken glass in the hall and out of the front door. We both freeze as bright white light dazzles us. I squint and see a black four-by-four pull into the drive. Someone is home and we've been caught in the headlights. The car draws to a halt and I look at Richard Hyam-Glass in the driving seat. He's looking at us. No, not us. At Fish. His expression is a mixture of surprise and fear. He wasn't expecting this and it seems he doesn't want it either. I look at Fish and say, 'Do you want to stay . . . ? Talk to—'

'Fucking *run!*' she yells.

――――――――――――――――――――――――――――― 6.32 p.m.

I've been waiting for her to speak since Hampstead. As we climb onto a Central Line train at Tottenham Court Road, she breaks the silence: 'Your telly wasn't fucked when I got it in off the roof. I dried it in front of the radiator and it worked fine.'

'What happened to it, then?'

'I kicked it over and it kind of went *phut.*'

I don't say anything.

'I'm sorry . . . But when I turned it on . . . *he* was on it.'

I put my arm round her.

She pushes it away, angry.

――――――――――――――――――――――――――――― 7.29 p.m.

We're sitting in a curry house. By the time our biryanis arrive

I feel bold enough to go for the big one. 'Why did you run away?' I ask.

'I didn't. He kicked me out.'

'On the day you got your GCSEs? They can't have been that bad.'

'They weren't. Four As and five Bs. He'd just had enough of me. Figured he'd done his parental bit. Seen me through school. So he told me to piss off.'

'What did your mum have to say?'

'She wasn't there. She was in Italy. *Trial separation*.'

'Were you like . . . You know . . .'

'A teenage tearaway? I wasn't perfect. I did the usual boys and drugs and staying out late stuff, but no worse than any of my mates. Honestly, I wasn't *that* bad. We just didn't get on. Never did.'

'But after what he put you through at his trial, don't you think he owed you?'

'He didn't put me through anything. Getting up in court and lying for him was *my* idea. I persuaded him to let me do it.'

'Why?'

'All I wanted him to do was . . . I just wanted to win him over, I suppose. Stupid, huh? After I fucked it up for him . . . Well, we were doomed after that.'

'You didn't fuck anything up. You were *thirteen*. He should never have let you do it. Apart from anything else he should have known how vicious Channel Four's barrister was capable of being.'

'That cunt? I still have nightmares about him.'

You and me both.

'You know, maybe your dad really regrets it now . . . Maybe you should have stayed today. Maybe that would have been your chance to—'

'I couldn't have stayed. I totalled his study.'

241

'Looking for your passport?'

'No, found that straightaway . . . I did it because I felt like it. It's *his* room. A fucking shrine to him. He's got this shelf full of awards. One of them was for Best Daytime Programme . . . I put it through his computer screen. He's mad about awards. And he *loves* his computer. His whole life's on it. I went through his files. Nearly finished volume two of his memoirs by the looks of it.'

'If he has any sense he'll have backed up.'

'Yeah, I did think of that,' she says resignedly.

Then she reaches into her jacket. She pulls out a bulging passport, holds it over the ashtray and empties out a small stack of disks.

_____ 8.17 p.m.

We changed subjects after that. I told her about the call from Jakki. Fish's reaction was a shrugged *so what*. 'Why care who knows? It's your life, man. Fuck 'em.'

Which, knowing her as I do now, was exactly what I'd expected her to say. Know what? I found it comforting.

As our coffees arrive I decide to go back to it.

'What were you called back then?'

'If I tell you, promise you'll never call me it?'

'OK.'

'Isabel,' she spits.

'*Isabel* . . . That's a lovely—'

'I fucking *hate* that name. *Understand*?'

'OK . . . You never answered my question earlier. Why haven't you got in touch with your dad?'

'He tried to find me,' she says, emptying a third sachet of sugar into her cup. 'About a year ago I got in touch with Jody – she was my best mate at school. Dunno why, but I was really depressed. Anyway, she told me I had to go home. She said my dad was going out of his mind and that he'd hired a detective to find me.'

'See what I mean? The guilt must be doing his head in.'

'This was over a year after he'd chucked me out,' she snaps. 'Why did he suddenly feel bad and want to find me?'

'Sometimes it takes time to do the right thing.'

'How long has the bastard had his TV show?'

'I don't know . . . About a year, I suppose.'

'Don't you fucking get it? He tried to find me when he got the deal. As soon as he was about to get his face out there again he got scared. I could *ruin* him with the shit I know. You saw how frightened he looked today. He doesn't want to find me because I'm his kid . . . I'm just a fucking time bomb.'

'So why don't you?'

'What, rat him out?'

'You could go to someone like Max Clifford, cut a deal with a tabloid, make some money. They'd love to get their hands on you. I'm surprised they haven't come looking for you already . . . I mean, you were *famous*.'

'They only haven't looked for me 'cause he's told 'em I'm backpacking in China or somewhere.'

'Well, he's kind of right – east London rather than East Asia.'

She's not smiling.

'Sorry . . . Hang on, how come you know what he's telling the press about you?'

She looks down at her food.

'You keep up with him, don't you?'

'Fucking don't,' she lies, poking at a piece of chicken.

'Look, you obviously care about him. I think you should get in touch and—'

'I don't give a *shit* about him, right? End of story.'

My turn to poke at a piece of chicken.

'I've thought about going to the papers,' she says after a couple of minutes. 'Ruining the twat.'

243

'What's stopped you?'
'What do you think? He's my dad.'

There are two messages on the machine when we get back to the flat. I press *play*.

'Whoops-a-fucking-daisy,' singsongs Vince – chock-a-block with remorse then. 'Just had a call from Jakks. Can't remember much from yesterday, but she tells me I fucked up. Sorry, Muzza. Beer talking and all that. Gimme a bell and I'll make it up to you. Promise. But don't call tonight. Obviously. It's fucking Saturday, innit?'

The second message is an unfamiliar voice: 'Hi . . . Hi. I'm trying to reach Murray Colin. Hope I've got the right number.' (The likely reason for her uncertainty is that it's still Megan's voice on the announcement – I haven't been able to bring myself to delete it.) 'Anyway. Right. My name's Stevie Tyler. From *Campaign* . . . Magazine. Anyway. OK. I just hoped you might be able to help me. Vis-à-vis a story I'm following up. To do with. Er. Your apparent. Um. Departure from Blower Mann. Anyway. Be vee, *vee* grateful if you could call me. And sorry to disturb you on a Saturday. Bye, then . . . Oh, yes. *Duh*! My number . . .'

She has left three phone numbers, a pager code and an e-mail address. She really does want me to get in touch.

'Vulture,' I mutter.

'You're not gonna call her back, then?' Fish asks.

'Why should I?'

'Well, the cat's out of the bag now . . . And she'll talk to your old bosses.'

'So?'

'Bet they've got some lovely things to say about you.'

She has a point.

I pick up the phone.

244

twenty-one: **it's gonna be chocker with dusky totty**

Fish and I wait by the Victoria taxi rank.

'He should've been here over fifteen minutes ago,' I mutter.

'Chill. He's got a kid to organise. That can't be easy,' Fish says.

'How would you know?'

My irritability has been growing these past couple of days and other people's tardiness bugs me as never before ... Like I'm running out of time.

'I'll give him another two minutes and then we're—'

I stop as a beaten-up Toyota screams into the station, cutting up a black cab before pulling up in front of us. The door bursts open and Vince tumbles out clutching a multicoloured collection of bloated carriers and – though my eyes don't quite believe it – a bucket and spade.

'Got here in under fifteen minutes. Sanjay Schumacher at the wheel.' He turns and beams at the Asian minicab driver, who beams back – obviously on the receiving end of a generous tip. Vince dumps the bags at our feet and climbs back into the cab. He re-emerges clutching his double. Except she's barely two feet tall. Any curiosity I might have had regarding what Muttley looked like as a puppy is now satisfied.

'C'mon, Bubbles,' Vince tells her. 'Let's say hello to your Uncle Muzza.'

245

Before I can object, I'm holding her. I'm not used to children and my body has stiffened. She doesn't seem to mind, though, and asks, 'Are we at Spain now?'

Verbal skills: C+.

Geography: Unclassified.

The Gatwick Express slides through Croydon. Vince and I raise stiff fingers in the general direction of the Schenker Bunker.

'What's that for?' asks Fish.

'Old times' sake,' I explain.

Vince has Bubbles on his lap and he's helping her open a packet of Quavers. One of his many carriers contains nothing but Quavers, Hula-Hoops, Monster Munch and Cheesy Puffs – 'In case she's funny with foreign food.'

'Was her mum cool about you taking her away for Christmas?' I ask.

'She was hysterical, but she's like that if I take Bubbles out to the park.'

'Mummy is gone to get her bum wash'ded,' Bubbles announces.

'She's booked herself in to some spa. She's having the Deluxe Colonic Flush.' Vince expands. 'They'll find bugger all up there, mind.' Then cooing to Bubbles, 'Mummy doesn't eat up all her din-dins, does she, baby-boo?'

I have got to tell you, this is *freaky*. Vince with tot on lap. Vince indulging in squeaky baby talk. Actually, it is bloody weird that Vince, the man who shopped me to my secretary who shopped me to the trade press, is here at all.

After spending the rest of my weekend fuming about him, we finally spoke on Monday. By then I simply wasn't that angry any more. Grudges have never been my thing. As they say, life's too short. Besides, when I called him I had reason to feel bad on his behalf. He'd only just emerged from Garry Mann's office. He'd been fired.

After my e-mails they decided to have a purge, though it wasn't exactly a Cultural Revolution in its scope – it started with me and ended with Vince. They couldn't forgive him for his unauthorised visit to Schenker.

'I'm really sorry, Vince,' I said. 'That was my fault.'

'Muzza, it's cool. It keeps my record up.'

'What record?'

'Being fired. Three jobs. Three firings.'

'That's not good, CV-wise.'

'Nah, keeps me on my toes. And saves me writing a resignation letter. That'd be a calamity. Can't spell to save my fucking life.'

'What's Brett going to do now?'

'Wants to resign in sympathy. That's what he did the last two times. Told him he'd be mad. Told him to think about it over Christmas . . . Then, if he ain't followed me out by the end of Jan, I'll never talk to the cunt again.'

'So, what you doing for Christmas?' I asked.

'I've got Bubbles. We'll just hang out in Battersea. Maybe go to a panto or some shite on ice.'

'Fancy coming to Spain?'

He was thrilled at the invitation. He sees it as more of a research trip than a holiday. A chance to check out the marinas for submarine access, as well as to indulge his hobby and meet some real crooks. I explained that my mum's house in Javea is several hundred miles from the Costa del Crime, but that didn't put him off. He figures there must be some overspill.

'You never know, maybe Sharkey's got a gaff there. It'd be like him to retire somewhere off the beaten track,' Vince speculated. Some people dream of spotting Elvis/Tupac/the blonde bloke from the Sweet in their local launderette. Vince Douglas has fantasies about running into a crime legend – one vicious enough to have committed several murders and wily enough to have gotten away with it.

—————————————————————————— 11.47 a.m.

The train pulls into Gatwick and Bubbles asks, 'Are we at Spain now?'

—————————————————————————— 12.21 p.m.

We've checked in our luggage. One suitcase. Mine. It contains everything I need, plus all of Fish's worldly goods, which fitted in the zip-up pocket that runs down the case's length and still left room for my toiletries. Vince wasn't prepared to check through his carrier bags. All of them contain items that Bubbles may need at *any moment*. This transformation in Vince is remarkable. Watching him simultaneously wield wet wipes, a small stuffed kitten and a non-spill cup is like watching a master juggler. He still looks and sounds like the drug-addled drummer from a not especially *together* indie band, but he's acting like a supermum in a Pampers ad.

Now we're trailing through the departure lounge, Vince's carrier bags stacked on a trolley, Bubbles on top of the heap like a chubby pink cherry. Fish isn't with us. I was worried about the fact that she was travelling so light. Well, what's she going to wear by the pool? One of her three pairs of knickers plus her single tattered bra? I sent her shopping with three fifties. She took some persuading.

For someone who has until recently made her living from begging and stealing she's surprisingly reluctant to take my money. She didn't want me to buy her plane ticket. 'We're going on Tuesday. How will you raise the cash in two days?' I asked.

'I can get it in fifteen minutes if I pick the right house.'

'You're not doing that to someone just before Christmas. I've been burgled, remember? It's a pretty crappy experience.'

'You seemed happy enough doing it to my mum and dad.'

'That was . . . *different*.'

It was too. She was simply going home to pick up some stuff . . . with menaces.

'Anyway,' I went on, 'you might get caught.'

'I can't take your money, man,' she said firmly.

'It's not *my* money. I *stole* it.'

'You *borrowed* it.'

'Oh, and just when do you think I'm going to pay it back?'

I rested my case there and we headed for the travel agent.

'So, you and her? You know, are you . . .?' Vince asks me in the duty-free shop.

'Are her and me *what*?'

'You know,' he says, executing a couple of unsubtle hip thrusts.

'*No.*'

'Why not?'

'Why should we be?'

'She's pretty cute . . . for street slime. And you're bankrolling her, aren't you?'

'Oh, is that how it works? Basically, you cover their financial needs and they repay in flesh?'

'I wouldn't've put it like that, but I s'pose . . . yeah.'

'Well, thanks for setting me straight, Vince. I never realised you had to *pay* for it. No wonder my sex life has been such a nonevent.'

'No need to be sarky. I just wondered, that's all.'

'Look, Fish and I are just mates. Anyway, I don't feel much up to . . . *that* at the moment.'

'Sorry. Wasn't thinking. So if you and her ain't . . . You know . . . Do you mind if I give it a whirl?'

'Er . . . Feel free. You fancy her, then?'

'Well, she's got tits under that baggy clobber, hasn't she?'

'She's a fantastic girl, Vince. And not as tough as she makes out. You'd better not muck her about,' I say, not really knowing from where this well of fatherly concern has suddenly sprung.

'Would I?'

'Yes.'

'I'll treat her like royalty, I swear.' Then looking at Bubbles, 'Wouldn't want my wickle pwincess gwowing up thinking all men are bastards, would we?'

12.39 p.m.

I'm standing in Waterstones looking at the books.

This is taking me *ages*.

I've always taken the pre-holiday airport book browse seriously. Like a lot of people I only read on holiday – three books a year crammed into a fortnight. This being so, it was important to get it right and the process always took me an unnervingly long time. Unnerving, that is, for Megan. Typically she'd make her selection in two or three minutes. Then, as I agonised, she'd drum her heels naggingly at my side, waiting for the Tannoy announcement: *This is the final call for passenger Colin to make up his bloody mind between Patricia Cornwell and Kathy Reichs (as if there's a difference anyway) and get on the sodding plane . . . And put back the Proust. You'll just look like a ponce reading that by the pool.*

This time, though, it is pure *hell*.

Because as I sift through the titles, reading the back-cover blurb, trying to make *important* decisions based on overblown copy and slyly edited review quotes something *big* strikes me. These will be the last books I ever read.

Jesus Christ, as if the whole fucking book-buying thing wasn't tough enough already.

All the slightly pissed conversations I've ever had come back to me; the stupidly hypothetical ones that start *If you could shag one woman/see one film/listen to one album before you die, who/what would it be?* Dumb filler conversations. Conversations where the answers to the questions simply didn't matter so long as they got a laugh.

Well, now they do. The answer to *every* question matters *intensely*.

Romance or thriller? Ellroy or Leonard? Coffee or tea? Aquafresh or Colgate? Everything is final. Absolutely.

Does the condemned man have any last requests?

Quite a few, actually. Trouble is that all this pressure you're putting me under is *not* helping me to make up my mind.

'Earth to Colin . . . Earth to Colin . . . You in a trance, Muzz?' Vince is getting good at timing his interruptions. He invariably manages to grab me as I teeter on the edge, about to plummet into the bottomless abyss of despair.

'Can't decide,' I say.

'Well, you don't wanna bother with that bunch of arse,' he says, pointing at *Howard's End* at the top of my pile. 'I had it at school. Thought the title was a knob gag, but there ain't no fucker called Howard in it, let alone his veiny schlong.'

He's right – about putting the book back, and also, I suspect, about the absence of schlongs. I only picked it up because it's one of the several dozen English classics that I haven't read and I felt that, well, I *should*. Ridiculous. Aren't I supposed to have stopped doing things because I *should*? I toss it back onto the display and head for the till with the fourteen other titles in my grasp. As I peel two fifties from my roll and hand them over to the cashier I spot the copy of *Campaign* beneath Vince's arm. I'd forgotten it was coming out today.

'Where did you get that?' I ask.

'WH Smith across the way. Page four,' he says, handing it over.

And there on page four I am: BLOWER MANN IN CANCER FIRING SHOCK.

'Whaddya think?' Vince asks as I finish reading the short piece.

'I can't believe it,' I reply truthfully.

'I know. It's got you down as twenty-nine. Lying twats. And can you believe Blower said that? Actually, I can. The man's a cunt out of the cunt's top drawer.'

He must be referring to Marcus Blower's quote:

'We offer Murray our deepest sympathy at what must be an extremely difficult time. However, by his own admission he acted in flagrant breach of his contract. If we gave him his job back, it would set a dangerous precedent. We'd soon find ourselves on a very slippery slope where anyone with a sniffle could flout company policy and assume immunity.'

But Vince is missing the point. 'No,' I say, 'I can't believe it's *out* there.'

I look around at the milling throng of travellers, expecting them to be staring at me, as if suddenly they all know. But I'm still as anonymous to them as they are to me. It doesn't stop me *feeling* different though. It's a far from pleasant sensation.

Vince says, 'Don't worry, Muzza. It's only *Campaign*. No fucker reads it.'

The incomprehensible mush of distress is rapidly replaced by a more concrete concern. 'Of course people read it, Vince. And what if *they* see it?'

'Who? Clark and his mates? The Russians ain't gonna be keeping tabs on British advertising and the only reason Clark'd go near it is to rip it up and turn it into wraps – it's that nice glossy paper dealers like.'

Vince has logic on his side, but he hasn't stopped the panic that's washing over me as I imagine *extwemely pwejudicial* ways of being *wubbed out*. My breath quickens and my knuckles bleach as I grip the luggage trolley. But Vince doesn't notice. His attention has flitted elsewhere. 'Where the hell's Fish? Ain't we got a plane to catch?'

We can't find her anywhere and after the final *This is the final call* we make our way to the gate. 'Chill, Muzza, she'll show,' Vince soothes. 'You know how it is with birds and shopping. Anyway, if she don't turn up, not to worry. It's gonna be chocker with dusky totty over there.'

'For God's sake shut it, Vince,' I snap at the very moment Fish appears at the far end of the corridor leading to our gate, a dot in the distance walking infuriatingly slowly. 'C'mon!' I scream as loudly as my poor lungs will allow. She acknowledges my desperate urging by . . . slow . . . ing . . . down.

When she reaches us there's no time to ask for an explanation and she isn't about to offer one. I bundle us aboard, feeling the plane door slam against my back. We stumble down the aisle, Fish sneering menacingly at any passengers that dare look at us disapprovingly, Vince decapitating several others with his bag lady's collection of carriers, and Bubbles and I following behind, me mumbling, 'Sorry . . . Sorry . . . Sorry . . .' – the wimp's mantra.

The captain doesn't wait for us to stow our luggage before he starts taxiing. As it happens there is no locker space left on the packed flight and Vince has to wedge his bags beneath a seat. As Fish and I take our seats in front of them I listen to the sound of Bubbles' potato-derived snacks being crushed to powder.

'What happened, Fish?' I ask.

'It was a nightmare, man,' she replies irritably. 'The last time I went clothes shopping was for a fucking school uniform. If you'd sent me off to nick the stuff, I could've coped. Deciding's a piece of piss when you're not paying.'

'You got something, though,' I say, looking at her one lonely carrier bag.

She reaches into the bag, pulls out a shoebox and flips off the lid.

'They're . . . really . . . lovely,' I say, looking at the pair of sci-fi Nikes lurking beneath a layer of flimsy tissue; training shoes in name only.

'Yeah, they should be for ninety-nine quid . . . Sorry.'

'That's OK.'

'I wouldn't've bothered, only my DMs are minging.'

I'd never have noticed.

She fumbles in her pocket for the change.

'Please don't,' I say. Then after a pause, 'Anyway, we're going to have to go shopping when we get there and get you something more . . . *summery*.'

She looks down, embarrassed, and mumbles, 'I wish I could pay you back.'

'How many times do I have to tell you I don't want any money.'

'I'm not talking about money.'

'Well, you are paying me back . . . just . . . by . . . being here.'

Though I mean every word, the sentiment makes me wince – I'm not used to saying stuff like this. But Fish is smiling at me with a warmth I haven't previously seen. Then we're pressed back into our seats as the pilot boosts the engines and the jet accelerates down the runway. It is now that I notice that something is missing.

Fear.

At this point on a plane journey I'd normally be gripping the armrests and looking resolutely at the back of the seat in front of me so as to avoid seeing moving ailerons and rapidly diminishing trees and buildings – anything, in other words, that hints at leaving the ground.

Not this time.

I turn my head and gaze through the window as the plane takes off. It rises, then banks and I find myself looking directly at the M25 a few hundred feet below. It seems different somehow.

It isn't of course. I'm the one that has changed.

_____ 2.41 p.m.

Bubbles hasn't stopped whinging since we took off and her tiny feet are drumming a rhythm on the back of my seat, which might be slightly less irritating if she could only maintain a proper beat.

Show me one childless adult that can abide the presence of kids on planes and I'll show you his lobotomy scars. On one flight that was particularly kindergarten-ish, Megan and I whiled away the tedium by dreaming up solutions to the menace of airborne under-fives. As I recall, having them shrink-wrapped and placed in the overhead lockers was the clear favourite.

I glance to my left and see that Fish has managed to fall asleep. I've noticed that about her; her ability to nod off on demand, any time, any place, any contorted body position. An essential survival skill for the homeless, I guess.

I need a distraction.

I peer into my holdall at the fourteen books – my fourteen *last* books – but I can't face the agony of choosing one. I go for the complimentary *Daily Mail* in the seat pocket. I don't like the *Mail* – partly because Megan hates it . . . Mostly because my stepfather loves it. But needs must. I flick through it, glancing at the headlines, willing myself not to be sucked into the stories . . .

And then I stop, catching my breath.

HAVE A GO HYAM FOILS BURGLAR reads the headline.

Would you credit it? Thirty-one years without so much as a mention in a school newsletter, then *twice* in one day.

Below the headline is a picture of Fish's dad standing amidst the wreckage of his study – I have to hand it to her, the girl did a demolition job worthy of a bunch of Iraqi looters. I read the story and become more enraged at each new line. By the end I'm mentally composing a splenetic letter to the editor.

Sir,

I refer to your report headlined HAVE A GO HYAM. *As the 'burglar' in question, I feel obliged to correct some errors. I didn't, as was claimed, attempt to flee by using Hyam-Glass's son as a human shield. I wasn't wrestled to the ground by Hyam-Glass and I didn't eventually escape by biting his ear. And while I may be no Ben Affleck, I'm neither 'weak-chinned' nor 'low-browed'.*

Finally, I'm not, as Hyam-Glass suggested, homeless. I don't, as he seems to think, need 'a warm and loving hug rather than the cold hell of jail.' But there is someone who does: my accomplice, whom your story neglected to mention. She is called Isabel and yes, she is the daughter that your 'have-a-go hero' inveigled to lie on his behalf during his own brush with criminality; the same daughter he ejected from the family home on the very day she achieved nine GCSE passes, including a creditable B in home economics.

I'm prepared to accept that you were simply reporting what you were told by Hyam-Glass – or more likely by his publicist. I would suggest, though, that in future you urge your reporters to dig a little deeper.

Yours et cetera,

The letter, of course, will never be committed to paper, let alone sent, but it leaves me feeling a little vindicated, if only in my own mind. I sit back and look at Fish sleeping peacefully. Then I tear the offending page from the newspaper, screw it up and stuff it into the pocket of my jeans.

Why would I want to ruin her Christmas by reminding her what a cynical and worthless liar her father is?

—————————————————————————————— 4.11 p.m.

A bumpy landing. A bit crap, actually. Like it has been a long year, the pilot is tired, he really can't be bothered. As the jet slows and wheels around at the end of the runway a sleepy little voice behind me: 'Are we at Spain now?'

twenty-two: **i won't sink**

A scream penetrates my dream (about Megan) and I sit bolt upright. I hear it again. It's not an adult scream. A kid. Bubbles. I relax – let Daddy deal with it. I lie down and put the pillow over my head. But the noise doesn't stop. I flop out of bed and walk across the cold tiled floor to the sitting room. There's no sign of life, only evidence of the living that went on last night – the empty wine bottles, dirty glasses and swollen ashtrays on the coffee table, all under the narrow-eyed gaze of Clint Eastwood. He's staring down from the _For a Few Dollars More_ poster on the wall, definitely disapproving. I slide open the French window that leads to the veranda and step into the dawn. Out here Bubbles' screams are loud enough to pierce tank armour. I run to the stone parapet and peer over the edge at the garden and swimming pool some ten feet below. There she is. Naked and cast away on a saggy silver Lilo that's drifting over the deep end – though, of course, when you're Bubbles' size, the entire pool constitutes a deep end. She looks up at me, her face set rigid with terror. 'It's _cold_,' she wails, as if _cold_ is the limit of the danger she's in.

'Don't move, Bubbles,' I call out in my best attempt – for just gone six in the morning – at calm and soothing. 'I'll come and get you.'

I run down the steps to the garden and across the expanse of terracotta tiles that surround the pool. They're wet with dew and my feet fly out from under me. My body keels over and my head hits the pool's ladder-rail. My bandage-free, though not fully healed right hand takes the brunt of the fall and it _hurts_. '_Fuck_!' I yell.

The screaming stops and all I can hear is the water gently lapping around the Lilo. I look up, fully expecting her to have slithered off into the eight-foot depths. But she's still aboard and she's staring at me with narrowed eyes. *'Don't* say that,' she says firmly. 'It's *Daddy's* word.'

It took several minutes to pull her from the pool and there were a few unnerving moments. Now she's nestling in my dressing gown and we head inside to wake Vince.

'You're bleeded,' she says, pointing at the cut on my head, which reopened after connecting with the ladder.

'I'm fine,' I reply. 'That was really dangerous, Bubbles. You must never, ever go near the swimming pool on your own. Do you understand?'

'I won't sink,' she says, her confidence restored now that she's on dry land.

'Don't do it again, OK? You scared the shit out of me.'

'Don't say that.'

'Daddy's word?'

She nods.

We reach the bedroom that she's sharing with Vince and I swing open the door. Bubbles' single bed is a mess of tangled sheets and blankets. Vince's double is as smooth as the day my mother made it. 'Do you know where Daddy is?' I ask.

She points down the corridor to Fish's room. I feel sick in the pit of my stomach. The unpleasant taste of last night is repeating on me.

We hired a car at the airport and raced the hour or so to Javea. Before we came to the villa we stocked up at the supermarket (or *supermercado* as my mother has it. She has about ten words of Spanish – more than enough to make her feel fully assimilated). We bought tea, coffee, bread, milk, some vacuum-packed ham and chorizo, a few other bits and bobs. And booze. Lots of booze. Then I knocked for Judith next door, got the keys and let ourselves in. Vince put Bubbles to bed and we started drinking. By the end of the third bottle he'd moved in on Fish. I watched them flirt drunkenly on the sofa from the other side of the room, and allowed myself to sink slowly into a glum silence. As I looked on, the gleaming-eyed optimism that I'd felt on leaving Gatwick quietly evaporated. Not much after ten I made my excuses and went to bed. I didn't feel well. I told myself it was the cancer. Which it was, but I wasn't certain that was all of it.

Now I *know* it wasn't – not by any stretch.

I stand uneasily outside Fish's room. The door is ajar and I can hear the sound of two bodies snoring peacefully. Bubbles is eager to go in, but I'm holding back.

'You must be starving,' I suggest. 'Fancy some breakfast?'

'Bacon!'

'I believe we have bacon.'

———————————————————————————— 8.54 a.m.

'So what are the rest of Daddy's words, then?' I ask as Bubbles tears into a Spanish sausage – after the bacon and a banana, her third breakfast.

'Fuck . . . Shit . . . Wanker . . . Um . . . Bastard . . . Knob . . . Gobshine . . .'

'I think you'll find it's *shite* . . . Is that it?'

She nods, adding, 'Only Daddy's allowed to say them.' Then her little face widens to accommodate a big smile and she says, 'Got another one. Cu—'

'Daddy must be very proud of you,' I say, cutting her off in the nick of time.

Between breakfasts Bubbles has been playing. She has the attention span of a guppy. Probably a function of being three,

260

but I guess it's also genetic – her father is hardly the most focused of individuals. As I watched her flit from 'Twinkle, Twinkle' to cloth dolls to rocking the fish tank on its stand I had an overwhelming sense of *déjà vu*. It was an action replay of a half-hour spent in Vince's office watching him *work* (for want of a better word). 'This, girl,' I said to her, 'is as good as it's gonna get.'

I've been keeping busy too. Taking my mind off stuff with the help of a dustpan and brush and my mum's decrepit vacuum cleaner. Clint has been watching me all the while, still disapproving. Not big on cleaning, I suppose. I don't recall him picking up a duster in *High Plains Drifter*. It's been infuriating, actually. Not Clint. The vacuum cleaner. The bloody thing barely sucked at all. I opened it up and the bag was jammed with about five years of compressed filth. Nothing's changed. I remember yelling at Mum when I was sixteen: 'What do you think happens to the dirt once you've vacuumed? Do you think it magically disappears inside the Hoover?' She looked at me as if she'd never considered it before, but now that she did, well, yes, that's probably exactly what happened.

Bubbles returns to her dolls, lining them up carefully on the sofa.

'Do they have names?' I ask her.

'Yes.' She points at each one in turn. 'Pinky . . . Madonna . . . Pinky's Sister . . . Pop Star . . . Cassidy . . . Belinda Fairy . . . Verity—'

She stops abruptly at the sound of shuffling feet. We both look up at Vince. He looks rough – grey-faced, crusty-eyed, stubbly – but he also bears the sly grin of *victory*. As he nears us he crouches and Bubbles runs into his arms. 'How's my baby?' he whoops. 'Uncle Muzz been looking after you?'

'I nearly drown'ded, Daddy,' she exclaims proudly.

'T'rific,' he replies encouragingly.

'She's not kidding,' I grouch as I run a cloth over the coffee table.

'You what?' Alarm spreads across his hungover face as he registers the blood that has dried on my forehead.

'While you were sleeping off your shag, she was in the swimming pool. You should take more care.'

'Jesus, fuck, Bubbles, what've I said about not going near the water?'

'It's not her fault, Vince. She's only three.'

'Three and a *half*,' Bubbles interrupts.

'I feel crap,' I say, ignoring her. 'I'm going back to bed.'

_____ 1.46 p.m.

I hear the door open and I snap my eyes shut. I listen to footsteps approaching the bed and then to a whispered, 'Murray . . . You awake?' I don't reply. I feel a hand touch my hair and stroke it lightly. 'Please don't die,' she says before leaving as quietly as she came.

_____ 6.10 p.m.

I'm woken by a gush of toddler giggles. The room is dark now. I've been asleep all day. Some holiday. *Some Christmas.* Call me naïve, but this is not what I had in mind. Feeling knackered. And ill . . . And . . . *jealous.* Of the living. And loving.

I'd better get up, if only for a wee. I push back the covers and climb to my feet. I feel weak and unsteady. I follow the smell of onions and head for the kitchen. Vince is hunched over a frying pan, wooden spatula in hand. He's singing: the noisy bit from 'It's Oh So Quiet' – Björk has nothing to worry about. He looks me up and down and I realise now that I'm only wearing underpants. 'That a malignant tumour in your pocket, or are you just pleased to see me?' he asks.

I have absolutely no answer to this.

'Sorry . . . Don't suppose you're in the mood. How you feeling?'

'Been better,' I reply.

'You need to eat. I'm making spag bol,' he announces as if he's Nigella Lawson and I should somehow be *turned on*. Then: 'Thanks for saving Bubbles' arse.'

'Probably more than her arse, Vince. Anyway, forget it . . . Where's Fish?'

'Chilling on the balcony whatsit.'

I go back into the living room. I peer out of the window into the gloom of the veranda and see nothing. Then I catch the faint red glow of a cigarette. It intensifies, illuminating Fish's profile. For a brief moment she looks more beautiful than anything I have ever seen. Almost innocent, as if her complexion has been scrubbed of squalor and cynicism. She catches me looking at her and lowers her cigarette, fading to black again. I turn away quickly.

—————————————————————————— 7.14 p.m.

Dinner is muted and sober. No way could you tell it's Christmas Eve. It strikes me that cancer must be infectious. My disease has dragged the mood into the gutter. Even Bubbles is quiet as she spreads bolognese sauce across her face, the table and the floor. Vince and Fish show no sign of wanting to repeat last night's flirting – not in front of me at any rate. Now I feel guilty. This is supposed to be a holiday. It's more like the hospice scene in a disease-of-the-week TV movie; one where the actors have forgotten their lines. I'd better say something.

'So, what did you guys get up to today?' It doesn't come out as breezily as I'd hoped.

Fish looks at me awkwardly but Vince gratefully accepts the

opening. 'Had a look round the seafront whatsit. Bubbles built a sandcastle.'

'It was *Cind'rella's* house,' Bubbles corrects. Then they're off, an improv double-act filling the void with every rubbish detail of their day. It continues until Vince announces, 'Bath time, baby,' and whisks Bubbles off to Matey, story and bed.

Fish and I look at each other nervously. Neither of us wants to be the first to speak. But eventually she cracks: 'I suppose I'd better wash up, then.'

'I'll give you a hand.'

'No, it's OK. Think I can manage.'

I let her get on with it, though I feel that washing up is one of the few pleasures I have left.

<hr>

8.22 p.m.

I'm alone on the veranda when Vince reappears. 'Little mite was shattered. Out like a light.' He takes one of my fags (yes, I'm still a smoker) and lights it. Then he says, 'Mind doing a spot of babysitting?'

'Wasn't planning on clubbing tonight,' I reply. 'You and Fish going out?'

'Well . . . just me really. Thought I'd check out this place I heard about today. Out on the N322, wherever the fuck that is.'

I know exactly where he's going. 'Jesus, Vince,' I snap, 'you're a bastard. What did I say about not mucking her around?'

'Hang on, matey, I think you've got this one arse about tit.'

'What are you talking about?'

'You're a bright boy, Muzz. You'll figure it out. Any road, I'm off. Won't be late – gotta get back and stuff Bubbles' stocking. She'll have me up at the crack of fanny tomorrow.' Before I can say anything else he turns and leaves.

I listen to him start up the hire car and set off – I presume –

for the N322, which winds into the hills outside town. Unless he has taken a sudden interest in Spanish rural life and wants to check out the farms, there's only one place he could be going to out there – Javea's licensed brothel.

8.39 p.m.

Fish appears on the veranda with a bottle of wine. 'Wanna glass?'

I nod and she sits down beside me on the wicker sofa.

We drink in silence for a few minutes. Then she says, 'It's a bastard.'

'What is?'

'They don't sell my fags out here.'

'B&H? They're everywhere.'

'B&H *Silvers*.'

'I didn't realise you were that choosy. Is that how it was on the street? Some kindly passer-by would offer you a B&H and you'd say, "Ain't you got any Silvers?"'

'You taking the piss?'

'Yes.'

'That's OK, then.'

A bit more silence before I pluck up the courage to ask, 'What's going on with you and Vince?'

'God . . . Big mistake. Don't get me wrong. He's a laugh and everything, but . . .'

'But what?'

'Look, it was a stupid drunken fuck. Can we talk about something else?'

'Sorry.'

'No, I'm sorry.'

'What for?'

'Because . . . I didn't come here because of him, did I?' she says.

'Why did you, then?'

She reaches her hand across the gap between us and puts it on top of mine.

'Now you're taking the piss, Fish.'

'I'm not. I . . . *like* you.'

'That's stupid.'

'Why? Because you're dying? I don't care. I mean, I *do* care. That's the point.'

'So you're happy about getting involved with a bloke who's not going to be here in a few weeks?'

'I already am involved,' she says, her hand now gripping mine.

I pull away. 'It's a *stupid* idea, Fish. It couldn't be any more stupid if it dipped itself in treacle, rolled about in crushed hazelnuts and joined the Young Conservatives. I'm going to be a bedridden vegetable soon.'

'I *don't care*.'

'And you're only eighteen.'

'Like you're sixty or something?'

'*And* I still haven't got over my bloody ex – not completely anyway. I'm sure that any agony aunt would have something to say on that. Must be page one in the training manual: *Do not under any circumstances advise your correspondents to get involved with a bloke who's terminally ill and who still has a thing for his ex.*'

'Look, if you don't . . . you know . . . like me or something, just say it.'

'It isn't that,' I say softly.

'So what happened to the bloke who was going to do whatever the fuck he wanted? Screw the consequences . . . What do you *want*, Murray? You'd better decide because . . . Well, have you seen the time?'

I turn and look at her. She's as beautiful as she was earlier in the cigarette glow. Her face is close to mine . . . and moving closer.

So I do what I've wanted to ever since she gave me the world's warmest smile on the plane. She tastes of fags and wine and bolognese and – vaguely unsettling this – tongue stud . . . and it is the *sexiest* thing.

twenty-three: why couldn't he have met a nice spanish girl?

I pick up the home-made cracker – a toilet-roll tube, wrapping paper and a couple of bin-bag ties. As seen on *Blue Peter*.

'You've been busy, Vince,' I say.

'Like I said, up at the crack of fanny. Bubbles helped . . . didn't you, angel?'

'*Yeah*, I help'ded,' Bubbles says, her face lighting up. This is saying something. Being Christmas Day, it has been burning at maximum wattage since, well, the crack of fanny. 'Pull it, Uncle Muzza,' she squeaks.

'Yeah, pull the fucker,' her dad echoes.

I hold it out towards Fish, who takes the other end. It splits in two without a bang – that would have been asking too much. A plump joint falls out onto the table. Yes, very *Blue Peter*. I wonder how Bubbles helped with this one – licked the Rizla?

'Thanks, that's . . . Just what I always wanted.'

'Good, 'cause you can't take it back. Didn't get a fucking receipt, did I? There's a joke and all.'

I stick my hand into the toilet roll and fish out a scrap of paper.

I read it out. 'What do you get the bloke what's only got weeks to live?'

Fish blanches. Vince titters. Bubbles giggles loudly as if I've reached the punchline already.

I turn over the paper: 'Perishables.'

'*Vince*!' Fish shrieks. 'That is not fucking funny.'

She's wrong though and I'd tell her if I weren't doubled up.

Svetlana appears from the kitchen, aroused by the commotion. Honestly, *Svetlana*. Vince met her last night out on the N322. I don't think she's a farm girl. With the excess of goodwill I'm feeling today I like to believe that his inviting her to Christmas dinner was an act of unbridled charity and has absolutely nothing to do with her thigh-length wet-look work boots.

She calls out to Bubbles. In Russian. 'Choc'late . . . No, *v'nilla*!' Bubbles replies excitedly. Svetlana heads back into the kitchen to fetch the ice-cream. Fish, Vince and I exchange bemused looks. 'Christmas. Time of miracles,' I say, lighting the joint. I look up at Clint on the wall. He seems to be smiling now. Approval at last. Maybe they used to put something in those cigars he chewed.

3.10 p.m.

It's a beautiful day. Unseasonably hot. Maybe eighty. Fish, Vince and I bask outside a café. It's closed, but the tables are out and we're taking advantage. We watch Bubbles playing with Svetlana on the beach some fifty yards from us. A game of chase. Svetlana is having trouble keeping up. The boots aren't helping.

'Aren't you going to put any sun block on her, Vince?' I ask.

'Nah, she's a heat-seeking missile, my baby,' Vince says. 'You shoulda seen her at the nursery sports-day. Thirty-seven degrees. Kids were dropping like flies in Ethiopia, 'cept for Bubbles. She just kept on going. Won everything that day. In the three-legged race she practically had to drag her partner's fucking corpse down the track. Wish they'd had an on-course bookie there 'cause I'd have made a fortune on her.'

'She and Svetlana seem to be getting on,' I say.

'They ain't got two words to rub together, but they're OK,' Vince agrees.

269

'She's quite a role model for the kid.'

'I thought that. You reckon too? . . . Hang on, you're being sarky, aren't you?'

'Uh-huh. It's called irony.'

'*That's* irony? Fucking Brett's going on about it all the time. I didn't like to ask . . . You know, he'd think I was . . . a mong or something.'

'No one would ever think that, Vince.'

'That weren't irony, was it?' he asks through clenched teeth.

I shake my head.

'Where's the marina?' he asks.

'Other side of that,' I reply, pointing to the headland at the far end of the Arenal. 'It's in the old town.'

'I'll check it out tomorrow. See if it's deep enough for a sub.'

'It's not exactly crawling with millionaires' yachts, Vince. You'd be better off in Marbella or Puerto Banus for that.'

Hang on, why am I taking this seriously? Like it's ever going to happen.

'Well, I'm here now,' he says. 'Be dumb not to have a—' He stops abruptly, his eyes bulging at something over my shoulder. Then: 'Fucking *hell*! I do not be*lieve*. Gotta check something out. Back in a mo.' He springs to his feet and hares off down the Arenal, dodging the strollers.

'Where's he going?' Fish asks, stirring from her daydream.

I can only shrug.

_____ 4.01 p.m.

A sand-coated Bubbles is back from the beach. Svetlana is looking at the time on her mobile. 'Vurk now,' she says with an apologetic shrug.

'You need to get back to the office?' I ask.

She looks at me blankly.

'You go. I'll tell Vince.'

'Tell im I don drive submarine,' she says haltingly. 'I big scare underwater.'

Everyone – even Russian hookers – knows about his sodding plan.

She bends down and hugs Bubbles. Then she goes, swaying on her eight-inch platforms like she's in training for the Moscow State Circus. Bubbles starts to cry – no daddy, no mummy substitute. Fish scoops her onto her lap.

'Daddy will be back soon, Bubbles,' I say. 'Probably went to buy you a toy.'

'H'*raaay*! A *toy*!'

_____ 4.48 p.m.

'Any sign?' I ask as Fish returns to the café.

She shakes her head. She has twice walked the length of the beachfront in search of Vince. I did it once and it wasted me. It's not that long, but my health . . . Well, it's not what it used to be. I look at Bubbles, who has found a distraction – an uncleared bowl of sugar sachets. She's tearing them open and probing inside them with a surprisingly dexterous tongue – demerara seems to be her favourite.

'He's been nearly two hours,' Fish grouches. 'He's taking the fucking piss.'

'*Yuck*!' screams Bubbles, her tongue coated with Canderel.

'This is stupid,' Fish says. 'Let's go. He knows where we live.'

_____ 10.26 p.m.

'Do you think we should call the police?' I ask.

Fish shakes her head. But I imagine that we could be sitting among stacks of dismembered corpses with serial killers queuing up to take turns on us and she'd still think calling the police a poor idea. She's not a *hey, let's call the police* kind of girl.

Things haven't got that bad yet, though there's still no sign of Vince. We're by the swimming pool, huddled on two sunbeds pulled together. Bubbles is inside, asleep. The night is cool, black and almost silent. The occasional car passing on the road immediately above and behind us makes the only sound, muffled by the high whitewashed wall that runs along the edge of the pool terrace.

'You worried?' Fish asks.

'Kind of . . . No, not really. I've never spent this amount of time with him, but I'd be more surprised if he didn't pull a stunt like this. He'll probably turn up at breakfast with a couple of Transylvanian hookers and an STD.'

We lie back and gaze up at the black sky pocked with tiny silver stars. I feel my eyes brim with tears as the emotions I first experienced at the traffic lights on Battersea Bridge bubble inside me like a burst main. This time the sense of missed chances is worse. Much bigger and more saddening . . . Well, it has been triggered by trillions of shimmering stars rather than the bridge's few hundred fairy lights. Fish pulls herself into me. 'You don't believe in God, do you?' she says.

I shake my head.

'Me neither . . . Shame.'

———————————————————————— 10.39 p.m.

We haven't moved or spoken for ten minutes. I feel better though, as if I could open my mouth without sobs spilling out. We hear a car wind up the hill towards the villa, the first in a while. It stops immediately above our heads on the other side of the fifteen-foot wall. The engine idles, a door opens.

'That him?' Fish says in a hushed voice.

'Could be . . . Could've got a taxi back.'

We wait and listen . . . to the sound of another door opening and feet scuffing tarmac. I tip my head back on the flattened sunbed and peer up towards the noise—

Just as something flies directly over us, appearing from the other side of the wall, a blurred, black bundle. Our bodies lock together as it descends and crashes into the pool throwing up a wall of chilly white water. We jerk upright, soaked now. We look at the half-submerged bundle as doors slam and the car squeals away.

'What the fuck is it?' Fish whispers, frightened.

I don't answer, just gaze at the mass in the pool. It moves, comes to life like Arnie the naked Terminator unfurling himself from the foetal position. As the mass produces arms and legs and transforms into a body it releases a thick cloud that seems black at first but then shows crimson in the underwater lights.

'It's Vince,' Fish gasps.

'Jesus, you're right,' I say, watching his body turn in the water, seeing his face through the blood. He isn't moving, just rolling.

'I can't swim,' Fish says.

She's called Fish. She has a cod tattooed on her hand. She *can't swim*. Great. I'm stripping off my shirt, pushing my shoes off my feet and, let me tell you, I am sick and bloody tired of pulling the Douglas family out of the pool. I don't want to do this; I *so* do not want to do this. But I feel my body lean and then drop into the water. *God*, it is *cold*. I tread water for a moment, feeling sharp pain in my chest, feeling myself drain of energy before I've even attempted to do anything useful, never mind heroic. Then I flinch as a hand grabs my leg and starts pulling me down. I grasp the rail built into the pool wall and cling on, but I sink as Vince's body slides up alongside mine. When I come back he's beside me. He's panting, looking at me through the mixture of blood and water that's pouring off his face. Then he opens his mouth and says through the fresh gaps in his teeth, 'What the fuck you taking a swim for? It's fucking freezing.'

'How're you feeling?' Fish asks as I emerge from the bedroom in dry clothes.

'Crap, but probably better than Vince.'

'What the fuck happened?' she asks.

'Must be something to do with Svetlana,' I say.

This is our only theory. We figure that where there are Russian prostitutes, the Russian gangsters can't be far behind and he has been monopolising her time. Vince refused to answer any questions beyond saying 'I met these blokes.'

'Why couldn't he have met a nice Spanish girl?' I say as his bedroom door opens and he joins us. He limps to the sofa and flops down. Fish and I look at him. His right eye has swollen shut. The cut above it and the one on his ear have stopped bleeding, but they look as if they could do with some attention.

'You want me to take you to hospital?' I ask.

'Nah, I'll be fine,' he slurs through swollen lips.

'How many teeth did you lose?' Fish asks.

'Hard to tell. Might be three, but maybe only two.'

'What the hell happened, Vince?' I ask.

'I told you, I met these blokes,' he mumbles.

'That much is pretty obvious. What blokes? I think we deserve an explanation. You made a right mess out there. My mum's pool is like a piranha tank.'

'Sorry.'

'Are you still in danger? Are *we* in danger? Should we leave the country?'

'Just these blokes,' he mumbles. 'Sorted now.'

'*Sorted*. That's supposed to make us feel better, is it?'

'Look,' he says with a tooth-free grin, 'I could tell you, but

274

if I did I'd have to fucking kill you. Now who fancies some tea?'

As he limps off to the kitchen I can't help but marvel. He's just so *resilient*. Like a Weeble – the ones that wobbled but wouldn't fall down.

twenty-four: **i won't say it**

Fish was right: trance *is* the bollocks.

Can't believe I'm thinking that. Can't believe I'm *dancing* to it. Actually, the way things have been turning out lately, disbelief has been suspended until further notice.

The last few days have been building up to this moment. Every hour has seen a barely perceptible rise in my levels of joy. Now I'm so dazzled by it that I can't see beyond it. Something to do with the weather, the wine, the fresh, salty air . . . Oh, and Fish.

'I *love* this song,' she shrieks.

'Me too,' I yell.

What am I saying? I hate this song. It's that old Belinda Carlisle number. The manic tranced-up version – DJ Probablya-Dutchbloke featuring SomeEuroblonde. I really *hate* it. So why is my body flailing and *why* am I singing?

Me singing!

Heaven is a place on earth.

_____ 11.59 p.m.

Diez . . .
   nueve . . .
   ocho . . .
   siete . . .
   séis . . .
   cinco . . .
   cuatro . . .

três . . .

dos . . .

uno!

The club erupts.

An explosion of love.

'I won't say it,' Fish whispers as we fling our arms around one another.

'Don't say anything.'

As we kiss tears mingle on our lips.

If I could die now . . .

_____ jan.

one: **mike said why didn't they put a sainsbury's there? something to benefit the *whole* community**

────────────────── thursday 1 january / 1.12 p.m.

I haven't come down yet. The general sense of New Year euphoria is still with me. Maybe my body has gone into industrial-scale endorphin production in anticipation of what's to come. Whatever, I feel *good* (like, as it happens, I *didn't* know that I would). Hard to explain why and, to be honest, I'm not attempting to – I'm afraid that the sharp scalpel of analysis will burst the bubble.

Best go with it for now because it has to stop.

Everything has to stop.

'You ready?' I ask Fish.

'Do I look OK?'

'You look beautiful.'

And she does. She's wearing the clothes she had on last night. A tiny-weeny silver top and a pair of extremely baggy para-chute pants festooned with dozens of dangling straps, both items bought in town. She looks like . . . Well, like a Pop Star. Megan had plenty going for her, but she never – *not once* – looked like a Pop Star.

'Let's go, then,' she says nervously.

Her anxiety is understandable. We're heading next door. The neighbours are having a barbecue. Judith stopped by with an invitation yesterday afternoon – 'You *must* come. Your mother would be mortified if I let you miss it.' I know from Mum that Judith and Mike's New Year Barbecue is an established ex-pat

281

tradition. A good proportion of Javea's Brits will be there, most of them middle-aged or older and as respectable as you might expect. Poor Fish hasn't done much mingling with middle-aged respectability of late, unless it was to pick their pockets.

Neither, I should think, has Vince and he's not about to start today. We join him by the pool, which is still tinged bloody-red from his death dive.

'You sure you don't want to come?' I ask.

'Couldn't face a barbie at the mo,' he says, flat on his back on a sunbed in his tiny orange Speedos. He's still severely battered and doesn't look as if he could face anything much. Bubbles sits at his feet squashing ants with the tip of her index finger. 'Hey, it must've been like the opening of *Sexy Beast*,' he says, seeming to pluck the thought from nowhere.

'What are you talking about?' I ask.

'You know, Ray Winstone standing by his pool and this fucking great rock rolls down the hill behind him, flies over his head and lands in the water – spur-*lash*! Wish you'd had a camera on it.'

'Yeah, that's *exactly* what I was thinking while I was jumping in to save you. This is *sooo cinematic*, baby.'

'Too right – Hang on. Is that the irony thing again?'

'No, Vince, I'm being serious.'

It's the first time he has spoken about that night since, well, that night. He has been putting on a brave face – quite an achievement with all the cuts, bruises and missing teeth – but he's clearly scared. So much so that he hasn't left the villa in a week. But he's bringing it up now so perhaps he wants to talk about it. Whatever, I want to *know* about it. 'What happened?' I ask.

'When we were sitting at that caf I saw someone,' he says.

'What, someone you know?'

'Kind of. By sight.'

'*Who*?'

'Anyway, I thought I'd catch up with him,' Vince goes on,

deliberately ignoring the question, 'introduce myself, see if I could interest him in an investment opportunity.'

'What investment opportunity?'

'You know, that little undersea project I'm trying to get going.'

'*Vince!*'

'Well, if you don't dream it you ain't never gonna live it ... Any road, Muzz, he weren't up for it.'

'He's got a lovely way of showing it. Who the hell was he?' Fish asks.

'Don't matter now. No one you know.'

'It was Brian Shark,' Bubbles squeaks.

'Brian *Sharkey*?' I squeak.

'Shut up, Bubbles,' Vince says. 'Course it weren't Brian Sharkey.'

'Brian Sharkey?' Fish says. 'The gangster Brian Sharkey?'

'Brian *Shark*. He's the *baddest* motherfucker that *ever* motherfuck'ded!' Bubbles recites, very excited now.

'*Shut it*, Bubbles,' Vince snaps. 'Look, it weren't Brian Sharkey. Brian Sharkey's dead. And even if he weren't, do you think I'd be soft enough to tap him for cash?'

I don't answer, but my expression says *Yes and double yes with knobs on*.

'It *was* Brian Shark,' Bubbles says under her breath, indignant at being contradicted.

Vince looks at the doubt and confusion on our faces and says. 'She's three for fuck's sake—'

'Three and a *half*!' Bubbles corrects, tears filling her eyes now.

'Whatever. You gonna believe her? If she told you Humpty fucking Dumpty did it would you believe her?'

'Humpty's maked of *egg*. He *can't* have bash'ded you in,' Bubbles argues, not without logic.

'It wasn't Sharkey, all right?' Vince says finally. 'Can we fucking drop it?'

We sit in silence for a moment. I exchange looks with Fish.

The jury may be out on who beat the crap out of Vince, but our money is going on the evidence of the witness that still believes in Santa and the awesome power of fairy dust. I'm scared now.

I stand up and say, 'C'mon, Fish. We'd better hit the barbie.'

'Will *Barbie* be there?' Bubbles chirps, recovering fast.

'It's a barbe*cue*,' I explain. 'Like burgers and chops and stuff. Want to come?'

She nods and looks at her dad.

'Go on, princess . . . Remember, if anyone offers you crack—'

'Jus' say *no*,' she says.

She takes Fish's hand and we head out of the front gate. 'Barbie *might* be there, mightn't she?' she says hopefully. Then, 'I smell'ded *sausages*.'

I can *see* sausages. Carbonised in a ribbon of dense smoke that's rising above the high garden wall. Some corner of a foreign field . . .

——————————————————————————— 2.33 p.m.

'Is that her?' Bubbles asks pointing at the big-haired blonde talking to Terry Venables.

'Might be. Do you want me to find out?'

'No . . . It's *not* her. Barbie's skin isn't orange . . . And *he's* not Ken.'

She's sitting on the steps at the shallow end of the pool while I feed her pieces of burger. Fish has gone to get drinks, the first time in over an hour that she has ventured from my side. We haven't done much mingling. Judith and Mike's garden is full of reminders of my mother's life here, which is uncannily similar to her old one in Essex – just with added suntan. It's funny – no, *bizarre* – how these people took the momentous decision to sell up, leave all behind and create a new life with new friends in a new world . . . only to end up at parties where they talk

284

about the same stuff they did in Britain. House prices, schools, crime rates, the weather. The *weather*. What's to talk about? It's sunny. All the time. *Get over it*.

We have *got* to get out of here. My euphoria has faded and despite acres of clear blue sky I'm feeling hemmed in. Suffocated. And ill. I'm on a clock now. T minus . . . Whatever . . . Something very imminent anyway. I can't be sitting here waiting to die while all around me talk about the *weather*.

'What happens when you're deaded?' Bubbles asks.

Miniature bloody mind reader.

'I don't . . . I'm not exactly—'

'Mummy says you go to *heaven*. It's all *pink* and there's *angels* and they're pink and it's in the *clouds*, but you can't stand on *clouds*, can you?'

'I'm . . . not . . . sure.'

'Daddy says that's *bollocks*. He says *worms* eat you all *up* and you go *rotted* . . .'

I'm trapped inside an episode of *Kids Say the Funniest Things – Uncut*.

'. . . and slimy and you turn into a *zompie*.'

'A *zombie*?'

'Or a vampire. What's a zompie?'

'It's like a—'

'How can you be a zompie if worms have eated you all up?' she asks, spotting the flaw in her father's hypothesis. 'What's there to eat in heaven? Where do you poo? Are there worms there? Is there Pizza Hut when you're deaded? And telly?'

'*Wow* . . . Bubbles . . .' I'm starting to hyperventilate. 'So many questions. Let's go and find Fish. Maybe she knows.' I take her hand and we weave our way across the lawn to the bar, which has been set up beneath a lemon tree. Fish is clutching two beer bottles. Judith has cornered her. *Cornered* is the right word because she looks tense and she's gripping those bottles as if they're live grenades. Seems I'm not the only one ready to escape.

'Murray!' Judith calls, waving me over. 'So em*barr*assing. I thought your *friend* was Megan with purple hair. A *solicitor* with *purple* hair.' She laughs uproariously at her own stupidity – at her own crass insensitivity.

Fish smiles through clenched teeth and I look at her apologetically – I'd forgotten how dim Judith is, and so much dimmer for having a stomach full of gin.

'Fish, we'd better be go—'

'Murray,' Judith says, gripping my arm, 'I was just telling your *friend* about how much happier Mike and I have been since we came out here. Best decision we ever made. We get the *Mail* every day and all we read about is the street crime and the asylum seekers. Everywhere apparently . . .'

Little wonder Fish's hostility is beginning to show. I've heard this garbage a dozen times before, always nodding and smiling stoically through the torrent of bigotry from Judith or Mike, or on a bad day both. The twisted image of England as a termite mound of thieving, raping, looting immigrants. I never dared to say anything contradictory. I'd curse myself afterwards, but salve my conscience with the thought that it was uninformed drivel from a couple now living hundreds of miles out of harm's way. I'm not alone. I've never heard anyone challenge them. Though my mum's politics are pretty half-baked, she's no bigot, yet she grins and bears it. Well, who else will feed her fish while she's away? And Megan listened to it once. Megan who represents asylum seekers and sits on a committee campaigning to get more black judges on the bench. Guess what? She sipped her wine, ate her chorizo and pineapple chunks on a stick and didn't say a word. She joked about it afterwards; wondered if Judith and Mike were hiding Martin Bormann in their pool house, but she stayed silent as she drowned in racist swill. Didn't want to upset my mum, I suppose.

'. . . Gangs of them roaming the streets. Apparently they all drive Mercs back in their own countries. Of course, that's what made us move. Mike could see it coming. Mark my words, he said, that Berlin Wall comes down and they'll be on us . . . Like *rats*. I know it's not terribly *Pee Cee*, but it has to be said . . .'

Oh my God, here we go. She's up to speed now. We have *got* to get out of here.

'. . . Immigration has ruined everything. It's just not . . . *England* any more.'

'Sorry, Judith,' I say, 'but we've really got to make a—'

'Hang on, Murray,' Fish says, keeping a lid on it no longer. She looks at Judith and asks, 'Where did you say you came from?'

'Surrey, dear. Woking.'

'Yeah, that's right. *Surrey*. All those five-bed semis overrun with *niggers* and *Pakis*. Bloody mosques on every corner.'

Judith is shocked – noxious as her opinions are, she's careful to avoid the N and P words. She's confused as well, too squiffy to figure out whether Fish is having a go at her or she's a neo-Nazi masquerading as the new girl in Sugababes. I'm sweating now. Hemmed in is turning into full-blown claustrophobia.

'Well, I wouldn't have put it like that,' Judith says at last, 'but, yes, it was getting more and more . . . *dusky*. There was talk of them building one of their temples up the road from us. On a prime piece of land as well. Mike said why didn't they put a Sainsbury's there? Something to benefit the *whole* community. I don't mind them having their own religions, but they don't have to rub it in our faces, do they?'

'Come on, Fish,' I say, desperation in my voice, 'we'd better—'

'No, they're as bad as the *queers* and the *homeless*,' Fish spits, ignoring me.

Judith gulps her G&T and giggles. 'Lord, don't get Mike started on *them*.' She has obviously made up her mind about Fish and decided to go with the flow.

287

'You people make me sick,' Fish snarls.

'Excuse me?' Judith says, her deep orange tan visibly leaching of colour.

'I said you make me *sick*,' she repeats, loudly because I've grabbed her arm, scooped up Bubbles and we're halfway across the lawn.

'Thanks for the support,' she says as we march towards the gate. 'How can you listen to that and not say anything?'

'Because . . . Because . . .'

'*What?*'

'My mum's got to live with these people,' I say.

'So? If Adolf Hitler moved in you'd let him chuck a few Jews on the barbecue 'cause he was your mum's neighbour?'

I stop in my tracks.

'What's wrong?' Fish asks.

'You're right,' I mutter.

I turn round and march us back to the bar.

'Where we going?' Bubbles asks.

'We're going to give Fish some support,' I say.

'*H'raay!*' she squeaks. 'What's s'port?'

'Watch and learn.'

Judith beams as she sees us return, seemingly oblivious to the fact that only moments ago she was on the verge of being deeply contradicted in her own home. 'Back for another already?' she cries tipsily. 'Hey-ho, the more the merrier.'

'No . . . No thanks. I just wanted to say . . . What Fish was trying to say was . . .' I look at Fish looking at me expectantly. I know what she was trying to say, but what am *I* trying to say? '. . . She was trying to say that . . . The trouble with immigrants is the way they *refuse* to fit in.'

'That's *right*,' Judith says, putting her hand on mine and squeezing.

'They don't learn the language, adopt the culture . . .' I'm up and running now, slipping up a gear, '. . . make friends with the locals. They just set up their little ghettos, read their own papers, watch their own telly . . . It's an insult to the hospitality that's been extended to them.'

'You put it so *well*, Murray,' she says approvingly. 'They set up little *ghettos*.'

'Like you, really.'

Jesus. There, I said it.

'Pardon me?' she says, though she heard me clearly enough.

'Correct me if I'm being stupid, Judith, but aren't you an immigrant?'

The bleach flushes through her tan again. 'I suppose . . . In a way,' she says as she tries to figure out where this is going. Then forcefully, 'No. *No*, it's not the same at all.'

'How so? Do you take a full and active part in Spanish life? Send your kids to the local school? And how much of the language have you learned?'

'Everyone speaks English here.'

'God, how arrogant is that? How would you have felt if the Indian who ran the corner shop back in Woking expected you to learn Gujarati?'

'Gujar-what?' This may be her own home – her *castle* – but she's on new and challenging ground here.

'And how many Spaniards did you invite today?' I ask.

'How *dare* you? Some of my best friends are Spanish.'

I can't help laughing. 'So where are they?'

Her mouth flaps uselessly.

'I'll tell you where. They're down some bar slagging off you lot – the *immigrants*. They probably want to flatten this place and put up a *supermercado* – something to benefit the *whole* community. I'm sorry, Judith, but when Fish said you made her sick, well, now you know why.'

Silence. Ice cracking in glasses the only sound.

Fish squeezes my hand. I was *good*, wasn't I?

I look at the circle of shocked faces, people who, whether or

289

not they share Judith's views, are clearly stunned that someone has been so vocal about *not* doing so.

I hear a voice behind me: '*Beautiful* day for it.'

Fish tugs my arm – time to go – but I'm on a roll now and I snap, 'Jesus, will you *piss* off with the bloody *weather*.'

Hang on, I know that voice.

I turn round and see her.

'Mum, what are you doing here?'

'I was going to ask you that,' she says, reaching out to hug me and at the same time staring at me in disbelief.

two: **poor megan**

It must have been a shock for her. To sum up: she arrived home to find that her (inexplicably red-tinged) pool had been occupied by a human punch bag in tiny orange Speedos, her son was next door insulting her neighbour in front of her closest friends, and that furthermore (a) he looked poorly and emaciated, (b) he was with a purple-haired girl who definitely wasn't a solicitor and (c) he was holding a toddler, thus raising the entirely unforeseen possibility of grandmotherhood.

I'd have been pretty gobsmacked in her espadrilles.

She's putting a brave face on it though. Emphasising that she's pleased to see me, while glossing over that she'd have preferred to find me looking a little less *peaky* and with a different entourage. One that included Megan. Mum put her right up there in the girlfriend performance league. Something we agreed on, then.

Fish and I are by the pool now. Not relaxing, but subdued and tense. Mum and David are inside unpacking.

'You gonna tell her?' Fish asks quietly.

I shrug.

'You've got to. She has a right to know.'

This is rich coming from someone whose own family couldn't be more dysfunctional if it moved from Hampstead to a trailer park on the Jerry Springer studio lot. I don't point this out. Mostly because she's right. I have to tell my mum.

'Why are they back?' Fish asks.

'Mum said something about my stepdad getting a call. Some business thing.'

291

'I thought you said he'd retired.'

'Best not to ask with him.'

David has been more than usually standoffish since he got home. Unlike Mum, he didn't seem shocked by the freak-show invasion of his turf. When we came back from Judith's party we found him calmly straightening the Clint posters in the living room. I asked him where Vince was. 'Gone for a kip. Looked like he needed it,' he replied coolly.

'I've made us all a snack,' my mum calls out from the veranda above us.

'We're still full from the barbecue,' I reply, wincing at my own mention of the party that has more than likely cast her into social oblivion.

'Well, I'm sure the little one could do with something to eat,' she says, looking adoringly at Bubbles who is playing at our feet. 'Come on in.'

5.16 p.m.

'You should've seen their villa, Murray,' Mum says as she washes and I dry. 'It was stunning. Chrissy's entire bedroom, *every*thing. *Pink* leopard skin.'

'The pink leopards of the Great Rift Valley – hardly any left in the wild.'

'Oh no, it wasn't *real* fur. Chrissy's an animal lover like me. She did have a mink, but she said it's OK because they're vermin. The journey back was terrible. The camper kept overheating. Oh, did I tell you about their statue? No, those blue plates go in the top cupboard, dear. It was overlooking their pool. Ours seems to have turned red while we were away. It was absolutely awesome – Anthony and Cleopatra. Only it wasn't. It was Chrissy and Jimmy! Did I say the top? The *bottom* cupboard. Well, their heads on Richard Burton and Liz Taylor's bodies. Imagine seeing yourself in marble! They don't

292

have the RAC over here. Poor David had to walk five miles to get water. Actually, Chrissy said it wasn't marble. Fibreglass, but you really wouldn't have guessed. I didn't know there were pink leopards. You live and learn, don't you? Do your friends prefer fried or scrambled? Just thinking ahead to breakfast. Don't worry, I'll do both. I wonder if it's those new chlorine tablets we put in before we left. I've never heard of red chlorine. They should warn you if they're going to change the colour . . .'

A thought strikes me. Talking to Mum isn't so different from talking to Bubbles. Both of them tend to steer the conversation, but with such a lack of directional control that you can dip in and out at any given point without losing the thread – no thread to lose.

'. . . Chrissy gave me the name of the sculptor, you see. What do you think of that? David and I as Romeo and Juliet. Of course, we could go for something Greek. Homer . . . Or is he that cartoon?'

'They were teenagers,' I say.

'Who, dear? The ancient Greeks?'

'No, Romeo and— Never mind . . . You'd make a good Juliet.'

Mum peels off her rubber gloves and looks at me. 'You look terrible, Murray.' The brave face has finally cracked.

As far as Mum is concerned I always look terrible. I could always eat more, wrap up, get a haircut, *a good night's sleep*, see a doctor . . . Just your average motherly hyper-concern. Except that this time it isn't. This time it's my cue to tell her.

So I say, 'I'm fine. It's just . . . flu.'

'You don't *look* fine. Have they been working you too hard?'

'I'm . . . not working. I . . . left.'

You see, I know my mum. I know how to handle her and I've got a plan. Gradual disclosure: hit her with the little things; acclimatise her in my personal nightmare's gently rolling foothills before I whisk her up to the terrifying summit with its sheer drops and virtual absence of oxygen. It worked for Edmund Hillary . . .

'You've packed in your job?' she gasps, her eyes welling up. 'My God . . . It's *Christmas* . . . That's . . . What were you thinking?'

OK, maybe it won't work for me, but it's the only plan I've got.

'I didn't actually . . . You know, hand in my notice . . . As such.'

'They *fired* you? What did you do?'

'I had an accident in a company car.'

'How can they fire you for an *accident*?' she cries, a tear rolling down her cheek. 'Was someone hurt?'

'No . . . Not really. It was just a bit of a flash car. And, you know, advertising . . . Any excuse to clear a desk.'

'How could they do that? You'd been there ever since university.'

'It doesn't matter, Mum. It was a crap job. Really, it's so unimportant.'

Which is the truest thing I've said so far.

'Your career *is* important,' she sobs, abandoning all attempts at self-control. (Oh yes, the plan is right on track.) 'It was a very good job . . . What's happened to you, Murray?'

What's happened to you? The Big Question, the one that has been hanging on her lips ever since she clapped eyes on me at Judith's.

I don't answer it. I look at her and feel a painful mixture of pity and guilt.

'What's *happened*, Murray?' she repeats as she dries her eyes with a tea towel. 'What was going on at Judith's? Your friend has really upset her.'

'She didn't upset her. I did. I'm sorry . . . But Judith's full of shit. I couldn't listen to it any more.'

'Who is she?'

'Fish? She's my girlfriend.'

This sets her off afresh. She bites on the tea towel to stifle the sobs, having received final confirmation that her son has hit rock bottom.

'Mum, she's really nice. Give her a chance. Get to know her.'

'Poor Megan,' she whispers.

'*Poor* Megan dumped me.'

'Why? What did you do?'

'I didn't do anything.'

The truth again – four words that explain in full why Megan left me.

'You must have,' Mum says. 'She wouldn't just . . . Not Megan.'

'Well, she *did*. Get used to it. I've had to.'

That sounded far crueler than I'd intended. Mum isn't good with cruel and I watch her collapse over the sink, hunching, ageing before my very eyes.

I've been here before.

'Well, he's *dead*. Get used to it. I've had to.'

I said that to her when I was fifteen. Nine months after Dad died. Nine months in which she hadn't taken a single baby step towards acceptance. On the day of his funeral she was so destroyed that she did actually throw herself on his coffin as it slid through the velvet curtain. It took four policemen in full dress uniform to prise her off. It freaked them out. All their experience manhandling thugs, rioters and feisty drunks didn't stand them in any kind of stead. Removing widow (hysterical) from coffin (moving) wasn't on the syllabus at Hendon and I could see them suppressing their natural inclinations to get her in a throat hold and slap the cuffs on. The honest truth? Just beneath my own trauma was a faint but discernible tingle of embarrassment. Dad's superintendent stood beside me and – presumably not knowing what else to say – said, 'He's with God now, Murray.'

Not yet he isn't, I thought, *and nor will he be if Mum doesn't let go of the bloody coffin.*

As we left he consoled us with, 'Time is a great healer.'

Which turned out to be as untrue as it was trite. Time made things worse. As the vestiges of Dad gradually disappeared – starting, I suppose, with his XXL coffin – she had less and less to cling to and fell headlong into a deep well of tears. I couldn't get near her. I could only watch and clear up after her. Actually, I reckon that's where my cleaning fetish took root – following Mum's trail of balled-up tissues with a wastebasket. And every moist, salty Kleenex I picked up watered my growing hatred for the driver of the Nissan Sunny – she'd killed *both* my parents.

After nine months, the eve of my sixteenth birthday, I snapped – *He's dead. Get used to it. I've had to.* It sounded callous, but, actually, it was a cry for help. She didn't hear me though.

And she forgot my birthday.

A few weeks later David turned up – riding into Colchester Avenue like Clint in *Pale Rider* – and everything changed. Not literally overnight – it took a couple of weeks. At first I was grateful. I had my mum back. Once again she was worrying about breakfast while cooking tea, juggling a dozen conversational balls over the washing up and telling me I needed to eat more, wrap up, see a doctor . . .

Then it struck me. *Why hadn't I been able to save her?* You really don't want to see the can of troubled, bitter, sad little worms *that* revelation prised open.

And here we are now. Sort of *here we go again.* I wonder if she'll throw herself on my coffin? Probably. I mean, look at her. Sobbing and scrunched up. And all she has lost is Megan – a hypothetical daughter-in-law who isn't even dead. She can't cope with *this* . . . More to the point, I'm not sure that I can cope with her *not* coping. I've *been* there. I couldn't help her the last time and nothing makes me think I could make a better job of it now.

But I have to deal with it. Get it over with . . .

'It's OK, Mum,' I say, my arm going around her shoulder. 'Megan and me . . . It had run its course. It was the right thing.'

'She looks so young. And what kind of a name is *Fish*? . . . She's got purple hair,' she snuffles.

'It's only hair. It might be pink next. Like Chrissy's leopards.'

This doesn't seem to help.

'Mum, there's something else. It's not . . . It's not good news . . . I've got—'

'Haven't you two done the dishes yet?'

I turn round to see David in the doorway.

And hateful though he is, am I glad to see him?

Neither Mum nor I speak. David scrutinises her, then me, but I should think it takes none of his detective's intuition to figure that he has walked in at a difficult moment. Then he says, 'Sweetheart, can I borrow your boy for a tick? Wanna pick his brains on my radiator.'

This, of course, is a ruse. *I* know that he can strip and reassemble an engine blindfolded and *he* knows that when it comes to anything more mechanical than a plug I am, in the words of more than one judge, 'worse than a girl'.

———————————————————————— 5.40 p.m.

'Pass me that ring spanner,' David says.

He's in luck – I know what a ring spanner is. I hand it to him and he disappears under the bonnet. I watch him work, thinking this is the perfect setting for one of those father/son moments – man and boy connecting over a busted engine. But my real dad and I had few of those and it's not going to happen with David. Conversationally we're on different planets. In different solar systems. In separate galaxies. David is a geezer and, well, I'm not. The much bigger part of the problem is that he's the flashy sod who waltzed off with Mum when grief was still raw and I am – at least as far as he's concerned – the wet, over-indulged only child. Even if we managed to crack the code of small talk, we'd still have light years between us.

'It's got more leaks than the sodding Welsh,' he says as he hauls out the worn-out radiator and lays it on the ground.

'Can I do anything?' I ask, knowing full well . . .

'Don't think so.'

'OK, then, I'll just be—'

'Murray . . . Before you rush off,' he says, turning to face me. 'What the fuck do you think you're playing at?'

He stares at me, his muscular arms folded across his green Lacoste shirt, his bald head glistening in the low sunlight like an orange bowling ball. His heavy neck chain is throwing darts of light at my eyes. He loves his jewellery. The only other men I'm aware of who wear that much gold with the same lack of self-consciousness live in hoods and rhyme *trigga* with *nigga*.

I don't – *can't* – answer his question.

'Don't get me wrong,' he continues. 'I couldn't give a monkey's who you drag down here – I've seen a lot worse than those two in my day – but your mum . . . Well, you know your mum.'

'David, I'm sorry . . .'

Jesus, why am I apologising? He said it himself; she's my mum. And I've been a part of her life for, ooh, sixteen years and one month longer than he has.

'. . . but I wasn't even expecting you to be here.'

'And neither was I, sunshine, neither was I. We were having a whale of a time in Marbella. I was in no hurry to schlep back and find my pool had been turned into a blood bank . . .'

Didn't think he'd suspect the chlorine tablets.

'. . . By rights your mate shouldn't be alive. He *wouldn't* be if I hadn't put a word in and promised to get back here to . . . tidy up.'

'Hang on, you know who did this to him? What the hell's been going on?'

'You really have no idea, have you?'

I shake my head. I'm too stunned to speak. I've always known that David is *dodgy*. But this side of him has always been kept at a safe remove. Actually, I honestly thought this side of him had retired – perhaps occasionally seeing other dodgy types for rounds of golf and talk of the old days. Apparently not. It's active and mixes with people who think nothing of knocking my friends senseless and tossing them into swimming pools. I remember the conversation with Vince and Bubbles earlier today and I say very quietly, 'Has it got anything to do with Brian Sharkey?'

'You what?'

'Brian Sharkey,' I repeat. 'Did he beat Vince up?'

David bursts out laughing. He's really laughing, as if I've told him the funniest joke in the world . . . Or, more likely, as if I've just said the stupidest thing in the world. Finally he stops and says, 'Number one, Murray, the likes of Brian Sharkey never do their own beating up. That's what they've got staff for. Number two, if your mate had run into Sharkey he'd be suffering a lot worse than minor abrasions. Number three – and this is the clincher – Brian Sharkey is dead.'

'That's just a rumour, isn't it? No one knows.'

'*I* know, sunshine, *I* know. There isn't a death certificate, but I have it from reliable sources that Sharkey's body is propping up a bridge on the M11 extension in Leytonstone. He's a pillar of the community in death as he never was in life.'

'Who did it, then?' I ask.

'Best you don't know. Anyway, I've had a word with your mate. Where the hell did you dig him up, by the way? He looks like that cartoon dog. Whatever, he's agreed that the smart thing to do is to get on the first plane out of here. Hopefully he's packing his bags as we speak. Now . . . I don't want you to take

299

this the wrong way, 'cause I don't mind having you around and I know your mum is thrilled to see you, but it might be an idea if you and your girlfriend joined him.'

'What, are we in—'

'You're safe enough. At least you will be once I've put in a call and assured certain people that you're as clueless as I know you are . . . But – no offence – you look like shit. I don't know what chemicals you've got swilling round your system, and frankly, I don't care, but I don't much appreciate you doing it under my roof.'

'It's my mum's home too,' I say peevishly.

'That makes it worse. I can understand you disrespecting me, but your own mother? You can see how upset she is.'

'That's because I've got—'

'Why don't you go home, clean yourself up and come back when you're straight?'

'I'm not doing drugs,' I say weakly.

'Well, you don't look too clever. Something's not agreeing with you.'

I can't really argue with that.

'When I arrived on the scene your mum was in pieces,' he says. 'She took some putting back together. I'm not having a pop at you – I know we've never spoke about it, but I suppose you were going through your own hell back then. My point is that I don't fancy going there again. You get my drift?'

I don't protest, though I could with justification. The odd thing is that, although we've got there by entirely different routes, we've both reached the same conclusion.

three: i'm *fine*

As I fasten my seat belt I wish we weren't going back.

Though I'm also glad we didn't stay.

'You should have told her,' Fish says.

'Can we talk about something else?'

I've tried to explain it to her, but she doesn't get it. And, unless she'd been around when my dad died, why would she?

'You should have told her. Look at the state of you.'

'Drop it, please. Anyway, I'm doing fine,' I lie.

Before Fish can contradict me a flight attendant appears with the free *Daily Mails*. She fixes me with a concerned expression and says, 'Are you feeling OK, sir?'

'I'm *fine*,' I reply a little too testily.

'Is there anything I can get you?'

'No . . . Thanks,' I say, trying to force a smile.

But I can't deny it. While Fish and Bubbles glow as if they've just had a holiday, and even Vince is sporting a tan on the limited areas of body that haven't been beaten blue, I look the way I feel. I'm colourless, pinched and underweight. I spend most of the time short of breath, and feverish beads of sweat – once merely the mark of stress – have made a permanent home on my forehead. After all these weeks of *knowing* I'm dying, I now *look* as if I am.

I really don't want to go home. To cold, grey January. Maybe we should have stayed. Taken the hire car and driven down the coast. But after our respective words with David, both Vince and I were subdued, depressed and – I think I can speak for Vince on this – scared. Cold, grey January seemed fitting.

301

Fish has her head in one of the books I bought (and haven't been able to touch). Vince and Bubbles sit across the aisle. Bubbles is dismantling a set of BA headphones and Vince is reading his *Mail* through bruised, slitty eyes. He lowers it and looks at me.

'What's up?' I ask.

He passes me the paper and points to the story at the foot of page five. I read the headline: DYING MAN GETS BULLET. The report that follows is – give or take a comma – the same as the one in *Campaign* ten days ago, rehashed for the benefit of well over two million *Mail* readers. I honestly couldn't care less any longer except that one of them is my mother. And I could possibly handle that if I didn't have to deal with the thought that Clark may be another. Vince has already got there.

'Here, Muzz,' he says, 'you planning any more trips?'

'Pony trekking up the Andean spine of South America?'

'Probably the best place for you, matey.'

four: call me completely crazy but i think a byzantine theme might work in here

I stand across the street from my flat. I've been here for ten minutes, hiding behind a lamppost – relatively easy given how much weight I've lost. I'm gazing up at my windows. No sign of life. I stub my cigarette and cross the road.

At Victoria, Fish and I had said goodbye to Vince and Bubbles, and taken a cab to the Dorchester. Not the bolthole of choice for the average fugitive, but does the average fugitive have £46,357 on his person? We checked in and then I caught a cab to South Woodford.

'Do you have to go?' Fish asked before I left.

'There's some stuff I want.'

'Like what?'

'Some clothes, CDs . . . My mobile.'

'Your fucking *mobile*. Buy another. Look, it's the first place they'll try and find you. Even if they think you're not stupid enough to go there, they're bound to turn the place over.'

'I'll be in and out in fifteen minutes. Back before you know it.'

'I'll come with you, then. Give you a hand. Watch your back.'

'No need. I'm fine.'

'You look like shit, Murray.'

'I'm FINE!' I wheezed as I slammed the door.

She was right. Coming back was a stupid idea. Why *am* I here? For my mobile and some fresh socks? As if I couldn't manage without them. I think the only reason I've returned is completely irrational. The flat is home and, well, I'm a homebody. When

303

the implications of the *Mail* story sank in I figured I wouldn't be spending any more time here and I had a need to see it one last time; say goodbye.

Now all of that seems utterly ridiculous. But I'm here now, so I might as well get it over with. I climb the steps and slot my key into the lock of the big front door. The hall is exactly as it was eleven days ago. Gloomy and shabby, the brown carpet still wrinkled and threadbare. I check the post on the table – junk, bills, credit-card threats and a couple of letters from Saint Matthew's. I leave it there. On my way to the stairs I decide to give Paula a knock and ask if I've had any visitors. I tap on her door and after a moment she appears in her away-from-the-office dykey clobber.

'Hi, Paula. Happy New Year.'

She looks bothered. 'Hi . . . Murray.'

'What's up?' I ask nervously. 'I had any callers?'

'We only got back from Wales at lunchtime . . . But the police were here about an hour ago,' she says.

I freeze.

'They wanted to know if we'd seen that girl you had staying. I told them you'd gone away for Christmas and I didn't know if she was still with you.'

Her father must have decided to turn her in, though God knows how the police tracked her down to here. Looks like we're both on the run now.

'She's not in any trouble, is she?' Paula adds.

'No, no, nothing like that . . . She . . . She had a load of gear nicked a while ago. Maybe they've found it.'

Paula doesn't look convinced, but I'm not going to hang about and reassure her. 'I'll see you later,' I say. 'I'm in a bit of a hurry.' As I climb the stairs she calls out, 'Is everything OK?' but I don't answer. Isn't it obvious that *OK* doesn't come close to describing the status quo? *'Is everything crashing around your ears, threatening to crush your half-baked plans to make happy and*

304

joyous what little remains of your pathetic life?' would have been nearer the mark, but would still have understated it.

The door to my flat is ajar. *Shit.* Not again. I'm getting heartily sick of this. Coming home to the probability of intruders. This is the third time in a matter of weeks, and it does *not* get any less terrifying. If anything, prior experience makes it worse – I *know* how bad it can turn out.

I stand stock-still and peer through the gap in the door. There's no movement, no sound. I suspect they're long gone. I should leave now as well. Turn round, walk away, never come back . . .

But I can't. This is my home.

I tiptoe inside and head for the living room. I peer into the gloom and see . . .

My idea of hell, actually.

I remember the mess that Fish and the Geordie made, but that was nothing. They were amateurs. *This* is how to make a mess. This is horrific. Absolutely bloody horrific. Like a bomb has hit the place. Actually, a bomb blast would have pulverised everything, turned it into dust, but the broken things in my living room are still recognisable as my possessions and somehow that makes it worse. My leather sofa and armchair are on their backs, the upholstery slashed in several places, the stuffing leaking out and spread across the carpet in fat white lumps. The TV no longer has a screen. It's sitting on its stand floating in a sea of splintered glass. The yucca pot is shattered. Smears of damp brown soil cling high on the wall, the point of impact.

I pick my way through the debris and head for the kitchen, then my bedroom. Same story. My whole flat has been gutted, wrecked, beaten up.

I realise I'm crying. Everything that represents my life is in ruins. It isn't that I had anything of *real* value. No art. No jewels. Nothing to raise expert eyebrows on *Antiques Roadshow*. If I'm honest, the place was filled with rubbish. Even the leather sofa was a nasty brown thing, £499 from Universe of Sofas and only just on the legal side of the Trade Description Act. But it was *my* nasty brown thing, like all the other crap was *my* crap. All of it stood for *me*. Now I feel as if my entire existence has been trampled on, sledgehammered, kicked into a wet, dirty gutter. And I'm not even dead yet. Though I feel a lot closer than I have to date.

I've got to get out of here. I head for the front door, but stop in the corridor. I've spotted my mobile on the floor. I didn't leave it there. And I didn't leave it charging up – I've just seen the wire snaking out from it, running along the skirting board and up to the charger plugged into the socket. I bend down and pick it up with clammy hands, as if it might be a booby trap.

Why did they leave it? And also show me the consideration of recharging it?

I switch it on and it immediately bleeps. I drop it as if it's a grenade and jump backwards. I stand petrified, staring at it. It doesn't spark and fizz or explode or ooze green toxic gas. None of that. Not being a prop in an episode of *The Avengers*, it just sits on the carpet. Inert . . . Except for something blinking on the display. The little tape spool icon. I've got a message.

Better listen.

Though it's the last thing I want to do.

I pick up the handset and dial my voicemail. The flat voice tells me I have three messages. I play the first. A sweet, slightly West Country voice that takes me a moment to place.

'Hello . . . Murray Colin? . . . Murray, this is Doctor Morrissey from Saint Matthew's. I diagnosed your . . . Er . . . We need to talk. I think the best thing is that you get in touch with me. Or with any of my colleagues. Urgently. There's been a—'

I delete the message.

Right now I don't want to hear her tell me I was rather

ill-advised to forgo treatment. Or that there's a radical new therapy that will bring me out in pustulant sores but give me an extra fortnight to live. Or that – *whoops* – they misplaced a decimal point in their reckoning and why aren't I dead already?

I play the second message.

'Hello . . . Er, hello. This is a message for Murray *Colin* . . .'

A male voice. Again it's familiar.

'. . . This is Mr Hersh. You may remember me. I'm the . . . er . . . Senior Consultant Urologist at Saint Matthew's . . . Hospital . . .'

Why is Hersh calling me? Alarm bells are ringing, but I'm not sure whether they're clanging for good or ill. Surely he doesn't want to berate me for walking out on my op, standing up the surgical team – like there are cancellation charges or something. It doesn't sound as if he wants to berate me for anything, actually. He sounds too hesitant. I recall him withering under Megan's onslaught of questions. He was scared then and he sounds it again now.

'. . . Something's come to my attention . . . And I'd be very grateful if you could get in touch with us . . . With *me*. It really is quite . . . *Very* urgent. My number . . .'

He recites a couple of numbers, but I can't hear them for the deafening bells. What the hell is going on? As the message ends I'm none the wiser. And I'm panicking. What to do? . . . *I know*. Find a pen, replay the message, jot down the bloke's number, *call* him . . . But how am I going to find anything to write with in this mess? *Hang on*. There's a third message. Maybe it's Hersh again. Maybe a slightly more forthcoming version.

I play it.

'Muwway . . .'

Fuck.

'. . . Cancer hey? That is *majorly* depwessing. Imagine how *sad* I was to wead about your pwedicament. Hope you're not too dejected though . . . Anyway, if you're listening to this, you've obviously awwived home . . . We stopped by to collect the motor, but you must be off having fun in it. Well-deserved under the circs . . . Oh, just wemembered. My bwother's girlfwiend does some cwystal healing gig. Pwobably bollocks, but nothing ventured, eh? . . . I'll give you her number when we catch up.'

Fuck, fuck, FUCK.

Did I say I was panicking a moment ago? *This* is panicking. Panic that I can taste in the form of warm, acrid bile at the back of my throat. Panic that started to heat up when I found the police had been calling, that came to a simmer on seeing the remnants of my flat and that is now *seething* because I won't ever find out what either the cops or doctors want if Clark finds me first. Which he surely will once he does the obvious and visits Vince.

Vince.

Call Fish.

I fumble in my pocket and find a box of Dorchester matches. I read the number on the back and dial it.

'Fish!' I yelp as she picks up.

'I fucking *love* this place,' she says. 'I'm on the bed eating ice-cream and I'm watching a cheesy porn movie about a—'

'Fish!' I yelp again.

'What's up? You OK?'

'Call Vince. *Now*. Tell him he can't stay at home. They'll find him. He's got to get away somewhere—'

'*Murray*. Slow down. What's happened?'

'Can't explain now. Call Vince. Tell him he's not safe.'

'What's *happened*?'

'Later. Call him *now*.'

I cut the line and pocket the phone. I turn to leave when it vibrates against my leg. I freeze. I have *never* been this scared of a phone. I pull it back out of my pocket and stare at it. I briefly toy with the notion of switching it off, burying my head in the sand, but I don't. I press *answer* and put it to my ear.

'Hullo . . . Hullo?' asks a nervous voice. 'I'd like to speak to Murray Colin . . . Hullo? Is anyone there?'

'Speaking,' I say at last.

'Hullo, Mr Colin. I'm glad I've managed to get hold of you. This is Mr Hersh from . . . er . . . Saint Matthew's. Did you get my message?'

'Yes.'

Funny. I have some fairly pressing questions at this point, accompanied by an inability to ask any of them.

'Good . . . er . . . Good. Do you think you might be able to come in and see us? As I said it really is terribly important.'

'Yes . . . No,' I say, flustered, wanting to find out what this is about, but still not knowing how to go about it. 'Look, I'm really . . . strapped for time at the minute. What's going on?'

'I'm sorry, Mr Colin, but I don't think it's the kind of thing I can go into on the phone . . . We do need to see you.'

'What's going on? . . . I'm sorry I ran out on my operation, but – you know – this has been pretty bloody stressful.'

'It's nothing like that. There's been a . . . I really can't say over the phone.'

'There's been a *what*?'

'We need to see you, Mr Colin. Can I schedule an—'

A penny is dropping. The fear in his voice . . . I know it. I've felt it myself. The executive's terror upon finding out he has screwed up – a misdirected invoice, a ballsed up cancer diagnosis . . .

'You've made a mistake, haven't you?' I say. 'You've screwed up.'

I'm finding my voice now.

'Well . . . I wouldn't characterise it exactly like that, but there have been some . . . um . . . administrative . . . er . . . *complications*. Can we schedule an—'

'You've *screwed* up. You've found a tumour in a bit of my

body that I didn't even know existed and you forgot to mention it. Jesus, until two minutes ago I thought this was only an averagely bad day.'

Really finding my voice.

'Jesus. Shit . . . *Fuck*,' I rage.

'Please . . . Mr Colin, *please* calm down. It really is nothing like that.'

'What then? *What*?' I shout.

'I'm sorry, but it's not something that I'm at liberty to discuss on the phone.'

'Well, you've got to tell me *some*thing. You've got to give me a bloody clue.'

I say this with more urgency than I've ever said anything. This is because I've realised that any second now I'll very probably be dead. I've realised I'm not alone.

Clark is standing in the open doorway to my flat.

His hair is long, shimmering and fragrant.

His clothes are immaculate – sort of tailored hippy.

He might have stepped straight out of a Summer of Love spread in *Arena*.

Except he's holding a gun.

'*Please*,' I beg – both Mr Hersh and Clark.

'I can't say any more than . . . Well, it isn't *bad* news . . . as such.'

Clark is doing the finger slicing across the throat gesture – which could mean *cut the call* or *I'm about to cut your fucking throat* or both.

'*Please* tell me something,' I plead, 'because I am about to *die* here.'

'Mr Colin. *Murray*!' Mr Hersh squeaks, panic in his voice – probably picturing me teetering on a parapet. 'Please don't do anything precipitate. It's *good* news. You haven't got – We *have* made a mistake. You're *not* going to d—'

I don't hear the rest because Clark has taken the phone from

310

me. He presses the gun to my forehead, forcing me back against the wall. He puts the phone to his ear and says, 'Muwway's busy wight now. He'll wing you back, yah?' Then he shuts it down and slips it into my trouser pocket.

He stares at me. Unblinking.

I stare back, feeling the gun's stubby muzzle make an indentation in my skin.

Eventually he speaks. Softly. 'Muwway, let me explain. The way my colleagues opewate . . . It isn't so diffewent to a high stweet bank, yah? You know, you fill out the application, sign the declawation stating you've been honest . . . Declared *all* welevant details. Well, your avewage high stweet bank would be miffed in the event of a less than full disclosure. Likewise, my colleagues are *extwemely* disappointed. You weally should have mentioned the cancer.'

But I haven't got cancer. That's what the man was trying to say, wasn't he? There has been a glorious, wonderful cock-up at Saint Matthew's and I, Murray Colin, HAVE NOT GOT CANCER!

I should be dancing a jig of joy now, shouldn't I?

I'm sure I would be if my head weren't sandwiched between wall and gun.

'They're *well* disappointed with you, Muwway,' Clark goes on. 'But it's worse than that, because they're also pissed with Vince and me. He weferred you to me. I passed you on to my colleagues. It's like the Amex wecommend-a-fwiend thing, except we don't get a fwee hibachi barbecue. No, our weward is that – assuming evewything turns out OK – we get to live. That is, we *don't* die, dig?'

That's what he was going to say! Mr Hersh was definitely going to say 'You're not going to DIE' when he was so rudely cut off. I, Murray Colin, have NOT got cancer and I am NOT GOING TO DIE.

Clark presses the gun into me hard, as if he's trying to bore a hole in my head with the barrel, kill me without actually firing the thing.

But I'm not supposed to die.

The *strangest* thing. I'm experiencing a moment of perfect clarity. A floaty out-of-body moment, where I'm looking down on myself and seeing not only a beautiful man drilling a gun into my brain, but also the irony, the comic timing. One man tells me I'm reprieved at the *exact* moment another prepares to pass a death sentence.

The Good News: you're not going to die.

The Bad News: well, actually, you *are*.

I do what anyone in this position would do . . . Thinking about it, I don't suppose *many* people have been in this *precise* situation, but if they were, there's a fair chance they'd do what I do now.

Giggle.

Well, it *is* funny.

But more than that, I am crapping fat bloody bricks of *terror*.

So put the laughter down to nerves.

It's clear, though, that Clark isn't sharing the moment. 'You're a cocky twat – I'd love to kill you now, Muwway, I'd weally like nothing better . . .'

I'M NOT SUPPOSED TO DIE.

'. . . But we have to twy and sort out this *fucking* mess. Obviously we can forget Apwil the nineteenth. No, payback day is gonna be earlier . . . Let's say Monday. If I don't get the money in *full* by midnight on Monday, well, I'll kill you then.'

But don't you understand? You can't do that. I HAVEN'T GOT CANCER. I'M NOT GOING TO DIE. Dying is no longer in the script.

'Obviously, you being *terminal*, that might not bother you . . . So you should know that I'll also kill Vince. Then I'll find any mums, dads, bwothers, sisters and girlfwiends you might have and *kill* them. You see, I won't give too much of a shit because if I haven't got the money, I'm going to die too . . . Dig?'

To emphasise the point, he reaches down to my crotch and

312

wraps his manicured hand around my scrotum, as if a mere gun against my head isn't enough.

'Clark,' I whisper.

'Whassup, dude?'

'I haven't got cancer.'

'You must think I'm weally vewy stupid. I wead the paper, wemember? And – *fuck* – I can feel the fucking *lump*.' He whips his hand from my groin and instinctively wipes it on his shirt. 'Shit, they didn't say it was on your fucking gonads, man.'

'It's not cancer. That was the hospital. On the phone. Just now. They made a mistake,' I gabble. 'It's *not* cancer.'

'Have you looked in a miwwor, lately? You look like *shit*. You've got a fucking lump in your twousers the size of a . . . It's *big*, dude.'

He has a point. I have a lump. I look like shit. I *feel* like shit. What the hell is going on?

'No, you took me for a pwick in Momo. Don't twy it on again. Midnight, Monday, yah? One hundwed and fifty gwand.'

'One hundred,' I protest. 'You said one hund—'

'There's a penalty for being a lying cunt . . . *One hundwed and fifty*.'

I try to nod, but the gun prevents my head from moving. So I whisper 'OK' just as the doorbell buzzes. Clark jumps and so does the gun, the barrel sliding terrifyingly up my forehead. He takes a half pace back. 'Who is it?' he asks.

I shrug – I really have no idea.

We stand and stare at each other in silence.

It buzzes again.

'What shall I do?' I ask.

He grasps my arm and marches me the short distance to the door. He pushes his gun into the back of my head and nudges it towards the entryphone.

'Find out who it is,' he hisses.

Another buzz. I push the intercom button. 'Who is it?' I ask, praying it's the *Reader's Digest* Prize Draw people, here to give me the excellent and timely news that I've won £150,000.

'Police . . .'

Bugger.

'. . . Can we come in, please?' replies a woman's voice.

I look at Clark and see my fear mirrored in his face. And anger.

'I didn't call them . . . I swear,' I say.

'What the fuck do they want?'

'I don't know – *honestly.*'

'Hello . . . *Hello.* Can we come in, please?' the voice nags.

'OK, OK,' Clark says, rubbing his forehead, working things out. 'Give me thirty seconds to get the fuck out of here and let the bitch in. You know what'll happen if you mention me or my fwiends, yah?'

I nod.

'And wemember Monday – one hundwed and fifty gwand. Don't twy and do a wunner – you're being watched now . . . Evewy fucking step.'

Then he goes, disappears into my front room. I hear the window slide open and a clump as he hits the flat roof – the way Fish first gained entry. I ignore the angry buzzes, count silently to ten . . . And let the policewoman in.

As I listen to her climb the stairs I fly into a fresh panic. I recall the story in the *Mail*, the one about the burglary at Hyam-Glass's house. It made no mention of Fish. No, the only intruder was a bloke . . . *Me.* In the few seconds it takes for the police-woman to come up the stairs I try to think of an alibi . . . And, of course, I can't.

She's here now, standing in the open doorway of my flat. I'm looking at her ID. 'I'm DS Bruce, Woodford CID,' she says. She's a short woman with cropped brown hair and shocking pink eyeshadow. 'This is DC Vine,' she adds, indicating her younger male colleague. 'May we come in?'

I usher them into my hall, hoping to keep them there – the rest of my flat poses questions that I don't feel prepared to answer – but she bowls past me and into the living room.

'My goodness,' she gasps, taking in the wreckage. 'What happened here?'

'I . . . er . . . I've been burgled.'

'Burgled is hardly the word for it. Looks like you've had a visit from my colleagues in the drug squad – not known for their subtlety, are they, Des?' she says, glancing at her side-kick. She spots the distress on my face and says, 'I'm sorry, sir. Hardly something to joke about. It seems we came at a good time, eh? . . . You were going to report this, weren't you?'

I nod.

'Anyway, my advice to people in your shoes is to look for the positive. An experience like this is devastating, but once the dust has settled you'll perhaps see that this is the perfect opportunity to give the place a bit of a facelift.' She surveys the room for a moment. 'I'm a sucker for all those makeover shows. Call me completely crazy, but I think a Byzantine theme might work in here . . . Purples and golds, mosaics, embroidered throw cushions . . . a bit of gilt on the cornice perhaps. You could go quite *exotic* with it . . . Crikey, just listen to me going on. I don't know the first thing about your personal taste. I don't even know your name.'

'Murray Colin,' I reply, relaxing a little.

'Ah, yes, it said *Colin* on the doorbell. Thought that might be a first name.'

'A lot of people do . . . Anyway, how can I help?'

'We're looking for a homeless girl. She calls herself Fish. Some of her street friends told us that she'd been seen popping in and out of here.'

'She was here,' I say. 'She left before Christmas, though. I've been away for ten days. I don't know where she is now.' Well,

315

some of it's true. The first bit. 'Why are you looking for her?' I ask, my face – I hope – a picture of innocence.

'We're investigating the death of a friend of hers. A hit and run. Only a hop, skip and a jump from here, as it happens. We understand he was looking for her on the night he died. He may have seen her and we were hoping she might be able to fill in some of the blanks.'

I wasn't expecting her to say that and I'm tossed into panic's whirlpool again. All of my half-prepared answers are redundant now and my head is filling up with the – frankly *unhelpful* – vision of Geordie flipping into the air on Hermon Hill.

'Now I think about it,' DS Bruce continues amiably, 'we have a witness who tells us she saw someone kneeling by his body. The description we've been given could match you . . . Mind you, it was so vague it could also match about a million other blokes. That's the trouble with police work. The public is usually willing to help, but your average eyewitness couldn't accurately describe Mel Gibson if he plonked himself in the next seat on the bus. The witness says the man didn't wait for an ambulance. Apparently he got in his car and drove off . . . Do you own a car, sir?'

'Er . . . Yes.'

'What make is it, out of curiosity?'

'A VW . . . um . . . Polo.'

'*Really*,' she murmurs, very interested now. 'Where is it?'

'I . . . I don't know . . . It was stolen. Before Christmas.'

'It's hardly been the season of goodwill for you, has it? Did you report it?'

'Um . . . No . . . I was going to, but I didn't have time before I went away . . . And it was worth next to nothing . . . And—'

'You should always report these things,' she says with a smile. I smile back, though mine is so forced that it must resemble an insanely contorted Joker grin. 'Can I ask you where you were in the early hours of December the twentieth, say between midnight and two?' she continues, still in the same amiable tone.

I look back at her blankly. I have no idea what to say.

'It was a Saturday,' she nudges.

I know that.

'I was . . . here . . . I think.'

'Was Fish with you?'

'Probably . . . Yes. Why?'

But I don't want to hear the answer. She doesn't give me one, because her sidekick coughs and says, ''Scuse me, ma'am, maybe you should take a look at this.' He's crouching on the floor. He has cleared away some of the debris and he's looking at a large reddish-brown stain on the beige carpet, the one that Megan told me not to get because it would *show up everything*. I *wish* I'd listened to her, especially as she had her eye on a lovely russet Wilton . . . pretty much the colour of dried blood. And I also wish that in the few days between Geordie dying and me leaving for Spain I had made an attempt to clean it up. The old me would have shifted into stain eradication overdrive. The old me would have looked at that unsightly splodge of blood much as Shackleton must have gazed at a map of Antarctica – as a challenge to be vanquished. But, oh no, my inner Jimi Hendrix had taken temporary control of things and – let's not mince words – he's a bloody slob.

DS Bruce joins her colleague on the floor and rubs delicately at the dark patch with a pink-polished fingertip. 'Can you tell me what this is, sir?' she asks.

'I can't remember.'

'Come on, a big stain like this on such a lovely carpet?'

'Red wine or something.'

She raises an eyebrow, indicating that she's going with the *or something* part of my answer. Then she says to her sidekick, 'Call SOCO. Hang on until they get here.'

'What's going on?' I ask, though, of course, I *know* – this room

ceased to be my living room the moment Clark and his demolition crew visited. After a few hours in undefined limbo it has
now been officially redesignated as a *Scene of Crime*.

DS Bruce raises herself up from the carpet and turns to me.
'Mr Colin, the incident we're investigating was a little more
complicated than a simple hit and run. Apart from what our
witness tells us, the victim also had injuries that weren't consis-
tent with being hit by a vehicle.'

I don't say anything. It's not that I'm exercising my right to
silence. It's because my vocal chords are paralysed. DS Bruce,
probably an expert in body language as well as Byzantine decor,
is studying me as if I'm a textbook case. Then she says, 'I think
you'd better come back to the station with me.'

'Why . . . What for?' I splutter.

'I'm hoping you can tell me that when we get there.'

five: **please don't jump**

I'm sitting on a bum-numbing plastic chair in a small police interview room.

A few hours with DS Bruce spent *not* talking about interior design felt more like years. Now I'm exhausted. I haven't been able to move since she left me with, 'I think we both need a little space to consider our options, Murray.'

Mine seem distinctly limited.

She hasn't actually said it yet; she hasn't called me a murderer. But that's surely what she's thinking. After all, she has a blood-stain on my carpet – presented like some gift-wrapped clue in a country-manor whodunit evening. She has a witness – an unseen curtain twitcher – who has me fleeing the scene in a Volkswagen Polo . . . Which has rather conveniently been stolen. What more does she need? A confession? Well, I gave her one near as damn it. I told her what happened that night, though I did understate the money – if fifty grand isn't motive for murder, then how much? As my story was unfolding it struck me how plausible it must have sounded . . . Except for the bit with the psycho-driven BMW. I mean, how likely is that?

And at the time I thought it was my lucky night.

I've been on my own for well over an hour . . . *Considering my options*. Going round in pointless and diminishing circles, actually. I look around the bleak, cheap room and I feel as if I'm in *The Bill* – an in-and-out in one episode part. Except this is real. It isn't a studio set with wobbly plywood walls – I've tested them and they're all too solid. I light a cigarette and, in the absence of anything else to look at, gaze at the packet . . .

at the slab of black type: *Smoke contains benzene, nitrosamines, formaldehyde and hydrogen cyanide.* My chemistry was never up to much, but that doesn't sound good. I flip the box over and get the punch line: *Smoking kills.*

Shit. Smoking causes cancer. I haven't got cancer.

Have I?

I frantically stub out the barely burned fag in the dirty foil ashtray. And once again – for the millionth time today (and I believe I mean that *literally*) – I'm desperately trying to remember what Mr Hersh said before Clark cut him off.

You haven't got . . .

Haven't got what?

Cancer?

The ability to carry a tune?

A rat's chance?

What?

Then *You're not going to d—*

A word beginning with D that might have been *die* . . . Or one of several hundred feasible alternatives that a dictionary could throw up.

But what else was it he said? That it wasn't *bad news – as such.* He said *as such.* It sounded like executive code for something. But what? I try to remember my days as a suit. Did I ever – in a weaselly, suit-y way – say *as such*? Probably. I used to say more or less anything to fuzz up the truth. But he also very clearly said it was *good news.* He used those exact bloody words and he didn't hedge them with any *as such*es, *in a manner of speaking*s, or *looked at perspectively*s (which, to my eternal shame, I did say at least once). *Good news* he said. Good news, good news, *good* fucking news.

So why has the initial rush of elation given way to infuriating, tail-chasing confusion? Because I look like *shit.* I *feel* like shit. I have a *lump.* A lump that until only a few hours ago was *definitely* going to kill me – and let's not forget I had *that* on

320

very good authority. I reach my hand down to my crotch . . . Maybe it has gone. But no. Still there. Larger than life . . . Maybe it's my imagination, but it seems to throb gently beneath my touch. It's taunting me: *Don't get your hopes up, matey*.

I've *got* to find out.

I take my mobile from my pocket and switch it on. The sign on the wall makes it plain that I'm not allowed to use it in here, but – come *on* – I'm facing a murder charge. I'm a bad boy now. I replay Hersh's message, listen to his numbers. He probably won't be at the hospital at this hour, but one of them is a mobile. I play the message again, memorise it, then dial.

It's answered on the fourth ring.

'Mr Hersh?' I say. '. . . It's Murray Colin.'

'*Murray*, Mr Colin, thank heaven you've phoned back,' he says, suddenly breathless. 'I'm so glad you haven't done anything . . .'

He trails off and I remember that the last time we spoke I had him picturing me balanced on a parapet about to leap.

'You've *got* to tell me what's going on,' I say.

'As I explained, the best place to do that is at the hospital,' he says, reverting to the party line. 'I can fully understand your desp— your *concern*, but it would be most unethical to go into detail over the phone. Look . . . How about this? We could do it tonight. Yes, we could do that. If you can . . . um . . . get yourself to Saint Matthew's I'd be happy to go back in and take you through things.'

Under normal circumstances I'd love to, but . . .

'I need to know *now*.'

'Please, you have to understand that I can't tell you anything over the phone.'

But I know now how to play this and I say, 'I'm sitting on a window ledge, Mr Hersh. The street is six floors down. If you don't tell me what's going on they'll be scraping me off the pavement.'

(This is preposterous. I'm terrified of heights. If I really was going to end it all, the last place you'd find me is on a window ledge . . . But he's not to know that.)

'God. *Please* . . . Oh my bloody *God*!' he says. 'Please don't . . . Don't do anything you might regret, Mr Colin.'

'I've got terminal cancer. *Weeks* to live. Why should I regret ending it now?'

'Because you *haven't* . . .'

'Haven't what?'

'You haven't got – I shouldn't be telling you this, I really shouldn't . . . There has been a mistake. Your situation isn't terminal . . . as such.'

There he goes *as such*ing again.

'What do you mean, *isn't terminal*?'

'Your diagnosis. You have got cancer. Probably. But it isn't . . . *isn't* as bad . . . Not nearly as bad as we thought.'

'What do you mean? I'm not going to die?'

'Well, in all likelihood not any time soon. If you come and see us right away and begin treatment there's an extremely high probability you'll make a full recovery . . . Mr Colin? . . . Mr Colin? . . . Are you there? . . .'

I can't speak for the raging confusion. I've got cancer *probably* but I'm not going to die *as such*. What the hell . . . What the *fuck* is going on? I can hear a strange sound . . . It's me choking, sobbing.

'Murray? . . . *Murray*? Please tell me you haven't jumped . . . *Please.*'

'I'm here . . . I'm here,' I say between deep, forced breaths. '*Shit* . . . I haven't . . . What . . . *How*?'

'If you promise to climb down from the ledge, I'll explain . . .'

Let's be absolutely clear about this. There's bad news. I have got cancer. *Probably*. But there's good news too. My cancer won't kill me. *Probably*. I don't fall into the category of No Chance, file under *Doomed*. Stick me under L for Lucky Blighters, the ones who more than likely recover and return to the community wiser for the experience – that is if they're not too busy making an utter dog's mess of their lives.

My *probable* cancer is in my left testicle. They still can't be certain until they take it out and poke around at it. But IT ISN'T ANYWHERE ELSE. Remember the CT scan that told them my lungs and liver were riddled with the disease; the scan that said I was going to die? Well, get this: it wasn't *my* CT scan. It was somebody else's – somebody else with very bad cancer. Mr Hersh won't tell me anything about him except that he has my build and he's about my age. No one realised that his film had gone into my file and mine into his until just after Christmas. While I was wilting in Spain, he was rushed to hospital showing all the symptoms of a man dying from cancer. They couldn't understand it at first, having only a few weeks previously given him a clean-ish bill of health. So they took another look at his scan. That was when they saw that the little label in the corner displayed a name that wasn't his.

A truly terrible blow for the poor guy. I *know* what he must be going through.

And wonderful, fantastic, *stupendous* news for me. Except I can't *feel* it.

Because as Mr Hersh finishes his explanation it's dawning on me that since the day I was diagnosed I've been working on a single project – and I've been performing with more determination than I'd ever thought myself capable of. It's just about finished. My self-dug grave is, give or take the odd clod, ready. I'm lying in it now, waiting for them to toss in the earth.

'But I feel like *shit*. I'm *ill*,' I say once he's finished his explanation.

'There could be any number of reasons for that, Mr Colin,' Hersh says, sounding calmer now that he's no longer picturing me on a window ledge. 'The thing is that as far as we can tell your cancer – if indeed it is cancer – *hasn't* spread. At least it hadn't at the time of your scan and there's good reason to suppose that it hasn't in the fairly short time since then. But you do need to come to the hospital so—'

'How is he?' I ask.

'Who?'

'The other guy.'

'I'm not at liberty to divulge confidential patient information,' he says, slipping seamlessly back into official speak . . . But there's something about his voice.

'He's dead, isn't he?'

'I shouldn't be— New Year's Eve . . . Sooner than any of us expected . . . Sometimes these things just . . .' He doesn't go on. *He* sounds choked now.

'I've screwed up before,' I say. 'I sent an invoice to the wrong client a few months ago. Stupid mistake. I got a right bollocking. These things happen.'

These things happen. Mistakes. Administrative blunders. Clerical errors. Cock-ups. But as was said of mine – as you can say of ninety-nine-point-nine per cent of them – *nobody died*.

'It's kind of you to say that,' he sighs. 'You're being very magnanimous . . . Look, you really must come in to see us. We need to begin treatment as a matter of urgency. Your operation shouldn't be delayed any longer. And the shock and confusion you must be experiencing . . . We have people you can talk to about that.'

It's my turn to go quiet.

'Mr Colin?'

'I've got to go now.'

I *do* need to talk to someone.

'Please, don't hang—'

'Don't worry. I'm not going to jump,' I say before cutting him off.

I pull the Dorchester matches from my pocket and read the number. The receptionist answers, then puts me on hold and I pray – and I mean *pray* – that when she connects me someone answers, and that someone is Fish, and that she's alone and not in the throes of bleeding to death, her throat slashed by vicious money lenders.

'Putting you through now, sir.'

It's picked up first ring.

'Fish?'

Please let it be.

'Murray!'

Yeeesss!

'Are you OK?' I ask.

'Never mind me. Where the fuck are you?'

'Woodford nick.'

'*Shit*. What happened?'

'Later. Where's Vince?'

'He's here. He booked into the room next door. He's fine.'

'Thank God. So he hasn't heard from Clark?'

'No . . . Murray, I've been worried sick. What's going on?'

'They're questioning me about Geor— Andy's death. They know he was round my flat.'

'But you didn't do anything.'

'Apart from bust his nose and get spotted driving away from his body.'

'Fucking hell. I'm coming down there. I'm gonna tell them what happened. That mad fucking twat was gonna kill me.'

'For God's sake don't do that. They'll probably arrest you too.'

'But I need to get you out of there,' she says, crying now. 'I'm going fucking mad without you.'

'I know, I know, me too . . . I need a lawyer.'

'Where am I gonna find one of them?' she asks, genuinely thrown.

325

'Call Megan.'

'Your ex?' she asks, a smidgen of new girlfriend insecurity creeping into her voice, but not enough to make a meaningful dent in the panic that's already there.

'Her numbers are in my address book. She might be in Scotland, but tell her she's got to help me out, even if it's just to give you the name of another solicitor.'

'OK, OK, I'll call her.'

'There's something else. I'm not going to . . .'

I can't get the words out. Because I still can't believe it and also because DS Bruce has stepped into the room. 'I'd like you to end that call immediately,' she says through gritted teeth.

'Who's that, Murray? Is someone there?'

'I'm *not* going to *die*,' I yell as DS Bruce walks purposefully towards me.

'What the fuck are you on about?' Fish pleads, crying and confused. 'Don't hang up. *Don't*. Murray, I lo—'

For the second time today my mobile is taken from me – snatched forcibly this time – and switched off. The call is dead, but I heard enough to send my heart into a little spasm . . . of welcome delight . . . mixed with nauseating dread. Because I don't want her to *luh* me. I don't want her to have to deal with the *shit* I'm in. That's because maybe-but-who-the-hell-knows-any-more I'm beginning to *luh* her too.

'Would you like to tell me what that was all about?' DS Bruce asks, sitting down opposite me.

'Just a friend. I wanted her to know . . . I want her to get me a lawyer.'

'A lawyer. A pain in the bum from where I'm sitting, but probably a good idea.' She pauses and looks at me deeply. 'Murray, I hope you don't mind me saying, but you look like shit. Are you OK?'

'Yes . . . Er . . . Yes. I've been . . . It isn't ca— I've had the flu. Quite badly.'

326

'Let's hope you're on the mend. Now, I'd like to talk about this money . . .'

'Take me through it again, Murray. This *five grand*, this money you won on a *horse* . . .'

Can you tell that I haven't done this before? I'm pretty sure that Detective Sergeant Bruce can. The horse thing. Somewhere lodged in my head – based probably on a half-remembered episode of *Taggart* or *Morse* or (who the hell knows?) something PC Plod said in *Noddy* – was the notion that the best way to explain away a suspicious wedge of cash is to put it down to a lucky win. Trouble is I've never been into a betting shop in my life. The places scare me – as far as I'm concerned they're in the same category as lap-dancing clubs and crack dens. Horses make me nervous and odds simply confuse me – I wouldn't know an each-way bet from a two-way radio. So I hope she doesn't ask me . . .

'What was it called?'

'What?'

'The horse?'

That's the one I was hoping she wouldn't ask me.

'I can't remember.'

'Come on, a big win like that. If it had been me, I'd be putting up a plaque to the nag in my living room.'

'I can't remem— *Bubbles*.'

'Excuse me?'

'That was the name of the horse. Bubbles.'

Jesus, Bubbles herself would be able to tell I haven't done this before.

'Where did it win?'

'She. It was a girl horse.'

'A *filly*. Where did *she* win?'

'Um . . .' Shit, shit, *shit.* ' . . . Er . . . Kenton. That was it. Kenton Park.'

'I think you'll find it was *Kemp*ton.'

The door opens – thank God the *door* opens – and Bruce's sidekick walks in. He bends down and whispers something in his boss's ear. She scrapes her chair back and stands up. 'You'll have to excuse me, Murray. I'll be back as soon as I can . . . And maybe you can give me some racing tips, eh?'

10.21 p.m.

This has been the longest hour.

I think it must be about an hour. I'm not wearing a watch and my only access to the time was my mobile. DS Bruce took the battery as she left me – a sensible precaution against further unauthorised calls.

I'm hoping desperately that Fish got hold of Megan.

Worrying, that one. Getting new girlfriend to call the old one. Not something, I suspect, that a relationship expert would advise. Especially when old girlfriend played a small part in new one's swan dive into destitution . . .

Shit.

What if Fish called Meg and he *picked up the phone?* She may have forgotten *his* voice – it was over five years ago, after all – but I doubt it. I'll take Sandy Morrison's monstrous Celtic boom to my grave and all he did was nick my girlfriend – he didn't blight my entire adolescence and effectively end any hope I had of making peace with my family.

In all of my conversations with Fish about her father – there've been a few since we broke into his house – I never once mentioned that my ex was on the legal team that was ranged against him . . . Or that she's now living with Fish's tormentor in chief. I chose not to tell her because – I assured myself – I didn't want to hurt her by bringing events from the dim past

328

into the harsh light of the present. *Ha.* I didn't tell her because I didn't want her to associate me with *them,* and therefore like me any less.

And now, maybe, that act of selfishness has earned precisely what it deserves.

10.37 p.m.

'Sorry about that, Murray. An unrelated matter,' DS Bruce apologises with apparent sincerity. 'You know how it is with crime. Nothing doing for a day or two, then four come along at once.'

No, I wouldn't know how it is, Detective Sergeant, being fairly new to this crime thing.

'We'll move on from the money. Getting us nowhere fast, that one. Now, my colleague has called British Airways. They confirmed you went to Spain. They told him you didn't travel alone, though. Who's Isabel Hyam-Glass? She wouldn't be the elusive Fish, would she?'

I nod.

'Unusual name, *Hyam-Glass.* She wouldn't be related to—'

'I honestly hadn't thought about it,' I say too quickly. I'm panicking afresh as I watch DS Bruce take a first tentative step towards a crime that she so far hasn't thought to link me with – a widely reported break-in at a Hampstead des res.

I wish Megan were here – for once, *nothing* to do with lovesickness. As DS Bruce looks at me, irritated now, I imagine a scenario where Fish's call is answered by Sandy who says, '*Ach, if it isnae the wee Hyam-Glass lassie – I ne'er forget the voice of a courtroom adversary, even one as naïvely inept as your sweet self,*' whereupon she slams down the phone, leaving me to rot deservedly in jail. Why the hell did I ask her to call Megan? Why, when I've already dug myself into such a deep hole that I'm in danger of breaking through the earth's crust, did I have to get my spade back out?

'Look, let's not piss about any more,' snaps DS Bruce. 'I'm not in the best of moods. My evening has already gone for a burton. I was supposed to be at my eleven-year-old's drama club tonight. They're doing *Bugsy Malone*. He's playing a gangster, would you believe? My husband will have videoed it, but it's not the same . . . Now, let's *focus*. Fish – *Isabel* Hyam-Glass. Related to him off the telly or not?'

'His daughter.'

'Alive or dead?'

'Alive.'

'Where?'

I don't answer. I'm wondering what Megan would advise me to say.

'Well?' DS Bruce nudges.

'I'm not obliged to tell you, you know,' I mumble, imagining that Meg would probably be shoving me in the general direction of taciturnity.

'Advising me on suspects' rights? I've done this before, you know. Where's Fish? You claim you were saving her life on the night Andrew Edwards died. I'm inclined not to believe you, but who knows? If I could talk to her maybe she could help you out.'

Maybe she could.

But I. Just. Can't. Do. It.

'She's still in Spain,' I blurt.

'BA told us she came back with you – the *rotten* liars.'

'OK, she isn't in Spain, but I haven't seen her since we got back.'

'Don't believe you.'

'We got a train into town together, but I said goodbye to her at Victoria. She's probably back on the streets now.'

'You're trying to tell me that after you'd bought her a holiday abroad she happily returned to the street? To a cardboard box? . . . You're seriously expecting me to believe that? . . . I thought you agreed to stop pissing me about.'

Well, I didn't strictly agree.

'I gave her some money. I think she booked into a hotel.'

'Which one?'

'I've no idea.'

'*Which one?*'

'The Dor . . . The Dor . . . The *door*. There's someone at the door.'

Jesus Christ, that was close.

DS Bruce turns her head to see a constable sticking his head into the room. 'Sorry to interrupt, ma'am, but Mr Colin's brief is here and she'd like to see him.'

'Wouldn't you know it? Just when we were getting somewhere,' she sighs. 'Better send her—'

Megan doesn't wait for the rest of the invitation. She pushes past the policeman and into the room. The sight of her washes over me like warm, bubbly, sweet-scented bath water. The sight of me, on the other hand, appears to slap her hard in the face. She is visibly shaken – well, I look like *shit*. But she's a professional – God, is she a *pro* – and she pulls herself together in a flash.

'I'm Megan Dyer, Mr Colin's solicitor,' she announces, thrusting out a hand towards DS Bruce – not to shake; it contains her business card. 'I'd like a few moments alone with my client.'

DS Bruce, as I've by now gathered, is also the consummate professional and she isn't fazed by Megan's impersonation of a crack NATO rapid-deployment force. 'I think that Mr Colin was just about to reach the punch line,' she says in a measured voice. 'Perhaps we could be allowed to finish. You're welcome to sit in, of course.'

'I don't need an invitation from you for that,' Megan responds testily. 'Frankly, I can't believe you're keeping my client here. Given his condition it amounts to a clear case of police brutality and it's going to stop right now.'

331

'Excuse me, Ms Dyer. What condition?'

'You must know that Mr Colin is in the late stages of terminal cancer.'

'No . . . *No*, I did not know any such thing. Is this true, Murray?' DS Bruce shoots me her most sceptical look yet.

My mouth is flapping like a carp's because . . . Well, I'm not in the late stages of anything, am I? Unless I count generally fucking up my life.

But I nod. I *nod* frantically because I have seen a chink of light. An *escape*.

'You said you had *flu*,' DS Bruce says.

'If my client chooses to keep his illness private, *then that is his right*,' Megan interrupts. 'I think, however, that under the circumstances his interests are better served if you know.'

DS Bruce is still looking at me in disbelief. 'I presume I can verify this.'

'My client has been receiving treatment at Saint Matthew's. I'm sure he'll let you speak to his doctors and confirm the *gravity* of his condition,' Megan says.

I almost interrupt her because they'll verify no such thing, but she's looking at me for a sign of agreement, and making it perfectly clear that anything less would be utter madness . . . So I nod my head again.

Then she walks round to my side of the little table and scoops my jacket from the back of the plastic chair. She holds it up behind me as if she's a waitress in a posh restaurant. I accept the invitation without pause and slip my arms into the sleeves.

'What do you think you're doing?' DS Bruce splutters.

'Look at my client, detective . . .'

'Detective Sergeant Bruce,' DS Bruce murmurs, finally completing the introductions.

'Does he honestly appear to be in any fit state to carry on being interrogated?'

She's right. She's *so* right. Everyone says it: *I look like shit*.

'He needs rest and medication, and he needs it now,' she continues before turning to me and saying, 'Come on, Murray, I'll take you home.'

six: *exquisite*

I'm sitting in the heated leather passenger seat of Sandy Morrison's Bentley. It's parked about a quarter of a mile from the police station. After Megan had negotiated my release and made a show of driving me off under DS Bruce's still befuddled gaze, she pulled over at the first opportunity so that we could talk.

Well, we've talked. Or rather I have. I've told her everything. I related it as a single contradiction-free narrative as well – DS Bruce should have been so lucky. Now Meg grips the wheel, though the car is stationary. She hasn't spoken for a couple of minutes, and she's looking at me as if she doesn't know me at all.

Which, I suppose, she doesn't. The Murray she knew was a lily-livered account supervisor too wet to handle the metaphoric knives of advertising, let alone mix it with those that flashed the real steely kind. He wasn't a crook. They were what she went to work for. After a long day of counselling criminal waifs and misfits she seemed to enjoy coming home, kicking off her shoes and falling into the embrace of a bloke who was safe, cautious – all right, *dull* – and so *dis*inclined towards criminality that the thought of parking in a disabled bay brought him out in a cold, prickly sweat.

Not that I've transformed myself into a swaggering gangster – a swaggering *anything* would be nice. However, the story I've just spun – pockmarked with drug dealers, loan sharks, a dead street-kid, a wad-stuffed kebab bag – must have her wondering how much deeper I could possibly sink.

'What can I say?' she manages at last. 'I remember you telling me you wanted to make things happen . . . But, *Jesus*, I didn't think this was what you had in mind.'

'It wasn't,' I say. 'Things kind of . . . you know . . . snowballed.'

'Jesus, Murray,' she gasps, shaking an incredulous head.

'Look, thanks for getting me out of there,' I say, attempting to pull her back to earth. 'I can't tell you how grateful I am.'

'Don't be silly. I'm just glad we came back early from Scotland.'

'Why did you?'

'Oh, nothing serious. You'll probably like this, actually. Sandy sprained his ankle. We weren't halfway up Ben Nevis before you ask. He did it dancing on Hog— . . . New Year's Eve.' She gives me a weak smile.

I think back to New Year's Eve – *Hogmanay*. Me uncharacteristically dancing like a demon and Sandy Morrison – whom, I imagine, is only too keen to cut a rug – sustaining a mild yet satisfying injury. I'm not superstitious, but I'm tempted to think that there might have been some voodoo magic at work.

Megan hits the steering wheel with her palms, a trademark *let's get organised* gesture, and says, 'Right, we have to plan some sort of strategy before I take you back in for questioning on Monday. You're going to have to tell her about the loan, you know. You'll have to get your friend Fish to see her as well. Disclosure will buy you some peace in your last . . . Jesus, this is hard. I'm sorry, Murray, but you're going to have to face up to this. You haven't got long . . .'

Did I say I'd told her everything? Well, I might have forgotten to mention one thing. The stop press, oh-my-God-doesn't-this-put-a-whole-new-complexion-on-things bit of news. The fact that . . . you know . . . I'm not actually terminal. I couldn't tell her. I feel too guilty. She has been living the last few weeks under a fallacy – not my fault, admittedly, since I've been its victim as well. But when I did have a chance to put her right in the police station, I didn't. I let her *lie* for me. Megan hates dishonesty. In her professional life. In her personal life. She *really* loathes it. Of the many principles she lives by it's the most important.

I can't tell her now. She'll kill me.

Though she'll have to join the queue.

'. . . Maybe I can get Sandy to—'

'Hold on, Megan.'

'I'm sorry, I know you probably don't want to hear his name, but there isn't a better defence lawyer in the country. We'd be mad not to pick his brain.'

'It isn't that.'

'What then?' she asks.

I can't continue the lie.

Out of respect to the bloke who got my scan as well as to Megan.

Anyway, she'll find out the truth soon enough.

It really pains me to concede this, but better she discovers it from me. Now.

'Meg . . . There's something I have to tell you . . .'

'. . . And you came into the police station like such a whirl-wind that I couldn't get a word in edgeways and – Look, I'm sorry. I should have said something. I shouldn't have let you tell her.'

'No, you shouldn't . . . You shouldn't have done that. I'll have to phone her and explain. She's going to think I'm such a bloody shyster.'

A *shyster*, I know, is the one class of lawyer that Megan would hate to be thought of more than any other – apart from, maybe, a tax specialist.

'I'm sorry, but I was desperate to get out of there.'

'I'd have got you out, Murray. She wasn't ready to charge

you with anything yet and even if she had been . . . *I'd have got you out*. You should have trusted me.'

'I'm sorry,' I mumble.

'I can't believe it,' she says quietly – finally absorbing the enormity of my news, I guess.

'Neither can I,' I say. 'I'm still reel—'

'I can't believe what a complete bloody *idiot* you've been.'

'*What?*'

'Look at you. Just *look* at you. You're facing a *murder* charge. Vicious thugs want to *kill* you. Look at the mess you're in. *Jesus* . . .'

'I thought I was *dying*, Megan.'

'What if you hadn't run away from the hospital that day? Have you even considered that?' Wild anger flashes in her eyes. 'Don't you think you'd have found out a lot sooner that you're *not* dying? You wouldn't have got yourself into all this shit. God, you might even still have a job.'

'You hated that job.'

'That's not the point.'

'It is the point. It so *is* the point,' I say, feeling indignant anger of my own well up. 'When I found out I was – when I thought I only had a few months I decided to do what *you* always wanted me to do. Change my life. *Do* something.'

'Oh, you did this to *impress* me? Well, a big round of applause for Murray. Who'd have thought a man could burn so many bridges, piss so many people off in so little time. God, I am *so* impressed. *Bravo.*'

Once again she shakes her head at me – though this time it's out of contempt rather than incredulity. 'This is typical of you. It's exactly why I left you. You spend years pointlessly flapping around like a . . . like a bloody great wet thing, then . . . Then *what*? You go mad. A headless chicken would look calm and rational next to you. You never think *anything* through.'

337

I'm stunned. This is my dumping revisited. With big bloody knobs on.

'I can't believe I was having second thoughts,' she mutters.

'Pardon?'

'Second thoughts,' she spits. 'You know, maybe-I've-done-the-wrong-thing kind of thoughts. They kicked in when I came back to collect my stuff. Then when we started seeing each other again – you know, all those hospital visits . . .'

'You were having *second thoughts*?'

'I guess it was just pity,' she says coldly. 'Imminent *death* does that.'

I can't speak.

'Murray, there's something you should know . . . I suppose I should have told you . . . No, I don't owe you explanations any more. Whatever, I'm telling you now. Sandy and I are engaged.'

'*Wow*,' I whisper. 'Since when?'

'Does it matter?'

'Well, no, I don't suppose—'

'He asked the weekend after you tried to do his car in, if you must know.'

That was . . . How many weeks ago? *She could have told me.* And there was me fretting about withholding something from her for . . . ooh, all of fifty minutes.

'Well . . . I suppose . . . Congratulations,' I say quietly. 'I guess he gave you a great big bloody—'

I don't finish because I have just spotted the great big bloody thing sparkling on her ring finger. As I focus on it I feel the single diamond's glints of light shoot out and stab me like acid laser pulses . . . And all I can say is, 'It's . . . *exquisite*.'

And it really is every bit as exquisite as the day JP Stein sold it to me in Hatton Garden.

seven: **you're a dead bloody cert, chief**

My legs ache from walking. I'm in Hackney. Not sure where exactly. A busy high road. People are hanging out, mooching aimlessly, walking home. Stumbling mostly. Wired, dangerous-looking people. It's not the sort of place a fudge-soft twonk like me wants to be at nearly one on a Saturday morning. But on the morning after the day I had yesterday I think I can make an exception. I see a sign. Mare Street. Very fitting because I'm having one. My head is a mess, and for someone who craves tidiness and order (preferably alphabetical) this is not a happy state of affairs.

Such a God-awful *mess*.

Where do I start?

Just where the hell do I start?

The not being riddled with cancer. Megan's righteous and – fair dos – justified anger. The not being riddled with cancer. The impending murder charge. The one hundred and fifty grand by Monday. The murder charge joined by the burglary charge. Mum reading about my cancer in yesterday's *Mail*. The *not* being riddled with cancer. The murder charge joined by the burglary charge and – how could I possibly forget this? – the crashing-into-a-cop-car-while-drunk-out-of-my-skull-and-being-sucked-off-by-six-foot-Saffy charge. One *hundred* and *fifty* grand by *Monday*. The not being riddled with cancer . . . . Which means that – ha, ha, bloody *ha* – I *will* have to pay off my credit cards, my back rent. My *wrecked* flat. Megan's *hate*-dipped anger. Megan's *engagement* to that smug, pompous *fuck*. The not being riddled with ca— *That smug, pompous, arrogant, tight-fisted . . .*

339

I'm sorry, and excuse me for digressing for just one minute . . . *but what a thieving fucking tight-wad JOCK.*

That is a *very* un-me thought. I was being politically correct in the days when PC merely described my dad – a bloke in a navy blue suit with shiny silver buttons and a pointy hat. There may have been the occasional lapse, but I've always gone out of my way to avoid the thick Irish/boring Belgians stuff. As for the Scots . . . While I admit that I've yet to come across an exciting Belgian, I have never met a mean Jock. And I have never, ever, not once suggested that they are tight. But . . . *But* . . .

Forgive me, *please* forgive me.

But what a mean, miserly, ungenerous, niggardly, parsimonious, penny-pinching, cheese-paring, stingy, skinflint, scrubby, Scrooge-like SCOTTISH TIGHTWAD.

The guy earns a million a year in fees alone. Whack in the book royalties, TV appearance money and maybe even the odd spot of cash for opening chichi Islington delis and you're looking at the swaggering definition of Seriously Loaded.

I presume the *cheap, mingy, penurious, short-armed-deep-pocketed CELTIC CUNT* found the ring on the floor of his car. Being – as Megan *repeatedly* told me – one of the sharper brains at the bar, he must have known how it got there. He must *know* that he has not only thieved my girlfriend, but also my expression of undying devotion to her. Maybe he enjoys the neatness, the fully-rounded *completeness* of sacking my life so thoroughly. If so, he is not only as *tight as a mayfly's arse*, but also a deeply disturbed *fuck* who no more has a conscience than did Idi Amin.

No, I'm not suggesting that he'd bump off his enemies and pop their dismembered bodies in the fridge . . .

Hang on, I *am* suggesting *precisely that*. Sandy Morrison QC is such a heinous, scum-sucking rat that the *only* reason he doesn't chop up and chill his opponents is that he has calculated the odds and figured he won't get away with it. Unlike how he has managed to steal *my* ring before giving it to *my* ex-true-love and get away . . .

Ha! Scot-free. Very nice.

But why the hell should he get off the hook? I may have been so senseless with hurt and rage that I flung myself out of his gross scarlet *pussy wagon* without telling Megan the truth about the *mingy gobshite* to whom she has pledged herself, but there's still time . . .

Well, not much. Bugger all as it happens.

But I *swear* that if by some direct-from-Hollywood miracle I'm still breathing come 12.01 Tuesday morning I will have my revenge. Which, like the severed body-parts of Idi Amin's enemies, is a dish best served cold.

That's what I can't get past. Lying here at the bottom of my self-dug grave, looking up, seeing *him* gazing down at me. He's dabbing at his eyes with a black silk hankie, but he can't wipe away the sly twinkle. And there she is behind him. His *fiancée*. Shaking her *bloody* head . . .

Hang on. Where does she get off being so indignant, so *pious*? She said *yes* at the back end of November – *forty-plus* days of betrothal – yet she didn't tell me until a little over an hour ago. All those mercy trips to Saint Matthew's, knowing that as she held my hand she'd already slipped *my* ring off her own to avoid having to tell me the truth . . . So much for Megan and honesty.

And if I'd been a little more honest with myself I'd have admitted long before tonight that I've been making excuses for her. She was sleeping with someone else *at least* three months before she left me, but I told myself that it was *my* fault. Teach me to be *so* boring, *so* sucking up to Mammon, so *not* in the seven-figure income bracket, wouldn't it? But she was a cheat. Plain and simple. How many *emergency client conferences* did she have when really she was sneaking off to screw Sandy

Tightwad-Jock QC? And what other grubby little secrets don't I know about her?

And *why* do I care so much?

She's not my girlfriend any more. I've got Fish. Megan can rot in . . .

Oh, sod it. I *do* care.

She claimed to have been having second thoughts. The truth is I've never stopped having my first lot of soppy Megan-filled thoughts. Jesus, my head is such a *mess*. My cancer is *curable*; as curable as cancer gets; more curable than a bloody cold, for heaven's sake. I should be kissing strangers, hugging lamp-posts, embracing *life* . . . But yesterday morning my disease was all I had to worry about. The rest of it . . . None of it mattered. No consequences . . .

I walk past a kebab shop, its extractor chugging greasy smoke into the street. The smell . . . onions, fatty lamb and . . . *mmm*, burning bridges.

Next door a convenience store hums with white fluorescent light. I stop and look inside. It seems familiar – maybe I was here once photographing the chiller cabinet. I see the cigarette logos behind the counter. I left mine at the police station and, God, I need one now. *Ha*, on top of everything else I'm a *smoker*.

1.09 a.m.

'Twenty Silk Cut Ultra, please.'

That's my plan – wean myself off by switching to something so laughably mild that I'd get more of a hit sucking a disposable biro. I reach into my pocket for money and feel a fat roll of the stuff. Before I left the Dorchester for my flat yesterday, I put my cash into the room safe, but I kept back a thousand. *Stupid.* I never used to carry wads of cash around. But yesterday – still living with a terminal disease – being liquid was important. When time is of the essence the idea of impulse purchasing assumes a much higher priority.

Hang on. I'm still on death row. Midnight *Monday*, unless I can come up with a hundred and fifty grand. As I take my cigarettes I see the Lotto till on the counter.

'Can I have some Lucky Dips as well, please?'

'How many, chief?' asks the young Indian serving me.

'A thousand . . . A thousand quid's worth.'

1.37 a.m.

'Want me to count 'em again?' he asks, still reeling, but now a grand to the good.

'No, it's OK, thanks. I'm sure it's right.' I take the block of tickets and put them in my pocket. 'Goodnight,' I say, turning to leave.

'Hang on . . . You wouldn't do us a favour, would you?' he calls out. 'Can I have my picture taken with you?'

I must look confused.

He blushes and says, 'Well, you're gonna win, intcha? I mean, a *thousand* lines. You're a dead bloody cert, chief.'

My grasp of statistics isn't all that, but I'm pretty sure he's some way off the mark. Even so I smile my first smile in what seems like forever and say, 'Yeah, a picture. Why not?'

'Great!' He grabs a disposable camera from a display and rips it from its pack, then yells out towards the back of the shop, 'Here, Sunny, come and gi's a hand.'

As we stand in front of the counter and say *cheese*, my brand new friend puts his arm around my shoulder and says, 'Here, when you're a millionaire I'm gonna blow this up and stick it in the window . . . If you don't mind?'

'No . . . No, I don't mind at all.'

When I'm a millionaire he can explode it to giant poster-size and stick it in Barnsbury bloody Square – directly opposite Sandy and Megan's house.

343

The photo call over, I finally leave the shop and realise I'm buzzing. Actually *buzzing*. I have a good feeling about this – let's face it, stranger things have happened lately. Maybe I am a dead bloody cert. Maybe everything will work out fine after—

I stop in my tracks, half-in half-out of the shop door.

I've spotted a car across the street. No big deal. There are lots of cars across the street. But this one is shiny black, sporty-sleek and Italian. Not so many of those in Hackney at this hour. And I could be wrong – the light isn't great – but I'm pretty sure the hairdo sitting behind the wheel is his. From here it looks every bit as shiny-sleek as his car. I remember his parting words: *You're being watched now . . . Evewy fucking step.* Surely he hasn't been stalking me since I left the police station? Surely I couldn't have been so blinded by rage and self-pity not to spot a Ferrari kerb-crawling a discreet distance behind me?

No, I'm being paranoid – perfectly *normal* paranoia. If I weren't feeling at least a little paranoid after everything that has happened, that alone would be reason to seek immediate psychiatric help. I take a couple of deep breaths, step onto the pavement and see a black taxi rattling towards me. I stick out my arm and it squeaks to a halt in front of me.

'Dorchester Hotel, please,' I call through the window.

I climb in and the cab pulls out and swings into a tight U-turn across the width of Mare Street. As we reach the other side we pass close to the parked Ferrari. Inside, Clark's narrowed eyes glare at me from beneath a flop of jet-black hair.

So much for paranoia.

I turn in my seat and watch from the rear window. Panicked, sweating, my thrashing heart trying to prise open a gap in my ribcage. The Ferrari's lights fire up. It nudges forward then jerks out into the traffic . . . Literally, actually, because it smacks hard into the side of a dirty white van that's bowling along some fifty yards behind us.

Mirror, signal, manoeuvre, Clark, *mirror, signal, manoeuvre.*
I face forward and settle down for the ride.
'You all right, mate?' the driver asks through the partition.
'Yes . . . I think I am.'

eight: **like lena zavaroni**

'You should've woken me,' I say, rubbing my eyes and focusing on the time.

'You needed sleep,' Fish says flopping onto the bed beside me. Her body moulds itself to mine through the sheet. She feels soft, relaxed, carefree. A new woman. 'I can't believe it,' she whispers into my chest.

'No . . . Neither can I,' I say, slowly waking to a fresh reality. 'Am I *really* OK?'

'That's what you told me last night. Fan-fucking-*brilliant*.'

'Well, not exactly.'

My fresh reality's complicated little details are slotting into the picture.

'I still need an op. And radiotherapy most likely. And there's the police . . . The *money* . . . A hundred and *fifty* grand.'

'We'll find a way,' she says calmly. 'Just *think*. You're not gonna *die* . . .' Then, 'I'll run you a bath.'

Well, what else is there to say?

Up to my neck in . . . *creamy* Dorchester bubbles.

I wonder why I've been feeling so ill lately. Why the chest pains, the tiredness, if I'm not riddled with cancer? Is it psychosomatic? It wouldn't be the first time. I remember the gangrene in my leg that turned out to be a combination of a twisted ankle and pea green dye leaching from my trousers onto my skin – look, I was *eleven*, OK? But I *do* have cancer. Is it spreading;

riddling? I've got to sort this out. Get myself to a hospital. First, though, I've got to get out of this mess alive.

'What's Vince up to, Fish?' I call out.

'He took Bubbles to the zoo,' she replies from the bedroom. 'Dunno if he's back . . . Hey, I could bust into my dad's place again. He must have something that's worth a hundred and fifty grand.'

'I think he might have changed his alarm code after the last time,' I reply. 'Anyway, I've got a foolproof plan,' I add, remembering my Lucky Dips.

'What's that?'

'Look in my jeans pocket.'

After a moment she appears at the bathroom door, a black look on her face.

'What's this?' she says holding up a piece of paper. Not a Lotto ticket.

Something I'd forgotten. A story in the *Mail* about a burglary in Hampstead. Balled up and shoved into my pocket while she slept on the flight to Spain.

'Why didn't you show me?' she demands.

'I . . . I'm sorry . . . It just seemed pointless. Hasn't he already hurt you enough?'

'He's a *cunt*, Murray. Sometimes I forget that and I need to be *reminded*,' she yells, waving the article at me. 'You should've shown me. You don't need to protect me, you know. The shit I've put up with . . . I don't need protection.'

'I'm sorry.'

'You shouldn't hide things. Secrets are *crap*,' she says, sitting down on the toilet seat to read. When she reaches the end she drops it between her legs into the toilet bowl.

'The twat didn't even mention me,' she says, tears filling her eyes.

'That's why I didn't—'

'You should've fucking told me,' she shouts before curling

347

into a furious ball, her knees pulled up tight to her chin.

She's right. Secrets are *crap*. And if this is the first day of the rest of my life, then I'd better start as I mean to continue.

'Fish, there's something I've got to tell you . . .'

I tell her about Megan's engagement. She listens quietly, her forehead furrowing, causing the rows of metalwork in her eyebrows to clump together. She is clicking her tongue stud against her teeth. I'd say she's agitated.

'Why are you telling me this?' she asks. 'Aren't you over her?'

'Yes . . . No . . . I don't know . . . Nothing's ever black and white, is it?'

'Yes it is. You're either over her or you're not. Fucking simple.'

Unexpected shades of clear-minded, decisive Megan here.

'Look, I'm angry with her for not telling me. I'm *mad* with him about the ring. And, no . . . I'm not over her . . . I'm getting there, but . . .'

'Well, let me know when you're done,' she says flatly, getting up from the toilet. 'I'm gonna order something from room service. You hungry?'

'No . . . There's something else.'

She sits down again and I tell her about her connection to Megan and Sandy.

'I'm really sorry,' I say as I finish. 'I shouldn't have kept it from you.'

'No, you fucking shouldn't,' she says after a moment. 'Wanna know something about that *bitch* you used to go out with? When their side found out I was gonna be a witness they did some digging. They sent her to my school. I saw her a couple of times hanging around the gates. I didn't think anything – she just looked like some kid's nanny.

'Then one afternoon she turns up at this caf in Belsize Park where we used to hang out. I wasn't there, but some of my mates were. She said she was my cousin and asked if they knew where I was. Then she started asking stuff about me. They were

all a bit cagey, but she told them she was worried about me
'cause I was having trouble at home. That didn't surprise them
'cause the trial wasn't exactly a secret. Then she said she wanted
to help me, but she needed to know how I'd been at school –
like had I been in trouble. So they fell for it and told her.'

'Told her what?' I ask.

'That I used to make things up.'

'How do you mean?'

'It was harmless. Fantasy stuff to make me look cool. It was
just stupid lies kids tell . . . Anyway, your *girlfriend* told my mates
I'm making up stories to mask my low self-esteem and – get
this – she asked them to be especially *kind* to me. *Can you fucking
believe that?* . . . You know all that shit came out in court. That
Scotch twat used it to make me look like a headcase. I didn't
stand a chance . . . How the *fuck* could you not tell me who she
was?'

I don't have an answer.

'Stupid thing is I'd've recognised her when she came round
your flat if I hadn't been off my face,' she goes on. 'Anyway, if
you feel *anything* for the bitch you can forget about you and
me.'

She stands up and walks out of the bathroom and closes the
door. A moment later I hear the bedroom door open and then
slam shut.

===================================== 6.35 p.m.

I let myself back into the room and flop down onto the bed.

I've looked everywhere for her and all I discovered is that
the Dorchester's management doesn't take kindly to guests
wandering around the public areas in white fluffy dressing
gowns – even their own white fluffy dressing gowns.

There's a tap on the door.

At last!

349

I cross the room and look through the peephole. It's Vince. Only Vince.

'Hey, it's Muzz the Miracle Kid,' he says as I let him in. Bubbles is asleep on his shoulder. 'Who's that geezer in the Bible who came back from the dead? Les, Larry . . .?'

'Lazarus.'

'That's you, that is. How're you doing?'

I shrug and say, 'How was the zoo?'

'Boring. All the animals were kipping. Someone should tell the lazy fuckers there's a public to entertain. Where's Fish?'

'She . . . er . . . went for a walk.' I watch him lay Bubbles gently on the bed and I ask, 'Wouldn't she be safer with her mum?'

'Probably, but I can't find the daft bitch. I must've phoned every fat farm in the Southeast trying to track her down . . . Anyway, I dunno why we're so worried.'

'He carries a *gun*, Vince.'

'He's not the only one.' A smirk spreads across his face. He lifts up his T-shirt to expose a narrow strip of midriff . . . and something lumpy tucked into his jeans.

Please, God, tell me it isn't what I think it is.

He pulls the lump from his waistband and holds it up. It's black, not very big, with a stubby square muzzle. Very similar to Clark's, which I've seen up close. They probably got them from the same shop – or wherever it is you get these things.

'*Vince*, what are you doing with that?' I say, instinctively edging away from him as he waggles it about. 'You're not a crack baron. You're an *art director*.'

'Gotta be prepared these days. You never know when some wanker client is gonna piss on my ads.' He points the gun at me and snarls. '*Suck lead, marketing scum.*'

'Don't point it at me!' I yelp. 'Where the hell did you get it?'

'This bloke down Cam—'

'Actually, don't tell me. I don't want to know. Please, just put it away. Things are bad enough without you turning into Jean Claude Van Damme.'

'Do me a favour. I'm Lee Marvin in *Point Blank*. Hey, I'm starving. Fancy some room service?'

'You go ahead. I'll wait for Fish to get back,' I say, though I'm thinking I may be waiting forever.

'Here . . . I'm picking up a vibe. You and her ain't got a . . . *situation*, have you?'

'Sort of.'

'Tell me about it. I am Doctor *Lurve*.'

I don't know why, I really don't, but I tell him.

———————————————————————— 7.03 p.m.

'Wow, so she's kind of a sleb,' Vince coos as I finish.

'Not through choice . . . And it was a while back. She was only thirteen.'

'A *child* star . . . Like Lena Zavaroni.'

'You're not taking this seriously, are you?'

'Course I am. Any road, I dunno why you're worried. She'll have to come back for her stuff.'

'What stuff?'

Fish arrived in my life with sod all. Looks as if she's left the same way.

'Nah, she'll be back . . . And even if she ain't, it's not like you love her or anything.' He stops and looks at my face. '*Fuck*, you fucking love her, don't you?'

'Can you leave me alone for a bit, Vince?'

'You're not gonna do anything daft, are you?'

'No . . . There's just some stuff I need to do.'

———————————————————————— 7.10 p.m.

I'm sitting on the edge of the bed taking deep breaths.

I have well and truly screwed up. *The first day of the rest of my life . . . Start as I mean to go on.* What a world-champion screw-up.

But I've got to get my head together because there is something I need to do. I need to call my mum. She must have read the *Mail* and she'll be hysterical. I pick up the phone and dial. I listen to the ring tone and hope David doesn't pick up. And I force myself to think *happy*.

'Hullo,' she says as breezily as usual.

'Hi, Mum.'

'Murray!'

She knows. The way her voice broke in the middle of *Murray* – just between the two Rs. She knows all right.

'Thank God you called,' she exclaims. 'You left in such a . . . I didn't even say a proper goodbye.' I can smell tears. 'I feel terrible.' Yes, she's crying now. 'You've . . . You've . . .' She can't get the words out.

'Mum, it's OK, really it's *OK*.'

'It's not OK. How can you say that? It's *terrible*. You've lost *everything* and—'

'Listen, Mum, *listen to me*. I haven't got cancer.'

This is my tactic: lie; deny everything; tell her I haven't got cancer *at all*. This is because if I tell her that I do have it – even an insignificantly tiny lump of the stuff – she'll flip. So I'm going to skate over the whole cancer thing, get out of this mess, get cured, then Mum need never know anything about anything.

Absolutely foolproof.

'Of course you haven't got cancer,' she says – which throws me off balance somewhat. 'I'm just saying that you've lost your job and Megan and I feel—'

'Hang on, what do you mean *of course* I haven't got cancer?'

'I know what you're thinking, Murray. That your silly mother is overreacting as usual – *God, it's only a job and a girlfriend. I haven't got flipping cancer*. Well, I know it's not the end of the world, but it doesn't stop me worrying for you.'

'You didn't read the *Mail* yesterday, did you?'

'No, it wasn't delivered for some reason. David had to drive into town and get an *Express*. How did you know?'

'Just a guess.'

'My God, you *have* got cancer, haven't you?'

'No, Mum, I promise you.'

'But why did you say—'

'*I haven't got cancer*. It was just a . . . It was a figure of speech. Anyway, how's things with you?'

'Oh, you know, always sunny, always the same. We solved the mystery of the red pool. David said it *was* the chlorine. He drained it after you left. It's lovely and blue again now. That reminds me, you left your mauve shirt. I'll give it a wash and stick it in the post. He had to fly off to London last night. Some business or other came up. Don't ask me what. Is that a cobweb? Sorry, just looking at the ceiling. I told him to look you up, but he said he'd be too busy. Oh, you couldn't start taping *EastEnders* for me? I just got off the phone to your Auntie Helen and she said it's ever so good at the moment. Apparently Alfie Moon is . . .'

I tune out. Situation normal . . .

11.31 p.m.

. . . All fucked up.

Vince and I have just finished checking my lottery tickets.

And, yes, nice man in the convenience store, I *am* a winner.

Eight lines of three numbers, one of four.

How to turn a grand into one hundred and fifty pounds.

A trifling £149,850 short.

'Wanna do 'em again?' Vince asks wearily, hoping I'll say no.

'I reckon four times is enough to know I'm well and truly stuffed . . . Jesus, this is a *total* disaster.'

'Course it ain't,' he chirps, heading for the minibar. 'You're only a grand down. How much you got left?'

'I don't know. Forty-four, forty-five? What difference does it make? I need a hundred and fifty. By *Monday*.'

I hear a crack. I look up and see him twisting the cap off a bottle of Johnny Walker.

'What are you playing at?' I squeak. 'I've got to pay for that. Don't you think I'm in enough shit already?'

'Cool, Muzza. You're Lazar-whatsit, remember?' he says, taking a big swig. 'You pull off the coming back from the dead stunt once, you can do it a dozen times.'

'I don't believe in miracles.'

'Neither do I, matey. That's why I've got a plan.'

'What, you've got a miniature sub on a meter on Park Lane? We're gonna rob a couple of yachts in Chelsea Harbour?'

'Don't be soft. That kinda thing takes months of organising . . . Hang on, that were irony, weren't it? Nah, this one's *fool*-proof. Guaran-fucking-*teed*. Even an idiot like you couldn't fuck it up. And the best thing is we can do it tonight.' He offers me the bottle, then asks, 'You got a tux?'

neuf

'Are you a member of this place?' I ask as we climb out of the taxi.

'No, but I know a guy who works the door. If he's on tonight we're in luck,' Vince replies. 'Gi's a minute and I'll check it out.'

He hands me his sleeping child, crosses the pavement and walks into the Prince Regent Club. I pull Bubbles into the lining of my tuxedo. Not *my* tuxedo. Conjured up from God knows where. The staff at the Dorchester are *out*standing. No request is too stupid. A room-service waiter produced a brace of them in minutes and it only cost me two hundred of my dwindling pounds. Of course, mine doesn't fit – it's a good two sizes too big. Neither does Vince's, but I should think that tailoring clothes to his bruised and beaten body would be a fashion challenge too far.

I look at the club – the *casino*. I've never been inside one. Way too scary. This one especially. It's in Saint James's Square for a start, which marks it down as posh. The entrance is discreet and far too English to advertise itself with Vegas neon. Las Vegas I might be able to cope with – in all the holiday shows I've seen it looks like Disney World with slot machines – like they probably have height restrictions on some of the more *extreme* gaming tables. Harmless, childish fun. The Prince Regent Club looks anything but. It clearly takes gambling seriously. The kind of place where James Bond nonchalantly bets thousands while he exchanges arched eyebrows with the Ukrainian beauty he's going to shag in the next scene but one.

I really don't think I can go through with this. But like Vince

355

said as he clipped the bow tie to my collar, 'You got a better fucking idea?'

He emerges from the club grinning toothlessly.

'We're on, Muzza. It's our lucky night.'

'Really?' I quaver. 'Vince, are you sure about this?'

'Trust me.'

I ignore the fact that only the fundamentally unreliable ever say *trust me*.

'Look,' he says. 'We'll be in and out in under half an hour. And you'll be going to sleep with a hundred and eighty K under your pillow.'

'I don't know . . . Maybe they'll take the forty-five as a down payment and I can pay off the rest in instalments.'

Vince looks at me as if this is an utterly ludicrous suggestion – which it is. '*Trust* me, Muzza. We *cannot* lose.'

'This is a *casino*. It's only here because idiots like us *lose* on a regular basis.'

'You're forgetting something.'

'Oh yeah, this *secret* of yours. What is it then?'

'Well, if I fucking told you it wouldn't be a secret, would it?'

'I'm not going in unless you tell me. If you expect me to cheat or something . . . I know what they do to cheats. I've seen the bit in *Casino* with the circular saw.'

'It was only a *hammer*. And don't fucking worry. We're not gonna cheat . . .'

Like I'm not going to worry, my face screams.

'All right, I'll tell you. But not a word to no one, OK?'

I nod.

'I've been a punter for years,' he says, 'horses, dogs, flies on fucking windows . . . You name it, I've backed it. I lose all the time just like any other punter, but get this . . .' He drops his voice to a whisper. '. . . I have never, ever lost when it mattered. When the chips are down, when my fucking *life* depends on it, I win. Every time.'

'Is that it? Your secret? You've got a gambling fairy looking out for you?'

'Don't be stupid. *Fairies*! No such thing. It's more like *fate*. Lady Luck. She pulls me out of the shite every time.'

'Jesus, you must think I'm mad.'

'Look,' he snaps, 'you got a better fucking idea?'

Of course I haven't, which is why I'm here outside an upmarket gambling den shivering violently – and only partly because of the cold.

'What about Bubbles?' I exclaim, spotting a last minute escape from this hell. 'I bet they don't have a crèche.'

'Sorted. The bird in the cloakroom is an angel. She's making my princess a little nest of minks as we speak . . . C'mon, Muzza, let's F.E.A.R.'

It's everything I imagined and worse. A rich, classy club to which I could *never* belong. Men in suits that *fit*. Women glued decorously to their arms as if they've been supplied by the same gentlemen's outfitter. The place is hushed. Just a light hum of conversation, the chink of ice in glasses and the rattle of little white balls on roulette wheels. There are no signs banning mobile phones but I should think that if one sounded its owner would be frogmarched off the premises before he'd had a chance to answer it. I haven't got mine with me, which is a worry. Not because I want to make a call now, but because I've lost it . . . No matter. Far bigger things to fret about. Like the Amazonian hostess who's striding towards us, her muscular legs slithering rhythmically in and out of the long slits in her satin gown. Probably wants to inform us about the house rule re wearing of suits (ill fitting).

She reaches us, cracks a delicious smile and tinkles, '*Vincent*, how's my *favourite* submariner?'

You see? *Everyone* – even athlete-limbed casino hostesses with voices like Julie Andrews – knows about his ridiculous ambition.

'You've been in the wars,' she continues, inspecting his bruises.

'Nah, it's nothing,' Vince replies. 'I'm great, darling, t'rific. Better for seeing you. You're looking *well* minxy tonight.'

'You're too kind.' Her dark skin blushes slightly. 'What can I get you?'

A new identity and a one-way ticket to Bolivia, please.

'Two G and Ts, easy on the T,' Vince says.

As she heads for the bar Vince grips my arm and says, 'Now remember, do everything *exactly* like I say . . . And when you win—'

'If.'

'*When* you win no whooping and hollering. This ain't Mecca.'

'Not with you, Vince. What's this got to do with Islam?'

'*Bingo*, you twonk. You know, two fat ladies, *housey, housey!* Fuck, you ain't lived, have you? . . . Gi's the money and I'll get some chips.'

'It's OK, I'm not hung— Oh, you mean the gambling sort, don't you?' I reach into my waistband and fish out the brown envelope stuffed with nine hundred fifty-pound notes. Forty-five thousand pounds. Vince wanted me to bring the lot – 'It's the only way this will work. You've gotta put it *all* on red.' – but I stubbornly held back the spare two hundred and fifty quid. I have to have something for emergencies – as if life hasn't become one long emergency.

'I'm not sure, Vince.'

'Don't bottle it now. If you do we'll both be dead on Monday.'

He takes the envelope and walks across the club, disappearing through a door. As I watch him I can't help but marvel. At roughly this time only ten days ago he was flying over my head into a swimming pool, lucky, apparently, to have got away with losing only three teeth. He is just so resilient . . .

In*vinc*ible. I recall thinking of him as a Weeble. But that was wrong. He's the real-life equivalent of John McClane in *Die Hard*. McClane spent two hours being ricocheted around a tower block like a ball on a pin table. After each knockdown he got to his feet, dusted himself off and carried on. His face got a little bloodier, his vest a little ragged-er, but he *carried on*. If Vince's life were ever to become a major motion picture, only Bruce Willis could play him – OK, Bruce with a prosthetic Muttley snout.

—————————————————————————— 1.57 a.m.

I'm huddled next to him, needing to feel his arm against mine for comfort. We're standing at a roulette table. In front of me are four unequal stacks of chips. My future reduced to forty-five discs . . . Which really are very pretty.

We didn't happen on this particular table by chance. Oh no, Vince has a *system*. I'd love to think it involved objective assessment of the odds, preferably supported by enough convoluted maths to give Stephen Hawking a migraine . . . Actually, it's based entirely upon gut feeling. Which, frankly, is a worry – call me unadventurous, but I find it unsettling when a man bypasses his brain and does his thinking with his lower intestine.

After a tour of the four tables available, Vince had picked up sufficient voodoo vibes to announce that *this* is the one. I'm holding back from playing not because I'm terrified – though I am. I'm obeying orders. Vince hasn't given me the nudge yet. He's adhering to the system, studying his gut, reading his own entrails, which – for now at least – are still safely tucked inside his abdomen. Each time the ball is tossed onto the wheel he calls the colour, whispering either *red* or *black*. At first he got it wrong as many times as he called right. But for the past seven spins he has been unerringly right – *red . . . red . . . black . . . black . . . red . . . black . . . red*. My grasp of statistics is rudimentary, but

359

I know that this is remarkable. What are the odds? Two to the power of seven. That's . . . two, four, eight, sixteen, thirty-two, sixty-four, *one hundred and twenty-eight* to one.

Maybe there's something in this secret. Maybe the Force is with us.

I get it – the nudge. *'Red,'* he whispers.

We're on.

With trembling hands I push my chips across the baize until they're sitting on the red diamond to the side of the numbered grid. The ball is already coasting around the edge of the wheel. As it drops and rattles in and out of the wheel's thirty-seven numbered compartments I close my eyes tight . . . Until the rattling stops and Vince's hand grips my arm, squeezing my skinny muscles painfully hard. I wait for the croupier . . .

'Neuf, *rouge.'*

ROUGE.

That's *red.*

'You *beauty!'* Vince hisses and my eyes open in time to see the croupier nudge forty-five one-thousand-pound chips into place beside my stack. Ninety grand! Over halfway there! 'What do I do?' I whisper breathlessly. 'Leave it on there?'

'Nah, get it off. It's gonna come up black.'

'Shall I put it on black then?'

'It's gotta go on *red.'*

I'm forgetting the plan. It *has* to go on red. Every last chip of it too. Don't ask me why. The answer lies in Vince's gut, where it's sloshing around with a semi-digested room-service club sandwich.

I pull the chips – ninety thousand British pounds! – towards me and wait as the ball once again circuits the wheel. If Vince has called this one correctly it will make nine in a row – that's five hundred and twelve to one.

The ball settles.

'Vingt, *noir.'*

The boy is a shaman. I *believe*, not in God but in Vince's weird juju powers.

He nudges me again.

But I can't do it. Suddenly I'm paralysed by fear. Paralysed by *reason*, actually. Because this isn't magic. There is no Lady Luck. Vince has been the beneficiary of a remarkable run of coincidences, no more. And sooner or later he's going to blow it. Why not sooner? Why not *now*?

'I can't do it, Vince.'

'You've *got* to.'

'OK, *you* do it.'

He gives me a despairing look and pushes me out of the way. Then he shoves the chips forward. The ball goes onto the wheel and I turn my back. I can't watch. I can't even listen to it ping and rattle.

So I walk. I stride away from the table until I reach the far side of the room. I gaze up at the big oil painting that hangs on the wall. A portrait of the Prince Regent. He looks splendid in his wig and regal silks, but some deeply buried history lesson surfaces in my head – Prince Regent, louche womaniser, feckless gambler, enough debts to cripple an emerging economy . . . Not helpful.

I close my eyes.

I hear a noise. No, a commotion. I open my eyes and see Vince's arm flailing in the air. He's cracking the blackest, most toothless grin in the history of happiness.

The Amazonian hostess appears at my side. 'Can I get you something, sir?'

Yes, you big, gorgeous posh thing, you can get me something all right – a great big bloody wheelbarrow to take away my cash.

_____ 2.10 a.m.

'God, I *love* you, Vince,' I say, hugging him.

'Leave it, Muzz. Just never knock the secret, OK?'

'*Never*. I swear. What number was it?'

'Dunno. One of them French ones. Who cares? It was red.'

'A hundred and eighty grand. I can't believe it.'

'Three hundred and sixty.'

'What?'

'It's three sixty.'

'Hang on . . . How . . . But . . . *How*, Vince?'

'While you were across the room shitting your pants I got to one eighty and I had another punt. Couldn't resist. I could *feel* it.'

'You're *mad*.'

'Yeah, you cunt, and now you're fucking *rich*.'

'Jesus – three hundred and sixty. *Jesus*. Vince, I love you.'

We're walking behind the Amazonian hostess who is carrying a tray. No drinks on it. Just stacks of pretty chips. I say we're walking. Floating is more like it. I feel happier than . . . Maybe than I've ever felt. I have got three hundred and sixty thousand pounds. I'm going to find Fish, tell her I'm sorry, tell her I *love* her. Then I'm going to deal with this murder thing. Of course I can sort it out. I haven't *murdered* anyone. I'm not going to die. From cancer. From gangster bullets. From *anything*. For the first time in my life I feel in*vinc*ible.

We arrive at the cashier's counter. The hostess puts the tray down and says, 'I'll leave you to it, gentlemen. Congratulations, by the way.' Then in a whisper to Vince, 'Should buy you two or three lovely little submarines.'

The cashier looks at the chips, then at us. 'I'll have to get the manager to authorise this, sir,' she says nervously. 'Any amount over—'

'Don't worry, that's fine,' I reply. 'We've got all night.'

ten: **it's the fucking pig bin**

I'm staring at his silver hair, his tanned face, his Colgate smile. I'm listening to his cool David Niven voice and I can't believe what I'm hearing. He's smiling at me. He can't say a thing like that and *smile*.

Vince clearly feels the same way because he's saying, 'You what? Hold up a minute. They're not fucking forgeries. They *can't* be.'

'I'm sorry, sir,' the casino manager says, 'but the notes you brought in are quite worthless.'

We're in his office; a big room furnished with antiques. A Stubbs horse hangs on the wall behind his leather-topped desk. In the corner a fireplace – unlit logs in its grate, a pair of muskets above its marble mantelpiece. The room is someone's idea of genteel homeliness. It is not the venue for the conversation we're having now.

'But you accepted them,' Vince protests – as if that makes it all right.

'We didn't know,' I say quietly, finally managing to speak.

'Of course not, sir,' the manager says soothingly, though I doubt sincerely. 'I'm sure that this is as big a shock for you as it is for us.'

You have no idea.

'You fucking *accepted* them,' Vince says again.

'Regrettably we did, sir. Our people are trained to be vigilant in these matters, but . . . Well, I don't wish to point the finger. However, the young lady who took care of your money this

363

evening is new. In her defence most forged notes are tens and twenties. To the best of my knowledge no one has managed to fake an adequate fifty, but these are really jolly good.' He holds one up to his desk light. 'The watermark is passable, and look at this.' He rubs the fifty against a notepad, then holds up the paper to show the smudge of peachy-pink ink that has transferred itself.

How the hell did we not spot that? The bloody ink isn't even dry.

'The sign of excellent work . . .'

Oh.

'. . . One usually only gets a smear with the real thing. These are indeed remarkable.' He gives us his most indulgent smile yet. Is he complimenting us? We didn't *make* the things. 'The police will be delighted to get their hands on them.'

The *police*? I look at Vince. His toothless jaw is trailing round his midriff.

'They should be here soon, so if you'd like to make yourselves comfortable.'

Police? *Here*? Make ourselves *comfortable*? This cannot be happening.

'Nah, we gotta split,' Vince says, reading my mind. 'You keep the money. I mean, it's fucking *forged*. We don't want it. *Obviously*. We'll just be off-ski, yeah?'

'I'm sure you'd rather help the authorities get to the bottom of this,' the manager says. 'They'll be here . . .' he pauses to glance at his watch '. . . oh, quite soon. I'm certain the whole thing can be cleared up with the minimum inconvenience.'

Minimum inconvenience? The authorities already want to put me away for murder and once I'm inside, the bloody gangsters will no doubt pay some psycho lifer his weight in cigarettes to string me up by my shoelaces in the shower block. Tell me, Mr David Niven Junior, just how minimally inconvenient is that?

'Please, make yourselves at home. If there's anything you need, don't hesitate to ask. My colleagues will be just outside.'

He gestures at the brace of heavy doormen who've been standing silently behind us throughout this interview.

As he gets up to leave Vince mumbles, 'My little girl.'

'Excuse me, sir?'

'My kid. She's . . . um . . . in your cloakroom. She's asleep on some coats.'

'That is most irregular,' the manager says, letting his disdain show for the first time. '*Most* irregular. I'll have someone bring her to you.'

2.32 a.m.

'The *cunts*,' I mutter. 'How fucking dare they? I mean, how *dare* they? *Forgeries*.'

Vince, who so far hasn't responded to my rant, turns to me and snaps, 'Will you shut it? They're *criminals*. Ripping people off is what they *do*. It's their *job*. Any road, whaddya gonna do about it? Tell the fucking cops? Who'll be here any fucking minute. Now will you help me?'

He's looking for a way out. I don't know why he's bothering. The window is locked and two heavies guard the door. Oh, and we've got a toddler for baggage, the sort of thing that usually stymies the best getaway plans. Was Steve McQueen hampered by a three-year-old in *The Great Escape*? And he still didn't bloody escape.

'Get up,' Vince says.

'What?'

'Just get up off your arse, will you?'

I lift the sleeping Bubbles from my lap and stand up. Vince takes my chair and carries it to the door, where he wedges it beneath the brass knob. Then he drags the manager's weighty oak desk across the room and jams it against the chair.

'How long's that going to keep them out?' I say.

He ignores me and goes to the window. He grabs one of the curtains, gives it a yank and the hooks snap free of the rail. He hands me the fabric. 'Wrap her up.'

'You what? She'll suffocate.'

'Just *do* it.'

I put the curtain on the floor and lay Bubbles on top of it. Then I roll her up until she resembles a maroon velvet slug, her little face barely visible at one end.

'Cover her right up,' he orders. 'I don't want her getting scarred.'

'*Scarred*? Vince, what are—'

'*Please*, Muzz, we ain't got time to argue.'

I do as I'm told as he heads for the fireplace. He reaches up and grabs one of the muskets. After a couple of tugs it comes away from the wall and he holds it in his hands, gauging its weight.

'We can't shoot our way out,' I squeak. 'It's an *antique*. It won't even work.'

'Will you put a fucking sock in it? Jesus Christ, what is it with you? All this fucking whinging – *can't do that, this won't work*. You've turned into a right fucking *suit* again. I preferred you when you had cancer.'

'I *do* have cancer,' I whinge.

'You know what I fucking mean,' he says, stomping to the window. He grips the gun at the end of its barrel and swings it. The glass shatters and a beat later the alarm sounds – louder than the one at Fish's dad's house – louder than anything I've ever heard. Bubbles wakes. The velvet slug is squirming. I can hear shoulders whacking the door, trying to force a way in. Vince ignores the pandemonium and concentrates on dislodging as much glass as possible from the smashed window.

'What the hell are you playing at?' I shout.

He doesn't hear me because he has jumped.

I run across the room and look through the jagged hole. Vince is ten feet below on a flat roof at the back of the building. He looks up at me and shouts, 'Chuck her down.'

'I can't. I'll kill her.'

'She's *my* kid. She ain't gonna die.'

I look round at the door. The thumps are getting harder. The chair and the desk have started to move, pushing the carpet up into fat ripples.

'Come on! We ain't got long,' Vince yells from below.

He's right. I feed my writhing velvet bundle through the hole. I look at Vince's outstretched arms and . . . let go. His legs buckle, but he doesn't drop her. Clutching his baby to him he stands back and shouts, 'Whaddya waiting for?'

I take a final look at the door. The gap is getting wider with every body slam. I climb onto the windowsill, ball myself up and roll forwards through the hole. I feel glass pull at my shoulder, tearing fabric and skin . . . And I'm falling. I hit the lead roof knees first, followed by elbows, followed by breath leaving my body. Still winded I pull myself up, amazed that nothing seems broken – the pain in my cut shoulder seems to be the worst of it.

Without waiting for me to recover Vince sets off at a slightly limping jog. I follow. The roof extends a long way beyond the back of the main building – I imagine we're running along the top of the actual casino, the scene of our crime. I steal a single backward glance at the window. No faces have appeared at it yet – Vince's barricade is proving more effective than I guess even he'd hoped.

He stops. He has reached the end. Seconds later I'm beside him and we're both peering down into a narrow black alley.

'See that skip?' he says. 'Let's hope it's full of paper and not busted bottles.'

He shoves Bubbles into my arms and drops off the edge. Fifteen or so feet later he hits the skip with a wet splat. I look

367

down, but I can't make out anything. I can hear him though. 'Aw, *fuck*. It's the fucking pig bin . . . Chuck us the kid.'

2.39 a.m.

We're up to our knees in kitchen waste, Vince at one end of the skip and me at the other. We're peering at the streets at each end of the alley. I've just seen a second police car flash past. So far Vince hasn't had any and his end seems our best bet . . .

But I can't help thinking that this is it.

Over.

Though there haven't been any bodies on the roof above us yet, the police are obviously arriving and the casino staff must be out and about by now.

'Am I in the zone tonight or what?' Vince croons.

I turn round and look beyond his end of the skip . . . at the black cab pulling up in front of the gap, its orange light beckoning.

'C'mon,' he says, hauling his body out of the ooze and over the rim. I pass Bubbles to him. She's no longer wrapped in the curtain. She's no longer screaming either. She's paralysed and can only stare at us in terror. I follow them out and we walk towards the taxi, silently pleading for it to stay put for a few moments more.

We're less than thirty feet from it when a silhouette turns the corner and heads down the alley – a silhouette that's instantly recognisable on account of its peaked cap.

I freeze.

'Keep walking,' Vince hisses.

I force my terrified feet to set off again . . . to certain arrest – I might as well hold out my wrists for the handcuffs. But before we reach the policeman Vince points frantically behind us. '*Quick*,' he yells. 'We got their kid. They just dropped her in the skip and legged it – evil *bastards*.'

The copper is sprinting up the alley before Vince has even finished the sentence. We head for the waiting cab and he says, 'In the *fucking* zone. Now I bet you're glad I made you wear a tux.'

eleven: **bermuda? barbados? somewhere hot beginning with b**

'I don't know how you can eat.'

'I'm starving,' Vince replies, sucking on a piece of fried bread until it's mushy enough to swallow. 'We were fucking *outstanding*, eh?'

'*You* were outstanding. I just slowed you down.'

'Nah, mate. We're a team. Bonnie and Clyde. You're the one with the tits.'

We haven't slept since we got back to the hotel. At first we were both surfing on adrenaline. Vince is still full of it, stopping only to refuel with a room-service breakfast, but mine has long since dissipated. Reality has bitten. Reality has very sharp teeth. I can't believe how happy – how *optimistic* – I was for a few minutes last night. But then I had three hundred and sixty thousand pounds. Now I've got . . .

An exhaustive inventory of my assets runs to £150 in winning Lotto tickets, £250 cash (forged) and some loose change. Some distance short of a bright future. Money may not buy you love, but it pays for freedom and hope – and rooms at the Dorchester. I wish Fish were here. I miss her. And she might even come up with a brilliant plan. OK, I doubt it, but I do miss her. I wish she'd at least call.

Vince and I have spent the last few hours going through the options. Once we'd discounted the more exotic rob a bank/mug a billionaire/invent cold fusion and patent it by Monday lunchtime scenarios, there was only one.

Run away.

When I was trying to reinvent myself at the peak of my cancer frenzy it wasn't as a fugitive. Maybe that was my problem. Trying to reinvent myself and, typically, not having even the haziest clue where to begin. Thinking that if I grabbed at whatever half-baked thought popped up, the answer would somehow come. Well, the answer has come. I am no longer Murray the Rubbish Suit. Give a big Butlins welcome to the new me: Murray the Terrified Fugitive. Gasp as I dodge the police who want to charge me with everything from murder to fraud to receiving oral favours in someone else's car. Hold your breath as I evade scary men with bad accents and big guns. Groan as it all goes horribly, spectacularly wrong.

'I can't believe it, Vince,' I say.

'I told you, I'm starving.'

'Not that. I can't believe they gave me fifty grand's worth of *forgeries* and now they've got the cheek to want it back – *three* times over ... I've spent the last two weeks flashing *forged* money. Great big *wads* of the stuff. I could have been arrested anywhere. In the bank when I was getting my euros. In the bookshop at Gatwick ... This is terrible. That nice bloke in Hackney who sold me the Lotto tickets. I gave him a grand's worth of dud notes ... *Terrible.*'

'You and your conscience, Muzz. Must be a real pain having to drag that fucker around.'

'He was a really nice guy. He wished me luck, took my picture ...'

Vince bursts out laughing.

'What's so bloody funny?'

'You are, mate. Letting him take your picture. *Here, I'm just gonna rip you off, but why don't you take my mug shot – you know, save you having to describe me to the cops.* You soft twonk.'

'I didn't know it was forged, did I?' I pout.

'That's the killer – neither did any of us. Know what really fucks me off?'

I do know – he's told me four or five times already – but I let him continue.

'I've never had a streak like last night's. *Never*. Three hundred and sixty *grand*. I *had* it in my hands. And that glossy-locked *gobshite* fucked it for me. . . . But whaddya gonna do? I mean, I'd happily slice his knob off and post it second class to his mum, but I ain't gonna take on his mates in the Red Army Mafia, am I? Whaddya gonna fucking do?'

He's right. What am I going to do? Complain? I never complain. I *hate* complaining. I can't even send back a rare steak when I ordered well-done. I'd rather retch as I force down raw, bleeding meat than make a fuss. Now, in my experience, when challenged, waiters don't generally whip guns from beneath their aprons – a withering look has always been sufficient to deter me. So am I really likely to *complain* to Clark and his friends?

I'm not a brand-new me. Vince was right last night. I'm still a suit. All I can do now is resort to the suit's first tactic in a crisis – slip away as quietly and unobtrusively as possible. Which, now I think about it, is also the fugitive's first tactic. See? I haven't reinvented myself at all. I'm just like any one of the half-dozen product relaunches I've worked on – shiny new packaging, same crap contents.

'I think we'd better leave here now,' I say.

'Can I finish my breakfast first? Any road, what's the hurry? They don't know we're here and neither do the cops. There's no point in going till we know where we're headed . . . We'll sneak out first thing tomorrow and hit Thomas Cook. Pick somewhere sunny. You ever been to Miami?'

'Vince, I can't even afford Bognor bloody Regis.'

'I've got a bit in the bank. Not much, but it might get us to—'

'I can't take your money. I got us into this mess.'

'We both got us into the shite . . . We'll both find a way out.'

372

'Look at me,' I say. 'How far am I going to get? I look terrible. I *feel* terrible. God, I feel *terrible*. What's wrong with me? I'm not supposed to be dying any more.'

'Coupla years ago I was running around like a blue-arsed fly on a dexy binge,' Vince says, though why I don't know. 'Juggling two birds, working my bollocks off and trying to do my bit on the Bubbles front. Going mental, I was. Any road, I just crashed one day. Looked as fucked as you do now. I had pneumonia.'

'You reckon I've got pneumonia?'

'Well, it figures, dunnit? You have been giving it large lately. Burning the candle at both ends and torching the fucker in the middle while you're at it.'

'*Pneumonia*,' I gasp.

The new party monster me: in a different league, clearly, to the bloke who wouldn't even light it at one end.

'It ain't so bad. Bit of kip and you'll be right as rain in a coupla weeks.'

'Thanks, Doctor Douglas. I feel so much better now.'

I wish I could share his optimism. As he noisily sucks on a sausage I lie back on my bed and stare into space . . . Looking for an answer . . . Finding a ceiling.

—————————————————————————— 8.37 a.m.

What's that?

Something on my foot.

I open my eyes. Bubbles is tugging at my sock. I must have dozed off. 'Daddy's crack'ded it,' she says.

'What's that?'

'I've only fucking cracked it,' Vince says, walking through the connecting door, a brand new spring in his step. See what I mean? He's John McClane.

'Tell me,' I say, desperate to hear his scheme and hoping to God that it isn't another *I heard there's this secret tunnel in Boots on the Strand that brings you out in the main vault of Coutts Bank.*

'Sooz's dad,' he exclaims. 'Bubbles' granddad. He was the chairman of ICI or Tesco or some bollocks. Any road, they sacked him a year ago. He got the biggest golden piss-off in corporate history. He's rolling in loot.'

'And he likes you enough to give you a hundred and fifty grand?'

'Can't stand me, but he won't wanna see *you know who* become an orphan.'

'What's an *or*phan?' Bubbles asks.

'A kid with a dead dad, princess. Whaddya reckon, Muzz?'

'Well, it's the closest to a plan I've heard today,' I add, perking up. 'Can you get in touch with him? Where's he live?'

'That's the tricky bit. Him and his missus pissed off – Jesus, you wanna see her. Younger than Sooz and baps like pink Florida grapefruits. Any road, they're living in . . . Bermuda? Barbados? Somewhere hot beginning with B. I just need to get hold of Sooz. She still ain't home . . . I could try my place.'

'Why would she be there? I thought she . . . you know, couldn't stand you.'

'She's got a key. You never know. She might be there waiting for her baby. She ain't no other place I can think of. It's gotta be worth a punt.'

He picks up the phone by my bed and dials. After a moment he speaks. She must be there, I think, but then I realise he's talking to his answering machine.

'Sooz . . . It's me . . . Pick up if you're there . . . It's really fucking important . . . OK, gimme a bell. I'm staying at the Dorch—'

It takes me only a second to roll across the bed and hit the phone rest.

'Whaddya do that for?' Vince snaps.

'Are you completely stupid? What happens when *they* turn up at your flat and listen to your messages?'

Annoyance turns to sheepishness. 'Me and my big gob . . . They'll've done my gaff over already, won't they? They won't be back.'

I don't look convinced.

'OK, we'd better check out I s'pose,' he mumbles.

'And how're we going to pay the bill?'

'Dunno . . . I might be able to blag it on my plastic,' he says without managing to sound optimistic. Then, 'How hard can it be to do a runner from this place?'

'We'd better pack,' I say, mentally adding another crime to my charge sheet.

'You pack. I'm going round Sooz's place, see if I can find her dad's number.'

'You can't bugger off now, Vince,' I squeak.

'She only lives in Bayswater. I'll be back in half an hour.'

'But she's not even there. Don't tell me you've got a key to hers as well.'

'Course not, but she's got these old sash windows and no locks. Mind looking after the Bub for a bit? Reckon she's still a bit young for her first B 'n' E.'

'Please don't go,' I whimper.

'Don't worry. If they're coming at all, they ain't gonna be here *that* quick.' Then he reaches into his waistband and pulls out his gun. 'Keep this,' he says, tossing it onto the bed, where it lands next to Bubbles.

'I don't want that.'

'You'll feel better with it . . . And don't worry. The safety's on.'

9.59 a.m.

Back in half an hour? I don't know where Vince learned to tell the time. I can only think the worst – that he has fallen at the first hurdle and been arrested for burglary.

Packing took ten minutes. This went against the grain. No, that's an understatement. It actually *savaged* the grain with a great big chainsaw. Packing is, next to cleaning, the closest thing I've ever had to a hobby – more of an obsession, actually. I imagine great painters experiencing a frisson of nervous excitement as they stare at a blank white canvas. I feel that when I gaze at an empty suitcase. Filling it – achieving an order so perfect that no shirt emerges creased, no suit is ever in need of a Corby Trouser Press and every sock knows its place – is an operation that can take hours, if not days. If packing were an Olympic sport, I'd be Mark Spitz, with golds in seven different luggage classes from overnight bag to steamer trunk.

Today, though, I flew round Vince's and my rooms with a plastic Dorchester laundry bag, throwing in the few items I deemed essential. Most of them belong to Bubbles. I chose the laundry bag over a more traditional set of luggage because I have a vague idea that we're less likely to be challenged walking out with it. What do I know, though? If nothing else, the last few weeks have shown me that crime isn't my forte. If it were an Olympic sport, I'd be arrested in the starting blocks.

I'm now sitting on the sofa surfing through the TV channels. I'm not watching, though. I'm far too preoccupied. Mostly by fear.

Bubbles sits next to me. 'Is Brian Shark a *real* shark?' she asks out of nowhere.

'Er . . . Yes, he is. Kind of.'

'Does he live in the sea?'

'He doesn't live anywhere, Bubbles. He's dead.'

'Why? 'Cause he bash'ded up Daddy?'

'What makes you think he bash'ded – *bashed* him up?'

'Daddy told me . . . When's Daddy back?'

'Soon,' I reply without a shred of conviction.

Bubbles is stuffing her face with Dorchester cashew nuts. Should she be eating cashews? I have no idea. I've turned off the TV. Now I'm drumming my fingers agitatedly on the coffee table. Occasionally I steal a nervous glance at the gun – or at the corner of its butt, which is poking out from the pillow I hid it beneath. Vince was wrong. It doesn't make me feel safer. My jacket is on. I'm ready to go the moment he shows up. Where the hell is he?

Something else has been bugging me – besides the terror of a violent death, the fear of a life sentence and the nagging worry of a small but significant tumour. The whereabouts of my mobile. I'm certain I had it when I got back from the police station. I decide to search the room for it. Not because losing it adds significantly to the sum total of my despair, but because it will give me something to do.

Still no sign of Vince. No mobile either. I can only think that Fish took it. The idea gives me a tiny rush of hope. If she has it . . . If she turns it on . . . Then I could call her . . . And if the battery isn't flat . . . If she can be bothered to answer it . . .

My search did turn up something. When I was going through my pockets I found a piece of paper. It was limp with fatigue and covered with fluff and crisp crumbs, but I knew what it was even before I'd unfolded it and flattened it out.

A handwritten receipt from JP Stein of Hatton Garden.

For one diamond solitaire ring. Total: £6,499.

I'm staring at it now. And I am seething.

Tight Thieving Bastard Jock Twat . . . QC.

I can't quite believe the level of my anger. Who has ripped me off more: the crooks or the Jock? The crooks by a total of

£43,501 – and that's not including interest at an incalculably gargantuan APR. But I don't want to kill them half as much. There's only one thing for it. I get up, go to the small desk and find a pad of Dorchester notepaper.

'What're you doing?' Bubbles asks.

'Writing a letter.'

Dear Megan,

I'm sorry. For everything. Being such an idiot. Dragging you into it. All of it. I may well need a lawyer at some point, but don't worry; I won't be calling you.

I'm especially sorry for misleading you at the police station. I should have been honest. Having said that, no doubt there are times when you could have been more honest with me. And Sandy could be a lot more honest with you right now.

Ask him where he got the beautiful ring that's on your finger. He might lie. Or he might tell you the truth. Brilliant lawyer that he is, he'll probably argue that he was perfectly entitled to it – citing the Finders Keepers Act (1932) or something. Whatever, I've enclosed the receipt. He'll find it useful if he wants to insure it.

The above probably makes me look vindictive. I don't care to be honest. I don't mind you knowing that I dislike Sandy intensely. I do want you to know that I don't mean to upset you – though I suppose you will be. Despite everything that's happened I do care about you. You deserve to be with someone who's straight with you.

I wish you the best, Meg, I really do.

Murray

I fold it up without even reading it back and put it in an envelope along with the receipt. I scribble her address on the front.

'Can I lick it?' Bubbles squeals from the bed.

I hold up the flap and she runs a glistening tongue across it – SWALK indeed. I intend to post it if it's the last thing I do . . . If I'm down to my final thirty pence I'll gladly blow it on a stamp.

As I'm slipping it into my pocket I jump . . . A noise. A door opening. Someone moving around in Vince's room.

'Daddy!' Bubbles squeaks. She leaps off the sofa and runs across the room to the connecting door. I follow and grab her because I have a bad feeling . . . though it could just be the chambermaid. I put my hand to Bubbles' mouth and my ear to the door. I can hear someone rummaging, opening drawers, clattering cupboards . . . Doesn't sound like maid service.

'We have to be very, very quiet, Bubbles,' I whisper. Then I tiptoe to the door that leads to the corridor and peer through the tiny peephole. My body jolts and goes so rigid my bones might snap under the tension. I have just seen Large standing guard outside Vince's room, his form made even more monstrous by the peephole's fisheye distortion. This can only mean that Clark is next door, no doubt performing the thorough kind of search he made at my flat.

'Is it Daddy?' Bubbles asks.

'*Shhh!*' I hiss insistently and she does.

C'mon, Murray, think.

Hide! That's it, we'll hide.

'Let's play hide and seek, Bubbles,' I whisper. Her little face lights up. 'Do you think you can be really, *really* quiet?'

She nods enthusiastically. She's good at this game. We played it in Spain and couldn't find her for nearly an hour, by which time I was ready to call the police. She'd hidden in the little bunker that houses the swimming-pool works. She was surrounded by hot pumps and lethal chemicals – quiet as a mouse, though that could have been due to chlorine fumes.

'OK, let's *play*,' I whisper.

Before she has a chance to reply I drop to the floor and push her under the bed. Then I follow her.

But not before I've reached under the pillow and retrieved Vince's *shooter*.

Bubbles *is* good at this game. We've been under here for ages and she hasn't made a sound. From my position wedged between bed base and carpet I can see the bottom of the connecting door. I know it isn't locked and I can only hope that Clark doesn't think to try it.

I'm not optimistic.

'Can we play something else now?' Bubbles asks.

'In a minute,' I whisper. 'Be really quiet, yeah?'

I hear a click and my heart stops. I watch the connecting door swing slowly open. Two pairs of feet walk into my room – Large's size-twenties and Clark's, which are still clad in those ridiculous slippers. I put one hand over Bubbles' mouth and grip the butt of Vince's gun with the other. God knows what I'd do with it. 'The safety's on' were his parting words. What's a safety catch look like? I feel up and down the weapon's flanks with my thumb and index finger, probing for something button-y and safety-catch-like. Then I stop myself . . . *As if I would ever fire the thing.*

I watch Clark's and Large's shoes shuffle around the room. 'Someone's been packing, Val,' Clark says. I hear a rustle as he picks up the Dorchester laundry bag. More rustling as he roots around inside. Then, 'Looky-looky. Passports.'

Shit.

'This one's Muwway's . . . This must be his bitch,' he says, finding Fish's. 'He likes 'em young. *Pervert.* Here's Vincent's . . . Definitely here, dude.'

A grunt from Large – *Val* – who probably didn't understand a word of that.

'I'll keep hold of these. Not a good time for Muwway to take a holiday.'

I watch Clark's feet head towards the door. *What*? Isn't he even going to try to find me?

380

'C'mon, Val. The maid's down the cowwidor. Don't fancy explaining ourselves if she comes in to clean. We'll gwab a dwink downstairs . . .'

Yeesss!

'. . . and catch up with the cunt later.'

Wish you hadn't said that because . . .

'That's *Daddy's* word!'

twelve: **you should get some west and welaxation. spend time wecupewating**

Let me tell you how it is.

Me: standing in the middle of the bedroom on wobbly legs, feet planted a yard apart, arms outstretched, left hand gripping the right which is clutching the butt of Vince's gun. This is as close as I can get to the classic, as-seen-on-TV, gun-toting stance. Out of the corner of my eye I've stolen a glance at myself in the mirror and I *think* it looks convincing. Like Charles Bronson in *Death Wish*. Imagine Bronson looking pale, sweaty and, frankly, extremely scared and *you are there*. My hands are pretty steady under the circumstances and I keep the tip of the barrel mere inches away from the beautifully coifed head of jet-black hair belonging to . . .

Clark: who is also holding a gun – remarkably similar to Vince's, definitely the same shop – its tip gently resting on the unblemished cheek of . . .

Bubbles: who is wide-eyed but calm and resting comfortably in the crook of a giant arm, which belongs of course to . . .

Val: who grabbed Bubbles when she crawled from under the bed to berate Clark for his use of the C-word. Val seems to be a natural with kids – must have left a big family behind in Chechnya or wherever. He can also do two things at once because the arm that isn't cradling Bubbles is holding a gun. It's identical to Clark's and it's pointed at . . .

Me: I'm amazed at myself. The gun is having an effect on me. I feel *powerful* – like (if it weren't for the tiny matter of Bubbles being held hostage) I'd *definitely* have taken these two *cheating* bastards out by now . . . If only I could figure out where the safety catch is.

'We only came to discuss wepayment, yah?' Clark soothes in his bank manager's voice. 'Nobody has to die here . . . Well, you do . . . *Cancer*. That's some heavy shit, man.'

'Let the girl go and we can talk about the money,' I say, sliding the index finger of my left hand up the side of the gun in the hope of finding the catch. It touches something. A little button. Must be the safety.

'Vince's ickle baby,' Clark coos, stroking her cheek with his gun. 'Tell you what, give us what's left of the cash and the car keys and we'll leave you in peace.'

'The car isn't here,' I say slowly. Meanwhile my index finger pushes against the button . . . *It moves*. Funny. I was anticipating a click, like flicking a switch. I wasn't expecting it to slide. No matter – what do I know about guns? I push it all the way – a distance of maybe a centimetre – until it stops. Now that it's no longer disabled the pistol feels a little heavier, a little more *serious*. I continue my improvised story about the Porsche. 'It's still in the garage . . .' (Which I imagine to be true.) '. . . I'm picking it up tomorrow.'

'We'd be weally glad to do that for you. You look wun down. You should get some west and welaxation. Spend time wecupewating . . . Where's the money?'

'You said I had until tomorrow. Midnight Monday. *You told me.*'

'Let's just say that we've been wowwied about you giving us the slip – cwawling off under a wock to die. I didn't like that stunt you pulled in the taxi the night before last. I weally should charge you for the wepairs to my . . .'

Please don't say it, please don't, because I don't want to laugh.

'. . . Fewwawi.'

Damn, you said it.

'It's not *funny*,' he snaps. Then more softly, 'I guess they must have you on some spacey fucking cancer dwugs, dude. Makes evewything seem like a giggle, yah?'

'I haven't got cancer. *Honestly.* Well, I do, but . . . Look, it's complicated.'

'No, it's *bullshit*,' he says, back to snappy. 'You've been wipping us off.'

'A bit like you've ripped me off.'

Did I just say that? Did I *complain*? I think I bloody well did and under the circumstances I'd say it more than compensates for a lifetime spent *not* saying '*Waiter, this cow isn't dead yet.*'

'Excuse me?' Clark says, seemingly as amazed as I am.

'I said you've ripped me off . . . The money . . . The notes were forged.'

He laughs. He actually bloody laughs. Then he says, 'Aw, diddums . . . As they say in wetailing, my fwiend, please check your change as mistakes cannot be wectified later. You can take it to the Citizens' Advice Buweau once we've finished teawing your limbs off. Now, where's the fucking money?'

So much for appealing to his conscience.

'I said *where's the money*?'

I can't tell him the truth. He'd never believe the truth – I can barely believe it myself. Panicking, my mind runs through possible lies and settles on 'It's in there.'

Why did I say that? And why am I pointing at the open cupboard which contains the safe – the *empty* safe? As fibs go this one is *spectacularly* stupid. At best it'll only buy me a couple of minutes, after which Clark will be madder than ever.

'Gimme the combo,' Clark says.

'Er . . . Six . . . Three . . . Three . . . Um . . . Six . . . *No*, Five . . . I . . . I can't remember.'

And, honestly, this isn't a ham-fisted delaying tactic – I *can't* remember. I did know what it was, but the digits have fled my brain and gone into hiding. What can I say? I've never been good under pressure.

'Well, *think*,' Clark snarls, his mood deteriorating rapidly.

Val presses his gun hard against my face. The muzzle of Clark's is pushing against Bubbles' chubby pink cheek. Not surprisingly she has picked up the vibe and does what she does best. She starts to cry.

'The number,' Clark snaps.

'I don't know . . . *Honestly*. Look, there's no money in there. Vince . . . He's gone to get it. He'll be back soon.'

Clark isn't buying this new approach. 'Bull*shit. What's the fucking number*?'

'The safe's *empty* . . . And I honestly don't know.'

The phone rings, making three trigger-fingers flinch. I feel a surge of excitement. Bubbles feels it too because she wails '*Daddy*!' through the tears. She's right. It *must* be Daddy. He's phoning to tell me he's seen Sooz, talked to her father, that the money is being wired to his account at this *very moment*. It's *got* to be that.

'Clark, let me get that. It'll be Vince. I told you he's getting the money.'

'Shut the *fuck* up. I'll count and if you haven't given me the combination by the time I weach five, baby loses her bwains . . . One . . .'

'Clark, it's *empty*. Let me answer the—' I don't finish because it stops ringing.

'Two . . .'

I look at Clark's finger twitching on the trigger and feel big Val increase the pressure against my cheek, and I know the only thing stopping them firing is the fact that they think I know the number and that the safe contains money. Bubbles' sobs increase in intensity and I feel despicably guilty that she's about to be murdered in a mess that is entirely of *my* making.

'Thwee . . .'

'*Please*, if I could remember the number I'd tell you and you could see for yourself that it's *empty*.'

'Four . . .'

I know what I have to do. It will be the last act of my life, but I have to do it *now.* I grip Vince's gun and close my eyes and silently intone F.E.A.R.

Then I squeeze the trigger.

Click.

No bang.

No BANG! No wrist-jerking recoil, no splatty crunch of bone and brain, no thump of a body being flung to the floor by the impact . . . No nothing. Just *click* . . . Followed by a strange *whoosh* . . . And now screams of pain.

I open my eyes and see why. Clark's hair, his lustrous black locks are in flames. Yellow, orange and, oddly, green. My hands are shaking violently now and I drop the gun onto the floor. All I can do is stare at Clark's head. It is *really* burning. Crackling and popping like dry straw. It smells too. Of burning hair, of course, but also of chemicals. God knows what brand of mousse he uses, but he should have read the fire hazard warning. Smoke gushes from his head and rushes up to the ceiling. He has dropped his own gun and his hands flap uselessly around his face. And blood starts to pour from his mouth. Maybe the gun did fire. Maybe I simply didn't hear it. Why, then, isn't he dead? And why is his hair on fire?

So many questions. I really am in the remedial class when it comes to *shooters.*

I look at Val. If he'd been at all professional he'd have blown my face off the moment I squeezed the trigger, but it seems that size isn't everything, and when it comes to the crunch he's as inept as the rest of us. He's rooted to the spot, his gun lowered, and he's staring at the inferno that used to be his colleague. Now Bubbles' screams are drowned out by a new noise, the deafening jangle of the fire bell. I turn back to Clark who has fallen to his knees, screaming at Val for help. The big guy gets his act together. He drops Bubbles and jumps to Clark's aid.

Which leaves me to bend down and scoop up Bubbles. I also pick up the gun. Then I walk from the room.

I head briskly to the lift and press the button. I glance back over my shoulder, fully expecting Val to remember his job description and pile out of the room spraying lead. He doesn't, though. I look at Bubbles and say gently, 'It's gonna be OK' – I almost believe it myself now. The words seem to work and the crying abates at last. The lift pings, though it's barely audible above the fire bell, and the doors slide open. I'm faced with a sixty-something couple, her clutching an *A–Z* and him with a battery of cameras swinging from his leathery neck. I step inside and the doors close just as the sprinklers in the corridor burst joyously to life.

'Is this just a drill?' the woman asks me in a twangy American accent.

'I think so,' I reply.

'That bell's spooked your little one,' she says warmly, her finger reaching out and brushing Bubbles' salty cheek.

We smile at each other, but the moment is cut short by her husband who lets out a gasp, grabs her and pulls her away from me. I follow his frightened eyes down to my hand. Though I'd stopped being aware of it, I'm still clutching Vince's gun. I stare at it in wonder. It didn't work. *It didn't fucking work.* But there was blood in his mouth. And the flames. The gun did do *something*, unless, that is, he was merely the victim of a miraculously timed display of spontaneous combustion.

'I don't know what the hell's goin' on here, son, but I think you'd better put that away,' the man says nervously – probably thinking he flew three-thousand-plus miles precisely to escape this kind of irresponsible weapon brandishing.

Bubbles sniffs and says, 'It's not *real*. It's for lighting Daddy's fags.'

thirteen: **this isn't a suntan. it's teflon**

I stare at the clock on the cooker, willing it to change ... The green lights flicker and one minute to twelve turns into ...

... Midnight.

The deadline has passed. It's official. Monday 5th January is no more. The bad guys haven't got their money, I've still got my life and I haven't even been arrested yet. How lucky am I? I saw off two armed and pissed-off villains with a replica. No, even sillier, a replica that is also a *cigarette lighter*. Extremely lucky, I think. It wasn't until some time after we'd walked out of the hotel – past the arriving fire engines – that it dawned on me that the button I'd thought was the safety catch must have adjusted the gas flow. I must have set it on *high*. See what I mean? *Lucky*. If I'd slid it the other way, Clark's hair would merely be singed and Bubbles and I would be dead.

The kettle clicks off. I make my coffee and take it to the living room, where I sit down on the floor. I put the mug on the carpet next to Vince's *gun*. I'm not using it to light cigarettes. No, I've given those up – far too bloody dangerous. I keep it next to me because Vince was right. It does make me feel safer.

I lean back against the wall and marvel. At my luck, at my gloriously spick and span surroundings and at myself for rising to my greatest cleaning challenge yet.

Oh, did I not mention that I'm back at my flat?

After the Dorchester I didn't know where else to go. I'd have booked into the cheapest B&B I could find, but in the rush to check-out I left my wallet on the bedside table. I could have done a Fish and slept rough, but I had Bubbles with me ... And, frankly, even if I'd been alone I doubt I'd have been brave enough to sleep under an arch – I wouldn't even know where to look for a bloody arch. I had just under fifteen quid in change so we caught the tube to South Woodford.

My flat was the same depressing demolition site that I'd left on Friday, but it was still the only place I could call home. I know policemen or gangsters could smash in the door at any given moment, but I'm trying to convince myself that they'll think I couldn't possibly be dumb enough to hide here. Not much to get by on, admittedly, but there is something else. I'm hoping that if Fish has a change of heart then this will be the *first* place she'll head for. I miss her more than I would have believed – and more than I ever missed Megan.

Once here I rolled up my sleeves and did what I do best. I cleaned like a maniac. It took several hours as well as the contents of every bottle, jar and spray can of cleaning product in my cupboards. I spent ninety minutes on Geordie's blood-stain alone. I had quite a struggle with my conscience over that one. But in the end the Cleaning Impulse won, as ever, and there I was merrily destroying evidence with a combination of 1001, Vanish and old-fashioned elbow grease. I'm proud to say that that particular patch of my carpet is once again beige . . . -ish. The hardball cop in DS Bruce will want to throw the book at me, but the homemaker in her will surely be quietly impressed.

Bubbles is asleep in my bedroom now.

We've been out today. With the telly not working and no toys she'd have gone mad with boredom if we hadn't. I got double lucky this morning. A search through my jacket pockets for stray change turned up something much better – my winning Lotto tickets. They weren't, after all, in my wallet. So I cashed them and we went shopping. Toys, food and clothes. Not much change from £150, but at least we've got new dolls and supplies for a few days.

On the way back I phoned my mobile from a call box and left a message for Fish. I begged her to come and find me. *Insane* because I can't be sure she has my phone. If either the cops or the baddies have it . . . It doesn't bear thinking about, but the act was a measure of how much I miss her.

Oh, I did do something else. I posted that letter to Meg. I regretted it as soon as it had slid into the pillar box – I *hate* making a scene.

I've finished my coffee. I'm exhausted now. I stand up and go to the sofa. I spread a sheet over it, managing to cover most of the gaping rips. Then I lie down and pull the blanket up to my ears. I check that Vince's lighter is tucked beneath the cushion and close my eyes. I hope I sleep better than I did last night.

—————————————————————————————— 6.17 a.m.

I wake up.

Someone is in the room.

Bubbles?

I don't think so.

Someone else . . . Someone *big*.

My heart racing, I fumble for the gun – the *lighter*. I pick it up and peer into the blackness. I can't see any— Hang on. A shadow. A figure. Standing over me. I am getting *sick* of this – sick of being *this* scared. My arms shaking, I raise the *gun* towards it – *him*, I think.

'It's all right, sunshine,' says a voice. 'I've already got a light.'

—————————————————————————————— 6.48 a.m.

He knows everything. *Everything*. He knows more about my

situation than *I* do. I'm speechless as I watch him light another cigarette.

'What did you come here for?' he says, replacing the spent match in the box and putting it down on the kitchen table. 'I didn't think even you'd be that daft.'

'I don't know. I'm that daft, I suppose . . .' I can't get over how *much* he knows. I've got so many questions. Like . . . Like, 'David, how did you know it was a lighter?'

'You're the talk of the town, an underworld legend. Never thought I'd see the day. Torching that poncey tart's barnet . . . Let's just say it's not done his reputation a load of favours. Apparently he bit through his tongue as well . . .'

That would explain the gush of blood from his mouth.

'. . . No, he's not best pleased with you.'

'I can't believe you *know* him,' I say.

'Know *of* him . . . I know of most of these people – used to be my job. I can't believe you've got yourself mixed up with 'em. If your mum knew the half of it . . .'

Mum remains blissfully ignorant. She was wrong when she said the *Mail* wasn't delivered. It was, but David got to it first. He read the DYING MAN GETS BULLET story and had an attack of guilt. He felt terrible about . . . Not exactly throwing me out, but encouraging an early departure. He invented a sudden *business trip* and caught a plane to London. He planned to find me and take me back to Spain, where I'd do things properly – die in peace and dignity with my mother at my side and him at hers. He looked for me here, then tried the hospital, where he bumped into DS Bruce. Yes, he knows her too – 'She was a probationer at Hornchurch. Bit full of herself. Seen too many episodes of *Cagney and Lacey*.' She told him about the murder inquiry. And she gave him her latest nugget of information – the fact that her prime suspect wasn't, after all, on the terminal list. They went their separate ways. She went off to look for me . . . And so did he.

I'm going to have to radically overhaul my view of my

stepfather. It turns out that the dodgy connections I've always sneered at have got him to the heart of my predicament much more quickly than DS Bruce. He knows *everything*, even the precise damage to Clark's *Fewwawi* – new front wing, tyre and headlight, apparently. And despite knowing everything, he still wants to save my sorry arse. This is what I find most incredible of all. My *step*father is my saviour. He said it himself: 'Better get used to it. I'm the Seventh Cavalry.'

Only one problem. Didn't they all die?

'What made you come here?' I ask.

'To the flat? Well, I knew about the midnight deadline, didn't I? I've been up all night trying to find you before the Mafio-ski did. Didn't think you'd be thick enough to come here, but I figured it was worth a shot.'

He drains his mug of coffee and stands up – I think we're leaving.

'Where are we going to go?' I ask.

'Here'll do for now,' he replies, picking up his matchbox and rattling it.

I look at it and read where *here* is – the Travel Rest. I know it. It's a mile or two from my flat. One of those anonymous hotels that sit next to roundabouts and are used by sales reps and marketing execs looking for cheap conference facilities. And now, it seems, by retired policemen and fugitives.

'You can hole up there and watch the telly while I sort things out. You'd better get your stuff. You ain't got much, have you?'

'Not much,' I say as a still half-asleep Bubbles appears at the kitchen door.

'Want milk,' she says.

'Jesus, Murray, you don't like to make life simple, do you?'

_____ 7.27 a.m.

We're in David's car – a rented Astra.

392

'Is Daddy at work?' Bubbles asks from my lap.

'He's . . . Probably on his way there now,' I say.

'What day is it?'

'Tuesday.'

'I go nursery on *Tues*day. Are we going nursery?'

'No . . . Not today,' I say. 'Sorry.'

'It's *O-Kay*, you know. I don't like nursery. They make us eat sandwiches. I don't like sandwiches. They got cheese in. I don't like cheese. Cheese is maked of cows. I don't like cows . . .' And so on.

I turn to David and ask, 'Sort things out . . . What do you mean?'

'Get you out of the country. You'll need a new passport. They did you a favour when they nicked your old one – we'd've had a 'mare getting you through Gatwick as Murray Colin. Don't suppose you've got any snaps in your wallet?'

'I haven't even got a wallet. I haven't got anything. I can't afford a fake passport. How much do they cost?'

'Don't worry. You can owe me.'

'Are you sure about this, David? I mean, maybe I should just turn myself in.'

'Blimey, you *are* daft.'

'But I haven't murdered anyone.'

'Uncle Muzza setted a man on *fires*,' Bubbles says.

'Did he, poppet? Well, you can bet he had it coming . . . Look, Murray, I'd be gobsmacked if you'd actually killed anyone. I know you . . . But Bruce doesn't and she reckons she's not far short of making a case. I've put villains away with a lot less than she's got . . . And I didn't tell you this, but they found your old car.'

'That's good,' I say. 'It proves it was stolen.'

'It doesn't prove anything. It had been torched, which just makes Bruce think you've fucked her evidence . . . Even if you manage to get off a murder charge, what about the funny money

393

you've been spreading round town? You'll probably avoid a GBH 'cause your burns victim won't be pressing charges, but how about criminal damage at the Prince Regent and the Dorchester? There's your drunk driving, your burglary in—'

'I get the message.'

'You turn yourself in and you're doing time. Simple as that. And don't think you'll be safe inside. In case no one's mentioned it, prison is full of criminals . . . Who'll be queuing up to bid for the contract the Mafio-ski will put out on you.'

'Who's Matthew O'Ski?' Bubbles asks.

'A bunch of foreigners who've taken the fun out of things, poppet . . . That lot get me. They're bloody everywhere. Drugs, gambling, hookers – there isn't a pie left without a fat Russian finger in it. And they've got no *principles*. I mean, bunging you fifty grand in Toy Town money. Where's the integrity in that? Wouldn't have happened in my day. No, your British slag was basically honest. He might have been a vicious bastard, but he'd never stitch you up. We lost something when that Berlin Wall came down. Used to be that you knew where you stood . . . We've been sold down the bloody river to a mob of tooled-up ruble millionaires.'

Now I've heard it all. I've listened to plenty of anti-foreigner rants – mostly from David's next-door neighbour – but never one that accuses the immigrants of stealing the livelihoods of decent, hardworking British career criminals. But I have to say it . . . I'm with him on this one. Sod political correctness. If the last few days have taught me anything, it's that (a) your average Scot is a mingy tight-arse and (b) your basic Slav is a shifty beet-eating scuzzbucket.

'Why are you doing this, David?' I ask.

'Helping you out? Well, if you haven't already gathered, I don't like to see the Ivans stitch up one of my own.'

'Seriously.'

'You don't think I'm being serious? . . . OK, it's not just that.

I know you and me haven't got on like your mum's wanted, but believe it or not I've never disliked you – thought you were a bit soppy, maybe, but never actually *disliked* you. And even if I hated your guts, I love your mum. You saw what she was like when your dad cashed his chips – rest his soul. It'd finish her off getting the call that they'd found you face down in the Thames.'

We drive in silence for a while. Then he says, 'There's something else as well. A couple of days ago I was assuming I'd be taking you back to Spain on a stretcher. Or in a coffin . . . *Cancer*. I *hate* cancer. Wasn't sure I could cope to be honest. But this? This is *work*. I'm in my element.'

'I can't leave the country, David,' I say firmly. 'I *have* got cancer.'

'Yeah, but it isn't like you're at death's door with it. I mean, you look pretty rough, but that's probably the stress you've been under.'

'Rough? I feel terrible.'

He leans across the car and puts his hand on my forehead. 'You've got a temperature. Could be mild pneumonia.'

After Doctor Vince, a second opinion from Doctor Dave.

'Whatever,' I say, 'I've got cancer and I need treatment. I have to have an operation. And probably radiotherapy. I can't leave.'

'Why's that? Haven't they got hospitals in Spain? The doctors over there are the best. I'm not kidding.'

'What about the risk you're running? It's not fair to put you through that . . . What if we bump into the Russians? And the police. Won't they do you for aiding and abetting or something?'

'Ten years back the PCA had enough of a case to have me doing serious time. Don't make their mistake and underestimate me. See this face? This isn't a suntan. It's Teflon.'

I give in. 'Thank you,' I say. 'I really mean it. Tha—'

'*Filth*!' Bubbles interrupts in an excited squeak.

I hear the siren and my head spins round in a panic. Behind us a motorbike is flashing blue, its rider gesturing David to pull over. I half expect him – perhaps even *want* him – to put his foot down and burn rubber, but without a word he slows and pulls up to the kerb.

Bubbles puts her hand on my chest and says, 'I can feel your *heart*.'

Not surprising since it's threatening to fly out of my chest and do us both a serious injury. I haven't felt panic like this since . . . Oh, since the Dorchester bloody Hotel. I stare at David with wide, frightened eyes. As he winds down his window, he looks at me and says, 'Jesus wept, you couldn't look more bang to rights if you tried. Best keep it zipped, yeah?'

'Hide your stash, *maaan*. It's the bastard *filth*!' Bubbles squeaks again, pointing at the approaching traffic cop as she bounces deliriously on my lap.

'That goes for you too, poppet,' David adds – a futile gesture, I think.

The cop bends down at the open window and peers at us through the slot in his helmet. I attempt a smile, but he doesn't seem interested in me. He's looking at Bubbles who beams at him and says, 'Uncle Muzza setted a *man* on fires. Are you going to put him in *prisons*?'

Out of the mouths of babes . . .

But the policeman ignores her. He's looking at David now. 'Sir,' he says, 'I've been following you for over half a mile. Your speed hasn't dropped below thirty-eight, you went through *two* amber lights and you're carrying an unrestrained child on a lap in the front passenger seat. And I suppose you're going to tell me that you had no idea that one of your brake lights isn't working.'

'May I just say what a *pleasure* it is to meet an officer who takes the job seriously,' David announces. 'Been living in Spain a few years and you wouldn't credit how sloppy *el fuzzos* are. This one time I was driving to Valencia and . . .'

I don't hear any more because he has climbed out of the car. My heart still thumping, I watch the two of them talking, turning away my scared and guilty face each time the cop glances in my direction. David takes something from his pocket . . . Now the cop is writing something out . . . He gives it to David. A ticket? . . . But they're both smiling . . . No, laughing . . . They're shaking hands . . . The cop returns to his bike and David climbs into the car.

'What happened?' I ask as I melt with relief.

'I flashed him this,' David says. He pulls a battered leather cardholder from his pocket and flips it open to show me his ten-years-past-its-sell-by police ID. 'Just like Amex – don't leave home without it.'

'I thought he was writing you a ticket.'

'He was giving me his number. I told him I could swing him a transfer from Traffic to Special Branch. Modern coppers, eh? No wonder the Russians are running rings round 'em.'

fourteen: i love you

I lie back on the hotel bed and flick through the music channels. The sound is low because Bubbles is asleep on the single next to mine. David is out, *sorting* things. I feel safer than I've felt in a while. I feel better too. As if the feverish exhaustion *is* stress-related and now it's fading because David has lowered a ladder into my grave. But I feel lonely as well – I wish Fish were here. And something else, now I think about it . . . I feel bored.

Wow. When was the last time I felt *bored*? Life has been anything but boring for weeks. *Months*. I *like* boring. Boring doesn't involve gangsters or cops. Or putting forty-five grand on red or finding out you've just broken into the home of the king of daytime telly or friends turning up minus several teeth or leaping out of broken windows with tots wrapped in maroon velvet curtains or slipper-wearing Etonian psychopaths or getting blowjobs from stupid models in stupid cars . . .

OK, boring is what my life *was*, and how happy was that? But I can handle it for a while . . . Just a little while.

As I drift off to sleep there's a knock on the door. I don't jump. *I don't jump*. Because I know it's only David. That's what boring means. No surprises. I get up and open it.

Now I jump.

'Fish!' I whoop.

'Sorry,' she mumbles as she stands motionless in the corridor.

'*Sorry*? You're sorry? Jesus, *I'm* sorry.' I fling out my arms and put them round her, wrenching her towards me and into the room.

'How . . . The hell . . . Did . . . You . . . Find . . . Me?' I ask between long, wet, suffocating kisses.

'I've been looking for you for two bloody days, man. I called you at the Dorchester on Sunday morning.'

'That was you?'

'You were there? You could've fucking answered. Anyway, I was doing my head in trying to figure where you might be. I never thought you'd be dumb enough to go back to your flat . . .'

You too?

'. . . But I switched your phone on a couple of hours ago and picked up your message . . . Sorry – dunno why I took it. Can't help myself half the time.'

'Good job you did.'

'Good job you *called* 'cause I'd run out of places to look. Anyway, I went round your place and I freaked when you weren't there. I thought they must've got you – the cops, the other blokes, whoever. I *freaked*. Then I found a box of matches on your kitchen table. It had the name of this place on it.'

David must have left it. Sloppy – I thought he was a *professional* dodgy geezer.

'Did you pick it up?' I ask.

'No, I didn't . . . Fuck, I see what you're thinking. Shall I go back for it?'

'No . . . No, it'll probably be fine,' I gabble because everything is going to be all right now – Fish is here, with *me*, of course it's going to be all right. 'We're checking out in the morning. David reckons it's too public here. We're going to stay with some friend of his by the sea . . . Well, Southend. Apparently it'll take a few days to get a passport so it's just a matter of lying low before we fly off to . . .'

I stop as I register her disappointment.

'What's the matter?' I ask. 'You're coming with me, aren't you?'

'Am I? Is that OK?'

'Fish, I didn't tell you this before. I should have . . . but I didn't. I love you.'

Cue a kiss that would asphyxiate a water buffalo.

We're sitting on my bed. In between more kisses I've managed to tell her what she has missed – a couple of my life's more eventful days. She looks at the sleeping Bubbles and says, 'I thought my childhood was fucked up, man. She's gonna have some cool shit to tell her shrink one day . . . Where's Vince?'

'I don't know. That's a worry. I'm kind of hoping he just got sidetracked. You know what his attention span is like . . . What am I talking about? It's a major worry, actually. Anyway, what about you? Where've you been?'

'Oh, I've been busy. Looking for you and stuff,' she says casually. Then a sorrowful look draws itself across her face. 'I felt like shit after I'd run out on you. I'm really sorry . . . I shouldn't've gone into one like that.'

'Shut up. I'm the one who should be apologising. I should have told you about Megan sooner . . . Like straightaway.'

'You had other things on your mind – you thought you were dying for fuck's sake. I was being selfish. I was feeling sorry for myself after I read that *shit* I found in your pocket. It reminded me of what living with him was like – like I didn't *exist* . . . Anyway, fuck him. I'm over it now . . . I've got the money.'

'Excuse me?'

'The *money*. The hundred and fifty grand. I've got it. Mind you, it looks like you might get away without paying it back. Oh well, we'll just have to spend it, then.'

'Hang on. *How*? What the hell have you done?'

'I haven't actually *got* it yet,' she goes on, ignoring the

400

question. 'I'll have it in a few days. By the end of the week.'

'Fish, *tell* me.' My mind is racing through possibilities – none of them legal and some of them, frankly, terrifying. 'What have you done?'

'I'm not allowed to tell you. I'm not allowed to tell anyone.'

'*Tell me.*'

'Wait and see. It was your idea, actually.'

But I don't have ideas for rustling up small fortunes in double-quick time by means that are almost certainly against the law and very possibly dangerous.

'Please tell me . . . Please tell me we're not in any more shit.'

'God, I'd forgotten how much you *worry*, man.'

She leans across the bed and mashes her mouth into mine while her hand moves up my leg into my groin, and I don't know what's sexier – the thing that her hand is doing or the feeling of her tongue-stud inside my mouth. She pulls—

I should explain something at this point. We haven't done it yet. Had sex. It's not that we haven't wanted to. It's just that a certain thing has got in the way . . . Do I really have to spell it out?

But I am ready now.

So ready.

—my zip down and . . . stops abruptly. She pulls away and says, 'One question: you definitely over her?'

I nod the most sincere nod that I have ever nodded because I am so over Megan Dyer.

'Good,' she says, worming her hand inside my jeans. Surely the excitement I'm feeling *must* be confirmation that I'm *not* terminally ill. *Shit,* that is *wonderful* . . . And *fuck,* there's a bloody three-year-old asleep on the other bed. Who the hell put her there?

My turn to pull away.

'What's the matter?' she asks.

I nod towards Bubbles.

'So? She's asleep. Anyway, the violent shit she's seen lately, if she wakes up and sees us screwing it might do her some good.'

I think back to my one and only experience of public-ish sex. A toilet in Signor Zilli's with Megan. Her a little drunk, very hot and *very* up for it. Me wilting as dramatically as a tulip stem in the Gobi Desert. And – *honestly* – I'm not reminded of it because my head is still swimming with Megan, but because I'm feeling the same now as I did then – *wilting*. OK, a sleeping toddler barely constitutes an audience. This is hardly a live sex show before a crowd of paying punters that's also being captured on video for the American market. But this is *me*, Murray 'Are the doors locked, the lights off and the curtains tight shut?' Colin, the bloke who can only maintain an erection within a ten-mile exclusion zone. Repressed? You'll probably find my picture next to the dictionary definition.

I look at Fish. Chalk to my cheese because, well, given that she has spent the last two years living in squats and shop doorways, she can't know the meaning of privacy. And because, even if she did, would she really give a damn?

I've *got* to get over this because after a couple of false starts this is *definitely* Day One, the first day of the rest of my life. I *have* to get it right this time. I've *got* to stop being so *me*, not least because out of the corner of my eye I can see Morrissey (pop star, not doctor) on the telly and he's singing 'You're The One For Me, Fatty' and the song's joyful certainty is entirely fitting except that Fish isn't even remotely fat and it might be slightly more appropriate if he were pining 'Please, Please, Please, Let Me Get What I Want' and as he asked in a completely different song 'How Soon Is Now?' and, well, if it isn't right *now*, this minute, this very *second*, then when the hell is it? And now another song pops into my head and, frankly, I wish it hadn't because it's crap, but it does have at its core a clarion call for decisive action and though I'm more than a little embarrassed to admit it, it's Bucks Fizz singing 'Making Your Mind Up'.

So I push her back onto the bed and say 'Sod Bubbles' and *almost* mean it. I try to focus on Fish and what her hand is doing – which would be easier if Bubbles would stop bloody *snoring* – and I go to work myself, pushing up her top and pulling down her shabby bra and . . . *Wow*, I reckon this is going to *happen* because I've never seen her breasts before and they are bloody *fant*—

Another knock.

'Who the fuck's that?' Fish hisses, her body stiffening beneath mine.

I climb off the bed, zip myself up and open the door.

'Don't tell me,' David says, as he peers over my shoulder and spots Fish putting herself back together. 'Lemme guess . . . You want another passport.'

fifteen: **in this world there's two kinds of people, my friend. those with loaded guns and those who dig**

'You don't have to do this, Fish . . . Not for me, anyway.'

'I owe you. You saved my life,' she says, draining her cup.

'The bloke had a knife to your throat. *Anyone* would have done it.'

'I'm not talking about that. I mean the day I broke in and trashed your place and I looked like a piece of crap and I must've stunk and you still asked me to stay.'

'I did that for me as much as for you.'

'Whatever. You saved my life. Anyway, I'm doing this for me.'

'What about the police? They're still looking for you.'

'Been dodging them for two years.'

'There'll be no turning back if you go through with it,' I say, clinging to her hand across the breakfast table.

'There never fucking was. I'll see you in Southend.' She leans across the table and kisses me.

As she walks out of the dining room I call out 'Be careful' and then 'I love you.' I don't know if she hears because she doesn't look back.

'Is she going to work?' Bubbles asks.

'Kind of,' I say.

'Is Daddy still at work?'

'Yes. But he'll be back soon.'

'Will he have more tooths gone?'

'With any luck, no,' I say, though I have a bad feeling that Vince used up the last of his good fortune on the roulette table.

I refill my cup with coffee as David walks into the dining room, jacket on, ready for another morning's *sorting*. 'She left already?' he asks, taking Fish's empty seat. 'Did she really have to split? She'd have been a lot safer if she'd stuck around. The cops are dead keen to talk to her even if the Russians aren't.'

'She had to go, cops or no cops,' I tell him.

'A girl's gotta do . . . I'll shoot now as well. Get these developed,' he says, rattling the camera film containing Fish's passport snaps. 'I'll be back by lunch. You be ready to move.'

'Are you going to work?' Bubbles asks. 'Will Daddy be there?'

'If he is I'll tell him to come straight to see you, poppet.' He shoots me a look and I give him one back because I've begged him to make finding Vince his next job as soon as we're away from here. 'You'll see your dad soon, I promise,' he says to Bubbles. He stands up. 'See you later . . . And don't go talking to strangers.'

_____ 11.21 a.m.

It's a lovely day. Sadistic January sunshine that fools crocuses into sprouting and hedgehogs into waking before mugging them with a *vicious* cold snap. I'm sitting on a log at the back of the hotel. It's one of a few that mark the perimeter of the bark-strewn children's play area beside the car park. Bubbles has set up home in the Technicolor plastic Wendy house. I can hear her now, dishing out summary justice to her dolls: 'That's *bullshit*, dude. You *wipp'ded* us off . . . If you haven't gived me the *combention* by when I weach *five*, baby loses her *bwains*.'

I fear for Tiny Tears' hair – being nylon it'll be even more incendiary than Clark's. In a moment of weakness I let her have Vince's lighter to play with. I'm really not fit to look after her. She urgently needs positive role models. Even if Vince doesn't quite fall into that category, he should be here. I need him to take Bubbles off my hands, but I also need to know he's OK. David has promised to make some calls, but maybe I should do that too. I take my mobile from my pocket, switch it on and dial. After a couple of rings: 'Good morning, Blower Mann/DBA, can I help you?'

That takes me back ... To what seems like another lifetime entirely.

'Brett Topowlski, please.'

A few more rings, then a barely interested 'Hullo.'

'Brett.'

'Who's that?'

'Murray ... Murray Colin.'

'Murray! *Fuck*, how the hell are you? Sorry, *sick* question ... Jesus, we were gutted when we heard. What a twisted *bastard* world. I mean, there's plenty of twats round here who deserve some terminal shit, but not ... Look, I'm really sorry.'

'There's something I need to tell you, Brett ...'

_____ 11.29 a.m.

'That is ... Jesus, that is ... You couldn't script it, man. Unbelievable,' he gasps after I've explained. 'What a *fuck* up. You're gonna sue the hospital, yeah? Hey, I've gotta tell Jakki. She's been getting everyone to sign a petition – she wants Blower to get you sculpted in bronze and stick you in reception. I think he's close to buckling as well ... Maybe I won't tell her, then. Gotta tell Vin though.'

'That's what I was calling about. Have you heard from him?'

'Not a peep. Been trying him for days. I've got us an in at Leo Burnett and I want to get our book over there. Why do you need him?'

'It's ... kind of a long story. But he's disappeared and left me with Bubbles. I think he might be in trouble.'

'Wouldn't be the first time. Why isn't the kid with her mum?'

'She's disappeared too.'

'She's done that before. Forty-eight hours of arse-ripping childbirth, but it still slips her mind that she's a mother. She vanished for six weeks once. Vin found her in an ashram in Cardiff. Millions go off in search of Buddha, but only Sooz tries looking in *Wales*. Any road, back to Vin – what sort of trouble? You mixed up in this as well?'

'Sort of.'

'Sounds like suit-speak for up to your ears in it. You haven't lost it, have you, matey? Look, don't panic. I'll make some calls, see what I can find out.'

'Thanks, Brett. I really appre— Sorry, I've got to go. I'll call you later.'

I've got to end the call because I've just seen a car pull into the car park. No big deal. They've been driving in and out all morning. None of them have been bright red Bentley Arnage Ts, though. It squeezes into a space between two hatchbacks and after a moment Megan climbs out, blinking at first in the bright sunshine, then spotting me. I stare at her as if she's the last person I expected to see – which she is.

'What are you doing here?' I ask as she reaches me.

'*Hello* would have done,' she replies in a friendly enough voice. 'I could ask the same of you.' She looks me up and down for a moment before saying, 'You look well. A lot better than you did at the nick.'

'Thanks. I feel a lot better, actually. Much improved.'

'It's amazing what a slight change in diagnosis can do.'

'Amazing . . . How did you find me?'

'I went to your flat. I didn't think you'd be daft enough to go there under the circumstances, but I found a box of Travel Rest matches in the kitchen.'

'The matches,' I say in a panic. 'Did you pick them up?'

'Yes, I needed the address. Why?' She looks at me sag with

407

relief. 'Silly question. You're a fugitive from justice. That's what I came to see you about, actually.'

Here we go. She wants me to turn myself in. She's wearing her lawyer gear too. Any other day it would be sexy, but today it's just frightening.

'I got a call from DS Bruce this morning,' she continues. 'She asked me if I was still your brief. I told her I very much doubted it, but she said she had some news and she didn't know who else to call. She still wants to talk to you, but not about murder. You are bloody lucky, Murray. Your silver BMW exists. The driver turned himself in. He couldn't live with the guilt apparently.'

'Jesus,' I gasp. 'That is a *massive* bloody relief.' And it is because, though I'm hardly out of trouble, one thing that really bothered me was the idea of people thinking I'd *killed* someone – in particular the idea of twelve men and women on a jury thinking it. 'Thanks, Meg,' I say.

'Don't thank me. Thank the BMW driver . . . You'll like this. Bruce said the guy works in advertising. And there was me claiming you lot checked in your consciences at reception.'

'You didn't have to drive all this way to tell me that, you know. I'm glad you did, but you didn't have to.'

'No, I didn't, but I wanted to. There's something else as well . . . I got your letter yesterday,' she says as she sits down beside me on the log.

I wince. Did I mention I hate making a scene? 'I'm sorry,' I say.

'No, I'm sorry. I'm really sorry . . . I was out of order the other night,' she continues. 'Don't get me wrong. I still think you've been a prat. But I can't imagine what you've been going through the last couple of months. I've been thinking about that, trying to put myself in your shoes. I don't think I'd have borrowed fifty grand from men with guns . . . But I had no right to be so judgemental. I'm sorry.'

'Forget it,' I say. 'Anyway, you're right. I have been a prat. It wasn't supposed to turn out like this though. I was going to do something really good with that money . . . Something worthwhile.'

She gives me one of her sceptical eyebrows.

'Look, I'm sure it would have come to me if it hadn't all gone pear-shaped.'

'Fifty grand buys a lot of *worthwhile*,' she says. 'Mind you, I'd have settled for having some fun.'

'Really?'

'Really. You can't be right-on *all* the time. It's too much like hard work.'

We sit in silence for a moment. Then she asks, 'Murray, did you really buy me this?' The ring glints at me from the palm of her outstretched hand.

I nod.

'Why didn't you give it to me?'

'You kind of stole the moment. I was going to propose the day you announced you'd met Sandy.'

'Shit. Lousy timing,' she says, looking away. 'Tell me, how the hell did Sandy get hold of it?'

'You haven't asked him?'

'I would have done. He's at a human rights convention in Oslo.'

'I put it in the box of stuff you collected. It must have fallen out in his car.'

'I wish you had given it to me,' she says quietly.

'You think things would be any different now?'

'I don't know . . . Maybe . . . No, probably not. But at least I'd have known how you felt. That stuff I was saying the other day about having second thoughts. I wasn't just telling you to be cruel. I wish you'd told me how you felt.'

'I thought you knew.'

'That was your trouble, Murray – you always assumed I could read your mind.'

'Isn't that how it's supposed to be? When you've been with

409

someone for a while you know what they're thinking. I always knew what was in your head.' The words sound lame and I wish I could take them back.

'You knew what was in my head because I *told* you,' she says. 'Oh . . . Never mind. Too late now.'

It is too late. Way too late. But that doesn't depress me. Not any more. And something else doesn't get to me. She's twizzling her hair. Zero effect. *Less* than zero because now I find it strangely *annoying*. You live and learn.

'What are you going to do?' I ask. 'You know, about Sandy.'

'Leave him of course. How could I stay with him after a stunt like that?'

She hands me the ring.

'Keep it,' I say. 'It's not as if it wasn't intended for you – it's just that the wrong bloke gave it to you.'

'I can't keep it,' she says, forcing it into my hand. 'Fuck, this is a disaster.'

She's crying now. Automatically my arm goes around her shoulder, though it doesn't seem appropriate. 'I'm sorry,' I say. 'I knew the letter would upset you, but that isn't why I wrote it. I'm truly sorry.'

'Oh, stop it. Stop being so bloody sorry. I'll be OK.' She pulls a tissue from her pocket and blows her nose. 'You've got far worse things to worry about than my fucked-up love life. What are you going to do? About the police . . . the money.'

'Leave the country.'

'Just like that? Just leave the country? Where are you going?'

'Where all the best criminals end up.'

'Spain? What about your . . . You know.'

'My cancer? I'll get it treated over there. Best docs in the world apparently.'

'Please get it sorted, Murray. It'd be a bloody shame if you went and died now after all that's happened.' Then after a long pause: 'What about that girl?'

That girl.

'She's coming with me.'

'She seems very young.'

I raise an eyebrow.

'You're right. None of my business. Is she here?'

'No, she's in town . . . Getting the money as it happens.'

'*How*? I thought she was homeless. Please tell me she's not robbing a bank.'

'Nothing like that . . . I might as well tell you. She's selling out her father.'

I finally got it out of Fish late last night. She was right – it *was* my idea. She remembered a conversation we'd had before Christmas when I'd idly asked why she hadn't been to the papers. So, with her hatred re-ignited by the story in the *Mail* and the need for serious money suddenly more urgent, she rang Max Clifford. She went to see him on Monday morning and gave him everything – not just her own story, but stuff on her father that never came out in court. Some really sleazy shit. Clifford got on the phone and soon had the interest of the *Mirror* and the *Express*. She didn't go with them, though. She went with the *Mail*. Not for the irony, but because it was the only paper offering a quarter of a million. The price is a measure of how high her father has risen – it's worth *that* much to take him down.

That's where she is today. With the journalists, giving them the interview. They're doing the photos as well. They're taking her back to the streets, dressing her in rags and re-creating her old life.

'What do you mean, selling out her father?' Megan asks.

'She's doing a kind of kiss and tell with the *Mail*.'

'That's awful, *horrible*,' she says. I know how she feels about chequebook journalism – in her personal code of sins it's not much better than selling heroin to schoolkids. 'How could you let her do that?'

411

'I never told you who her dad is. He's Richard Hyam-Glass.'

'No . . . She's Isabel Hyam-Glass? . . . *Nooo*.'

'Small world, isn't it? She's the girl Sandy ripped to shreds in court.'

'*Jesus* . . . Now I know why she looked familiar when I saw her. This is incredible. Why didn't you say anything?'

'I didn't know myself for a while . . . She's still pretty mad about that stunt you pulled with her schoolmates – *Cousin* Meg.'

As she blushes my mobile goes off. I answer it, hoping it's Brett with good news about Vince. But it's better than that.

'Muzza! *Mate*. It's me.'

'Vince, where've you been? I've been going spare. I thought you were dead.'

'Nah . . . Nah, nothing like that. You know me. Got side-tracked,' he says in a *jolly* sort of voice that I have to say is really *inappropriate* given what I've been through since he got *sidetracked*. 'Been trying to get hold of you, but your mobile's been switched off.'

'I only just got it back,' I say flatly. 'Fish turned up.'

'Knew she would. Is Bubbles OK?'

'She's fine. Missing you like mad. Vince, what the hell have you been doing?'

'Later, Muzz. Where are you?'

'A hotel in Redbridge. The Travel Rest. On the A12. When can you get here?'

'Be there soon. Don't move, OK?'

'OK,' I say, but the line has already gone dead.

'Who was that?' Megan asks.

'Vince. The guy who helped me get the money. You've met him, actually. He used to work at Blower Mann.'

'Is he the one who wants to rob yachts in a submarine?'

'He's the one.'

'Who's Bubbles?'

'She is,' I say pointing at the little girl emerging from the

412

Wendy house with a headless Tiny Tears and a replica gun. 'Bubbles,' I call out. 'Daddy's coming.'

'*H'raaaay*! Daddy, Daddy, *Daddy*!' She runs up and flings herself onto my lap.

'*Amazing*,' Megan says. 'I have to say you've spent the last few weeks astonishing me, Murray. I always thought you hated kids.'

'So did I . . . But you live and learn, don't you?'

'You certainly do. *Jesus*, Murray, what the hell's she doing with that?' she shrieks, only now spotting Vince's lighter.

'Don't worry,' I tell her, taking it from Bubbles and holding it out in the palm of my hand. 'It's her dad's lighter. It's not real.'

'It bloody well looks real. Please put it away.'

I slip it into my pocket.

'Look, I'd better be going,' she says. 'I only came to tell you the good news about the BMW . . . And to give you the ring.'

'Are you OK?'

'Yes, yes . . . No, of course I'm not, but I'll be fine, honestly.'

As she stands up I say, 'Don't go yet. Stay for a coffee. Don't leave like this.'

I feel bad. Not because I have pangs of longing for her, but because I *don't*.

'No,' she says, 'I'd better—'

'Look, Meg, with any luck I won't ever see you again – I mean, I'm a fugitive now. We can't say goodbye like this.'

'All right then, I'll have a coffee,' she says, sitting back down on the log. After a moment she adds, 'I've just had a thought.'

'What's that?'

'You told your friend where you were. He wasn't with the bad guys, was he?'

'No, he was on his own . . . I think. Anyway, Vince wouldn't give me up.'

'*Astonishing*,' she smiles. 'Now you're even talking like a gangster.'

I don't smile back because she has got me thinking – *worrying*.

413

That jolly tone in Vince's voice sounded a bit unreal – like it was drug-induced . . . Or forced at gunpoint. Maybe the sunshine has been lulling me – as well as the crocuses and hedgehogs – into a false sense of security.

Another car pulls round the corner of the hotel and into the car park. A long black Mercedes with gold wheels and heavily tinted glass – definitely not a rep's car.

'What's the matter?' Megan asks, sensing the tension.

'I don't know. Nothing probably . . . But maybe we should take Bubbles inside.'

We stand up and set off across the tarmac, Bubbles' hand held tightly in mine. The car has pulled into a space and a door opens. Someone stumbles out, as if pushed. It's Vince. Who else? He straightens himself up and spots us. Bubbles has already torn her hand from my grasp and is sprinting towards him.

'Does her dad always get chauffeured around in a pimp mobile and look like he's gone ten rounds with Tyson?' Megan asks quietly.

'Not as a rule.'

'This doesn't look good, does it?'

'Not good at all. I'd go now if I were you.'

She doesn't move, though.

Vince has scooped Bubbles into his arms, but he stops himself from doing the usual whooping and spinning her around. He stares at me, the look on his bruised face saying only *sorry*. He walks slowly towards us, stopping when he's ten feet short.

'They had a bloke waiting at Sooz's place,' he says. 'I've really fucking blown it. I'm sorry, but if I hadn't made the call just now they'd have topped me and then gone after Sooz. I couldn't do that to Bubbles. I'm really fucking sorry.'

'Don't be, Vince. It's not like they gave you a choice. Who else is in the car?'

'You'll know him when you see him. He's pissed with you. *Pithed*, as it goes.'

A door opens on the other side of the Merc and a man climbs out. One side of his face is bandaged and he's wearing a big Rasta tea cosy. It takes me a second to recognise him – I imagine the hat is hiding the result of a recent bad hair day.

'Thith plathe mutht be a letdown after the Dorthethter,' he says as he reaches us. The brand-new speech impediment makes sense of Vince's last remark – I remember David telling me he'd bitten through his tongue when I set light to him. His hand is in the pocket of his long black cashmere coat. I guess it's clutching a gun, because a rigid lump juts out towards me, ruining the cut.

Instinctively I reach my hand into my jacket, feeling Vince's lighter. Clark steps up to me. Pushing the lump in his coat into my ribs, he reaches into my pocket with his free hand. He pulls out the *gun* and looks at it contemptuously. 'You weally think you could pull that thtunt a thecond time?' he says. 'I can't believe I wath thuckered by a fucking thigawette lighter.'

I can't believe he was either, but I don't say so.

He opens his coat and drops it into a wide breast pocket. 'I thuppothe you know why we're here, Muwway.'

'Why don't you let Vince and the kid go? I'll get you the money.'

He just laughs.

'My girlfriend's getting it now, I swear. She's in town sorting it out.'

'Firtht it'th in the thafe, then Vinthe ith getting it, now your girlfwiend ith *thorting* it out . . . You are twuly full of cwap, Muwway, my man.'

'He's not lying. She is getting it,' Megan says. I'm surprised to hear her speak – surprised, too, that she managed to understand a word of what he said because, frankly, I'm struggling to keep up.

Clark snaps now, whipping his gun from his pocket and

pointing it at Megan's head. 'Thut the fuck up, bitth. Who thaid you could thpeak? Who the fuck are you?'

'I'm Murray's lawyer,' she says with admirable calmness. 'I assure you he's getting your money.'

'It'll take more than a lawyer to ecthtwact you fwom the thit, *canther* boy,' he says, swinging the gun towards me.

'His condition isn't serious, you know,' Megan says. 'Nothing like as bad as the newspaper made out.'

'Hith condithion became theriouth fwom the moment he twied to make me look like a pwick. It'th gone way beyond the money.' He takes half a step towards me until his gun is pressed against my forehead. I feel my breathing quicken, then Megan's hand grasp my arm.

'Set him on fires, Uncle Muzza, set him on *fires*,' Bubbles squeaks.

'Thut the fucking wug wat up, Vinthent,' Clark says.

Vince's hand has already gone over her mouth.

Clark's finger tightens on the trigger.

'*Wait*.' It's Megan. 'You want your money, don't you?' she says.

'He doethn't have any money, thweetie,' Clark sneers.

'He's got a car,' she says.

Do I? Since when? She can't possibly mean the Polo.

'He's got a Bentley . . . It's over there.' She points at Sandy's car.

Clark follows her finger and spots it. Then he turns back to me and says, 'I think that pwhapth your lawyer ith jerking my chain.' He levels the gun at my head again. I close my eyes . . . And hear the jangle of a car key. I open them and see Clark squinting at Sandy's key ring.

'Look,' Megan says, pointing at the fob. 'B for Bentley. It's worth well over a hundred and fifty grand. Not even ten thousand miles on the clock. *Pristine* condition. Take it and leave us alone.'

Spoken like a saleswoman . . . And, *hell*, she must be *really* mad at Sandy.

Clark stares at her, thinking, figuring things out. Then with his left hand he reaches into his coat and takes out a mobile. Without lowering the gun he thumbs a button on his keypad before putting the phone to his ear. After a moment: 'It'th me . . . *Me* . . . *Yeth*, Clark . . . There'th been a development. You'd betht come.'

We wait as another body climbs out of the Mercedes. It's Little. He waddles towards us and in a moment he's beside Clark. He looks every bit as dapper as he did at Momo. But angrier. As if a trip to the borders of Essex to exact punishment on a pathetic cheat is playing havoc with his carefully constructed social calendar.

'Wha's 'appen?' he snaps at Clark while glaring irritably at me.

'Muwway'th lawyer claimth the wed Bentley over there ith hith. She thuggethtth we take it in wepawation.'

'Wha'?' Little snarls. 'Spik English, you stupee basta.'

'The big wed puthy wagon. Over there. It'th hith.' Clark's patience is fraying.

His boss gets it now and looks at the Bentley. 'Veery nice boossy vargen.' He looks at Megan and gestures for the keys.

'Tell your friend to put his gun away first,' she says.

Little doesn't like that one bit. I know this because he pulls a gun of his own and aims it at her head. 'Kih,' he grunts. She does the smart thing and tosses them to him. He inspects them and the corners of his mouth lift – a satisfied man. ''K, 'K,' he says to Clark. 'We 'ave boossy vargen . . . I drive, 'K?'

'Cool,' Clark replies. 'What about him?' He gestures at me with his gun.

'Stick 'im in boot.'

I feel Megan's hand grip my arm again. I look at Vince standing helplessly next to Clark, powerless to act other than

417

to clamp his hand over Bubbles' mouth and pull her head into his jacket. Clark steps forward and takes my other arm. I shrug helplessly at Megan. What else can I do but go? Clark starts to pull me towards the Bentley but stops as a car appears in the car park. He and his boss lower their guns as they watch it. I dare to glance at it too. It's a green Vauxhall Astra.

Yesss, the Seventh Cavalry . . . But wait, they all died, didn't they?

David pulls into a space and gets out of the car. He pauses for a moment, studying the situation. Clark and Little may have lowered their guns, but they haven't pocketed them. I expect David to climb back into his car, drive off, get reinforcements or something. But, no, he sets off towards us.

'You been keeping an eye on our Murray? Very kind of you,' he says breezily when he reaches us. Then to me, 'Right, let's make a move, eh?' He steps towards me and the guns come back up, both now pointing at him. 'Now, I knew you'd do that,' he says coolly. 'But best not be hasty, yeah? . . . I'm going to take something from my pocket. It's not a gun, I promise you. But you should take a look at it before you stick a bullet in me . . . OK?'

Clark looks at Little, who looks at David. Then Little gives a curt nod.

'Vewy thlowly,' Clark advises.

'As slow as you like,' David agrees. His hand comes out of his pocket. It's holding his leather cardholder. He lets it fall open to reveal his ID. 'You don't want to go killing a cop, do you? Always a piss-poor idea, that one . . . Now, before you panic I'm not here on official business. I'm just here to collect Murray – make sure he doesn't get into any more scrapes.'

He takes half a step towards me again, but Little jabs his gun at him. 'You take 'im nowhere. He come with us.'

'Look . . . *friend* . . . Murray's been a silly boy,' David says, 'but topping him isn't gonna get you a penny, is it? How about

418

I take him away and we can come up with a sensible repay-ment plan.'

'He's sorted out the money,' Megan says.

'What's that, sweetheart?'

'The Bentley, *Murray's* Bentley. Over there. He's offered them that,' she explains hurriedly.

David looks confused, but only for a moment. Then he's up and running, grabbing the thread and going with it. 'There you go. *Lovely* motor – one of Britain's greatest gifts to the world, the Bentley. It's right up there with Melton Mowbrays and the jury system. Should more than compensate you gentlemen. You coming then, Murray?'

'You take 'im *nowhere*,' Little snaps. ''Im and boossy vargen come with us.'

David looks puzzled so Clark interprets. 'My employer ith ecthtwemely upthet with Muwway, yah? He feelth that he thouldn't be allowed to get away with twying to wun wingth awound uth. Dig?'

'Sorry, I don't, sunshine. Speak English, will you?' David says.

'He'th been taking the *pith*. He'th going to pay the fucking pwithe . . . *Dig?*' Clark shouts.

'OK, OK,' David soothes. 'Know what? This reminds me of the best movie ever made bar none. *You see, in this world there's two kinds of people, my friend. Those with loaded guns and those who dig,*' he says, slipping into a fairly passable Clint Eastwood. 'I s'pose I'm one of the ones what's digging, eh?'

Clark and Little look at him, utterly confused.

'*The Good, the Bad and the Ugly,*' David explains. 'Blondie – that's Clint's character – he says it to . . . Never mind. My point is you've got the guns and you'll do what the fuck you like. I'm not gonna argue with you. But before you bugger off with Murray let me show you who I am.'

'You cop. We know,' Little grunts.

'There's a bit more to it than that.'

David's other hand starts to come out of his jacket pocket, immediately setting Clark's and Little's guns twitching. 'Calm, gentlemen, calm,' he says with a smile as he produces a small silver mobile phone. He flips it open and touches a button. The display lights up as he scrolls through the directory. Then he stops and holds up the phone for the benefit of Clark and Little. They peer at the screen, their eyes widening as if they've just clapped eyes on a ghost. Vince, too, squints at the phone in slack-jawed terror. Then Little pulls himself together and snaps, 'He dead.'

'That's just where you're wrong, as it happens,' David responds. 'He's got his feet up enjoying a well-deserved retirement. Can't say where, obviously, but it's someplace sunny . . . I say retirement, but it's hard to let go, isn't it? He still keeps up with goings-on back home . . . Looks out for his old friends . . . *Dig*?'

Little does and takes a nervous step back.

'Now, will I be leaving with Murray and his mates or would you prefer I put in a call?' David says, his thumb hovering over *dial*.

sixteen: **he likes his peace and quiet**

We sit in the Astra. Me up front with David. Megan, Vince and
Bubbles in the back. We watch in silence as the Bentley slides
noiselessly out of the car park. Little driving, Clark beside him.
The Merc follows and through the darkened glass I can make
out Val at the wheel. David starts the engine and we move off.
We follow them to a roundabout where we take separate exits.
Now I feel safe enough to speak.

'What happened back there?' I say.

'Just showed 'em a name,' David says quietly.

'What name?' Megan asks.

'Wanna tell them, Vince, or shall I?'

I look around at Vince. The terror I glimpsed in the car park
has returned. 'You tell 'em,' he mumbles.

'Someone Vince ran into in Javea. Actually, *ran into* doesn't
cover it. More like he stalked him down the length of the Arenal
before collaring him and hitting him with a half-arsed business
plan.'

'Who is he?' I ask, though I think I know.

'If I told you I'd have to kill you,' David says with a smile.

'Who is he, David?' Megan asks.

He stares straight ahead at the road, ignoring both of us. I
look at Vince who's looking at Bubbles, willing her to keep her
mouth shut. Now I *know* I know.

'Why did you tell me he was dead, David?' I ask.

'You didn't need to know otherwise.'

'He lives in Javea?'

421

'This doesn't leave this car, right?' David says, glaring at me meaningfully. 'He lives a few miles out. Jalon Valley. He likes his peace and quiet . . . doesn't he, Vince?'

'And you'd have called him?' I continue.

'Well, it's just about his siesta time, so he wouldn't have been best pleased . . . But if push had come to shove.'

'Excuse me, but who the hell are you talking about?' Megan says.

'Brian *Shark*. The *baddest* motherfucker that ever *motherfuck-'ded*,' Bubbles squeaks.

'Hang on . . . Brian bloody *Sharkey*?' Megan gasps.

No one says anything, but no one needs to.

'Brian *Sharkey*,' Megan repeats. 'I don't believe it . . . I'm probably committing gross professional misconduct even by *thinking* this, David, but you are *amazing*.'

Took the words right out of my mouth.

'As I told your ex, sweetheart, I'm Teflon-coated. Even bullets won't stick. Now, there's a minicab office coming up. You wanna be dropped there or are you fleeing the country with the rest of us?'

_____ 12.24 p.m.

'This is definitely goodbye then,' I say.

'Definitely,' Megan replies.

We're standing by her cab, which is waiting to take her back to town.

'Listen, what you did back there. It was incred—'

'Please, I don't want to hear it. Like a life isn't worth more than a stupid car.'

'Well, thank you. A million times over . . . What are you going to tell Sandy?'

'The truth. What the hell else? He *owes* you, Murray. The *shit*.'

'I'm sorry you have to go back and deal with . . . all that.'

422

'I'll be OK. Finding somewhere to live is the biggest of my worries.'

'There's a flat going in South Woodford if you're interested.'

'I don't think so . . . Fresh starts all round, I reckon.'

'Yeah, I reckon.'

We look at each other awkwardly for a moment. Then she leans forward and hugs me. 'Do something for me, Murray. Take care of yourself.'

'You too, Meg.'

I watch her climb into the car. As it sets off she winds down her window and calls out, 'I can't wait to read what's in the *Mail* . . . *Me* looking forward to the *Mail*! *Un*believable.'

—————————————————————— 12.31 p.m.

The traffic light ahead switches from green to amber and David pulls up, perhaps remembering yesterday's brush with the traffic cop. My peripheral vision picks up red paintwork and I turn my head just as a Bentley pulls up alongside us.

'What the fuck are they doing here?' David says, spotting it too.

'Twonks are probably lost,' Vince says. 'They had a 'mare finding their way out of the West End this morning.'

'That's the Ivans for you. Probably been driving round in circles since we left 'em. Now, should we tell 'em they'll end up in Clacton if they stay on this road . . . ? No, best they sort themselves out.'

I don't want to look, but I can't tear my eyes away. Little is at the wheel. He seems agitated. Next to him Clark seems cowed. They're clearly lost and it's obvious who's getting the blame. Little puts a long cigarette in his mouth and Clark reaches into his coat, producing Vince's replica from the breast pocket.

'Bastard's got my lighter,' Vince mumbles as Clark raises it to the tip of his boss's fag. Then, 'What the *fuck*!'

423

We heard the muffled bang. Far more shocking though is the fact that Little's face has disappeared. Obliterated in an explosion of blood, deep red and glistening. His head tips back against the window, which itself is now slick with blood. Clark sits perfectly immobile beside him, seemingly petrified.

None of us can speak.

The light turns green.

As David puts the car into gear and moves off he mutters, 'Yeah, best leave 'em to sort themselves out.'

I turn round and look at Vince and Bubbles. She seems unconcerned, oblivious even, but Vince's face has drained of colour – even his bruises look bleached. He's as catatonic as I am and he can only stare back at me.

After a long moment he shoves a cigarette between his lips with a trembling hand. Then he fumbles in his pocket and produces a box of matches.

Thank *Christ*.

You know where you are with matches.

_____ mar.

do you know what today is?

I point the camera at . . .

Sophie Dahl's prone and virtually naked body.

Elvis/Lennon/Tupac as he emerges from a cave deep in the Hindu Kush.

A multi-pack of Alpenchok bars nestling in a supermarket freezer cabinet.

None of the above, actually, though any – even the choc-ices – would be preferable to the reality.

The reality: I point the camera at . . .

I don't know. I can't see. My eyes are tight shut. Because I'm too bloody scared to look.

'Please move away from the edge, Fish,' I plead.

'Oh, stop being such a pussy and take the fucking picture.'

'I'm *begging* you.'

'OK, OK, I'm moving.'

I open one eye a crack and squint at her. She appears to have shuffled her bum a token six inches towards safety, but her legs are still dangling over the sharp rim of the rocky outcrop. She's still unnervingly close to plummeting hundreds of feet onto the . . . I don't know what she'd plummet onto because I haven't dared look, have I? Whatever, it's bound to be hard or jagged or in some other way lethal.

She's grinning at me. '*Cheeeeeeeeeeeeese!*'

I plunge my finger down onto the shutter release and hear the click. God knows if it was in focus, if she was blinking, if her face was being obscured by a passing bat making a freak daylight appearance. I wasn't paying that much attention and, frankly, I don't care. Job done. I've taken her sodding photo.

'Now will you come away from the edge?' I say.

She stands up and walks towards me, towards relative safety, though even being a good fifteen feet from the drop doesn't fill me with a sense of security. Who can say with absolute certainty that a freakish passing bat *won't* skim by, throwing me off balance and sending me rolling to certain death? OK, the chance must be slight, but I'm not prepared to take it.

'Can we go back down now?' I ask.

'What's the hurry? It's beautiful up here,' Fish replies as she takes a deep breath of slightly rarefied Mediterranean air.

Up here is the summit of Montgo, the hump of a mountain that stands guard over Javea. From the ground it looks a little like Rio's Sugarloaf (only squatter and less photogenic . . . Oh, and minus the neighbouring Jesus statue). I have to say that I much prefer it from the ground. I've never stood on the summit of anything, not even a gravel heap. Heights number high on my ever-lengthening list of *things to be avoided if at all possible*: hospitals, flying, awkward confrontations, casinos, cars (esp. when containing leggy models), guns . . .

Heights terrify me only slightly less than do submarines, but the difference is enough to have me up here with Fish rather than in Valencia with Vince. He has gone to check out his dream. A miniature sub that's being sold by a salvage company at what he assures me is a very reasonable price. Actually, the phrase he used was *rock bottom*. 'Vince,' I told him, 'the last thing you want to pay for a submarine is a *rock bottom* price.' It's probably more of a sieve than a sub. It'll do the going down thing. Most likely not so hot on the coming back up bit.

On balance I definitely prefer being up here. At the *summit*.

'*Amazing* view,' I say. 'Ready to head back down?'

'It took us hours to climb up and you wanna stay less than

five minutes? Chill, man.' She pushes me down onto a rock and sits beside me, leaning her body into mine. I feel safer sitting. Slightly. At least I can open both eyes without suffering an attack of dizziness. I put my arm around her and feel . . . almost . . . relaxed. She's right. It is beautiful up here. And the air is fresher than anything I've ever breathed.

'Do you know what today is, Fish?' I ask.

'Yeah, Saturday.'

'Saturday the twenty-first of March. Four months to the day since I was first diagnosed . . . I was supposed to die today.'

'What, they were *that* precise?'

'No, they gave me between three and five months. I just kind of averaged it out and, well, today was the day.'

'Well, you look kind of alive to me.'

'Yeah, I feel it, thanks.'

Quick medical bulletin: I had my testicle removed about a week after I'd arrived in Spain. They checked it out, gave me blood tests, x-rays and a CT scan, and confirmed that I did have cancer. A stage one teratoma. Stage one means it *hadn't* spread. They told me that without any further treatment my chances of recovery were pretty good, around seventy-five per cent. With radiotherapy they could bring the figure up to nearly one hundred. The choice was mine.

Surprise, surprise, I took the radiotherapy. My oncologist explained in uncertain English that treating cancer was like bombing Iraq. 'First we *ree*move tumour with the surgery. Very *pree*cise and exact. Ees beet like drop laser-guide bomb on Saddam palace. Next we do radiation. Ees beet like send hundred B-52 to blow *sheet* out of Baghdad jus' in case Saddam sneak out of palace when we no look.' He sounded like a Mexican baddie in one of David's spaghetti westerns and I wouldn't have been surprised if he'd addressed me as *gringo*. He didn't look like a *bandito* though, and I have to agree with David: despite their slightly inappropriate use of military analogies, Spanish doctors are *excellent*. Not that I've got any real grudge with their British counterparts. They could brush up on their filing protocols, mind.

The radiation carpet-bombed an area between my groin and my sternum. Fifteen minutes a session, five sessions a week. Afterwards I'd be exhausted and nauseous, more so than I'd ever felt. With the daily grind of treatments it was impossible to imagine it was making me better, not even after Mum had bought me a little book all about the importance of *positive visualisation*. I'm sorry, but Hitler was big on positive visualisation – the thousand-year Reich and all that – and look where it got him. No, I stuck to my tried and trusted technique – visualise the blackest possible outcome, then anything else is an improvement.

The course finished just over a week ago and it's hard to credit the transformation. Do I feel better? Well, the fact that I'm on top of a mountain must say something. OK, it's hardly the Eiger, but the biggest thing I'd ever climbed before today was a loft ladder.

I'm not officially cured. I have to have tests every six months for the next God knows how long to make sure the cancer hasn't returned. I'm not certain that I'll ever be cured *officially*. I think I'll always be in *remission* – like a life prisoner who's released knowing he'll return to jail at the first hint of mischief. But right now I *feel* cured. I feel alive and, more significantly, glad to be that way.

Not that I know what I'm going to do with my life. You know me. Ambition (as in *lack of*) has always been an issue. But something will turn up. Won't it?

And I'm happy for now. Very happy. I'm not being chased by the police or gangsters or disease. I've got my mum, my new friend David, more or less constant sunshine, a pleasant apartment with a partial sea view . . . OK, I've got Vince for a flat mate, but he promises it's only temporary and I can think of worse people to live with . . . Actually, I can't. The man is an unmitigated slob. I've lain awake at night compiling lists of Worse People to Live with than Vince Douglas, which so far contain not a single name. I don't suppose Pol Pot would have made a particularly congenial house guest, but I bet he would have at least picked up his socks.

But I have got the person I really want.

Right now she's pulling a cigarette from her pack and sticking it in her mouth.

'You trek all the way up here to breathe the freshest air in Spain and you're gonna have a fag?' I say.

'Ex-smokers. They're the *worst*, man.'

'Smoking causes cancer, you know.'

'Smoking can get your fucking head blown off,' she says with a grin.

Actually, after everything that has happened, after the insane, terrifying, couldn't-make-it-up ride that I've been on since last November, there is only one thing that really haunts me. I can't shake the image of Clark killing his boss with the gun I'd been carrying around for three days. The gun I'd waved in David's face. The gun I'd let Bubbles play with. All I can say is thank God I'd given up cigarettes by then.

It didn't take long to figure it out. That in the chaos at the Dorchester, I bent down and picked up Clark's gun, leaving him with Vince's lighter. 'Couldn't you tell the difference?' Vince sneered as we sped towards Southend. 'It had a hole in the butt where you stuck in the gas.' What can I say? The guns were indistinguishable to my untrained eye. A man was on fire. The alarm was blaring. It was a *pressurised situation*. Besides, I wasn't the only one who couldn't tell them apart.

Poor old Clark. A couple of weeks ago David told me his body had been found in an empty basement in Stoke Newington. I guess the Mafio-ski don't take well to their bosses being *wubbed out* with *extweme pwattishness*.

For Fish, Vince and David it's an endless source of amusement. For me it's the fount of all my nightmares. Dreams where a Russian gangster's exploding head is replaced by Bubbles', David's or, sometimes, by mine.

The American gun nuts are right. It's not the firearms that kill people. It's stupid bloody pillocks like Clark and me.

'All right, shall we go then?' Fish asks, stubbing out her fag on the ground.

We get to our feet and head for the path that brought us up here. As we stand at the top of it, I realise that going down will be a lot hairier than coming up. Going down entails *looking* down.

'*Shit*,' I say quietly.

'C'mon, baby, we can do it,' she encourages. She grabs my hand and sets off at a trot that I'd say is definitely too brisk for the conditions. But I'm moving now, gathering momentum and it's too late to do much about it.

'Slow down,' I say between pants.

'What're you talking about? This *is* slow,' she replies, speeding up a little.

'You're gonna bloody kill us both,' I call out immediately before my foot catches something and my body spills over and off the path. Fish spins round and grabs for me with both hands, but she's too late. I'm going over the edge, falling . . .

Not far, actually. About five or six feet into a hollow filled with scrubby little bushes and litter. Lots of litter.

'You OK?' Fish calls.

'No, I'm bloody not. I'm covered in crap.' I push myself up to a sitting position and look around me. I'm surrounded by food wrappers, bottles and cans. I stand up and peel a yoghurt carton off my arm, which is now coated in yellow-green goo. I can smell it. Rancid olive oil. I look down at the split plastic bottle from which it has leaked.

'Shit, shit, *shit*. That's the last time I go mountain climbing with you, Fish.'

She doesn't reply because she's laughing.

I scramble up the side of the hollow and back onto the path, where I stand in front of her looking and smelling like the Creature from the Municipal Dump.

'Sorry, Murray,' she says between titters. 'Sorry.'

Right now I would *kill* for a pack of moist travel wipes, preferably lemon-scented, but, *Christ*, I promise I wouldn't be choosy. I look around for something, *anything* to wipe the mess from my body. I see a clump of little plants that have gained themselves an unpromising foothold among the loose shale beside the path. They're dry and scratchy – spindly branches dotted with small dark green leaves – but in the absence of anything else they'll have to do. I bend down and tear off a handful of thin twigs. I ball it up and rub at the thick, greasy cocktail of filth on my forearm, gently at first, then harder. After some fairly frantic scrubbing that threatens to strip a layer of skin, I move my hand and look at my arm.

Something remarkable has happened.

My arm is clean. I mean it's *really* clean as in squeaky, fresh-from-the-shower clean. I look at the remains of the plant in my hand. Its little leaves are fractured and crushed and whatever is inside them is dissolving the oily mess that's caking them. I mean *really* dissolving it. It's like watching one of those *miraculous* demo sequences in a soap powder ad, where fat globules of black engine oil magically float out of a piece of fabric restoring it to virgin white. You know as you're watching that you're being duped, that life just isn't like that, nothing could be *that* good, but this is happening . . . It's *really* happening. Before my very eyes.

'What's the matter?' Fish says. 'You look like you're in shock.'

I am, but it's good shock. *Brilliant* shock. 'This is *incredible*,' I gasp. 'I'm *clean*.'

'Fantastic. Shall we go?'

I ignore her because I'm on my knees, gathering fresh bunches of the stuff.

'What the fuck are you doing, Murray?'

'Have you any idea what this plant is called?'

'Who cares? Crappy little weed or something. Can we go?'

'This could be *it*, Fish,' I exclaim.

'This could be *what*?'

She has no idea. Not a clue that I may have stumbled – almost literally – upon the future of household cleaning. A brilliantly effective yet *entirely natural* degreasant. I bring a handful up to my nose and inhale . . .

A fresh, ever so slightly pungent fragrance; distinctive like eucalyptus, but *nothing* like eucalyptus. I close my eyes and imagine walking into a kitchen and smelling this . . . And then into a bathroom . . .

Yeeeessssssssssssssssss!

The Holy Grail. A scent that would work in the kitchen *and* the bathroom.

This is overwhelming, too good to be true. It cannot be happening.

I wonder if it has germicidal properties as well. I mean, could it possibly *disinfect*? . . . No, that's asking too much. A spectacularly effective, *natural* cleaning agent with a truly versatile fragrance – I'll happily, *deliriously* settle for that.

'Murray, I'm worried,' Fish says, sounding it. 'What's got into you?'

'Come and give me a hand,' I say as I claw at the baked earth around the plants, trying to uproot them. My mind is racing ahead. I'm going to have to learn about cultivation, extraction processes, manufacturing, packaging . . . So much to do.

But it'll be worth it.

This is our future.

It could make us rich.

Maybe famous.
And it might even make the world a better place.
I just *knew* something would come to me in

The End